SO
NOT
THE
DRAMA

Paula Chase

SO NOT THE DRAMA

A Del Rio Bay Novel

DAFINA BOOKS FOR YOUNG READERS
KENSINGTON PUBLISHING CORP.
http://www.kensingtonbooks.com

DAFINA BOOKS are published by

Kensington Publishing Corp.
850 Third Avenue
New York, NY 10022

All Kensington titles, imprints and distributed lines are available at special quantity discounts for bulk purchases for sales promotion, premiums, fundraising, educational or institutional use.

Special book excerpts or customized printings can also be created to fit specific needs. For details, write or phone the office of the Kensington Special Sales Manager: Kensington Publishing Corp., 850 Third Avenue, New York, NY 10022. Attn. Special Sales Department. Phone: 1-800-221-2647.

ISBN-13: 978-0-7582-1859-9
ISBN-10: 0-7582-1859-1

First Trade Paperback Printing: March 2007
10 9 8 7 6 5

Printed in the United States of America

For my girls,
Princess A and Princess Bea,
and for Big Ed.

Acknowledgments

To: My fam, hubby Ted and the Princesses, who didn't have me committed when I said "I want to become an author." Going without dinner (breakfast and lunch, too) or attention when I went on mad writing binges. My parents, who instilled my love of writing and to this day are the curators of the "vault," a box in their closet of all the stories I've written since the age of five. I write by myself but not alone. My inspiration for the Del Rio Bay Clique (Two Plus Too, you know who you are!) . . . don't ya'll trip trying to figure out who is who. There's a little bit of all of you in each of the clique. The little girls I write for, rolling through the 'burbs in their multiculti cliques, making our world color-blind one friend at a time (if I shouted you all out, there'd be drama). My Lizzie, Miss Addy-O. Forgive me if I mangled the Spanish; I'll do better next go 'round. Nowhere near least, my agent, Jen Carlson, who saw the clique's potential and my eddy, Stacey Barney, who knows authors are Drama incarnate but loves us anyway! And this is why you shouldn't go all, "I'd like to thank the Academy," b/c someone might be left out—so to everyone who was there while I pursued this (ad)venture. Love!

Prologue

"They wanna know. Who's that girl?"
—Eve, "Who's That Girl?"

P opularity is a drug. You get a taste of it and suddenly the looks you get from people, the way you get treated, the things you get away with . . . you need it. You honest to God need it. People make pretend that being popular is no big deal. Either those people aren't popular and know they'll never have a chance at tasting its sweet addicting juices, or they're lying.

I got my first taste of popularity when I was four. No, seriously. My boy, Michael, and I attended Sunny Faces, a day care run out of his grandmom's house. The day care was downstairs in her basement, a kiddie wonderland of toys in every corner and hugantic paintings and colorful decals on the walls. There was also a big playground out back.

Now the basement is Michael's, remade over into a bedroom/gameroom/den of boyness.

But back then, when it was our playpen, even with all the dazzling odds and ends and kidgets, the one place we all wanted to go was upstairs. We never got to see the rest of the house. It was off-limits. So naturally, that's where we wanted to go. The stairs went up forever, gobbled up in the darkness near the top, with only a sliver of light coming from beneath the door.

With me leading the pack, we'd make up adventures about conquering the fantasy land beyond that door. Like, maybe it opened up into a lake of ice cream and trees of chocolate—since that's where Ms. Mae Bell came from with snacks. That became our favorite fantasy and eventually, the truth, as far as a bunch of four-year-olds were concerned.

If only we could get beyond the dreaded baby gate, we could take a dip in a big creamy vat of vanilla and take a bite out of one of the choco trees.

You know, to his credit, Michael never said a word to dispel any of our myths about the rest of his house being a candy land. Then again, why would he? How cool would that be to live in a land of candy?

Since his grandmother ran the joint, Michael was always allowed to go upstairs. Sometimes he'd toddle after her and she'd let him help bring down the snacks. If anyone else tried, Ms. Mae Bell would scoop them up, plop them down at the bottom of the stairs, and secure the gate with a firm, "You're gonna break your neck on these steps. Stay here. I'll be right back."

Man, but that gate made it irresistible. Some days we'd park right next to it and play because it was as close as we could get.

So, yeah, anyway popularity and how it found me.

I became popular thanks to workaholic parents climbing the corporate ladder. Thank you, Fifty-hour work weeks! My mom had just started her own PR firm and my dad was a techie at a big company based out of Northern Virginia. They were mad busy scrambling to the top.

One day my mom called. She was running late and she couldn't reach my dad. Could Ms. Mae Bell please keep me a little later than normal? Of course, she'd pay whatever penalty was required for having Ms. Mae Bell work beyond her usual grueling twelve-hour day of screaming toddlers and crying babies.

So as everyone else was leaving, Ms. Mae Bell announces, to no one in particular, I'm guessing—we were a bunch of four-year-olds—that I'd be having dinner with her and Michael. She lifted the latch on the baby gate and ushered us upstairs to watch television, while she waited for the parents of the three other kids still left.

My stomach sang and danced as my chubby, four-year-old legs carried me out of the dark coolness of the stairway into heaven. I was so excited walking up those stairs, so caught up in what I'd do when I got to candy land, that it took me a few seconds to realize that the plush brown carpet wasn't, in fact, a river of chocolate.

Michael's house was just like mine.

Where were the gummy rocks? The Reese's cup benches? The clouds of cotton candy (don't ask why he'd have clouds in his house)?

I'm not sure, but I think I cried. I really only remember Michael showing me his room and watching *Teletubbies*. I was too shocked to ask him where the candy stuff was hiding.

The next day, I was all set to report that candy land did not exist. But when everyone crowded around me, anxious to know what it was like, giving up their snack if I sat by them to share my adventures, wanting to team up with me for play circle . . . well, I discovered something better than candy land.

I had something everyone wanted—a glimpse into the other side—and it made me the It girl of Sunny Faces day care. It put me on the pop side or at least as popular as you can be with a crowd with very short attention spans. I think Shelly Mason was popular two days later for bringing a puppy in for Show-'n'-Tell.

No matter, my taste for popularity was born and my quest to remain ever the It girl sprouted roots.

I remember making up some story about not being able to talk about what was upstairs because it was top secret. Which was cool with them; they just wanted to be near someone who had crossed over.

I've never looked back.

Why would I? Being popular rocks!

When my rule of middle school came to a close, naturally, I had to hatch a plan to remain on top at Del Rio High School. Del Rio High is full of cliques. What high school isn't? But it's more full than most and the fate of your existence depends on where you get stuck, labeled, categorized, and otherwise boxed in by the governing clique—the Uppers.

So you see my dilemma?

Me and my crew have always been popular—but that transition from middle to high school is inevitable—and we're about to go from Middle School Royalty to High School Ambiguity. So, you know, I'm thinking I've gotta handle that.

It's not the same as starting over. Popularity carries over. So it's not that I'll be totally unknown. The Class of 2009 will know what's up and some of the sophs knew me before they left middle school. It's the junior class I'm worried about. I'll have to scrabble my way to the middle of the pack—which is to be the most popular in your class and more popular than some sophs and juniors. But, of course, never more pop than the reigning senior class. Lesson #10 from Pop 101.

All of this and classes too!

I'm an old pro at the tricks of becoming and staying popular and I could pretend that there's a true formula, or I can be real and let you know, it's a lot of work. Work that started the minute my pink Nellie Timberlands left Del Rio Middle School and strutted a few blocks down to the one and only high school, in the 'burbs of the DRB. Samuel-Wellesly, Del Rio Bay's only other high school, is another story. And we'll get to that later. But the best laid plans of popularity can and are disrupted by real life. So let me back it on up and let you peep how plans go right, left, back and forth before they land you at your destination . . . or at least somewhere really close.

63 Hours, 10 Minutes, and 40 Seconds to Go...

> "The princess is here!"
> —Ciara, "1, 2 Step"

"There are approximately sixty-three hours, ten minutes, and forty seconds left before we are officially Del Rio Bay High Freshmen!" Mina Mooney shouted.

Mugginess saturated the air like a warm, wet, sloppy kiss gobbling up the stingy breeze floating by.

Children splashed off the shore, jet skis skimmed the water's top, and the hazy curtain of smoke rings dancing off grills draped the beach, barely shifting in the Bay's scant breeze.

Mina dabbed sweat off her satiny brown face. In defiance of the heat, she scrunched deeper beneath the beach 'brella and tried the announcement on again for good measure. "Sixty-three hours, eight minutes, and three seconds!"

A few sun worshippers stirred. They glanced her way, mildly curious.

There wasn't a naked space for miles on the hot sand. But no one was interested in joining her strange celebration.

She grabbed a drink from the cooler. The hot beige sand prickled her knees and spilled into the body divots of her beach towel, stinging her butt as she pushed back into the shady retreat of the umbrella. Swiping dramatically at the piles of sand, she swept her towel clean until it was a sandless island once again.

Mina – 1, Sand – 0.

The hollow victory inspired another Paul Revere whoop. "Did you hear me, Liz?! It's almost time!"

Roused by the constant wake-up call, Lizzie propped herself up on her elbows.

"Mina." She lifted her head reluctantly. "I hear you. Thanks to your declaration, every five minutes, evvveryone here has heard you! School starts in sixty-three hours, blah, blah, blah."

She plopped down in a huff. "Now, shut up."

Mina kicked sand at her, forgetting for a second about her battle with the pesky granules. "Look, girl, we're about to embark on the last and final leg of our academic careers together. Celebration is in order, like it or not!"

Lizzie popped her shades. Her green eyes, droopy with sleep, flashed with mild irritation. "First of all, stop using words like 'embark' without a teacher around." She frowned down at the sand stuck to her arm, wiping at it absently. "Second, only you could find joy in the first day of school, Miss JV Cheer Captain and All-Around Pop Seeker."

School was the last thing Lizzie wanted to think about. She pushed her shades down and waited for the right moment to doze off on the conversation.

"You know what?" Mina asked in one of those bright-side-grass-is-always-greener tones. "Ya'll will be okay once it starts and we start hitting Friday night football, watching JZ get his game on and chowing down at the Ria afterward."

Rio's Ria was a small pizza restaurant and *the* place to be if you were an under eighteen DRB 'burbanite, awake and not on the beach. Not that the pizza wasn't good, but Rio's Ria was the spot by sheer luck. It happened to be within walking distance of Cimarra Beach, Del Rio Bay's middle and high schools, and more than a dozen communities.

"We eat at the Ria every Thursday no matter what time of year it is," Lizzie said. "That's hardly a reason to get excited about going back to school. And who is 'ya'll'?"

"Michael. I guess both of ya'll been drinking from the same bottle of hater-ade cause he's all bummed out about school starting, too," Mina said, ramping up for a full-blown conversation.

She'd spent half the afternoon daydreaming, waiting for someone to gab with. Now that Lizzie was awake, it was on. "Maybe class would be more interesting if you treated it like one of your productions."

Lizzie grabbed a spray bottle and pelted her belly and neck with lukewarm water. It still felt good on her steamy skin.

"Just act like a student," Mina reasoned.

"In case you can't tell, I'm rolling my eyes," Lizzie warned.

Mina tickled Lizzie's side with her toe. "Come on, you're excited about Freshman Lit. I know you are."

Lizzie giggled. "Only because we have it together."

"There ya go. I knew you could find something to get hyped about."

Having a class with Mina was one bright spot. But Lizzie refused to give Mina the satisfaction. School was not something to celebrate.

"I hate that we have Lit last period. Who is awake enough for Austen and Faulkner during fourth period?" she grumbled.

"But I know you're excited about being able to audition for . . . dun-da-da-dahhhh, Bay Dra-da's production." Mina made her skeptical eyebrows, daring Lizzie to say otherwise.

Lizzie didn't argue. The school's Drama and Dance Troupe was the one element of school she was down for.

Blond hair spilled down her shoulders as she sat up. For the first time she looked alert. "Of course. And if I could do it without the whole class thing, all the better."

"Yeah, well it's a package deal. See, for me . . ."

"Yeah, yeah, the Uppers, the café, yada, yada, blasé-blah," Lizzie said, spritzing her arms.

"See, you brush it off like it's nothing. But I'm doing this for Us," Mina said.

Lizzie's eyebrow shot up.

Plotting to score a spot in the coveted café, the beautiful people's–only section of the cafeteria, had been Mina's obsession since summer started. It was all she talked about. Sitting in the café with the Uppers, the high school's social glitterati, was school to her. She didn't mind attending class to improve her social status. As she always said, if not there, where?

Lizzie didn't worry about being the It girl. Mina worried, planned, and focused on stuff like that enough for both of them. If Mina didn't accomplish her goal—whatever the specific objective was—it would be something else she'd obsess over until she got it. So to avoid having to hear this every day until Christmas, Lizzie was rooting for her to earn whatever spot she thought she deserved among the potpourri of kids who ran the entire school from sports to debate team.

Uppers were the ruling class. They hailed from a variety of grades, backgrounds, and neighborhoods and had one thing in common: somehow they had made it to the top of their species, athlete, rich kid, smart kid. It was the mother of all cliques—the clique that decided the cliques.

JZ once said the first semester of high school was like the NFL draft, where the cliques picked you and decided where you fit. Whether you cared, bought into it or not, wasn't the point.

Mina was caught up in her favorite conversation. "Because you know once one of us has a solid in, it'll probably be all swazy for the rest of us." She parted her hair, putting it into two braids as she talked. Her fingers fought through the wavy roots, forcing it to behave. "I'm figuring I have an easy in because of cheerleading. But since the last two junior varsity squads were kind of sorry, I heard the cheerleaders fell off a bit. It's all about the Stomp Starz, now," Mina said, referring to the high school's hip-hop step team.

She thought it over. "Maybe I should go out for step team."

"Ha! Yeah, right." Snorts honked from Lizzie's nose. "Are you serious?"

"Yeah. I could do step team in the winter and cheer only for football. Why are you tripping so hard?"

"Two words," Lizzie said, thrusting two fingers skyward. "Jessica. Johnson."

Mina groaned. She had forgotten all about Jessica, sophomore, newest step mistress of the Stomp Starz, and the only black female rolling with the Uppers, specifically with the glam clique—the snotty, mostly rich kids.

Mostly, because Jessica wasn't. Mina still wondered how Jessica got in with the glams. She lived in The Great Melting Pot—or, at least, that's what everybody called Woodberry Ridge, the neighborhood where Jessica lived, because a lot of the residents were immigrants.

One of DRB's oldest 'burbs and most diverse neighborhoods, The Great Melting Pot had the most inexpensive homes in the city and drew lots of workers who ran Del Rio Bay's restaurants and retail stores. Also, a handful of teachers lived there.

Yet, even coming from The Great Melting Pot, somehow Jessica had befriended Mari-Beth Linton, blond-haired, green-eyed head of the glams and all-around snot. Mari-Beth was the type of person who only made friends with people who could benefit her. All the more reason Mina never understood how Jessica fit in. But the two were the best of friends. Mina had stayed as far away from Mari-Beth as was humanly possible in middle school. Jessica was bad enough and her, Mina couldn't avoid.

Mina had suffered through two years of recreational squad cheerleading with Jessica and Jess's fraternal twin sister, Sarah. The second year on the Raiders squad, when Jessica made captain, was the absolute worst season of Mina's life.

Everyone, except Sarah, called Jessica the Cheer Nazi behind her back because she wasn't just bossy, she was straight nasty. She took a special dislike to Mina and whenever the coach was out of earshot, all Mina heard was:

"God! Could your herkie be any lower? We're going to get points off if that's the best you can do."

"Mina, lock your knees!"

Sarah and Jess were like night and day, right down to their personalities and even looks. Cool, laid-back Sarah was the cream, light cocoa-complexioned, thick curly hair to her ears, to Jessica's coffee-bean skin, broad nose, thick lips, and extremely straight weavealicious hair down past her shoulders.

It wasn't enough for Mina that she and Sarah got along. She couldn't stand the thought of being disliked and confronted Jessica during practice one day.

"Jess, did I do something wrong?" she asked, warding off the urge to run far away from Jessica's hostile vibes.

"You do everything wrong. Maybe cheerleading isn't your thing." Jessica pierced Mina with hazel eyes (contacts) that looked odd against her dark complexion.

"I meant, did I say or do something to make you hate on me so much?"

Jessica craned her neck, checking on the whereabouts of the coach. "You're just the extra black token," she said through a phony, frozen grin. "Remember, everywhere you go, I'll have already been there, done that."

"Meaning?" Mina asked, not believing her ears.

"Meaning, there's not enough room for three of us on the squad. Take up soccer or something," Jessica said before gliding off, runway model style.

Mina was sick the rest of practice. As a matter-of-fact, being in the same room as Jess and her nasty cat-colored eyes made her nauseous.

Every practice after their little talk, Jessica made sure to point out some new cheerleading deficiency Mina had: *high Vs not high enough, low Vs not low enough,* and this one, whispered while the coach looked over her routine notes, Mina was sure Jessica had totally made up, *"Your head bobble is throwing off the eight-count."*

Mina never bothered trying to figure out how a small movement of her head, if she'd even made one, could throw off a whole segment of the routine. Instead, with Jessica's constant badgering ringing in her ears—*"Mina, your motions suck. Tighten 'em up!"*—Mina turned to blogging after especially brutal practices.

Teen Pop Star, her blog all about life in the popularity bubble, became her favorite boredom killer and her lifeline when Lizzie, Michael, or JZ weren't around for venting. That first year, Jessica, a proud, card-carrying member of the I'm so hot and you, you're so not club, was the star of most of Mina's blog entries as The Bee.

To protect the innocent and the not so innocent, in Jessica's case, Mina kept the blog's URL private and made up names for everyone, including herself, the Pop Princess. She hadn't shared the blog with the clique until this summer.

Lizzie laughed out loud at every entry and kept saying, "Mi, this would make a great book."

And just like that, Mina knew it would be one day, *I Was a Teenage Pop Star,* a secret behind-the-scenes look at life on the pop side, told by an insider. Who better to talk about the inner workings of the pop life than her?

And only Mina would know which parts of the book were real and which ones weren't. The blog/future novel was the only good thing that came out of two seasons with Hurricane Jess. Luckily, Jessica had lost interest in cheerleading as a freshman and picked up step squad.

Jessica would always be the one that "got" away, the only person to resist Mina's girl-next-door charm and now she was the ruling black chick of Del Rio Bay High. The thought of sucking up to her to get ahead made Mina woozy. Jessica's words echoed in Mina's brain, "Remember, everywhere you go, I'll have already been there, done that."

Yeah, no step squad for me, Mina thought.

"Still wanna do step team?" Lizzie asked, laughter glinting in her eyes.

"Not so much," Mina said. "But I'm not scared of Jess. Don't get it twisted."

"Yeah, but she's where you wanna be. You gotta at least play nice," Lizzie said.

"I'm more worried about impressing Kim Vaughn, the varsity cheer captain," Mina said. She knew she couldn't totally discount Jessica. If Jessica wanted to make Mina's life hell again, it could be done. But there were other ways to navigate the waters of popularity.

Lizzie twisted her French braid into a fat bun at the back of her neck, then turned on to her stomach and said, "Okay, girl, change the channel." That was their code for you're getting on my nerves and I'm tired of talking about this. "I plan to hold onto my forty hours and whatever minutes with a death grip." Lizzie yawned, her words muffled as she turned her head. "Wake me on the first day of school!"

Alone again and too wired to nap, Mina plugged in her earpiece. Young Jeezy burst into her ear. She mouthed along, not bothering to censor his inappropriately irresistible lyrics and cracked open her Journal of Random Thoughts (JORT), the mobile version of Teen Pop. Stretched out on her stomach, pen in hand, she closed her eyes, pushing thoughts of Jessica far away, and let the words swimming in her head form coherent sentences that described the day's jaunt to the beach.

Even the clique wasn't safe from Mina's portrayal of their adventures. Michael's Academy Award–worthy performance earlier was shaping up quickly as a new chapter. The downside to being with her friends all the time had started to show that morning.

She squinted against the sun's glare until her eyes found Michael, a dark drop of chocolate on a bright orange and yellow boogie board, skin and bald head glistening. Mina half expected to see a rumbling thunder cloud over his head, the perfect symbol for his mood earlier.

She and Lizzie were all of ten minutes late and Michael had a fit. He chewed them out and vowed in a snit that this was the last time he would bother showing up on time to meet them somewhere.

Cue the symphony and everyone sing opera style, "Dra-maaa!"

But, also typical Michael. You knew what was on his mind, because he painted a picture for you. But even Mina hadn't been able to penetrate his moods on days like today when he was an equal opportunity bitcher.

Mina had never seen him so sensitive.

It's not like she got mad over things he said to her.

Well, she didn't stay mad . . . long.

Today, she hadn't bothered to press the issue, figuring he was just tired of always hanging with her and Liz while JZ got his swerve on, talking up new girlfriend prospects.

Now that she thought about it, it was JZ, anxious to scope out potential beach honeys, who had rolled out, leaving Michael to set up the umbrella and gear by his lonely. There was no such thing as late to JZ—as far as he was concerned the party didn't start until he rolled through.

Michael should have fussed him out. She and Lizzie were just the easy targets. She rolled her eyes as she scribbled.

JZ could get away with murder. His mega-watt smile and willingness to strike up a conversation with anyone drew people to him, especially girls. She glanced up, head checking. She didn't want anyone to even see her admit this in writing. The truth was, JZ was fine. Nearly six feet of cinnamon handsomeness complete with a ripple of tight, smooth muscles thanks to a school year spent swearing off soda, sugar, and fast food, fine. The problem was he knew it and so did a lot of girls in the DRB.

Her stomach churned, fluttering at the thought of him ditching the clique for one of his girls aplenty. But she pushed the thought far away. *No one's breaking up the clique*, she thought with smug satisfaction.

A fresh, almost cool breeze rustled the JORT's pages as she penned her last thoughts for the day.

August 28, 2005

In exactly sixty-two hours, ten minutes, and eighteen seconds, I'll be a high school frosh. :::Dun, Dun, Dun, Dun, Dun, Dun DAH!!!::: My road to the "real word" and beyond begins!

Secret wishes:

❀ The Del Rio Bay Clique (my peeps, Lizzie-O, Mike-Man, and JZ "the lover," ha-ha) will make big things happen just like we did in middle school. That's what's up!

❀ My high school experience will be as awesome as I keep dreaming it will be. Café here I come!

❀ That I can squeeze cheerleading, track, and writing for The Blue Devil Bugle newspaper all into one school year (w/o flunking!!!).

❀ The "forever" in best friends forever doesn't just mean, "until we find something else more interesting to do."

❀ Life (in general) is really a bowl of cherries and not the pits!

❀ I'll always have my friends to help me through the tough!!!

Mina reread the last sentence and added a fourth exclamation point, one for each of them. As a final act of reaffirming the clique's tightness, she replaced the punctuation's usual dot with oversized hearts then shut the book on summer's memories. She rummaged quietly through the cooler. Tiptoeing, as if her sandy footsteps could be heard over the loud beach sounds, she stood over Liz's tanning body and let the icy cold water slowly drip down her back. She sprinted toward the bay as Lizzie leapt off the blanket, yelping and shivering from the sudden freeze.

Backpedaling into the water, Mina's voice carried back to the beach. "Hey, Liz!" She laughed maniacally, watching Lizzie shake off the cold shower. "Sixty-two hours exactly and counting!"

46 Hours, 0 Minutes

The loud hum of the vacuum cleaner mixed with the insistent twitter of a cell phone.

Mina squinted against the sun seeping into the room. Days like this she regretted choosing yellow as the color scheme for her room. It made the room bright, impossible to shut out once her eyes fluttered open. She squeezed her eyes shut and slammed a pillow over her head.

The racket droned on, penetrating her shield.

Without rolling over, or pushing the pillow off her head, she stretched her arm and blindly patted the nightstand, making contact with the phone for a second before it spun away to the farthest corner.

Mina groaned. The muscles in her right arm and along her side ached in protest as she pushed up onto one elbow, grabbing for the phone with her left hand. The tightness in her shoulder stopped her short. Her arm refused to inch closer.

Between the fierce game of chicken and the five hours in the muggy heat, her body had taken a beating.

It was worth it. Cimarra Beach was a popular hangout. Mina had met many a cutie strolling the shore. It was quite the hot spot, pun intended. But you had to get there early. Once the beach was full, new cars were let in only after a car left.

Not that it mattered to the clique. They took the twelve-minute walk from The Woods, Mina, JZ, and Michael's neighborhood, guaranteeing admission.

Ignoring the fresh shot of pain, Mina pushed hard off her elbow to sit up. She snatched the phone from the edge of the nightstand just as the last ring bleated.

"Hey, Mi," Lizzie said.

"What?!!!" Mina checked the clock. Could this really be her best friend calling her? Involved in theater all year round, Lizzie spent her nights rehearsing lines and was rarely up before ten A.M. in the summer.

"No, you're not dreaming." Lizzie giggled. "Did you ask your mom yet, about hanging out with me at my mom's company picnic?"

"Not yet. Hold on and let me do it now."

Mina's adrenaline pumped. Lizzie's mother was a regional buyer for May Company. She decided which clothes would represent the Teen Spirit apparel line for May department stores along the East Coast and the winter line was showcased every year, at the annual picnic.

Thanks to Lizzie's T-shirt and jeans taste, obsession if you asked Mina since Lizzie refused to wear much else, Mina copped a lot of hot outfits courtesy of Marybeth O'Reilly.

She couldn't wait to sport the yellow, fake-fur, midcut jacket she'd helped Miss Marybeth choose for the fall line.

Mina stood at the top of the stairs. "Ma?!" She went down a few stairs and then sat. "Ma?!"

Her mother looked up, frowning. She motioned to Mina to hold on, made two broad sweeps across a strip of carpet, then turned off the vacuum. "Good morning, Boo."

"Morning. Can I go with Lizzie to the May Company picnic?"

"That's today?" Mina's mother considered the question as she wound up the vacuum cord. "I don't think so. We have a lot to do later this afternoon."

"I know. But . . ."

"And Vera's coming to do your hair tonight."

"Ma, it'll be over waaayyy before Vera's doing my hair."

"No, not today, Honey. I still have a few things to buy you for school and you need to be there when I get them." Her mom thrust the vacuum in Mina's direction. "You should get started on your room."

Mina sat dumbfounded for a minute. Just like that it was a no?

"Can I vacuum later?"

"Yeah, later as in within the next few hours. Not later as in tonight when me and Daddy are ready to relax." Her mother fixed her with an and-I-mean-it look.

Mina nodded as she walked back to her room and picked up the phone. "She said no."

"Even if my mom comes to get you?" Lizzie said.

"I gotta be there when she finishes up school shopping," Mina said as if she couldn't understand the logic. She paced the floor, brain working overtime. "Oh, what if you come hang out with me? It's not a picnic but at least we'd be together."

"The picnic is boring anyway . . . to me," Lizzie added. She didn't enjoy the May Company sneak preview nearly as much as Mina and wouldn't enjoy it at all without her.

"Tell your mom that my father can pick you up. He's already out and can get you on his way back," Mina said.

Mina walked into the hall. Her mom was back upstairs in the master bedroom. "Ma, what if Lizzie hangs out with us? I'll call Daddy and see if he'll pick her up on his way home."

Mina's mother stopped folding clothes. Her eyebrows stretched in a look Mina knew meant she had pushed it. But Mina pressed, on the edge of whining.

"It's the last Saturday of the summer! We want to hang out. We're bored."

She stood at the entrance of her parents' room, lip drooping in an exaggerated pout.

"Exactly," Mariah Mooney answered. "It's the last Saturday, and when Daddy gets home we have a million errands to run."

"Lizzie doesn't mind running around with us," Mina countered, just as Lizzie's answer came back over the phone, a flat, "My mom said no."

"Why?!" Mina asked.

"Why what?" Mina's mother scowled in confusion.

Mina put up a finger to stop her mom's conversation. "No, I was talking to Lizzie," she said.

"Mina, now you know you're wrong. You should have asked before calling Lizzie. Now I've gotta break both your hearts," Mina's mother said. She shook her head. "The answer is still no. But maybe next weekend."

"Yeah, right, next weekend." Mina turned her back so she could roll her eyes out of her mother's sight.

Mariah tapped Mina's shoulder. "Have you finished folding your clothes?"

"Yes!" Mina snapped.

"What?" Mariah's eyebrows shot up again.

Mina fixed her tone. "I did it yesterday morning, remember?"

She walked off to her room, shut the door quietly but with force, and slammed herself onto her bed. "I don't see why I have to shop with them today! Or at least why you can't go with us," she complained to Lizzie.

"I'm going to be totally bored at my mom's company picnic," Lizzie said. "At least if you were going I'd have a hanging bud."

Crazy. Lizzie could care less about going and Mina would kill to see the sneak peek. It was better than running to the Super Wal-Mart.

"I can't wait until we can drive." Mina bounced a pink barrel pillow off the wall, playing a game of catch. "Michael will be able to get his learner's permit next winter. It is gonna be *on* by summer."

"Too bad we still have *this* year to get through," Lizzie reminded her, wanting no part in blowing through summer.

Mina laughed. "As usual, me and my September birthday . . . all late. It'll be second semester sophomore year before I get my permit. Ya'll need to start calling me De'las. 'Cause I'm always de last one to do stuff."

She laughed long and hard at her own joke. When she stopped, the phone was silent.

"Liz?"

"What?" Lizzie said.

"Oh, that wasn't funny?" Mina said.

"Now I see why French wasn't your thing." Lizzie giggled.

"Umph, let's not speak of the dead." Mina groaned at the thought of the class that had ruined her B-average streak. "I shouldn't have let you talk me into that."

Mina wasn't used to struggling in any class . . . except math. She'd come to terms with her math deficiency. But French was a nightmare. She used verbs in the wrong tense and mangled the language every step of the way. Madame O, the French teacher, had constantly used her as an example of how not to speak French. Even straight-A Lizzie could only tutor Mina to a C.

"It was pretty nasty," Lizzie said.

"Language just isn't my thing. The stuff is mad hard," Mina said.

"I wish Michael all the luck in the world helping you with Spanish this year," Lizzie said.

"I know, right. I'm hopeless," Mina said. "Mike loves Spanish, yet he won't touch an AP class with a ten-foot pole. . . ."

She and Lizzie chorused Michael's line about why he wouldn't take advanced English, "Thick books about dead people."

They laughed.

"He'll probably have the last laugh, chilling with his three-page papers while we're stuck writing a thesis," Mina said. "He can use all his extra time doing my Spanish homework for me."

"Yeah, like he ever would," Lizzie said. "But now you've messed up our plan. How are we gonna hitchhike our way through France after graduation with you only being able to say your name and pass the ketchup?"

Lizzie's laughter turned into deep, nose-honking snorts.

"I'll just let your smart butt do all the talking," Mina said. "Pass-ay la kat-sup."

Lizzie hooted, loud, forcing Mina to pull the phone away from her ear. "You're right. I'll do the talking."

"Well I'm glad my foreign language barrier is a great source of entertainment for you, but I'm gonna get ready to roll," Mina said. "Maybe Jay is up for a swim. May as well get in one last dip before I get my hair done tonight." She walked over to her dresser and pulled out a pink and brown polka-dot two piece. "I will not let this whole day go by with me just discount shopping with the 'rents."

"See! I wish I was there." Lizzie pouted.

Mina slipped on her swimsuit and gripped the phone with her chin.

"Girl, we'd tear it up if we still lived in the same nabe," she said, wistfully, thinking back to life BTM, Before the Move, when a breezy, five-minute walk separated her and Lizzie. Now Lizzie was several neighborhoods away in Falcon's Way, which was only five miles from Mina's neighborhood. But on days like this, it might as well have been five hundred.

"Yeah, well have fun for me, too," Lizzie said. "But not too much, please."

"Promise. I'll holler later."

Mina dropped the phone on the bed, wriggled into a pair of shorts and a pink baby doll T-shirt, then threw a beach towel and her JORT into a sling bag.

"I'm going down to JZ's for a little while," she yelled out to her mom from the hallway.

"I told you that when Daddy gets home . . ."

"I have my phone. Can you just call when he gets here? I promise I'll come right home," Mina said. "Please!"

Mina's mom came to the hallway shaking her head. "Always on the go. Go ahead, Amina. And don't play that mess about you didn't hear the phone or try that dead spot thing."

"For real, though, JZ's pool is near a dead spot. My cell never rings if I sit it too close to the pool."

Her mom chuckled. "Yeah, well, you better find an alive spot somewhere out there where you can hear the phone. Got it?"

Mina kissed her mom on the cheek. "Okay. I'm gone."

She let her legs carry her down the steps and out of the house as fast as she could before her mother realized she'd skipped out on vacuuming.

45 Hours, 40 Minutes

"Go ahead, envy me."
—Mary J. Blige (ft. 50 Cent), "MJB da' MVP"

Dogwood, the longest road in the neighborhood, stretched out in front of her. Tall oaks, firs, and maples dominated the roadside, dimming the sunny day and muting the sounds of the few cars moving lazily along the quiet street. Ten houses, mostly hidden by acres of full, mature trees, dotted Dogwood.

Mina sped up. Even in the daylight, being on Dogwood alone creeped her out.

Two plump women, jog-walking, waved at her, making Mina laugh at herself for letting the road spook her. The trees gave way to The Woods' park where two moms and their toddlers braved the hot August morning, passing time at the playground. Otherwise, the park's fields and basketball court were empty.

The road ended in a wide circle that held two homes. The first sat back from the road, out of view, a mailbox the only indication a home was near.

JZ's house was the other one. It sprawled in front of Mina, a large contemporary two-story on what was an old farm before The Woods homes were built. Mina pulled her phone out and started down the long drive.

"Are you in the back already?"

"Yeah. You here?" JZ said.

Mina jogged down the drive and turned the corner, expecting to see JZ on the NBA regulation-sized court his parents had built for him. It was empty. "Yeah, I'm here. I don't see you, though."

"I'm at the pool," JZ said.

Mina walked past the sideline bleachers, which held one hundred spectators. JZ's parents spared no expense to indulge his talents. The clique spent many days swimming or hanging out on the court where JZ and Michael's friends from the Raiders basketball team would show up for impromptu basketball tournaments that went on for hours.

Mina walked the length of the sideline. It took her around the pool house and to a patio. JZ waved to her from the deep end of the pool.

A stream of cold water splattered Mina's T-shirt.

"Jay, stop!" She jumped away from the jetting water.

JZ reloaded a bulky yellow and red water machine gun and fired her up.

"What's up, Mina-Moo?" He sprayed and loaded, sprayed and loaded, never giving her a chance to get her clothes off.

"That's not even funny." Mina scuttled away from the spray while twisting and turning her way out of the soaked T-shirt. It fell to the ground with a soggy thud. "Boy, look at my shirt. My JORT better not be wet!"

"It'll be dry when you leave. Stop tripping," JZ said, still squirting away with the high-powered water gun.

Stop tripping. Mina was always on the receiving end of his favorite phrase. Just because Mina wanted to keep her clothes dry so she wouldn't have to walk back home doing the wet duck waddle, she was tripping, of course.

Mina scurried behind a high-backed plastic chair to keep her shorts dry. But the streams of water found their way through every nook and cranny of the chair no matter where Mina squatted. She scrambled out of her shorts, threw them to the far corner of the patio, then jumped into the water, staying underwater until the shock of the cold water passed.

JZ nodded toward another gun when she came up for air. "Want one?"

"No. I'm not trying . . ."

She sputtered as water splashed her face.

"Chicken?" JZ flapped his arms like a bird. "Cluuuuccckkkk! Cluccckkkk! Cluck-cluck!"

"Okay. For real, you must have been mad lonely for some company." She dipped back under and stroked across the pool.

JZ was like a brother, at least if having a brother was like having someone make you the butt of their constant torture and jokes. He also insisted on being Mina's conscience. Not that she didn't do her fair share of setting him straight. The giving as good as the getting was the basis of their friendship and had been since they were five and they silently agreed to share Michael.

She'd known Michael a full year before JZ moved to The Woods. But JZ and Michael bonded over sports, which left Mina out. JZ did everything he could, at first, to boot Mina out of the picture—teasing, name-calling, and nearly breaking her nose.

The last thing was an accident and ultimately led to a truce.

Still, JZ was always the first one to set Mina straight when she got too mouthy or too opinionated. When she did, he'd point out one of her flaws or remind her of some embarrassing time. It was like his only goal in life was to remind her she wasn't perfect.

What infuriated Mina was, a lot of times JZ was right. He called Mina on her need to overthink things. Like, during cheer tryouts a month ago.

Mina sweated tryouts. The day after tryouts she wouldn't let it go. "Kim Vaughn frowned every time I did one of my jumps." "My jumps must not be high enough." "If she hates me, I might as well forget cheering at high school at all, ever."

Lizzie and Michael tried to reassure her. It was JZ who said simply, "Stop tripping," and refused to let her speak another word about tryouts the rest of the day.

When the squad roster was posted, Mina's name was among them and JZ was the first one with the "told you so." He was also the one who stopped Mina midsentence when she immediately began fretting about whether she'd get the JV captain position.

It was never ending between them and always had been.

Mina stroked her way around the pool then resurfaced next to JZ. She grabbed at a nearby float and climbed aboard.

"So you're as bored as I am, I see."

"Man, I just got mad energy, today." JZ tugged at Mina's float.

"Jay, for real, don't tip me over," Mina warned. It was an empty threat. If he tipped her she'd fall over, fuss, and that was it. He knew it and she knew it.

"I won't." JZ feigned innocence as he tugged harder until the float rocked. But Mina wasn't taking the bait. She sat calmly waiting until he grew tired of the game.

Propping himself on the edge of the float by his elbows, JZ pushed it around the pool. "Is Lizzie coming to your spot later?"

"No. My mom's not having it," Mina said.

"Word? My peoples said I could cook out later," JZ said. "I invited some of the team, too."

"Shoot! I gotta go shopping," Mina said.

"*You* don't want to go shopping?" JZ's eyebrows hitched in surprise.

Mina rolled her eyes. "Not for school supplies and household junk."

A sly smile spread across JZ's face. "Stankonia gonna be disappointed that you won't be here."

Mina groaned at the mention of Kyle Jenkins. Behind his back, everybody called him Stankonia because his breath was always kicking. He'd been trying to holler at Mina for the longest time. She had run out of ways to say no she didn't want to go out with him. She was considering sending smoke signals next time.

"Umph, I'm glad I have something to do then," Mina said. She relaxed into the float, enjoying the ride. "Is Craig coming?"

JZ shrugged. "He might come through."

Craig Simpson, junior and first-string varsity football player = yummy, was Mina's obsession, second only to the café. Tall, like she liked them, low-cut hair, lanky but starting to buff up a little, and slightly slanty brown eyes that made him look like he could be mixed, maybe of some exotic European descent. Except he wasn't. She'd seen his parents at a JV game last year and they were both black.

Mmm, mmm, mmm.

Mina let one leg fall into the pool and kicked gently against the water.

"I might have to risk getting in trouble to come down here and chill with Craig."

"Girl, please," JZ said. "You gonna sit right in Kmart or Wal-Mart or wherever Momma and Poppa Mooney want your tail."

Mina kicked water into his face.

"Oh it's on!" JZ said.

Mina fell in, slo-mo style, as he tipped the float over. She thrust herself up to the surface just in time to see JZ grab the water gun off the pool's ledge.

She plunged back down, kicking furiously to put distance between them. A shot of pain stung her as her knee scraped the pool's floor. Wiping at her eyes, she stood up and stumbled blindly toward the pool's wall.

Water sprayed her back as JZ attacked.

"Jay, stop, for real," Mina pleaded. "I banged my knee up." She hopped out of the pool, yelping in pain as JZ shot her right in the open cut. "Jay!"

The cut wasn't deep, which kind of made it worse. It throbbed. Mina hobbled to the pool shed where JZ's parents kept a freshly stocked first aid kit.

"Is it that bad, Queen of Drama?" JZ asked, eyebrow raised.

"It just stings when I walk. I'm gonna get a bandage."

JZ hopped out of the pool and mounted the diving board. "I see you stopped counting down."

Mina's head popped out of the shed. She made pretend she was looking at a watch. "No, I didn't. We have about forty hours left."

"You're a trip," JZ said, before diving into the pool.

Mina peeled the bandage back and carefully laid it on the scratch, which wasn't even bleeding anymore. She limped over (the cut stung a little) to her bag, grabbed her JORT and a pen, then took a seat on the concrete by the pool. Sitting on the pool ledge, she dangled her feet in the water and jotted a few sentences about her day as she waited for JZ to come up for air.

"No, you're a trip," she said when he bobbed up. "Why are ya'll acting like I'm the only one ready to get my frosh on?"

JZ shook his head free of the excess water and doggie paddled over to Mina. "I can't front like I'm not excited. But I can give you two reasons why I'm not as hyped as you."

"Alright, go," Mina said.

"One, Freshman Lit and Algebra II."

"That's two," she teased. "Okay, but can I bright side it?"

"Don't you always?" JZ said.

Mina ignored his sarcasm. "Yes."

JZ poked his wet finger at her journal page. "Just don't quote me for the daily news."

Mina wiped absently at the wet spot. "Whatever. The bright side is, you and Lizzie have the same math class, me and Mike have Spanish together, and me and Lizzie have Freshman Lit. At least the classes will be bearable." She grinned. "And it could be worse. You could be in Pre-Calc."

JZ shushed her.

He could have tested into Pre-Calculus, but just between him and the clique, he'd failed the test on purpose because he wanted to focus on the football season without worrying about struggling in a more advanced math class.

Leave it to JZ to work the system.

"Ooh and of course, the streak," Mina said. The clique was going on their fifth consecutive semester with the exact same lunch period.

JZ pounded his chest. "The streak lives!"

"So, what's reason number two?" Mina asked. She stuck her pen inside the journal, closed it, and slid the book across the concrete toward her bag.

"Man, 'cause I could have been on varsity if it wasn't for my pops." Bitterness edged his voice. "Bright side that one."

A former All-State High School baller, coveted collegiate athlete, and first-round National Football League rookie before a career-ending injury sent him back into the "real" professional world, Mr. Zimms knew the pitfalls of being an excellent and popular athlete well. He purposely stood in the way of letting sports take over JZ's world. Making him play on JV, no matter how badly the Varsity coaches wanted him, was Mr. Zimms's way of making sure JZ kept sports in the "right" perspective.

"It's not like you won't go on to play for a good college or whatever just because you don't play on Varsity your first year," Mina said. "You're smart . . ."

"And handsome." He grinned.

"Pssh, whatever. You're smart. I'll give you that."

The droplets fell short of their mark as JZ splashed at her.

"I'm just saying, you know how bad they wanted me on Varsity, though, right?" He was ready to share the story in case she didn't.

Mina rolled her eyes to the sky. "Yeah. 'Cause you've told me like"—she pretended to count—"twenty times since July."

"Alright, so you recognize the skill, right?" JZ flexed his biceps.

Mina laughed. "Yeah, yeah. Now guess who's gonna be flexing on JV."

The twittering of her phone saved her from another shower as she ran to the patio to get it.

"Mina, Daddy's home. So get yourself together," Mina's mom said on the other end. "We want to roll out of here within the hour."

"Do we have to hit the stores so soon?" Mina begged.

"Amina Mooney, don't pull this on me. I let you go to JZ's and—"

"Alright, I'm on my way," Mina said.

"Did you just cut me off?" her mother asked in her best oh-no-she-didn't voice.

"Sorry, Ma."

Mina made faces at JZ and made the chatterbox symbol with her hands, mocking her mother's lecturing.

"Ay, Miss Mariah!! Mina saying you talking her ear off!" JZ yelled.

"Boy, shut up," Mina fussed.

"Mina did you hear me?" her mom scolded.

"Yeah . . . I mean, yes. I'm getting my stuff on now." Mina shushed JZ.

"Be home in fifteen minutes, alright?"

"Okay." Mina slipped her shorts back on but threw the soaked T-shirt in her bag. "See I told you it wouldn't be dry," she muttered more to herself than to JZ.

JZ climbed out of the pool and walked Mina around front.

"So, do you think Kim will invite me to sit in the café if she has the same lunch as us?" Mina asked out of the blue. The thought of going shopping for school supplies sent her mind racing back to the fact that the first day of school was just hours away.

"Mi, are you seriously that pressed?" JZ asked.

"Yes, Jay, I am. You know how I do," Mina said testily. "I'm just . . . nervous I guess."

"For real, what you want me to say?" JZ ran his hands over his low-cut waves. Warm and fuzzy wasn't his style. It was usually Michael's job to pat Mina on the back and kiss away all her crazy neuroses. "That you and Kim gonna be girls and you'll be in the café flossing from day one?"

Mina grinned. "Uh-huh."

"Alright. Well that's probably what's gonna happen then." JZ shrugged. He dodged Mina's hug.

"See, now how hard was that?" Mina elbowed him playfully in the gut before starting up the driveway.

JZ hollered after her. "Yup, ya'll gonna be tight. Like this." He squeezed two fingers together. "Thick as thieves. Won't be able to pry ya'll apart. Kim is gon' be your girl. Your ace in the hole!"

When Mina got to the edge of the driveway he yelled. "Mi-naaah?!"

She turned. "What?"

"Not!" He broke out in a braying fit of laughter.

13 Hours, 30 Minutes

"Change clothes and go."
—Jay-Z (ft. Pharrell), "Change Clothes"

Mina's mood guided her sense of fashion. Tonight, with the first day of school just hours away, with her emotions swinging from excitement to a low-grade panic, with a closet full of clothes waiting to be *the* outfit for her high school debut, she was flustered and close to being the first person ever to go to school naked out of the sheer inability to decide.

Blocking out the sounds of the television coming from the family room below, for the second time that night Mina thought about giving up and joining her parents, leaving the outfit decision to tomorrow's A.M. mood. Knowing even as the notion crept in she wouldn't give in to it. Her, hastily pick out the outfit for her first day of high school, nearly bleary-eyed at 5:45 A.M.?

Not bloody likely.

Outfit selection for her first day was too important. It had to send the right message.

Was she shy but friendly?

Bubbly and approachable?

Or, cool with a slight touch of snootiness?

She sat cross-legged in front of her closet, head cocked, staring deep into the well-coordinated den of fabric. The clothing stared back, mute, challenging her to pick just one.

Getting nowhere, she narrowed down the looks. She selected two outfits that best fit the two vibes she was caught between, hung them on the closet door and sat down at her PC, knowing who could end the debate.

Michael was always styled out, not in a Mr. Bentley Diddy's manservant way but in a casual, coordinated, fresh kicks and matching lid kind of way. He would never be caught sbummy, a phrase born two years earlier when Mina, one day, came out of the house wearing fleece track pants and an oversized T-shirt.

"For real, you're wearing that?" Michael had asked.

"What? We're just going to the playground." Mina looked down at what she thought was perfect for a dusty, grassy park.

"I know but you don't need to look so bummy. People gon' think you homeless." He pointed. "And I can get in that shirt with you! That's crazy, Mina." He tutted, wrinkling his nose in distaste.

"It's a playground!" she shouted, embarrassed that he was calling her out.

"And you looking ragged. Change! I'll wait." Michael folded his arms and grounded his feet.

After a few seconds of glaring and debating if she wanted to fight him on the issue, she stomped back into the house, muttering. "Sbummy! That's what's crazy. People do dress down sometimes."

It was the last day she wore fleece or a big T-shirt outside of the house. And from then on, the phrase was used anytime they saw someone wearing ragged, dingy, or just plain ugly fashion.

Mina squealed happily when Michael's screen name popped up on her Buddy List.

BubbliMi: Hey, Boo! can u help a sister out?
Mike-Man: 'sup, baby grl?
BubbliMi: Need a fashion consult. Can u come over real quick?

Mike-Man: now, what if I'm busy?!

BubbliMi: 2 busy 4 UR girl?!?!?!??!?!

Mike-Man: ☺ Never. Give me a few min.

BubbliMi: Thanks, Mike.

With a load lifted off her shoulders, Mina logged off and snuggled between her parents on the couch until Michael's familiar double knock with a quick tap of the doorbell signaled his arrival.

Mina scooted off the couch and opened the door. "I got it."

Michael walked into the spacious sunroom, spied out in all black, tee and denim, even a black cap. "Hey, Deev," he said, before calling out hello politely to Mina's folks.

"How you doing, Michael?" Mina's dad said, looking up briefly from the television.

"Hi, Mike," Mina's mom sang. A smile spread across her face as she got up and walked toward him, arms open for a hug. In a fashion-forward nod to why her daughter was a style-head, she looked youngish and casual in a pair of cropped, yellow terry track pants and matching middie jacket. "I haven't seen your grandmom in a while. How is she?"

Michael met her in the middle of the room, accepting the warm embrace.

"She's good."

"Tell her Jack and I said hello." Mina's mom said, giving Michael's shoulder a squeeze. "What does Mina have you up to tonight?"

Before he could answer, Mina pulled him toward the stairs. "Michael trying to teach me how to stunt for the first day."

Mina's mother shook her head, smiling. "And that means?"

Mina walked back down the stairs, placed herself in front of the television, pooched her mouth out in a model's pout, and struck a pose. "Ma, stunt means to show off—you know, be sure your face is seen up in the place." She stroked her chin. "Umm . . . back in the Stone Age I think ya'll called it vouging."

"Oh, why didn't you say so?" Mina's mother asked. "Like this?" She walked over, stood next to Mina and began to hit pose after pose, stopping for a flash between each, giving the imaginary photographer time to capture her glory—hand on her hip, chin in the air, both arms up over her head entwined in a freaky snake move, and finally the ghetto pose, a deep squat flashing the funk sign.

Mina's father's laughter erupted, deep and loud, his attention completely drawn from the television for the first time. "Yeah, well, your face better be up in the place tomorrow, stunting or not. Or your butt is going to be on lockdown in this house."

Mina grinned as she tugged her mother's arm, pulling her up from the squat and led her back to the sofa. She patted her mother's head. "Alright, Daddy, as long as Mommy promises to never do that again."

"Now, see, don't be mad because I got it going on," Mina's mother chuckled.

Michael had found his way to the loveseat and was laughing along, always at home with Mina's family. Before he could settle in, Mina grabbed his arm and dragged him toward the stairs. She needed his focus on her gear. Some days she couldn't sandblast him out of long-winded conversations with her mom.

A spear of guilt poked her heart. She knew Mike loved her family. He was the son her parents never had and vice versa. He didn't know who his father was and never knew much about his mother, a free-spirited, gifted artist with three children by three different men. Everyone knew she had ventured back to Del Rio Bay only three times in the last twenty years, each time to dump her offspring with Ms. Mae Bell, her mother, before losing herself in a black hole of abstract art and trifling men. Or so the story went.

Michael had been the last drop-off fourteen years earlier and last he heard via his grandmother's casual, out-of-the-blue updates, his mother was a starving artist in New York City without two nickels to rub together.

His two sisters were ten and fifteen years older than him and had long since gone off to make their own lives. It was always just him and Ms. Mae Bell, which explained his classic, old-soul ways, wise beyond his years, full of advice, and more prone to pick a quiet game over a loud one.

"Your parents are wild. I could trip with them, anytime." Michael took a last look back toward the sunroom.

Mina hummed in agreement. Ignoring the bittersweet resignation in Michael's voice, she pushed her guilt aside. He could have his after-school special moment later. She'd let him run his mouth with her mom all night afterward. But first . . .

She motioned to the hanging outfits. "Alright, Mike, this is as far as I got. Which is the right one?"

Michael knew little of his mother but had inherited one good thing from her: artistic instinct. What started as doodling as a kid blossomed to graffiti art on his friends' backpacks, jackets, and pants at ten, and full-blown outfit sketches at twelve.

Mina was the sole keeper of the secret of that last skill. All anyone else knew was that he could hook up a graffiti pack and draw a mean caricature, literally. His Hall of Shame stood on the same wall that once held a huge decal of Mickey Mouse when the basement was Sunny Farms day care and not Michael's stylish "apartment." Cartoonish versions of people who had pissed him off, the Hall of Shame was packed with drawings of people that would probably have gladly paid him a few dollars to rip up their buffoonish image.

Lucky for them, only his closest friends ever saw drawings like the one that looked eerily like their elementary school principal, swaddled in a huge baby diaper, mouth wide in a wailing scream of, "I said stop running!" In case you were unsure if that indeed was Mr. Josephs, his name at the bottom of the drawing certified it and Michael's signature underneath confirmed the handiwork.

Michael paced in front of the outfits, his designer's eye keen and serious.

The rugby shirt and denim mini hung above a pair of glittery silver striped Adidas shell heads was definitely styling. Not stunting, but still, it was hot and he said so.

He ran his fingers over the plaid miniskirt paired with knee socks, a ruffle-sleeve shirt, and black Mary Jane clogs. The ultimate schoolgirl look. "Private school geek chic," he commented under his breath, sounding very art-buyerish.

Mina's head bobbed with each cluck of approval, waiting for the final verdict. She leaned forward to hear his muttering. Her butt gripped the edge of the bed.

"I like the plaid mini!" He took a seat at Mina's PC. "It's plucky, like you and your wide-eyed innocence."

"Whatever." She sucked her teeth. "I was with you up until the last comment."

She bounced off the bed and placed the outfit up to her body, twisting and turning for a good angle in her full-length mirror. Whirling the outfit around to catch it in the full light, she agreed once more. "Yeah, that's the one."

Mina hung the outfit on a hook on the back of her closet door then walked back over to Michael and sat down on the desktop. Resting her feet on his lap, she ignored his scowl. "So, you up for tomorrow?"

"Probably not as excited as you. But then who is?" Michael sat back in the swivel chair, arms folded.

The whole clique was singing the same song. Mina tried to explain her feelings for the thousandth time. "It's not really school I'm excited about . . . but, you know, what being in high school is about. You know, what I'm saying?" she asked.

His head nodded, slow, mechanical, going along to avoid an argument or worse, a lecture.

"But that's 'cause you see everything as some new adventure," Michael said.

"Well, what's wrong with that?"

"Nothing, Mouthy Mi. That's just you anyway. Everything has a happy ending . . . at least in your mind."

She formed her lips to argue but Michael swiveled the chair away. He walked back over to the outfit hanging on the closet door, talking more to it than Mina. "I didn't mean any harm. But, you know, you just always see things on the up side. And nothing is wrong with that." He mumbled, "For you."

For you. Mina decided not to ask what that was about.

Instead, she pushed herself off the desk, walked over to the closet, and linked arms with Michael, trying to kid away his dour outlook. "What's on your mind, brother man? Has Lizzie gotten to you and told you how hard tutoring me in language is?"

"Naw, nothing like that. I'm ready for something new . . . besides school," he added quickly before Mina could summon up another endorsement for the pros of starting school. The words poured as he paced from the closet to the desk. "I'm seriously thinking about applying to a school of arts or something. Del Rio is so weak! I'm just posing as a student here, biding my time. It's just not me!"

Mina studied him. "School of arts? You mean for college? That's good, Mike."

He was usually quiet whenever the clique's discussion turned to college. Even in middle school Mina would talk about finding a college with a good journalism program. Writing was what she did best. It came natural.

She and Lizzie had even talked about looking for a school that had strong theater and journo programs so they could go together. Mina assumed Michael kept out of the topic because, except for Spanish, his classes were more vocational than college-bound. She was glad to hear him talk about the future.

"No. I mean like now. Going to an arts high school in DC. Or maybe Baltimore. Or even New York."

"New York?!" Mina rolled her eyes. "You know you're not going to New York!"

The regret at bringing it up and hurt that she wasn't more understanding was on Michael's face, sending Mina scrambling to apologize. "I'm just saying, come on we only have a few years together." Her eyes lit up. "Hey, maybe you and I could ask the advisor of The Blue Devil Bugle to let us do a column on fashion. That would be fun."

Mina's eyes gleamed as the thought took hold and unfolded, in her mind, as a solid plan.

"Naw, you're the one who's so into writing," Michael said, unenthused. "Not me."

"I'm saying, with your drawings and my writing we . . ."

"Whatever, Mi. Writing for the school newspaper is still more you than me," Michael snapped. He lowered his voice. "I wanna be somewhere I can do my thing. Be me."

Michael was talking in riddles tonight. Mina pulled on her patience when she joked, "What does that mean? Who have you been all this time?"

"Yes, me!" He thumped his chest with his thumb as he talked. "You know me, right? Michael, the dude with the mad drawing and design skills, the chick for a best friend, and the faglike tendencies."

"Mike, nobody thinks you're gay," Mina sputtered, hoping that was the right response. She was on new ground.

His snort of sarcastic laughter called her a liar. He had caught her off guard and knew it. Why should she expect him to speak out loud what had been an unspoken question for years, if not within the clique, among their peers at Del Rio Middle?

They had all heard the whispers about how nicely he dressed, how clean he always stayed, and how it must mean something besides he cared how he looked.

It had gotten confrontational, but only once.

In sixth grade a few guys mistook his fresh and clean appearance for weakness and got in his face. The thumping he gave them was still legend at Del Rio Middle and enough to discourage any more challengers.

He patted Mina's arm like an old granny. "Nobody *knows* if I'm gay, but just about everybody wonders. I don't bother to talk about my designs because that would pretty much seal it for anybody keeping score on reasons for me to be."

At a loss for words, something new for her, Mina couldn't keep up with his string of admissions. Part of her wanted to blurt, "Well are you?" But Michael was stressing and that question felt wrong for a million reasons.

Michael was a neatnik, stylish with a nearly obsessive need to dress his butt off.

But gay?

It had occurred to her, not because of his style or because he could design on a dime, but because she'd never once seen or heard him gawk or talk about girls the way JZ made a part-time job of it.

Then again, the straightest straight man looked gay next to JZ's raging hormones.

Michael pecked her cheek. "Don't lose sleep over it, Diva. I'll be at Del Rio Bay High bright and early, crusty-eyed like the rest of our freshman class."

He left her standing in her bedroom doorway, mouth still open in an attempt to put together a coherent sentence.

12 Hours . . .

"I'm your girl. You're my girl."
—Destiny's Child, "Girl"

Hair wrapped and tied back in a scarf and in pink capri lounge pajamas with green elephants—her good-luck bottoms, the ones she wore the night before Craig Simpson chatted her up at the Ria for the first time ever—Mina settled in at her desk for a last-minute check-in with Lizzie.

She crossed her legs, loving how comfortable and well worn the pj's were since she had designated them as faves the second day of summer. It couldn't have been a coincidence that Craig noticed her the day after she'd worn them to bed. It had to have been the pj's. She couldn't find the actual connection but it made as much sense as anything else.

How else to explain that she'd seen Craig in Rio's Ria every week during the school year and he never paid her one bit of attention? Then, *bam*, she bought the pajama bottoms on a whim during a shopping spree one Wednesday, headed to the Ria the next night to kick it with the clique, and Craig came up and asked if her she was Mina, JZ's friend.

Mina didn't mind the tag "JZ's friend." She would have said she was friends with Magneto, the evil X-Men dude, if it meant getting Craig to talk to her.

She managed not to look too idiotic and answered "Uh-huh." He asked if she played any sports and when she said cheerleading he said, "Oh, right, JZ said you've been holding it down for the Raiders. Well our JV squad sucked last year. Try not to suck as much."

It wasn't your ideal ice breaker, but it was all she needed to officially crush on Craig. So he and JZ had talked about her, huh? Good sign.

She was willing to ignore his last comment since she was already on top of making sure JV was on point this year.

Ever since that day, she made sure to be close enough to say a few words to him whenever she'd seen him at Cimarra or Rio's Ria. Seeing Craig at the Ria wasn't coincidence, everyone was there, but him talking to her—that was special.

Lizzie popped on and Mina jumped right to it.

BubbliMi: What r u wearing? You ready pop ur collar?
Liz-e-O: Mi, ur the fashion diva not me. What's the diff what I wear? Worried I'll ruin ur rep . . . oh wait! U don't have one! LOL.
BubbliMi: OK u can't see me but I'm givin u the cold shoulder.
Liz-e-O: LMAO.
BubbliMi: Seriously. What u stuntin' in tomorrow?
Liz-e-O: La La La La La La ::::hands over my ears:::: I don't feel like talking about school—seriously!
BubbliMi: Alright Alright no more talk of school :::crossing my fingers:::
Liz-e-O: Thank U!
BubbliMi: But don't come looking sbummy . . . or I'm gon' have to joke u. U my girl and all, but . . . just no jeans okay? PLEASE!?!?!?!
Liz-e-O: Whatev!
BubbliMi: On another note. Mike was here earlier and dropped the G-bomb on me.

Liz-e-O: ???????

BubbliMi: He went off about people thinking he was gay and how Del Rio isn't his scene anymore. He's really tripping lately.

Liz-e-O: U know Mike—just in one of his moods probably.

BubbliMi: He needs to stop bringing the drama though, throwing a sister off w/that whole gay thing all casually. Send up a flare, put out a sign—something to let me know u dropping a convo that heavy. Dag!

Liz-e-O: Homophobe!

BubbliMi: So not, Lizzie. I'm just saying we never talk about him and his persnickety ways. To me that's Mike just being Mike. The seed is kind of planted though—now he got me wondering if it's bothering him. Do u think he thinks he's gay?

Liz-e-O: LOL. I'm confused now. What's the question?

BubbliMi: C u not being serious. One of our best friends could be battling with his sexual ID and u making jokes.

Liz-e-O: The only thing Mike is battling is probably a bad case of u gettin on his nerves about school starting.

BubbliMi: I'm gonna remember this when auditions roll around and u bugging me to death about that. Wait till I ice u. See how u like it Theater Chick!

Liz-e-O: Okay. U get to say one more thing about why it's so wonderfully great that prison—I mean school—starts tomorrow.☺

BubbliMi: Just one?

Liz-e-O: Pushing it!

BubbliMi: Ok. I get to see Craig Simpson EVERY DAY. :::cheesing::::

Liz-e-O: LOL. Now there's a good reason for school to start.

BubbliMi: Tru 'dat. OK. Eyes heavy must sleep.

Liz-e-O: Me too. C U.

BubbliMi: An' I'm out!

00:00

"Ch-ch-ch-ch-changes, turn and face the strange."
—David Bowie, "Changes"

The morning was too quiet. It was odd that no early morning commuters competed with the school bus for space on the road flush with high-dollar homes.

Mina swiveled her legs into the aisle, letting Michael slide into the seat, knowing better than to make conversation until the bus was at least out of The Woods and on the main strip—ten minutes worth of driving and just enough time for him to blink the sleep off.

She gazed down the aisle of the bus, scanning the mostly familiar faces of early A.M. zombies. She scrutinized everyone's gear. So far, jeans and T-shirts were the unanimous choice.

No gutsy fashionistas here, she thought, slightly disgusted with everyone's lack of adventure.

She sent a mental message across the silent city, hoping Lizzie had made a better choice. Mina knew it was futile. Dynamite couldn't blast the denim off Lizzie.

The bus screeched into the circle at the end of Dogwood. JZ walked toward Mina and Michael giving out high fives, pounds, and handshakes along the way. The somber quiet broke around him as his voice carried, greeting everybody.

"Ay, girl!" He plopped in the seat across from Michael and made his long legs at home in the middle of the aisle. Not caring about

Michael's unspoken rule of silence, he reached over Mina. "Mike-Mike! Man, Mina you missed it Saturday."

JZ and Michael slapped hands and touched elbows, nearly bowing Mina in the face.

"Don't rub it in." Mina swatted at their arms.

"Kelis and Shonda rolled through. They asked for you," JZ said.

"You know I can only take Kelis in small doses." Mina frowned at the thought of her cheer squad mate. She and Kelis had been co-captains on the rec squad last fall. Both wanted to be alpha cheerleader and sometimes argued over who was in charge of what.

It was no surprise, then, that after they both made the Blue Devils JV cheer squad Kelis had been Mina's only real competition for the position to lead the all-freshmen team. At least until when, only two weeks into practice, Kelis back-talked Coach Embry, all but locking it down for Mina. Coach named Mina head captain and Kelis co. Still meant they had to work together. But Mina took satisfaction in the fact that Kelis's title was literally co-captain and Mina's was just captain.

Ha!

Kelis's mouth was why Mina could only take her for an hour at a time. She thought she knew everything. And how could both of them know everything?

"Your boy Craig rolled through, too," JZ said. He leaned into the aisle to get a good look at Mina's face. "You want to know who he tipped in with?"

Mina shrugged, holding out for a second before blurting, "Who?"

"Kim," JZ said.

"Kim? Vaughn? Varsity captain Kim?" Mina brooded. Wasn't it bad enough Kim was already an established member of the senior pop crowd? Now she had Mina's crush, too?

"Yup. Your boy Craig down with that swirl," JZ teased. "I don't think he's into sistahs."

"Man, why you playing her like that?" Michael chuckled under his breath.

JZ gave Michael another pound. "She was trying play it cool, though, son."

"What?" Mina frowned. She missed so much Saturday evening.

"He brought Kim but they weren't hooking up or nothing," JZ admitted.

"How do you know?" Mina asked, openly pressed.

"Alright your boy did you a favor. I asked him on the low if Kim was his chick. He said she was just rolling with him for the night. She's dating some dude at North County High."

Mina's shoulders relaxed. Craig was still for the taking.

"Don't ever say I ain't do nothing for you," JZ said.

"It's 'cause you love me," Mina teased, happy once more.

"Yeah, like a distant cousin," JZ shot back.

"I owe you one," Mina said.

"I'll definitely remember that. I'm gonna need your mad writing talent to help me out in Lit," JZ said. "Help a brother out on the first essay."

Mina eyebrows squinched in concentration. "Wait. How is me helping you with like . . . a twenty-page paper equal to you just casually dipping in Craig's business for me?"

"Oh, it's like that?" JZ said.

"I'm just saying . . ."

He dismissed Mina with a talk-to-the-hand motion.

"Mike, does that sound fair to you?" Mina asked.

"Shoot that's on ya'll," Michael said, waking up little-by-little. "I'ma sit right back and enjoy my simple essays while ya'll up all night dissecting the meaning of life according to the Bronte sisters."

"I'm trying to help you out, girl," JZ said.

"Ummm . . . okay. How?" Mina asked.

"How you gonna write the next great American novel if you

don't practice?" JZ said. He was totally serious. "You can even thank me in your Pulitzer speech."

He mimed talking into a mic. "To JZ who was in my corner. Thank you for making me see the light. Practice makes perfect. I'll never forget Freshman Lit."

"We need to have a serious talk about balancing favors, 'kay?" Mina sat back in the seat and watched as the bus traveled deep onto Lake View Road where Lizzie once lived.

"Hey, ya'll know we got a new chick in the hood, right?" JZ asked.

"Who?" Mina asked.

It was never too early to squeeze the gossip juice.

"Ms. Phillips's niece?" Michael grudgingly joined the conversation.

"Yeah, shorty from Pirates Cove. She got cakes for days!" JZ leaned in and knocked fists with Michael.

"Stop reaching over me!" Mina hollered.

It figured JZ would comment on the size of the girl's butt before anything else. She had a few hundred questions herself. Was she nice? Why had she moved from one of the DRB's most notorious low-income housing projects, across the bridge, over to the 'burbs? Was she ghetto-fabulous or just ghetto?

But, no, "cakes for days" was pretty much in-depth analysis coming from JZ.

"I saw her with her aunt the other day. She cute in the face, slim in the waist, and got a serious apple bottom," he continued, his lowered voice still the loudest thing on the bus.

"Oh, here we go. This her stop!" JZ fell silent and stared toward the front.

Mina chucked JZ's open mouth closed, but gazed at the bus door, interested to see this new girl firsthand.

She couldn't count on JZ's description of anybody. The girl

could have two heads; as long as one of them was cute, it was all swazy for him.

"That's her," JZ said and had enough sense to whisper it.

Mina stared openly. She disliked her on sight. She was about five feet tall, Mina's height. Her curly, blond highlighted, close-cut natural was too short for Mina's taste but cute in an edgy, top model way. The blond, usually brash and artificial looking on a black person, complemented her golden honey complexion and made her look mature.

Mina felt elementary school next to GoldiLocks. Her own hair was wrapped bone-straight, flat-ironed, and then bent at the ends to give it some definition. She should have fought harder for some highlights or layers. But she kept her hair long and one length for cheerleading and moms wasn't feeling highlights. She liked her hair straight or in spiral curls, her next favorite style, but they may as well have been pigtails or the big dooky plaits next to this girl's brassy, well-styled 'do.

Jealousy pinched her chest.

Being the new chick could go one of two ways: either people would be drawn to her because she was new, exotic, and very unburblike, or the cliques would form quickly, circling like wagons to ice her out.

Mina secretly wished for the second one. She didn't need anybody stealing her thunder.

Mina almost felt guilty for the very Jessica-like thought. But she worked the crowd during middle school, busting her chops in cheerleading, track, student government, and yearbook to keep her face in front of her peers. She was well-known and liked, popular among her fellow freshmen. There was a rightful place in the Uppers for her and she didn't want some brown-eyed blonde from the projects to tip in and mess up her flow just for being "different."

Mina's eyes swept over Goldi's outfit, looking for anything to have something bad to say, and was disappointed there, too. Even though she told herself that the black gauchos with the ankle-length boots was way too fall for the first day of school, she knew the combo was hot. Topped off with a black baby doll T-shirt that read "Ask me if I care!" in jagged, white letters, the entire outfit had an upperclassman ring to it, adding to the girl's older vibe.

"Well let me go do what I do." JZ hopped up and weaved his way to the front as the bus lurched on.

He sat down in the seat behind the new girl.

Mina watched them converse.

"Well?" Michael raised an eyebrow.

"Well what?" Mina said, distracted.

"Opinion."

"About?"

Michael pursed his lips. "Mina, I know you. You already have an opinion on this new chick. So dish!"

"Not really."

Michael snorted—the same snort from the night before that called her a liar. "I see through you, diva. But the more you don't say, the more I know what you thinking anyway."

"Please." Mina waved him off, refusing to comment. She looked across the aisle, where JZ had been seconds before, and stared out the window. The new girl looked like competition, smelled like competition. The last thing she needed.

Del Rio Bay High was a big school. Half of the city's student population fed into it; the other half went to Sam-Well. It was easy to become just another face in the crowd of more than two thousand students—something Mina had always fought against. The new chick stuck out without trying.

The truth was any new chocolate face would stick out at DRB High. There were fewer than three hundred black students in the whole school. Within a day, all of the black kids would know there was a new member in their midst. The grapevine would handle that.

No, it was that shirt. The hair. The air like she didn't care if anyone talked to her—a package that would get New Chick noticed. The reasons people noticed didn't matter. She'd get noticed. Another new face at DRB High was like, so what. But getting noticed was only a half a step away from popularity.

It was official; Mina hated her.

As soon as she stepped off the bus, Mina had a crystal-clear moment of clarity. Call it a lightbulb moment or whatever you want, but for the first time Mina not only understood the saying "be careful what you wish for." She was living it.

Suddenly, standing there on the front campus of DRB High was the last place she wanted to be.

"Still excited?" Michael asked from beside her, as if reading Mina's mind or the slack-jawed numbness on her face.

Why, yes, I am . . . just terrified at the same time.

Mina and Michael fell into place among the streams of students flowing toward the school.

Mina refused to acknowledge the hint of "told you so" in Michael's voice or the accelerated pace of her own heartbeat. "Don't forget . . ." The nervous chirp in her voice surprised her. She cleared her throat, forcing it to be normal. "If you get to lunch first, try and snag a window seat."

Michael snapped a salute. "Yes, Ma'am."

"For real, Mike. We've gotta get near . . ."

"The café," he finished. "Like any of us are actually going to get to the cafeteria before you. You know you'll be the first person up in the joint."

"Maybe so," Mina admitted. "But just in case . . . don't forget."

She and Michael were swept through a set of double doors and into the school's front lobby. Bright blue and gold walls and GO DEVILS in huge letters across the entry welcomed them.

She was really here. Not in an empty shell for cheer practice, but here with everyone else.

Del Rio Bay High, baby, Blue Devil country.

The ice in her belly melted and Mina began to feel the flow. Clusters of students shrank, then grew again as new people replaced those filtering down the school-colors hallways, which were longer and brighter than DRB Middle. No more of the hokey "Today is the first day of the rest of your life" motivational signs hung. Instead, "Go Devils! Beat the Bruins" spirit signs lined the walls, rooting on all the school's sports teams.

The Rules of Engagement memorized after years of following them to the letter, Mina turned it "on." Head up, confident walk, broad smile and big hey to those she knew, coy smile and quiet hello to those she didn't, and the important, thin, pleasant-but-aloof smile and head nod to anybody she knew for a fact was an Upper.

Michael snickered.

"What?" Mina said through her well-placed smile. She waited for Michael to tease her for the momentary lapse in confidence, rub it in. Remind her that this is what she'd been counting down to. She was ready to pretend there was no glacier at the pit of her stomach a few seconds ago, but didn't have to. Michael only shook his head. He steered Mina by the elbow to the nearest stairwell where JZ stood, deep in conversation with a tall, thin blond guy.

Mina squinted in confusion when the guy reached out to exchange a pound and elbow bump with Michael.

"What's up, Mike?" he said, before turning a pearly white grin Mina's way. "Hey, Mina."

Recognition dawned on her. It was Todd, her favorite of JZ's jock buddies from the Raiders rec team and one of the many who always turned out for the all-day tourneys at JZ's house.

"Ohhh. Hey, Todd. When did you go blond? I likes," Mina said, admiring his newly highlighted locks. She followed automatically as

Todd, JZ, and Michael started up the stairs. Her class was in the opposite direction, upstairs but in the very back of the school. The familiar warmth of the fellas felt too good to leave right now. She'd just double time it once they got upstairs.

Todd grinned and ran his hands through his hair. "Thanks. Heather talked me into it last month. Said she was dying to know how I'd look with light hair."

"So you let her talk you into it, all so she could break camp and hook up with Brandon?" JZ said. His mouth turned down in a grimace. "Man, chicks are wack."

Todd and Heather's breakup had made the summer grapevine. She'd kicked Todd to the curb, by e-mail, while he was in California visiting family. The word was, Todd wasn't over it.

Way to rub it in JZ.

Mina poked JZ in the back. "Not all of us are wack," she reassured Todd. "The blond looks cute. Heather gonna be mad jealous when all the girls are up on you."

"Yeah, you know me. Play-ah, Play-ah," Todd joked.

When they reached the landing, JZ took off down a bright blue hallway. "Alright, ya'll. I'll see you at lunch," JZ said.

"See you guys," Todd said, heading behind JZ.

Mina called after them. "Jay, if you get to lunch first . . ."

"Window table. I know." JZ blended into the crowd.

Michael stopped in front of the computer lab. "This is me, Diva."

Mina stared down the corridor. In spite of a handful of teachers pushing along the clusters of students who held court in the middle, the amount of people between Mina and the end of the hallway grew.

"Dag, my class is way down at the end," she said, easing away.

"Better mootsie your tootsies, baby girl." Michael laughed.

"I know, right. Or Jimmy my Choo," Mina said, playing along.

"That's my girl. Had to pick a more expensive shoe and one up me," he said. But Mina saw the pride on his face. She was glad to be in on their little style joke. The first time Michael showed Mina his design sketches and realized they could talk fashion together, his face lit up like someone who had won the lottery. The warmth spread to Mina's feet, feeding her confidence.

She sped up, nearly heeling the person in front of her, and made her way through a pack of girls, squealing and hugging like they hadn't seen one another in years. Their screechy display annoyed and amused Mina. But before she could give them a second look, Mina spotted Lizzie near the end of the freshman bay of lockers. She looked a hot mess.

Mina zigzagged through the bodies, reaching Lizzie in seconds. She plucked at Lizzie's oversized T-shirt. It billowed out in a small puff then fell slack against Liz's thin frame, coming midthigh to her capris.

"What was all the window shopping and Internet surfing over the summer for if not to force you to recognize the Fashion Dos and Definitely Do Nots?" Mina said. "Okay, are you trying to piss me off?"

"Did I?" Lizzie laughed.

"The denim capris are cute. But the shirt!" Mina frowned. "Seriously, how could you come to school sbummy on the first day of all days?!"

Lizzie slipped the shirt over her head, revealing a retro baby doll T-shirt imprinted with the drama faces.

Mina beamed. "Okay, see, now that I like!"

She gave Lizzie's arm a squeeze of approval.

Lizzie threw the big shirt in her locker. "Just testing to see how shallow you actually are." She patted Mina on the shoulder. "You'll be glad to know you're still as materialistic and judgmental as ever."

"Thank youuu." Mina took a deep stage bow and blew Lizzie a melodramatic kiss. "Alright. Now that I see you're looking fly-i-i-i-i-i-i-i- I can go to class in peace. Later, girl."

Mina turned on her heels to head into the classroom and crashed into GoldiLocks.

"My bad," Mina said, drawing back.

Goldi walked by, never acknowledging her.

Jaw dropped, Mina turned back to Lizzie. "Did you see that?"

"She's in my home room," Lizzie said. "Her name's Jacinta Phillips."

"Yeah, that much I know," Mina said. "Quick, which clique will she go to?"

Lizzie squinted. "Ummm . . . the glams probably."

"Jessica's clique?" Mina shook her head. "Nah, almost all of them are rich chicks."

Lizzie turned heel. "You asked. That's just my guess. Gotta run."

Mina walked in the same direction as Goldi. A slow fog of realization dawned that they were in the same class. She had been psyched for this sociology class until just a second ago.

The study of social behavior was one of five Life Lessons (LL) courses—a curriculum based on real-world issues, created to get students more excited about learning.

No one would ever admit, to a parent anyway, that it wasn't a sudden thirst for education that made the courses so popular; LLs required no books and were taught by Life Gurus—very cool term—instead of teachers.

It also didn't hurt that getting into an LL course was about as easy as getting beyond the velvet rope at an awards show. LLs were elective classes like Home Economics, Information Technology, and Marketing. But the process for getting into the Life Lessons courses was nothing like signing up for Home Ec, where you checked it and a second choice elective off on the course selection sheet then waited to see which one you'd get first.

There was a process for getting into a Life Lessons class. It started in the eighth grade. Every eighth-grader, in public school, filled out a three-page questionnaire asking them everything from their favorite color to which ink blot resembled a horse standing on a cloud. Lots of odd stuff that Mina couldn't connect to Psychology, Sociology, Lifestyle Modeling, or any of the other courses.

Whatever mumbo jumbo the test results revealed, what the test reviewers called the students' "life choices," was used to place many of them into an LL course once they hit high school.

It didn't matter what course you requested, ultimately the top-secret answers determined which class the powers-that-be allowed you to have. And only one LL was allowed per student. Once you were assigned a course, you weren't allowed to take another. You might get an LL as a freshman, maybe as a senior. The class was a mix of grades.

Some students never got an LL.

Mina was the only one in the clique to get one. A fact she took as a symbol of her destined status. A theory Michael openly mocked.

"Getting an LL is like the lottery, you just got lucky, Diva," he'd said. "Get over yourself."

Mina refused to agree with him. She was a believer in signs. Everything meant something.

The confidential and highly controversial selection process for Life Lessons courses was fought by many parents for its exclusionary tactics, but embraced by students who felt they were special when chosen to take an LL.

Getting into Sociology, one of the LL courses she had actually requested, made Mina feel like a rock star. Now she just felt queasy.

She stood at the classroom's entrance, sulking. It took her a minute to realize that the room was chairless. A few people lounged on the table tops, but most people stood, uncertain. Mina wandered inside, confused, trying to find someone to make conversation with and ask what the deal was. Her mind raced over the rules of engagement:

1. Know your place. Hers was midstream popular—just well-known enough among her fellow frosh to be part of the in-crowd, but not recognizable enough among the more established set.
2. Treat those you're above with polite courtesy—the social winds change too fast and the peon you were dissing today could be the keeper of the key the next.
3. Treat those you're below with a modest indifference but with due respect—never be eager. Desperation is a scent called loser.
4. Be known for something—for now, she liked to think of herself as "that black girl who's captain of JV cheer squad."

Her eyes scanned the room coolly while her brain worked frantically to categorize everyone. She wanted to eliminate starting a conversation with the Unpops—she wasn't in the mood to make casual conversation with some nobody that might end up clinging to her as a friend beyond the bell.

She smiled in the general direction of Grace, an Upper, while still eying the area for the right someone to talk to so she'd look properly social.

Before she could step into the room, a voice from beside her said, "Umph, they just let anybody into these classes."

Mina's stomach clenched. Praying someone else had the same haughty, clipped voice she glanced to her left.

Jessica stood, model-thin in a pink and green plaid miniskirt, blush pink baby doll T-shirt, and a pair of pink, ankle-wrap espadrilles.

Mina tried not to stare at the skirt. She'd wanted that same exact skirt so bad, she'd gone completely kindergarten and broken into a full session of begging in the store.

Please, please, Ma. Please!

But her mother had flat-out refused. "Mina, you have a million minis already. Enough."

"So the fresh fish finally made it to the big pond, huh?" Jessica said.

"Hi, Jessica." Mina's heart raced. This couldn't be happening to her. Her luck was not usually this bad.

And she has on my skirt!

Jessica ran her fingers through her long weave, which Mina noticed was now wavy instead of straight. "So, are you still cheering?"

"Uh-huh," was Mina's only answer. She stood straight, mindful of her body language. She was uninterested but not intimidated, not much.

"That's cool. Oh you're on JV, right? I gave up cheerleading," Jessica said with an eye roll. "It was boring."

"I heard you were step mistress last year." Mina hoped she was still on the safe side of nonchalant. She decided to toot her own horn a little. "You were the freshman captain, huh? Like me this year."

"Yeah, I heard you made Junior Varsity Captain." Jessica rushed the conversation back to herself. "I'm captain of step squad again this year, too. Step is the hotness, girl. Cheerleading is so five minutes ago."

Naturally, Jessica didn't mention that cheerleading was now off-limits due to Mari-Beth dropping hints during Jess's second season that she was "so over" cheerleading. Mari-Beth hadn't cheered a day in her life. She was tired of Jess having practice and competitions interfering with the time she wanted to call Jess on the fly and be entertained or at least bored along with a friend.

Jess didn't mind the pattern of domination in her friendship with Mari. Jess knew her place. Rather than risk being cut off from vacations on the beach and weekend trips to the salon, Jess took every ounce of her high maintenance bud's demands.

So far Mari hadn't pulled any tantrums about Jess being on the Stomp Starz. Jess was good at step and wanted to stay on the team. But none of that was any of Mina's business.

Mina didn't know or care why Jessica stopped cheering. All she heard was Jessica baiting her to say something against step. Jessica's own twin was on the varsity cheer squad, so how five minutes ago could it be?

Jessica was an Upper and Mina knew where she stood, which was right there, on the outside looking in, letting the small talk linger. But she steered clear of the trap with a simple, "I've been cheering too long to stop now."

"Yeah, you need to stick to cheerleading," Jessica said. "JV was so weak last year! Keep up the tradition." She waved to Grace and sashayed out of Mina's face.

Mina's hands shook as she juggled a handful of notebooks.

Allowing herself a few calming breaths, Mina leaned against the wall. A small, plump white woman with a wild nest of shocking red hair walked in and stationed herself at Mina's elbow. She wore clogs, a tunic, and a pair of well-worn slacks, very 60s meets Old Navy.

Mina waited for her to launch into the usual My name is speech. The woman stood still as a tree, eyeing the students pouring into the classroom.

Mina swayed, fidgeted, and sideways-glanced along with her classmates, waiting for the Guru to relieve the stress of the unknown. She inched farther into the classroom, away from the door, turning so she could face the Guru head on.

More time ticked by. Still she said nothing, just stared at them. The students stared back, silently confused and too embarrassed to challenge her odd behavior. The whispy swish of shoe against carpet as someone shifted from foot to foot was almost as loud as the teacher's voice from the adjoining room.

The melodic boing of the final bell filled the room for a second. There were a few more seconds of confused shuffling of feet and throat clearing.

Mina's nerves buzzed. As a nonstop talker, silence was her enemy.

She jumped when the woman's voice finally cracked the silence like an egg. "Many of you are probably a little nervous about taking your first sociology class."

Glad for the release, a hiss of murmurs: "No not really," "A little," and the inevitable, clownish, "This isn't Algebra? I'm in the wrong room," caused a ripple of giggles.

Mina's nervous laughter caught in her throat when the Life Guru stopped inches from her. She had to force her eyes away from the halo of red, shimmering curls framing the woman's face to look her in the eye.

"Hi, I'm Mrs. Simms. Why aren't you sitting down?"

Mina looked around for help before stuttering, "I . . . I . . . um, don't have a chair."

Mrs. Simms seemed to consider this, snorted lightly, and then returned to the center of the room again. "On a scale of one to ten, how uncomfortable were you guys when I stood here just staring?"

A chorus of high-end numbers rang out. It seemed to please her. She laughed like someone had just told her a really good joke. "Good. Same scale, this time how uncomfortable you were walking into a classroom without any chairs?"

More nines and tens were called out.

"Well then, welcome to Intro to Sociology, the study of how groups influence how individuals think, feel, and act. Or as some students have labeled it in the past, That Crazy Old Bird's Class." She laughed at her joke, making her way around the room, weaving in and out between the tables as she gabbed on. "Get used to being faced with new challenges. In my class, there is no comfort zone. And I'm not going to waste a lot of time coddling you guys. We have a project to start." She opened a door next to Mina. "All of the seats are in here. They're in groups of four, which represent your project groups. Your name is taped to a chair. Find it."

The class peered around her into the dark space.

"Take your seats and place your groups around a table," she instructed from her desktop. Her legs kicked softly at the air. Her smile held on to whatever secret the project had in store.

Dazed, students made their way to the closet. They waited. When it was clear the teacher wasn't going to help them pass out the chairs, they bunched around the door, staring. Mina stepped inside and began calling names.

Mrs. Simms hopped off her desk and was at the closet in two steps. "Good for you. What's your name?"

"Amina Mooney."

"Amina, even though the rest of the group sat back and wondered what to do, you stepped up. Very good. You didn't allow the group's reluctance to influence your decision to take action."

Mrs. Simms grinned like someone who didn't have a grip on reality.

"I'm sorry. Go on, Amina." She took her place back on top of the desk.

Mina continued calling out names.

"Oh, this one is mine." She pulled out the next chair and stepped out of the closet. "I guess somebody else should take over."

She took the chair to a back table, nearly bumping shoulders with Jessica as she passed.

Mina kept her eye on the closet, curious who else would be in their group. She hoped she'd drawn Grace on her team.

Someone else jumped into Mina's role as chair distributor and called out "Kellita Lopez."

Mina watched as Kellita approached. Her long, full chestnut hair fell in soft, voluptuous waves to her shoulders. She put her chair down in a slow, fluid move then sat erect. She folded her hands primly on the table with what some people would call grace and others snobbery.

Mina was ready to vote for the latter when the girl spoke up in a near whisper.

"You can call me Kelly."

"And I'm Mina. No one calls me Amina except my mom . . . when she's mad," she chattered.

The name Jacinta Phillips was called, jolting Mina back to the chair handout.

She whirled around in her chair and caught sight of Goldi taking her chair. Mina held her breath as Jacinta walked to their table.

First Jessica and now this?

Mina glared as Jacinta situated her chair at the far end of the short table, aloof, no intros or hellos.

She held on to hope. Maybe the last group member would be Grace. *Come on, let it be Grace, let it be Grace.*

"Jessica Johnson," the person handing out chairs called.

Mina's mouth gaped open. The old nausea she'd get right before cheer practice rolled in and settled in the pit of her gut. What if Lizzie was right about Goldi joining the glam clique? Mina sized Kelly up quickly. She didn't look like someone that would offer much shelter from the storm if Goldi and The Bee joined forces.

Jessica walked stiff-legged back to the table and placed her chair opposite Mina's. She flipped her weave off her shoulder then gave each one of her group members a long hard look. But Jacinta beat her with the first smart words.

"*Three* black Barbies! Unbelievable." Jacinta pursed her lips and stared past the girls into a distant part of the classroom.

"Look, frosh," Jessica raised her eyebrows at Jacinta. "I don't know you and you don't know me. So check yourself. You don't even want to go there with me."

Mina was giddy. The shots exchanged between Jacinta and Jessica were music to her ears. Hope wasn't buried yet.

Jacinta eyebrows hitched then swan dived into a scowl. "Barbie, please! You don't want to go there with *me*. Mrs. Simms," she called out, voice husky with annoyance. "Are we in the same group because we all black?"

Mrs. Simms looked over and pondered the question for a second. Her hair rustled like a flock of cardinals taking flight as she laughed. "No. But if you girls end up discovering something about the sociology among yourselves because you're all of a similar racial makeup, then I might give you extra credit."

"You're gonna end up getting us in trouble, clashing with the teacher before we even know what's up," Mina fussed in a whisper.

"God, Mina, can you be more dramatic?" Jessica's perpetual frown deepened.

Jacinta pursed her lips as if she smelled something bad. She rolled her eyes at Mina and dismissed all of them with a slight turn of her head.

Kelly sat back from the table and kept her eye trained on the Guru.

Mrs. Simms launched into the assignment's purpose, her voice high and excited. Mina's group joined the rest of the class, listening, interested in spite of themselves as she explained that their job over the semester would be to eradicate their prejudices. When she explained that eradicate meant to get rid of, whoops of high-pitched, nervous laughter echoed throughout the room.

They looked around at one another, unsure if the Guru had lost her mind or if she seriously believed such a huge task, one that the world itself hadn't mastered, could be accomplished by their class of twenty-four, in one semester.

Mrs. Simms's voice boomed over the buzzing, startling the students into submission. "If you don't believe one person can change the world, then you haven't been paying attention!"

Her declaration made, she sat atop her desk, cross-legged until her outburst sank in. When it was quiet, a smile broke through her stern face. She softened her voice. "One day a young guy, fourteen years old, the age of most of you in here, made a comment to an older woman. A comment the woman felt was inappropriate. Days later that young boy was found dead."

With their attention wrapped around her words, she continued in a voice only a notch above a whisper, allowing the teacher's voice from the next classroom to filter into their silent space. The students leaned forward to hear.

"That young boy's name was Emmett Till. And his murder occurred in 1955, in Money, Mississippi. Emmett wasn't from the hot, steamy banks of the Mississippi; he was from the city, Chicago." Her hands rose, fell, clapped, and clasped. They constantly moved, emphasizing words as she took the class back in time.

"He was in Mississippi to visit an uncle. According to his cousin, who was also from Chicago, one day he, Emmett, and some friends went to a local store. Emmett took a photo of a white girl out of his wallet, claiming she was his girlfriend. Boys being boys, his friends challenged him. They dared him to go into the store and say something to the white woman behind the counter to prove he was such a big man with the white ladies."

She paused and outlasting the last wave of nervous whispers and giggles, resumed her story, never raising her voice.

"No one knows what Emmett said to the woman. Some say he whistled at her. The woman claims he grabbed her and told her not to be afraid because he had been with white girls before. No one will ever know the truth. What is well-known is days later, the woman's husband and his half-brother dragged Emmett from his uncle's home, beat him, shot him, and dumped his body in the Tallahatchie River. Another fact: the two men were acquitted of the murder by an all-white jury."

Mrs. Simms ramped up her lecture. Her voice was passionate. "Emmett Till's death breathed new life into the civil rights movement! His death, and the outrage it caused among blacks and whites, was the spark that would turn into a flame when later that same year Rosa Parks refused to give up her bus seat to a white person in Montgomery, Alabama. In death, Emmett Till helped to rid our nation of a little prejudice. Because, even though there was still a lot of strife between blacks and whites in 1955, times were changing. And a sign of that change was the fact that many whites were no longer tolerant of the vicious, cruel behavior rampant in the southern part of this country. The story of Emmett Till made many people think twice about discounting the importance of someone's life because of their race."

Her last words hung in the air.

Tiny goose bumps covered Mina's arms. She'd watched a documentary with her parents about Emmett Till once and had nightmares for days from the images of his battered face. The company of twenty-three other students in the brightly lit classroom couldn't push away her memories of those images. She was glad Mrs. Simms had spared them the photos.

Convinced the students had marinated long enough in the silence, Mrs. Simms hopped down from her desk and reached out to them, arms wide open. "What I'm asking you to do is open yourselves to prejudice and make a conscious choice either to embrace it or eliminate it from your life. The choice you make will change your world and the world around you."

Someone spoke up. "But, you're assuming we're prejudiced."

Others nodded in agreement.

Mina sat a little straighter, as if slumping would give away any of her own prejudices.

"Aren't you?" Mrs. Simms's eyebrows arched. She drew from a stack of papers and began passing a handout to the tables. "So the upperclassmen don't give the freshmen crap just for being new?"

A few snorts at that one.

"The geeks and jocks always see eye to eye on what's cool?" Mrs. Simms stared at a DRB baseball player.

He looked over his shoulder. Mrs. Simms was still waiting for his answer when he turned back around. Finally, he shrugged. "I don't know."

"No? What about the café?" Mrs. Simms asked, dropping the handout at Mina's table.

Mina's ears perked up.

"Whenever I have lunch duty, I love watching the café. How many of you know about the café?"

Most hands went up. Kelly and Jacinta were two of only four students without theirs raised.

"Well, you'll find out about it soon enough." Mrs. Simms laughed. "It's one of Del Rio High's best sociological experiments. At least that's how I look at it. Let me just say this, the café is proof that there are plenty of prejudices within the walls of Del Rio Bay High. Anyone disagree?"

Mrs. Simms walked among the aisle of tables, her eyes questioning the sea of shaking heads. She looked at each and every student she passed while she spoke. "There are many types of prejudice. Racial is just the most obvious. Even if you can't imagine prejudice resulting in something as horrible as Emmett Till's death, I'm sure many of you harbor some degree of prejudice against just about anyone who isn't exactly like you. So, over the next six weeks, your job will be to explore those prejudices and decide how to deal with them. Sociology is about collecting, analyzing, and then interpreting data. And that's how I want you to approach each and every assignment."

Mrs. Simms arrived at the head of the class. She held up a finger. "First, you will collect information about one another. Where you're from, how were you raised, what you like to do, what you want to do in the future. Whatever information you feel you need to understand who each person is." She thrust a second finger in the air. "Second, you will analyze the information you collect. How is each group member's lifestyle, likes, desires, and dislikes similar to your own? How are they different?"

She let the information sink in for a minute before punching a third finger upward. "Last, you'll interpret the information. Does what you know about this person affect how you feel about them? Did you feel differently before you knew these things?"

Mrs. Simms turned to walk away then stopped like she had forgotten something. "Oh, and after today, none of the group work will be done in class. So keep track of the packet I just handed out. It covers all of the details."

A collective "Huh?" rippled through the room.

"Since we only meet twice a week, we need class time to cover actual theories of sociology," Mrs. Simms explained. "So, you'll tackle learning about one another on your own time. The final exam will be a presentation of your findings."

She took a seat behind her desk and began writing.

The students were mute, waiting for more instruction. Slowly each group began planning when the class realized there was no more.

Low conversations built into excited chatter.

"Well, I'll start," Mina said. Her head ping-ponged among the three group mates as she spoke. "To me, this should be an easy project for us. We're all black, so how many prejudices do we have to get rid of?"

"You mean we're all black-*ish*," Jacinta said. She sniggled openly as she cut her eyes toward Kelly.

"That's ignorant," Jessica said. "I'm mixed."

Jacinta's bark of laughter made Mrs. Simms look up momentarily. "You mixed with what? Black and dark black?"

Mina was too startled by Jacinta's boldness to snicker at the joke.

Jessica held her head high and looked down on Jacinta. Answering this was a formality to set the record straight, her rigid posture said. "First of all my mother is white and my father is black. Second, it's 'you're mixed with what' not 'you mixed with what.'"

Jacinta peered at Jessica, pretending to take a closer look. "Obviously you convinced yourself you mixed. But good luck perping as a white chick in the real world."

Jessica pursed her lips, her stance icy and dismissive.

Mina didn't know whether to give Goldi some dap for busting on Jessica or warn her that she was making one evil enemy. She decided to put them back on track, instead of taking any kind of side. "Look, speaking as one of the three Barbie's, Jacinta you've already put in your own bias. It's not the best way to start out."

"Whatever, man," Jacinta replied. "The project not about making friends. It sound like I'm stuck with you Barbies, Bratz dolls, or whatever ya'll call yourself. I can't see how we won't be spending time together, like it or not."

"I vote for not," Jessica sneered.

"Okay, I know what we could do," Mina said. "Let's all write down our thoughts on one another, just based on meeting this first time."

Kelly spoke up for the first time since introducing herself. "So, like, our first impressions?"

When the girls looked at her, she nervously tucked her long hair behind her ear and shrank back into her chair.

"Exactly," Mina confirmed. She leaned in to be heard over the loud planning of other groups. "We won't share these first impressions with one another until the very end of the project. And we'll update our impressions throughout the semester."

"That's brilliant, Mina. Not!" Jessica said. "It still doesn't answer how we're going to get to know each other. And I'm using that strictly to mean for the class." She flipped her hair and cut her eyes at Jacinta. "I'm not interested in knowing more than I need to."

"We could plan to meet after school a few times," Mina said.

"And do what?" Jacinta frowned.

"I don't know. Talk or whatever. It was just a suggestion," Mina huffed in frustration. "Look, no one else is saying anything . . . useful."

Jacinta shrugged. "I don't get what we'd do after school. Just sit there staring at each other?"

"Well, Miss Grammar, the point of the project is to find out about each other," Jessica said. "We've got to talk at some point outside of class. I hate to agree with Mina, but after school in the library could work."

"Are you for real? 'Cause I know that hair ain't," Jacinta said.

Jessica and Jacinta stared one another down until Jacinta turned to Mina. "I'm saying, so we're just going to sit in the library and go around a circle and talk about ourselves? That's not getting to know somebody."

"Why not? How else do you get to know somebody?" Mina challenged. "Mind reading?" She knocked Kelly's knee lightly under the table and snickered, but Kelly sat wooden, distant from the drama.

Jacinta gave her a blank look. "I'll explain this once for the slow crowd. Sitting in the library taking turns talking won't work 'cause then we're only finding out what that person wants us to know. That's why it's not really getting to know somebody."

She sat back in her chair and folded her arms. Lecture over.

Kelly leaned in. "Well, what about spending the night at each other's houses?" She looked expectantly at Jacinta.

"Don't look at me." Jacinta raised an eyebrow toward Mina. "Obviously she's the expert on the best way to do this right."

"I didn't say all that," Mina said.

"Or, maybe Weavearella has an idea." Jacinta chucked her head toward Jessica.

"At least I have hair," Jessica said.

Jacinta raised her arms and shrugged. "But whose?"

"Oooh original." Jessica spoke up importantly. "Look, Quiet Girl, how is the sleepover thing different from the library idea?"

Kelly sat back in her chair, silent again.

"Hello," Jessica said. "We don't have all day."

Kelly pushed at her already tucked hair and cleared her throat. "Well, it's kind of the same. But I see what Jacinta means about the library." She threw Mina a quiet "sorry" look. "If we go to each other's house, we'll at least get to see where the person lives."

Kelly paused, waiting for someone to object. No one did. "If we do sleepovers, like on a Friday or Saturday, we meet each other's family and see how each of us lives." She shrugged. "Some things might come up that wouldn't if we only met at school."

"I think that's a really good idea," Mina gushed. A sleepover being homework was up her alley even if it did involve being in the same atmosphere as Jessica overnight. "So, Kelly, how about we have it at yours first? Since it was your idea."

"Oh, we don't have to . . ." Kelly said.

"Come on, Quiet Girl, it may as well be you," Jessica said. She took out some paper and began taking notes. "We'll plan who's next at each sleepover. I have a busy life, so I can't be spending every weekend with you"—she struggled for a word before settling on—"girls."

"Yeah, I'm sure you all's social calendars are like totally full," Jacinta said in a *Legally Blonde* accent.

Jessica flicked a finger at Mina and Kelly. "I don't know about theirs, but mine is."

"I think this could be fun, if we just . . . you know, put our differences aside," Mina said.

"Yeah, that's called the point of the project, Mina," Jessica snorted. "So if we're all on board with writing our impressions, we can decide what to do with them later. Let's do our first impressions now so we don't have to talk."

A look passed between Mina and Jacinta. Mina was almost certain they were thinking the same thing—"bitch."

Sociology

August 29, 2005

Jacinta Phillips

I'm not feeling this class, at all. No, I'm not feeling Del Rio Bay High, at all. Already!

My father wants me to give DRH a try and be open to the "experience." So how does the year start? I end up in a group with the Bobble head 'burb girls. I can't wait to tell Daddy that it's exactly like I said it would be—a whole bunch of vanilla faces and chocolate faces that act vanilla. Everybody knows, Del Rio Bay High is one of the snottiest, think-they're-all-that schools in the county.

My worst nightmare was being stuck in a school full of chatty white girls (and the halls are definitely filled with them). And I end up with their black clones! Oh my bad, Jessica is "mixed." Is she for real or what?! She's chocolate as a Hershey bar, don't have an ounce of hair on her that she was born with and have big thick Naomi Campbell lips. Mixed. O-kay!

Kelly barely said ten words. I have no idea what to think. Mousy? Scared of her own shadow? What's up with the hair tucking thing?! Oh, but her embroidered capris are hot! I've never seen them like that with the flowers patterned down the side.

Mina talks too much! I was surprised her and Swirl weren't friends. But obviously they're not because Swirl was straight rude to her. Grow a backbone to go with all that mouth, girl.

I think these girls are tripping. Everyone here is

fake. At least at Sam-Well High it would be fake girls I'm used to.

Is the six weeks up yet?!

Sociology
Project Prejudice
August 29, 2005
Observations by Kelly Lopez: First Impressions

We didn't have LLs at my old school, McKinley Stewart (McStew) school of the elite, shallow, and privileged. But my guidance counselor told Grand she'd pull some strings to make sure I got Sociology because she thought it would help bring me "out of my shell."

I'm not in a shell, not really. If people talk to me, I'll talk back. All of that bickering between Mina, Jacinta, and Jessica today—that wasn't talking. So I chose not to say anything. But here's what I thought:

Jessica is like every other girl I ever had the misfortune to sit next to at McStew. It's not enough, for girls like Jessica, to be (think they are, anyway) better than you. They have to announce it. I'm used to it.

I'll give it to Mina. Jessica was mean to her and Jacinta seemed to ignore her, but Mina never stopped offering her two cents. I could like her.

I get Jessica (kind of), but I don't understand Jacinta. Why was she so defensive? How can the first words you say to someone be, "Oh great, three black Barbie dolls," or whatever she said. The funny thing is, it seems like Jessica and Jacinta would hit it off—two ultraopinionated people, sounds like a match made in heaven. Then again, maybe a friendship between two people like that is the first sign of the end of the world.

If nothing else, this is an interesting way to start public school.

Project Prejudice
8-29-05
Jessica Johnson: First Impressions

I have nothing in common with these girls.

And what did I do to deserve a class with chatterbox, wannabe Mina? Last year without her was like a long vacation. Now she's back. Still the same old Mina, talk, talk, talk.

I smelled ghetto fabulous before Jacinta opened her mouth. Call it a gift. Obviously, she's not aware that certain rules apply here at DRB High and the first rule is: Know Your Place. Guess I'll have to play teacher.

I recognize Quiet Girl (what was her name? Kellina?). She lives a few streets down from Mari-Beth. Which means her family has money. First order of business, get the scoop on her; she may come in handy.

My first impression is that someone has played a cruel joke on me by placing me in this group.

Soc
8/29/2005
Observations by Amina Mooney: First Impressions

Okay, I'm going to ignore the fact that I must live

and breathe Jessica for the next six weeks. I will not let her or Goldi ruin the thrill of getting an LL my very FIRST semester.

I wonder what it means that I got the LL I wanted (good sign) but ended up with Jessica (hella bad sign). Or is it? Maybe this is our chance to become friends. Maybe this is how I make it into the café through the hard knocks of getting Jess to like me. It could happen . . . I guess.

This project is sweet. How often are you forced to get to know someone and decide for yourself if you truly have anything in common instead of basing opinion on all that surface junk (she thinks she's cute, blah, blah). And I'm going to tell Michael my whole theory that, this is a symbol of things to come, is right! Two Uppers in my class—one in my group (too bad it's the wrong one)—it's gotta mean something. Meanwhile, impressions:

Jacinta, AKA GoldiLocks, what's with the chip on the shoulder? Her 'tude is annoying, not scary. But okay, mad props for standing up to Jessica. For real! So she can't be ALL bad.

Jessica . . . what can I say? Still using your powers for evil instead of good. But you're gonna love me.

Kelly, I can't get a real read on you. She has this way of looking at you as if you're speaking a foreign language. Also, a few times (and I know this is mean) I felt like yelling "boo" to see if Kelly would like jump out of her skin or something. Totally deer in the headlights.

Lunch Outside of the Fishbowl

"I'm so fly, and you, you so not."
—Young Jeezy (ft. Mannie Fresh), "And Then What"

On her way to lunch, Mina took the scenic route, soaking in every moment. Resisting the urge to stand in the middle of the hall and twirl, Mina walked hurriedly as if she had somewhere important to be. Her simple goal: be noticed.

She strolled by the fancy computer lab, waving at an old friend who played field hockey.

Outside of the vast auditorium, which held 1,500 people and boasted the newest in sound and lighting technology, she joked with a Chamil, a mutual frosh friend of hers and Lizzie's. Chamil, short for chameleon, was Mina's name, approved by Lizzie, to describe people really good at acting—a nod to their ability to change into so many different characters.

She was wrapping up her convo with the Chamil when Lila, President of Bay Dra-da and a total Upper, came up to the girl, interrupting the conversation without even a hint of excuse me. Mina didn't take offense when the girl's full attention focused on Lila. It wasn't like she could help the girl get a good part. Turning on her heels, she went on her way, slowing down in front of the gymnasium. The new, shiny hardwood floor, free from scratches, gleamed through the open door. She scanned the room and seeing no signs of the teacher, cracked the door open.

"Hey, Ricky," Mina called out to a senior that used to hang around The Woods' park regularly to play ball with JZ.

A few guys looked her way before going back to their basketball game.

"I'm out," Ricky stepped away from the game. "What's up, Mina?" He pushed his sweaty blond mop out of his eyes. "Finally playing the big leagues?"

Mina's grin spread. Even though Ricky always teased that Mina was too young for him, they flirted like crazy anytime he played ball in The Woods and he always said he'd reconsider the dating thing, once she got to DRH, "joining the big leagues."

"Yup. So you're taking me out when?" She pretended to flip through a date book.

He chuckled. "Where you off to?"

"Lunch. I didn't see you as much this summer."

"I played summer league in Meade this year," Ricky said. "Trying to step up my game before college."

"Oh, did you . . ."

"Hey!" Lizzie popped up beside her.

Mina linked arms with her. "Hey, you!"

"Hey, Lizzie. Later, Mina." Ricky raced back to the game.

"Liz, my world is crumbling," Mina said, glad to spill the tea about her soc class.

"What? Craig hasn't fallen madly in love with you yet? The fool!"

"There's still time for that," Mina assured her. "No. You won't believe this. Jessica is in my soc class. AND we're in this group project thing."

"No!"

"Yes!"

Lizzie squeezed Mina's arm. "I'm so sorry."

"I know. And to top it off, that girl, Jacinta . . ."

"The girl from my homeroom? The one who igged you this morning?" Lizzie said.

Mina nodded. "Yeah. She's in my group, too."

"Poor, Mi-Mi. Let me bright side it. You only have soc every two days. Me and you have Lit every day," Lizzie said.

They skipped in a circle, relishing their silliness.

"I'm trying not to panic over the whole thing," Mina said. "I mean, who knows, maybe Jess will . . ."

"Not eat her young when she has kids?" Lizzie snickered.

Mina laughed so hard they had to stop walking.

"That's wrong, but so true." Mina shook, still laughing. "No. I was going to say maybe Jess won't . . . be such a . . ."

"Bitch," Lizzie finished. "Maybe. But don't count on it."

"I know. I can dream though," Mina said wistfully.

Lizzie lowered her voice. "Uh-oh, speak of the devil and she appears . . ." She nodded straight ahead. "Ouch and wearing that miniskirt you loved."

"Oh, I know. Don't you hate that?" Mina grimaced. "I'm so glad I didn't buy it."

"You mean your mom didn't let you buy it."

"Minor deet," Mina said.

She and Lizzie cut their conversation as they neared the cafeteria where Jessica stood with her best friend, Mari-Beth. The two mirrored one another in body shape and hair style. If Jessica weren't so dark, she and Mari-Beth looked more like sisters on the surface than Jessica and her own twin.

"Seriously, Mina, don't tell me you have this lunch period," Jessica said.

"Hate to be the bearer of bad news, but yup." Mina's stomach bubbled nervously. Standing up to Jessica took all of her energy. Her entire body had to get in on the act.

"This first day blows. There are wannabes everywhere," Mari-Beth said.

She tossed her hair, giving Jessica a look that Jessica promptly understood meant open the door. Jessica scuttled forward and swung the door wide. Mari-Beth walked through without a glance toward Mina and Lizzie. But Jessica gave them the proper this-means-you look before slipping through the cafeteria doors behind her evil twin in spirit.

"Honestly, Mi, I'm not sure why you'd want to sit outside with them," Lizzie said, knowing her words fell on deaf ears.

Mina answered Lizzie from her fog. "I don't want to sit outside with *those* two. But if they're part of the package . . ." she shrugged. "Come on."

Mina burst through the cafeteria doors like she owned the place.

"First day of lunch and year five of the streak," Mina said.

"The streak lives!" Lizzie said on cue. "Do you see the guys?"

"Nope. We're here first." Mina took inventory of open tables. She squealed in delight. "Look, there's still one empty window table. Let's go."

With one eye on the activity outdoors in the café, Mina speed-walked to the round table past the rest of the long grayish-white fake marbleized bench tables that blended in with the off-white cinder block walls.

The café was the bright, sunny spot of the bland room, and Mina was drawn to the round table, only one of four, that put her as close to it as possible. She plopped down, facing the window. Lizzie sat with the window to her side.

Mina pulled out her lunch and gaped at the outdoor fishbowl.

Twenty feet wide, twenty feet across, accessible by a single door at the far end of the cafeteria, the café was nothing more than an island of concrete surrounded by a patch of grass just wide enough to be a pain for the maintenance crew to cut. The students' slice of heaven. No teachers patrolled it. No wannabes penetrated it.

"Ooh, speaking of bad news, guess who my Algebra II teacher is?" Lizzie cracked open a yogurt. When Mina didn't answer, Lizzie tried again. "Mi, guess who my math teacher is."

"Mii-naa?" Lizzie sang, nearing the end of her patience.

"Huh? Oh, who?" Mina cutt her eyes between Lizzie and the outdoors. Thanks to the floor-to-ceiling glass panes surrounding the fishbowl, she wasn't missing a thing.

A strange urge to bum-rush the court seized Mina's brain. She just wanted her toe to touch the concrete. Just a toe. She had a vision of rushing out, inhaling the air, and running back in—all but ensuring she'd be labeled that crazy chick or worse, desperate.

Her neck strained as she turned to get a fuller view of the action, no longer taking peeks on the low. She itched to get up until the café door opened and closed with a whomp, spitting a poof of air in her face and bringing her back to her senses.

Unless you lived under a rock, freshmen came into the school knowing about the café's one and only rule: Invitation only!

Funny how Mrs. Simms had talked about it. Even she left the whole café thing in mystery. Made it seem even more like some bizarre lunchtime secret society.

Getting in wasn't a matter of if for Mina, but when, she thought, tapping her foot to faint strains of music flowing freely from the area.

She shook the cobwebs from her brain and turned her eyes away from the window and back to Lizzie's very tight face. "I zoned out, didn't I?" Mina asked.

"Uh, yeah. Just to have you back to earth, I'll be glad when you get called up to café land," Lizzie said, scooping yogurt. She spun around and tried to see the café like Mina did. People flowed between the five bistro tables—the only place to actually sit and eat—lounged against the one brick wall, and stood atop the sandy-colored concrete benches that anchored the corners, everywhere flaunting their freedom from a teacher monitor.

It was a nice day to eat outside. But that's all Lizzie saw, a chance to eat outside. The café didn't hold the same magical allure for her.

"My bad. So, what about your Algebra II teacher?" Mina said.

Michael sat down next to Mina. "Hey, Diva! Is that all you eating? What's up, Lizzie?"

He turned his nose up at Mina's "lunch" of apple juice and cheese crackers.

"Hi, Michael. Finally, someone who might actually talk to me," Lizzie groused playfully.

"I was too excited this morning to think about lunch. But I'm good," Mina said. Her stomach rumbled, reminding her that she'd regret being stingy with the calories come cheer practice.

Michael passed his burger under her nose. "Sure?"

Her stomach rumbled again, loudly. Michael laughed. He pushed his tray at her. "Share my fries."

Mina dug in. "Well, you know a chick won't turn down a fry."

JZ sat in a seat next to Lizzie, talking loudly.

"There go my girl. Liz! So you gonna get me the hook up!?"

"I've already said no," Lizzie ducked away from JZ's only-when-he-wanted-something hug.

"No to what?" Mina watched Kelly pass and head for a near-empty table in the middle of the room. She sat and opened a book.

"I just found out Lizzie has a class with Rachel Hall. I been trying holler at shawty all summer! But she got some boyfriend at Sam-Well." JZ followed Mina's stare. "What you looking at?"

"Jay, first of all, Rachel and I aren't hardly what I'd call friends. Second, hell-llooo." Lizzie did a cheesy Miss America figure-eight wave. "First day of school, calling. How will I look playing match-maker and we've had a total of one whole class together?"

JZ winked. "Like you have good taste. For real, hook a brother up, Liz-O. Get me that in and I'll do the rest. Let her know brother probably got more going on than some punk from Sam-Well."

He pulled at Lizzie's hair before going on to the food line.

"Mi, what are you looking at, now?" Lizzie scowled. "The café's in the other direction."

"Hold up. I'll be right back." Mina headed toward Kelly's lonely island, head-checking once more to make sure no one was going to join the table. "Are you waiting for somebody?"

Startled, Kelly's head popped up from the book. She shook her head no slowly in answer. She was alone.

"Why don't you sit with us?" Mina gestured to the window.

Kelly's eyes crinkled as she followed Mina's pointing finger.

Taking Kelly's hesitation for shyness, Mina addressed her the way she would a small, scared child. "Come on. It's cool. Consider it extra credit for soc."

She helped Kelly gather her books and led her to the table.

"Everybody, this is Kelly." Mina sat down. She motioned to Kelly to sit next to Lizzie. "Kelly, Lizzie, and Mike."

Kelly threw up a quick wave, sat down, and immediately opened her book.

Lizzie raised her eyebrow at Michael. Who reads during lunch? Well, unless they were cramming for a test.

Michael pointed to Mina and shrugged.

They knew how Mina was—always on the quest to earn brownie points where she could. Like she always said, staying on the pop side took a lot of effort and you had to schmooze the little people. It wouldn't be odd for Kelly to be her latest "little person" that they'd have to indulge until she moved on to another.

JZ returned to the table. He sat across from Kelly and openly leered. "What's up? My name is Jason. Everybody calls me JZ."

"I'm Kelly."

"So who should I thank for Kelly finding her way to our table?" JZ looked to the clique then inhaled a mouthful of burger.

"Me and Kelly have soc together," Mina said. "Which, seriously, if a house falls on Jessica, I think will be my best class this semester."

"Ahh, see, watch what you wish for," Michael said. "Jessica Johnson is in your LL?"

"Shut up, don't even go there, Mike." Mina palmed his face and gave it a playful shove.

"Aw, naw. I'm going there." Michael made his voice high and girlish. "I'm the only one who got an LL. Oh my Gawd, that must mean something. I'm special. Look at me, Mina Queen of the signs that don't mean anything."

JZ and Lizzie fell out laughing.

"Sorry, Mi, I'm on your side, seriously," Lizzie said between gulps of laughter. "But you did kind of go on and on about it."

Mina couldn't help but chuckle along. "I wasn't that bad, ya'll."

Michael jerked his head back and gave her a look. "Yeah, okay." He flipped a fry into his mouth. "Now look. So what sign is it that The Bee is in your class?"

"Not just my class. But my group. We're doing a project together. Right Kelly?" Mina said.

Kelly nodded.

A new round of laughter at Mina's expense made its way around the table.

"You gotta admit that's some funny ish, Mina," JZ said. "The one girl you're always competing with neck and neck."

"I wouldn't put it like that. We just had cheerleading in common," Mina said.

"Yeah, then. Now she's there." Michael pointed to Jessica at one of the café's bistro tables. "And that's where you want to be . . . correct or not?"

Mina smacked at his pointing finger.

"You're still lucky. You got the one LL you really wanted," Lizzie said. "I was hoping to get Psych."

"You still might, next semester," Mina assured her.

"I think ya'll sweat those courses too much," Michael said. "You could take the same class at community college if you wanted to waste your summer in school."

"Naw, playuh," JZ said through a mouthful of food. "The college versions have books and shit. None of the LLs have a course book. That's why I'm feeling 'em."

Michael pursed his lips and waved it off. "I tell you what, brother is gonna finish up his credits early. By senior year, I'll have three gym classes and Home Ec or some mad easy class like that."

JZ reached out for some dap. "I hear that."

"Please." Mina rolled her eyes. "JZ, try pulling that and your father would be on you so hard."

"I didn't say I could do it," JZ said. "But more power to Mike if he can. I'm down with three gyms a day and lunch. Now that's a school day."

"So, okay, give me the scoop." Mina picked more fries off Michael's tray. "Who has everybody met? Which teachers do you hate? What do you think so far?" She turned to Kelly. "Even with the two wacked sisters in our group, soc is gonna be bomb. Won't it?"

Kelly nodded, then went back to her book.

"Well this is what I was trying to tell *you* earlier." Lizzie made a face at Mina. "I don't know about JZ, but I hate how our math teacher lectures like it's a college course. Stupid Algebra II." She bit into an apple and crunched as she talked. "The bad part is, our teacher is Mr. Collins, the drama director."

Mina groaned. "Umph, so you have no choice but to be on your game in his class."

"Exactly," Lizzie said. "I didn't know he was the drama director until today. It used to be a woman."

"He's a little too prissy for me," JZ said. "I can tell he's into drama."

Lizzie frowned. "Are you trying to be offensive or does it just come naturally?"

"What?" JZ made wide innocent eyes.

"You know you're wrong," Mina said, laughing at his act.

"Don't trip, Liz. You gotta admit he is prissy, always putting his hands on his hips like a woman when he talks," JZ said. He took on a nasal tone, hunched his back, and put his hands on his hips as he mocked the teacher. "Now, Mr. Zimms, am I going to have trouble out of you. You athletes, excuse me jocks, are always my biggest nuisance."

Everybody at the table, except Kelly, laughed at JZ's show.

"Alright, you do have him down," Lizzie said.

"I don't know why you would think it was bad to have him as your teacher. Shoot if Coach was my teacher, it would be all good," JZ said.

Lizzie made a face at Mina, directing her head to a still reading Kelly.

Mina mouthed, "Say something to her."

"So, Kelly, did you just move to Del Rio Bay?" Lizzie hitched her shoulders as if to ask Mina, is that good?

The table grew curiously silent.

"No. I went to McStew Prep," Kelly said.

Everyone moved forward to hear her. Kelly seemed to have mastered the "inside" voice that teachers drilled into your head in kindergarten.

"Mc-Steewwwww!" JZ howled. "One of my favorite, honey pots. Mike, remember that chick, Katie?"

Michael nodded.

"She was a McStew honey," JZ said. "You know her, Kelly? I forget her last name."

Kelly shook her head.

"Okay, she's not interested in JZ's latest ventures in *Girls Gone Wild*, the McStew episodes," Mina lectured.

JZ made the gas face.

"Where do you live?" Michael asked.

"Folgers Way." Kelly shifted uncomfortably under everyone's intent staring.

Her eyes flitted from face to face for a second as an invisible debate settled among the clique. Who would ask the next question?

After clearing her throat, Kelly went back to reading her book.

Lizzie frowned and flashed Mina a "What's up with that?" gesture. She shrank away from Mina's smacking hand.

"Stop," Mina mouthed.

"Ay, my boy, Jake Phoenix lives in Folgers. You know him?" JZ said.

Kelly thought about it then shook her head.

"You sure?" JZ eyes were wide in disbelief. "He's JV quarterback this year."

"He didn't go to McStew," Kelly said.

"Naw, he went to Del Rio Middle. But I'm sure he lives in Folgers . . . has for a minute, too. I think he moved there three years ago," JZ said. "Jake is my man."

Kelly nodded then went to turn back to her book when Mina jumped in.

"Ignore JZ. He thinks if he knows someone everyone does. You'll get to know a lot of people this year," Mina assured her, going on, lost in her own chatter. "And, when I get into the café, I promise not to forget the little people."

Kelly lifted her head like a mouse poking out of a hole. "The café? Mrs. Simms mentioned it this morning." Her eyes questioned as her head stretched a little more out of its invisible hiding space. "What is it?"

The group exchanged looks of surprise. Private school or not, Kelly should have known about the café. There were two high schools in Del Rio Bay: DRB High in the 'burbs, and Sam-Well, across town and over the DRB Bridge in the city. The two schools were in tough competition in sports, fashion, cliques, name it. And people's allegiance to the schools started well before they ever entered high school. Del Rio Bay High's outdoor lunch area was just one more thing to hold over Sam-Well's head in the my-school-is-better-than-yours fight.

Lizzie flicked her thumb toward the windows. "That's the café."

"And where I'll be sitting by December 10! You heard it here first," Mina announced to three sets of rolling eyes. "Oh you doubt your girl?"

"Mina's on a quest!" JZ threw up a touchdown sign. He walked around to the other side of the table, stood behind her, and squeezed her shoulder. "So who you plan on doing to get in?"

"Don't be disgusting," Mina scolded.

Kelly's face was a question mark.

"Ignore him," Mina said. She didn't want to give credence to the urban legend about admission to the café. They were wild and ridiculous. "Some people say you only get in the café if you do an Upper a favor."

JZ threw his head back, laughing uproariously. "Yeah, that's a nice way of putting it."

"Favor?" Kelly asked, her book forgotten.

"Sex, gifts, gadgets," Lizzie explained, matter-of-factly. "Giving whoever gets you in what they want. I think it's all overblown. You know the administration would be all on that if it were true."

"Even you not that naïve, Miss Liz," Michael scolded. "Wilder things have happened under the teachers' noses."

JZ nodded. He demolished the rest of the burger. "Always will," he said, food spraying.

"Alright, ew!" Mina brushed crumbs away from her.

"Are you guys serious?" Kelly asked.

"Dead," Mina crossed her heart. "Me, I think it's about star power. Or whatever quality you want to call it. That's my ticket."

Kelly looked over her shoulder toward the café. No teacher chaperoned the area. No one manned the door. As far as Kelly could tell, people walked in and out of the area freely.

The tall bistro tables were barely visible between the shoulder-to-shoulder bodies.

"Who decides all of this?" she asked, her small voice strong with curiosity. "Has any freshman ever tried just going out there?"

When no one answered, she turned back to her book, interest lost in the topic. Star power and the It factor weren't things she cared about.

The bell announcing the end of lunch rang overhead.

"Later peoples." JZ dashed off.

Michael set off in the same direction. "See you, diva-girls."

"Bye," Mina and Lizzie chorused.

"What's your next class?" Mina asked Kelly, who had finally closed her book.

"Biology. It was nice to meet you, Lizzie," Kelly said. She slung her messenger bag over her shoulder and melted into the traffic leading out of the cafeteria.

Lizzie gave Mina a look.

"Don't even say anything," Mina warned.

"Kelly is a bit . . ." Lizzie gazed at the ceiling. "Odd."

Mina laughed as they grabbed their books and set off to Lit class. "Was it the reading?" she said.

Lizzie snorted. "Yes!"

"Don't get me started dishing," Mina said. "I gotta be joined at the hip with her and the rest of my group for six weeks." Mina smacked at the back of her own hand. "I can't judge. I will not judge."

"What do you mean?" Lizzie asked.

"The project is about eliminating prejudice." Mina's face went serious. "I can't be catty."

Lizzie's laugh came out a harsh bark. "Good luck with that!"

"That's wrong. I can do it!" Mina pretended to be offended.

"I'll pray for you." Lizzie bowed her head.

"The strangest thing is we have to do the project on our own time. No class time is allowed for it," Mina explained. "I've never heard of a project like this before. Hey is that even legal? To make us do the whole project outside of class?"

"Emm, weird," Lizzie said. "Probably not against the law, though."

She and Mina flowed with the hall's traffic, letting it take them to the stairs that led to the English hall.

"Probably not," Mina said. "It's actually kind of cool, though. We're doing sleepovers for our project."

"Wow, talk about an assignment you can pass with your eyes closed," Lizzie said.

"I know, right," Mina put her hand out for a high five.

Lizzie patted it lightly. "Are you going to ask Kelly to the table every day?"

"I mean, I don't have to. But I might as well be nice to her." Mina shrugged. "Not like you'll notice she's there."

Mina and Lizzie's laughter carried down the short hallway leading to English classrooms. They toned it down to muffled sniggling when one of the teachers gave them the Sssh! finger. They quick-stepped it into the classroom.

"You think we'll have assigned seats?" Mina asked, spying out the layout of the room. "How about over there?" She nodded to seats near the only window.

"Fine with me." Lizzie followed. "It's an advanced English class, for God's sake. Assigned seats are for the detention set." She stuck her tongue out in distaste.

"Snob," Mina teased.

"Takes one to know one."

"I know that's right!" Mina kneeled in a chair and gazed out the window at the courtyard below. She pointed to several people standing outside. "Mmm, it's Craig. He is too fine for words."

Lizzie stood by her looking at the action outside. "Knock on the window," she dared.

"He can't hear me from up here," Mina said.

Lizzie banged on the window. She flailed her arms until the person Craig was talking to tapped his shoulder and pointed up toward the window.

"Oh my God!" Mina ducked, bumping her head on the desk. "Ow!! Lizzie!"

Lizzie laughed. She waved down at Craig who squinted in confusion but waved back. "What!? Wave to him."

"I am not coming back up until you sit down," Mina squeaked.

"Ladies, let's settle down back there," the teacher reprimanded.

"Shoot, already got us in trouble," Mina grumbled. She rubbed at her forehead. "Now I know we're getting assigned seats."

Lizzie fell into a fresh round of laugh-snorts as she took the seat in front of Mina.

I Im j Im

> "My music so loud. I'm swingin'."
> —Chamillionaire, "Ridin'"

Clutter, clutter everywhere!

Mina squinted into the sea of folders, books, and binders surrounding her on the floor. It felt like she had twenty folders or notebooks for every subject. Desperate for order, she scanned the clutter of books, mentally ticked off her options, and decided on the glam system for academic organization—rearranging every subject by color. Yellow notebook, folder, and tabs for English; blue for history; Orange for soc; and gray for math, symbolic for how dull it was.

Lost in her coordination, a tickle of pleasure settled over her as the rainbow of books sat in neat piles around her. She laughed out loud at herself for enjoying the task way more than she meant to.

As she admired her work, the distant sound of horns blaring went unnoticed. When a second round of trumpets beckoned, announcing Lizzie had logged on, she jumped up off the floor and scrambled to the PC, anxious to turn it down before her mother hollered to stop running her mouth and finish her homework. She always did when she heard a million bells, whistles, and ringtones announcing that Mina was holding full conversations in cyberspace.

She was surprised to see she'd missed IMs from Jayizda-man (JZ), 1sexycheergrl (fellow cheer diva Kelis), and ColeyCol (Colby), platonic, cutie friend from math class, while she had been lost in geek time funning with her books.

Mina's fingers flew as she responded to the IMs.

Jayizda-man: Mi-naaaa!!! Holla back girl. I want cop that Lupe Fiasco. Burn it 4 me so I can save my .99 cents. Ha-haaaaaa
BubbliMi: Jay, I'll bring it w/me tomorrow.

JZ's away message popped up. "Take a number . . . I'll get back atcha."

She switched to Colby's message.

ColeyCol: u have 2days assignment? Pls say YES!!
BubbliMi: Dag Colby u slackin' after only 2 days? LOL

A minute went by before Colby responded.

ColeyCol: Ha ha. Lost my dam notes
BubbliMi: the homework is on pg 25
ColeyCol: Kewl. Ya just saved me from my 1st incomplete
BubbliMi: Y didn't u go 2 the homework URL?
ColeyCol: site iz down
BubbliMi: O
ColeyCol: thx

His name dimmed on Mina's buddy list.

She logged into Overdrive and let the hip-hop station stream. Her buddy list indicated that Kelis was still on. Mina's cousin, Keisha, was also online. She pinged them and Lizzie.

BubbliMi: What up, K? Did u want something?
BubbliMi: Hey Keish. What's happening in the ATL?
BubbliMi: LizO, what's up baby girl?

Mina waited for the messages to flow in. The music was loud enough to cover up the dings and whistles from her mom.

Kelis pinged back first.

1sexycheergrl: Hey boo-boo!

Mina laughed out loud. Kelis always talked like they were the best of friends. They didn't hate each other, but this would probably be a long season of the two of them trying to rule the JV squad together.

BubbliMi: what's going on?
1sexycheergrl: Kim hit me up, said we need to start planning for pep rally.

Mina's stomach rumbled as she read all types of things into Kelis—*the CO-captain* –getting a call from Kim about squad business that the Captain should know about first. She fought the urge to panic but couldn't help herself.

BubbliMi: Y didn't she call me?
1sexycheergrl: ::Shrugging::

Yeah, right, Mina thought. Kelis had probably been kissing butt and chatting Kim up behind her back.

BubbliMi: well what did she say? I mean what does she want us to do?
1sexycheergrl: JV squad has to plan the whole thing top 2 bottom.
BubbliMi: is there a theme?
1sexycheergrl: gotta come up with 3 and let varsity choose da 1 they like best.

Mina's blood boiled. Why hadn't Kim just come to her?

She had IMs from Lizzie and Keisha but couldn't pull herself away from the conversation with Kelis.

BubbliMi: we can talk about it at practice, I guess.
1sexycheergrl: cool w/me. Just giving u da headz up
BubbliMi: when did Kim hit u up?
1sexycheergrl: she caught me after practice. U had already left.

That was it. Mina would make sure she was the last one to leave practice from now on.

BubbliMi: OK. Thx.
1sexycheergrl: later cheer babe
BubbliMi: LOL, C U

Mina's fingers flew as she complained to Lizzie.

BubbliMi: Ooohhh I am so HOT!

While she waited, she answered Keisha's message.

Dereksgirl: Hey cuz. It's all good in A-town. N u?
BubbliMi: Cheer drama. U and Derek still going strong I C?
Dereksgirl: Um-hmm That's my Boo! How u living in the BF dept?
BubbliMi: ::frowning:: that department is closed
Dereksgirl: LOL
BubbliMi: still looking for Mr. Cute stuff
Dereksgirl: he better be Mr. BLACK cute stuff

Mina rolled her eyes. Keisha had moved to Atlanta the year they entered the fourth grade. Ever since, she was always going all black power on Mina. Last year, at the family reunion, she teased Mina, mercilessly, about how slim the boyfriend pickings were in Del Rio Bay. She tripped off The Galley, Del Rio Middle's yearbook, and the fact that there were only about twenty or so black dudes in each grade.

The 'burbs of Del Rio Bay were definitely no Atlanta. The only predominately black high school was Sam-Well, the school Jacinta would have gone to if she hadn't come to DRB High. Mina definitely had her eyes on a couple Sam-Well hotties. But without a car it wasn't like she could seriously date. Okay, it wasn't like her mother was letting her date where it involved her going out one-on-one anyway.

Keisha's high school was all-black. Every school Keisha ever went to was all-black. And she planned to continue the line by going to Spelman College. She wanted Mina to go to college there, too.

Spelman, backpacking in France—Mina had everybody planning for her life after high school. And all she was really worried about, at least tonight, was why Kim hadn't tried to call her at home about the pep rally.

Her IMs were ringing off the charts.
Dereksgirl: U hear me?
BubbliMi: Yeah, yeah. We do have some cutie white dudes up here, though.
Dereksgirl: whatever, Mina. Get u a brother, girl!
BubbliMi: Keish, I know u not saying my BF can be a serial killer just as long as he black.
Dereksgirl: there u go, exaggerating! It's different down here, that's all. U don't see a lot of the swirl on my block.

Mina wasn't up for this talk tonight. She was well aware she was boyfriendless. She didn't feel like hearing Keisha argue why when she found one he had to be a certain this and that. They'd had this conversation many times before over the last two years. Mina toggled to Lizzie's messages, which were one long string of where are yous:

Liz-e-O: what's the matter? Y r u hot?

Liz-e-O: Hello, Mi, what's up?

Liz-e-O: Mina!

Liz-e-O: Miiiii-naaaaaa. U better not be away from ur PC and forgot 2 put on ur Away msg!

BubbliMi: Sorry. Talking to my cousin, Keisha

Liz-e-O: O Thought I was out here by myself. what r u pissed about?

BubbliMi: Let me tell Keisha I'll holler later

Liz-e-O: Ok

Mina toggled back to Keisha, who was still lecturing.

Dereksgirl: 4 real cuz if u end u with a white boy I think ur dad would be hot

BubbliMi: r u done? Dag get off da soap box, yo. LOL

Dereksgirl: LOL Just trying save u from the madness

BubbliMi: seeing as how there are no candidates (white or black, Puerto Rican or Hatian 4 that matter) banging down my door for the job, I think I'm safe.

Dereksgirl: what about that cutie, JZ? The one who got that slamming body overnight!!

BubbliMi: Okay, ew! Urp . . . I think I just threw up in my mouth a little bit.

Dereksgirl: LOL Ewww. Girl, don't sit there like he is not fine!

BubbliMi: Not saying he is or isn't . . . just I don't see him like that.

Dereksgirl: JZ iz lucky I got a man.

BubbliMi: yeah I was just ready 2 remind u of that. Well now that uv upset my stomach . . . let me roll.

Dereksgirl: LOL c u Mi.

BubbliMi: Bye Keish.

She laughed and closed out all the boxes except the IM with Lizzie.

BubbliMi: Sorry. Keisha just grossed me out.

Liz-e-O: What?

BubbliMi: Asked how come I don't date JZ.

Liz-e-O: LOL guess u didn't admit u did have a little crush once.

BubbliMi: Okay what part about sworn to never speak of that again didn't u understand? That was a million years ago, anyway.

Liz-e-O: 6th grade is a million years ago?

BubbliMi: YES!

Liz-e-O: LOL. I think it's cute u crushed on JZ. u guys have been friends for a long time, I don't think anyone would think it was weird that u had a crush on him.

BubbliMi: HAD is the key word. And we were in sixth grade. AND I was just bored or whatever. It lasted all of a month.

Liz-e-O: thank God. I was running out of excuses for why u were acting so weird around him.

BubbliMi: but u had my back though! U my girl.

Liz-e-O: Always. SO, Y were u mad earlier?

BubbliMi: Oh, Kelis! She just casually drops that Kim wants the JV squad to plan the pep rally. I think Kim hates me.

Liz-e-O: Just b/c she told Kelis and not u?

BubbliMi: That's part of it. I mean why didn't she at least call me tonight and tell me the same thing she told Kelis??????? Y she dis-re-spekin? LOL

Liz-e-O: ROFL Maybe she fig'ed Kelis would tell u

BubbliMi: Maybe. Still it sux

Liz-e-O: Just write about it in ur blog

BubbliMi: u know I will

Liz-e-O: feel better

BubbliMi: thx

Liz-e-O: Gotta go. Algebra II homework:::retch::: calling. Every time I sit down 2 do math homework I get the shakes.

BubbliMi: LOL slight exaggeration I'm sure

Liz-e-O: Not really. I just really want to do well . . . in class and in drama.

BubbliMi: U will. U always have . . . in both.

Liz-e-O: first time for everything

BubbliMi: Yeah but this won't be it

Liz-e-O: Hope ur right. Figs I'd get Math Anxiety NOW after all these years of sailing through it

BubbliMi: LOL C U chick

Liz-e-O: Bye Mi

If You're Not Interested...
There's No Shortage of
Wannabes

"Come on and ease on down... ease on down the road."
—Michael Jackson and Diana Ross, "Ease on Down
the Road," from The Wiz

Lizzie walked into the lunchroom. She breathed in the energy of the cafeteria's noise and movement, thankful for the break from classes. JZ and Mina had already staked out their window table. After only three days, the routine was firm.

Lizzie watched as Mina, who hardly ever ate her own lunch, picked at a fruit cup. Most times Mina picked at everyone else's plate as part of her the-calories-don't-count-if-they're-somebody-else's diet.

Whatever calories Mina didn't consume, JZ took care of. Today he had two trays of lunch.

Michael made his way to the table with a taco salad. A little thrill slivered up Lizzie's spine. The table was Kelly free. Kelly was spooky quiet. Even when she talked she spoke so low that half the time Lizzie just pretended to hear what she said.

And you're kind of jealous.

Lizzie blanched, unable to push away the little factoid before it settled in.

No, it wasn't jealousy, she told herself, but annoyance. It got on her nerves how hard Mina worked to make Kelly a part of the conversation, usually referencing the sociology class. It was all, at least in Lizzie's opinion, they seemed to have in common. The soc class was taking the excitement out of her and Mina sharing Lit class, which was already off to a dizzying pace.

Lizzie regretted taking two advanced courses. I should have flunked out on purpose like JZ, she thought, knowing she'd never really do that. It would probably backfire if she tried. Knowing her parents and their "theater is a HOBBY," she'd flunk and the first thing her parents would strip were her drama ties.

She had two papers already assigned, one for U.S. History and one for English—no, Ms. Qualls, the Lit teacher, called it a "preview" of upcoming assignments. It felt like an assignment to Lizzie, though. The paper had a due date and everything. Freshman Lit and U.S. History teachers were no joke. Lizzie had a lot on her academic plate and the last thing she needed to ruin her lunch, the only downtime she had, was Kelly's wide-eyed questioning.

So there, she told herself, it's not jealousy at all.

Even, Mina, Miss Forty hours and counting, had finally admitted that there were some cons to the great new school year, like Freshman Lit. The first assignment was a doozy out the box.

The other day, Ms. Qualls handed out copies of both *A Tale of Two Cities* and *Silas Marner* along with a ten-page packet of questions and instructions.

"You have the semester to read both books," Ms. Qualls had said to a room full of groans. "Come on people, it's more than enough, time. We'll begin, right away, with *A Tale of Two Cities* and move on to *Silas Marner* by the end of October."

More groans and a few bold mumblings of "that's crazy."

Ms. Qualls had gone on, unfazed. "Then, I'll need a comprehensive essay revolved around the theme of change and redemption in individuals. How people change. What stimulates change and how likely is change. You'll understand better if you open your packets."

Lizzie had felt Mina's heavy sigh on the back of her neck. And Mina loved reading and writing more than anyone Lizzie knew. But 608 pages was too much, even for her.

"Maybe you read one and I read one and we compare notes," Mina whispered.

Lizzie turned her head slightly to the side, talking out of the corner of her mouth. "Dibs on *Silas Marner*."

"You would pick the shortest book." Mina kicked the back of Lizzie's chair.

All Lizzie could think was touché, told you so, and nah-nah-nah-nah!

Maybe next year Mina would savor summer, like every other person under the age of eighteen.

With a fresh batch of told-you-so taunts ready and spared Kelly's doe-eyed innocence, Lizzie's mood soared. She bounded down the steps, nearly knocking heads with Lila, head of the drama troupe. It was the second time she'd seen her since school started.

The first time was the first day of school at Rio's Ria. Standing at the counter, ordering a soda, she didn't know Lila was standing behind her. Turning to head back to her seat, to join the clique, Lizzie nearly spilled her open drink on her.

"Sorry," Lizzie had apologized, more than a little annoyed that Lila was so close she had practically been in her skin.

"Lizzie, right?" Lila had asked, a smirk on her face. She knew exactly who Lizzie was. They'd attended the same theater camp for the last three years, though they never hung out or anything. And just this summer they played opposite each other in the camp's production of *Grease*.

"Yeah. Hey, *Lila*." She'd emphasized, to point out they already knew each other at least by name.

"You were Rizzo in last year's camp production of *Grease*, right?" Lila's eyes rolled toward the ceiling.

She was really putting on the "now, where do I know you?" act.

Lila had a lot of pull in theater, so Lizzie went along, biting back annoyance at the game. Of course Lila knew very well she'd played Rizzo. Lila had played Sandy, the main character. She and Lizzie had half a dozen scenes together since Sandy and Rizzo were enemies in the play. Ironically, Rizzo was the dominant one. Now, in real life it was vice versa. Lizzie played her part.

"Yup, that was me." Lizzie smiled.

Lila nodded. "Yeah, you were pretty good."

And with that she had turned her back and stepped up to the counter to order, leaving Lizzie standing there wondering if the conversation was over or not.

Now here they were nearly colliding again. But school was Lila's territory for sure. She was the star of Bay Dra-da, no doubt about it. Lizzie knew she had to be the adoring newbie. She clicked her mind to go along, figuring Lila was ready to start the "don't I know you," game again.

"Hey, Lizzie. Why don't you sit with us outside." Lila flicked her head toward the café. It was a demand, not an invite.

Lizzie's mouth fell open. Her heart felt like it was trying to jump out of her throat. She looked toward the café, as always teeming with teens. Lila was inviting her out there. How did it go from barely recognizing her to this?

Lila was interested in her. With three commercials under her belt and dozens of regionwide productions where she played a lead or key role, Lila's reputation went beyond Del Rio Bay.

Lizzie wasn't exactly sure why Lila bothered with local school productions, but thought it was probably big fish in the little pond syndrome; Lila loved the attention too much to pass up even the local roles.

She nodded her head toward the window before finally answering. "Oh, um, I was going to sit with my friend, Mina."

Kind of a dumb answer, since this invitation would probably never be offered again. But it had slipped out. That whole honesty thing was a real pain sometimes.

Lila turned her long, elegant neck slowly toward the window. Her thin lips turned up into a snotty, condescending smile as she continued, unfazed. "Well, we wanted to talk to you about joining Bay Dra-da. We're doing two productions this year, and I think you should audition. You were really good in *Grease* this summer. Played your part without outplaying me. Smart." She arched her eyebrows high. "But if you're not interested . . . there's no shortage of wannabes."

Lizzie's mouth went dry. Her heart started doing the Kentucky Derby trot again. Was that all she was? A wannabe? She wasn't sure whether to be a little offended or a lot offended.

Lila's cold, steady stare unsettled her. Lizzie shifted her weight from one foot to the other as she considered the weight of the invitation and newly earned title and was shocked that her voice came out so calm. "Oh, no, I'm interested. Most def."

After she said it, she wasn't sure if she was interested in the invite or interested in the lead role. At this point, it seemed the two were connected.

She wondered if this was some new freshman hazing ritual. Maybe she was on a prank show. The sudden urge to search the cafeteria for hidden cameras struck her.

Lila's sharp voice slapped her back into reality. "We rarely select a frosh for principal roles. I was the last freshman to win a lead and that was two years ago." She paused for dramatic effect and Lizzie wondered if she was supposed to applaud or something. Then Lila continued. "But who knows, maybe you could snag one. Especially since I won't be trying out for any until spring." She paused again, then announced, "Because I'll be in the ensemble of The Players big winter production!"

Never above performing a little off the stage, Lizzie affected the wide-eyed surprise she knew she was expected to at the mention of

The Del Rio Players, a local theater company with a national repu-tation. Many of its actors went on to Broadway and a few had re-spectable careers in movie and television.

Pleased with the reaction, Lila continued, "So I'll see you in the café. You'll see my table."

Lizzie kept her excitement in check. "Well, I . . . let me tell Mina I'll catch up later."

Lila's curt nod said it all. Of course Lizzie would join them. Any other choice was career suicide.

Lizzie had only needed a second to calculate her options. Sit with the clique and stay true to the streak. Or ditch on lunch, breaking the streak and pissing Mina off to schmooze Lila and get in good with the drama powers. Winning a principal role wasn't just about having acting skill, which she had plenty of, it was also about know-ing the right people in the drama clique. Lila wasn't just one of the right people, she was *the* right person to know.

An invite to sit with senior members of Bay Dra-da in the café, by the troupe's president, was a golden ticket to anywhere in the world.

Add it all up and the jury had come back quickly. Sorry, Mina.

Reeling, Lizzie watched Lila's regal retreat, a slow stroll, head high, which gave people plenty of time to notice her.

"Go, Liz. Go, Liz!" she chanted in her head. The excitement poured out of her ears through her wide grin.

Walking to the table, she did some quick math on how long Mina would be peeved with her. Best calculation, any hurt feelings would be blown over by tomorrow. She would take whatever lumps she'd have to. The first school production was *The Wiz* and there were only a handful of key roles. If Lila thought she could land one of them she had to act. Lizzie smiled at her little pun.

Her cool façade crumbled once she reached the table.

"Hey, Mi, look, I hate to do this, but something came up. I gotta bail on lunch. But guess what?! I got an invite to the café!!!" Her words tumbled out in a hurried breath.

"See, Mina you're rubbing off on people," JZ said. He laughed. "Now you have Lizzie all pressed about the café."

Mina ignored JZ. She looked into Lizzie's flushed face and screamed. "What?!?! Okay, tell me everything. Who is it?" Realization dawned on her face. "Girl, it better be some senior hotness dying to sweep you off your feet. You're breaking up the streak!"

"No, nothing like that." Lizzie stole a glance toward Lila's table, already surrounded by four others. "The president of Bay Dra-da thinks I have a chance to snag a lead role in one of this year's productions. A lead, Mi!!"

"You'll be chilling in the café? It's only the first week of school. That's got to be some kind of record." Mina was barely able to disguise her disappointment, envious in spite of herself. She rebounded quickly, determined to be happy for her friend. She couldn't honestly say she'd honor the streak if she got the call. "Well, you go, Miss Liz!"

"Are you sure?" Lizzie forced herself to sound patient.

"Yup. Catch me up on every detail in Lit. Okay?"

"Absotively! Thanks, Mi." Lizzie sprinted off.

Mina watched through the window as Lizzie squeezed in at a tiny table, now packed with six others. Lila, a rail-thin redhead, was the girl Lizzie once called one of the area's best young thespians. She had actually used that word instead of actor. Until she saw Lizzie was serious, Mina had almost laughed. But Lizzie had known the girl's whole resume like Mina memorized who was in what clique. Mina believed Lizzie tried to model her own amateur acting career after Lila's. And why not? The girl even had her own groupies. They were always beside her giggling like hyenas and fawning over Lila as if she were already flossing on the E! channel walking the red carpet.

Riveted by the Lila Show before her now, Mina watched through the window as the attractive redhead made a grand gesture, sweeping her arms over her head then throwing her head back and letting loose a good strong laugh.

In an instant, Mina knew who the groupies were in the circle. They were the ones laughing extra hard. One of them even held her sides. Mina's eyes moved to Lizzie's half-smile, half-grimace and knew that the joke couldn't have been all that funny.

She shook her head at the phony scene. It nagged at her that Lizzie could be on her way to being one of Lila's drama flunkies. But acting was important to Lizzie. She would support her girl, even if it meant being a little phony herself.

Michael's voice cracked through her thoughts. "Uh-oh, there she goes."

Mina ripped her attention away from Lila. "There who goes?"

"Your girl. She's gone back to the other side."

He laughed. JZ chuckled along.

"The other side of what Michael?!" Mina ping-ponged from his face to JZ's missing the joke.

Michael crunched on his salad. "We all knew the day would come when she realized she was white and had to be with her own kind."

Mina's face fell. Her eyebrows scrunched so close together they looked like one.

Her face grew hot as fresh tears glossed her eyes. She blinked and swallowed hard, trying to get her words together, unsure if she was upset because Liz got an invite to the café on the third day of school or that Michael had pulled the race card on her.

She hadn't heard the "Lizzie is white" speech from Michael in years but had heard enough when she first befriended Liz to recite the lines: "Because Lizzie is white, . . ." fill in the blank, to name how it related to why they couldn't or shouldn't be friends or why they would never see eye-to-eye on anything.

Even though she wasn't feeling up to a debate, Mina challenged

Michael. Anger flared her nostrils. "You know, when we were nine years old, the whole black-white thing ran me hot. Now it's just played out." She folded her arms and stared him down. "I thought you'd come better than that, Michael. Unless you still really believe that mess a zillion years later!"

Michael's eyes bucked in surprise. "Mina, I was just playing. Chill. You know Lizzie my girl, too."

"Here she go!" JZ threw his hands up and pretended to duck.

Mina could admit it in her head—she was jealous of Lizzie's early invite into the fold of DRB High's upper crust. But she couldn't force her tongue to say it.

Why? Why did Lizzie get the call and she didn't even care about sitting in the café?

WHY?

Envy chipped away at her logic. She needed something to rant against and it might as well be Michael.

"Behind every joke lies the truth," she snapped.

"Son, she dropped the philosophy on you." JZ laughed.

Michael snorted, unsure how he'd started Mina quoting tired clichés. He chuckled to break the tension. "Okay, Diva. Well, it was mostly a joke. But I don't think it would be such an odd thing if Lizzie hung out with more whites this year."

"And what? You and Jay gonna start hanging out with more guys this year even though we been friends since the beginning of time?"

"Ass, how I get thrown up in here?" JZ asked, midgulp of his drink.

"That's different," Michael sniffed.

"Me and Lizzie have known each other since we were nine. How all of a sudden does her being white change things?"

He sighed long and heavy, like he was holding on to the last piece of his patience.

"Mina, I wasn't trying to start nothing. Joking, I was just joking at first." Michael shook his head. "BUT I'm not gon' lie. Every school year, I used to think Lizzie might end up ditching you and hooking up with more white people. I don't really think that no more." He chuckled. "Well, not much."

Mina rolled her eyes, refusing to encourage more discussion.

He squeezed her shoulder. "Diva, I was joking. Awright?! I know Lizzie your man fifty grand. Well your wo-man."

He leaned up against her, pushing her. "Am I your man fifty grand?"

Mina tried not to smile. She wanted to be mad with him.

He leaned in harder, pushing her.

Mina laughed, unable to hold it in. Michael's grandmother had introduced the old school phrase one day when they were talking about old school versus new school slang. Ever since, the clique blew the dust off the old references now and then, using them as a joke to describe their own friendships.

"Yeah, you my man fifty grand. Sometimes," she said.

"That's cold." He grinned.

Mina gave him a halfhearted smile before swiping up the half-eaten fruit cup and empty juice bottle. Her appetite was gone, lost somewhere between Lizzie's happy news and Michael's badly timed wisecracks. Joking or not, he touched on a nerve she hadn't been aware was so raw.

She walked past a nearby trash can and headed to one directly in front of the window where Lizzie sat with the theater clique. Taking her time, Mina dropped the spoon in the trash.

Lizzie looked at home atop the high-backed stools. Her freshly tanned face was shiny with joy. Already comfortable in the presence of the drama powers she talked with her hands as much as the rest of them. Her arms moved animatedly with each word then rested in between lines.

Eyes still fixed on the scene outside of the window, Mina cautiously placed the fruit cup on top of some other trash, careful not to splash juices on her white shirt.

Without missing a beat in the conversation, Lizzie flashed Mina the peace sign. It was quick; just two fingers cupping her cheek. It made her look like The Thinker sculpture. Then they were back down from her face in an instant. No one at the table seemed to notice. Their conversation flowed on.

The fleeting hand signal was part of the code she and Mina used to help each other out of boring conversations. One finger meant "help get me up outta here." But two meant things were all good. They had been doing it for years and had been caught more than once, when they first started, by the borer. Now they were pros at it.

Lizzie was letting Mina know, no need to save her, she liked it where she was just fine.

The bile of jealousy rose in Mina's throat, burning. She fought it back, determined to be happy for Lizzie if it killed her. Willing her jaws into a smile she waited a second more for Lizzie to look her way again. When she did, Mina threw the peace sign back.

Lizzie's smile widened.

Mina laughed softly to herself, glad Lizzie looked up when she did. Mina was running out of reasons to stand at the trash can.

She tossed her juice bottle in, turned her back on the window, and stepped into a face full of Jessica.

"Dreaming?" Jessica sniffed.

"Jessica, look, whatever . . ." Mina wasn't sure how to put it but settled for a neutral, nonoffending word, "differences we have . . ."

Jessica folded her arms. "Which are a lot."

"No doubt," Mina muttered. "But you don't want to fail anymore than I do. So let's just get through this class."

"As if I'd ruin my GPA over you."

Mina sipped air slowly through her nose, forcing herself not to speak. Her heart pattered rapidly.

Jessica pointed her chin toward Lizzie.

"I just wanted to let you know that just because your little friend has an in with the drama geeks, don't think you're in."

"Whatever that means." Mina played the whole conversation down. It crossed her mind that some of Lizzie's acting skill was rubbing off on her. She believed she didn't care about the café. But Jessica didn't buy it.

"I told you before, you're only following in my footsteps." Jessica kept space between them but her words, spoken low and strong, clutched Mina tighter than a hand. "When I graduate you can have this pit. But until then, I'm the head black chick."

"Don't you mean mixed?" Mina retorted.

"Ha, ha, cute," Jessica said. "Keep that sense of humor as you sit on this side of the fishbowl." She walked off, her stiff, runway walk drawing attention as it was meant to.

Caught Ya' Talking 'Bout Me

"Ya' acting real hard. But I know ya' faking."
—Brooke Valentine, "Girl Fight"

When Thursday rolled around, Michael waited for the rest of the clique at Rio's Ria. He leaned back into the booth and let the pizza joint's familiar Crayola-colored walls, splashed with photos, banners, and jerseys of local teams, close him in. The smell of fresh dough and spicy secret ingredients lingered around him before it filled his lungs.

Music strained over the usual clamor of ringing phones, chatting teenagers, and the dinging cash register.

Michael rubbed his hands over his stubbly head (time to shave it down again) and rocked in time to the distant music.

As usual, he was the first to arrive at the restaurant. The official seat-saver until the clique rushed in from their practices and rehearsals. He never used to care. Then one day, over the summer, Lizzie pointed out that as long as he was around they would never have to worry about having a table on lock.

After that, they all took their sweet time getting there. At least it seemed so to him. It pissed him off when they tipped in, first five minutes then ten, then twenty minutes, after the agreed upon time. Always running their yaps with their friends from whatever activity they had just left and strolling over like the table had appeared at their will.

It hurt him to let it ride, but it was true, he was always free to be the first one there, and he only had himself to blame. JZ played sports all year, training with teammates in between seasons; if Mina wasn't wrapped up in cheerleading, it was praise dancing at her church, student government functions, venting on her blog or journal, Pilates, hip-hop class, or whatever new fad exercise class she was into for the minute; and Lizzie acted—four productions a year and acting and singing classes to boot.

Michael did what?

Exactly what he was doing today, waiting on his friends and content to be the Advice Man.

He was okay with his role until Liz's comment made it obvious they were all more than content to have him just hanging on. He wasn't just sick of it, he was through with it.

He pulled out a shiny, silver binder and leafed through sheets of hand-drawn designs, detailed down to the buttons and coordination of color. He fingered the worn pages lovingly, smiling down at his big loopy signature on the first page.

The words of the drama director, Mr. Collins, rang in his ears. "They're exceptional, truly excellent. I'm quite impressed, Mr. James."

Mr. Collins could have said, "good," "okay," or "nice." But he said "exceptional"! Exceptional had to be good enough to get him a spot on Bay Dra-da's costume staff.

At first, Michael was deflated when Mr. Collins said he'd have to show the designs to the head designer first. He had expected an immediate answer. Looking over his drawings, he felt better. His intricate work was better than ordinary. He was good. Bay Dra-da better recognize!

When they did, he would resign his position as seat-saver. Let the clique see what it was like to wander the Ria like everyone else, waiting on an open spot. The smile tugging at the corners of his mouth pulled into a full grin when Mina popped up behind him and gave his head a playful shove.

Michael slipped the binder under his chair. "Hey, Diva."

"Hey, Boo. Why you have your design book with you?" Mina asked.

He waved it off. "I'll tell you later. Let's just say maybe I can put off the school of arts for a little while, 'cause sorry ass, Del Rio High might have something to offer after all."

"Hmm . . . gracing us no-talent, simple teens with your presence a little longer huh? We appreciate it." She bowed deep at the waist before sliding into the booth across from him.

They laughed.

"I'm glad to see you smiling. It's been a minute." She scooted closer to the wall as JZ and Lizzie swept in. "Ya'll gotta pardon me, I didn't have time to shower after practice."

"Lucky me, I get to sit next to you." Lizzie held her nose and refused to move closer.

Mina reached out and wrapped her arms around Lizzie. "Best friend love!"

JZ and Michael slapped hands and touched elbows.

Mina signaled to the server and ordered for the table, her official job. With that out of the way, she turned to Lizzie. "Well, since you've permanently broken the streak . . ."

"Two days in a row, too," Michael pointed out. "The chances that we'll have lunch together all through high school doubtful."

"Sorry," Lizzie said. "I'm just doing like JZ, getting my thing off."

Everybody laughed.

"It's getting your thing on," JZ said.

"Oh. Well you know what I mean." Lizzie smiled.

"So, how has life been on the beautiful side?" Mina asked. "Ya'll look like you're always tripping out."

Lizzie rolled her eyes to play down mention of the café. Every time Mina had brought it up, Lizzie said little before changing the subject. She knew how important making it there was to Mina. She didn't want to rub her success in her friend's face. "The same. Honestly, Mina, sitting in the café is no big deal."

"Spoken like someone who has sat there two times to my none. It's such a best friend thing to say." Mina gave Lizzie an affectionate squeeze. "That's why you my girl." She leaned back and raised her eyebrow. "Now tell me the truth."

"That is the truth." Lizzie laughed before daring to share just a little more. "Actually, it's a lot like being here. Music playing and people going from table to table gossiping."

Mina nodded, soaking in Lizzie's description. She imagined herself in the middle of the social swirl.

"The best thing is that being around Lila may help me get a juicier role. Politics, you know," Lizzie explained. "I gotta laugh at her jokes and pretend my next breath depends on hearing about her ensemble role with The Players."

"Well you a damn good actress then," Michael said. "You looked like you were having a good time out there to me." He clapped. "Bravo and you go girl."

Lizzie held up the no-applause-please hands and did a stage bow from her seat. She knocked shoulders with Mina. "You know, if Kim had lunch with us, I bet she'd invite you out there."

Mina wished she believed that. She'd seen Kim in the hallway before practice today and asked, politely, about the pep rally.

"Didn't Kelis tell you what I said?" Kim's blue eyes had flashed confusion. She didn't even slow down. Mina had to jog-walk to keep up with her on the way to the locker room.

"Yeah. But I wanted to make sure I didn't miss any details." Mina forced her voice to sound nonchalant.

"JV plans the whole thing. Pick three themes, we'll tell you which one we like and you guys go from there." Kim shrugged then swished her long hair. "End of details."

"Okay," Mina said, ready to let it go. But she couldn't help herself. "Well, um, do you need my number?"

Kim frowned.

Mina stumbled ahead quickly. "I figured you talked to Kelis because you didn't have it."

"I have your number but I saw Kelis first. Is there a problem?" Kim arched her eyebrow.

Mina took the hint. "No, not at all. I wasn't sure if you knew how to reach me."

"Yeah, I've got your number. We have a squad phone list, remember?" Kim opened the locker room door. "Come on, you know Coach loves giving demerits for being late."

And that was that. Kim wasn't mean but she wasn't giving out hugs either. It killed Mina that their relationship wasn't closer.

JZ snapped her out of her fog.

"Speaking of politicking, I've gotten to know Jacinta, Ms. Phillips's niece. She mad cool peoples," he announced.

Mina raised her eyebrows. "Is she?"

"Mad cool" wasn't her take on Jacinta. She hadn't warmed up very much since the first day of school. Today she'd sat by herself in sociology class instead of near Mina and Kelly. Jessica sat with Grace and Mina had thanked the pop gods for that small favor.

"C-c-c-cat fight," JZ whooped loudly at his own joke. He high-fived Michael who was meowing and clawing at Mina.

Mina dismissed them with a snooty turn of her head. "Whatever. Liz, you know what I'm saying?"

"Yeah. I only have homeroom with her, but I can't say she gives me the warm and fuzzies."

JZ wasn't surprised by Mina's reaction. She took it personally when someone had the nerve to feel anything but love for her. "Well, she jive straight alright with me," he said.

"Now, there's a surprise!" Mina shot back. "When cakes for days is your only qualification for someone being alright with you, it leaves the field wide open."

Now she and Lizzie slapped hands.

"Anyway, it's just like you to be down with chicks with the urban flava."

JZ's tone turned serious. "Everyone knows you're a boogee princess, Mina, but every girl from the PJs is not a chickenhead. You tripping."

"Oh no he not trying to preach up in here," Mina declared, clapping.

Lizzie came to Mina's defense. "Jay, every girl from the 'burbs isn't a stuck-up bourgeois snob, either."

"Exactly!" JZ countered. He threw his hands up. "Every girl from the 'burbs isn't stuck up and every one from the hood isn't a toughie. So, why ya'll assuming where someone lives is who they are? Miss Sociology should know better."

Mina wagged her finger at him from across the table. "First of all, I didn't make any assumptions about Jacinta. She's the one acting all hard."

"Liar." Michael coughed into his hand.

Mina gave him the evil eye, turning up the heat on her speech. "*And*, this isn't about PJs versus the 'burbs. It's about how Jacinta came off when we met . . . ignorant!"

"You sure you not mad 'cause she didn't come in bowing down to the Princess of The Woods?" JZ asked. His right eyebrow arched in a perfect steeple. A devilish grin lit up his face.

"JZ, nobody asking her to come in kissing our tail, but she came off like it was beneath her to talk to us," Mina said in exasperation.

She fixed her friends with a look and waited for agreement or argument. Getting neither she jumped back into her point. "Why is it okay for someone from the projects to say we're stuck up or not keeping it real? But when we say something about how they live or say they're ghetto, everyone gets offended and says we're stereotyping and being boogee?"

"She has a point, Dog," Michael interjected.

Mina's eyebrows dared JZ to finish the debate. She wasn't fooled by JZ's sudden act of chivalry.

Maybe he thought Jacinta was worthy of their friendship. But most likely this was more about him strutting the Player's role, trying to get closer to the girl, than it was about him thinking Jacinta was some poor, lonely soul in need of a friend.

Lowering her voice to show she was off the soapbox, she asked, "Did Jacinta mention we're in a soc group together?"

JZ shrugged. "No. She was just saying that she didn't know very many people this way and felt like she'd never fit in. I told her that she should roll with us sometimes, 'cause everyone was real."

Mina sniffed. "Umph. I'm sure she'd turn that offer down flat if she knew I rolled with you. But she better recognize. I AM the Princess of The Woods, so she's gotta deal with that."

JZ's grin spread. He slouched down in the seat and mumbled, "What's up, Jacinta?"

Michael burst out laughing and gave JZ's fist a double pound. "Playuh, no you didn't! That's just wrong."

JZ kept a straight face.

Mina prayed that JZ was joking about Jacinta standing right behind her. She bristled at Jacinta's soft greeting, "Hey, Jason. Hi, Lizzie." She paused. "Princess of The Woods!"

Mina was mortified into silence. She couldn't turn to face Jacinta.

"Caught ya' talking 'bout me, huh?" Jacinta said. She stood off to the side of the booth next to Lizzie. Anger flecked her brown eyes. "Why am I not surprised?"

JZ chuckled. "Mina was just . . . helping Lizzie rehearse some lines."

He barely got through the lie before braying into laughter.

"Yeah, right." Jacinta's eyes swept over Michael. "And I don't know you."

Michael nodded a hello and introduced himself.

Jacinta stepped aside as the server arrived with their food. "I obviously interrupted something." She stared at Mina, who still wouldn't look her way. "I can catch up with you later, Jason, since ya'll pizza here."

"Naw, naw, you cool. Sit down. You can share mine," JZ offered. He scooted in.

"Is it cool with you Princess?" Jacinta said.

Mina wriggled under Jacinta's smirk and tried explaining. "I didn't mean any harm. I was . . ."

Jacinta cut her eyes away, addressing everyone but Mina as she sat down. "So, Jason said ya'll the clique holding things down around here."

"He ain't never lie," Michael boasted.

"I can't believe Jason your homey, Mina. Your Highness seems too innocent to be hanging out with dudes."

"What?!" Mina scowled. She sat ramrod straight and forced herself to meet Jacinta's stare. She couldn't believe how normal Jacinta was acting—no scrunched eyebrows, no twisted mouth. Even the annoyance in her voice was gone. It wasn't quite friendliness but compared to the permanent pout she'd worn in class, it might as well have been.

"You just don't strike me as a down-ass chick," Jacinta stated bluntly.

There was a moment of tense silence as they stared each other down, neither willing to turn away first.

Lizzie tried to play peacemaker. "So, you and Mina have soc together?"

Jacinta shrugged. "Yeah. I couldn't drop it because independent study was full, so . . ."

"So, you're stuck with the boogee princesses, right?" Mina dug, finally recovered. She hadn't really said anything all that wrong. Why was she tripping over what Jacinta heard her say?

"Yeah, something like that," Jacinta shot back.

Michael and JZ looked at one another, silent laughter in their eyes. At five-foot, Mina was anything but intimidating, but what she lacked in height she made up for in very vocal opinions. She had met her match in Jacinta.

Mina rolled her eyes at their snickering. She kicked JZ's shin under the table, more annoyed than mad. This was so like him, getting her riled then watching her squirm when it led to drama. She still didn't trust that this wasn't one of his ploys to add Jacinta to his honey list. But when his foot rubbed her leg gently, his version of waving the white truce flag, Mina smiled, unable to stay mad.

She was being uppity—that much JZ was right about. If Jacinta could take the first step, she might as well meet her halfway. Jacinta didn't know anyone from their part of Del Rio Bay and they were going to get to know one another through the sociology project anyway. Plus, she couldn't be too mad at somebody that would go toe-to-toe with Jessica "The Bee" Johnson. Mina waved her own white flag, handing Jacinta a slice of pizza. "Well, the Princess of The Woods, on behalf of boogee princesses everywhere, welcomes you to Del Rio Bay."

Jacinta looked down at the cheesy thickness drizzling with grease. It was the only thing standing between her life back at home and life in the suburbs. If she took a bite, it would push her deeper into this fairy tale world where the black kids blended in with the white and the street corner hangouts were substituted with pizzerias and big, green front yards. How could this still be Del Rio Bay?

The side of Del Rio she was from was one hundred and eighty degrees different.

If she were home, right now, she would be chilling at the basketball court with Raheem and his best friend, Angel. But she wasn't home; she was sitting in a pizza place with the rainbow coalition, feeling like at any moment someone was going to break out in song like this was the Disney channel.

She contemplated for the umpteenth time how possible it was to get through the year without making new friends. Ever since promising her father she would give Del Rio Bay High School a chance for at least one year, she'd asked herself that question.

So far, sitting by herself in class was no big deal. But reminding herself she had friends back in The Cove didn't help much when she was sitting alone at lunch or at home bored after school. Calling Raheem every single night, soaking up every word about the latest happenings at Sam-Well High School, didn't even help much anymore. She was lonely. JZ had been the only person who hadn't treated her like she had a second head growing out of her neck.

So here she was.

Before JZ asked her to stop at the Ria and hang, she rationalized her distant attitude, almost convincing herself it was all good to be a loner. She told herself over and over she had nothing in common with any of the snooty, suburbanite clones she'd met so far.

But she wanted to be real with herself. She didn't know that first-hand, because school had only started four days ago and she hadn't made a single attempt, until now, to meet anyone.

She wanted to remain distant, so she could go home and rag on the 'burb kids and their corny hangouts to Heem and Angel. But she was already tired of being by herself.

When she'd told Raheem that over the phone the other night, he didn't say much to help things. "Yeah, well make sure you don't cure that loneliness by letting some gray boy holler at you," was his only answer.

That's all he ever talked about, how Del Rio High had a bunch of gray boys, black dudes trying to act white. Jacinta had seen plenty over the last few days. But she had to admit—not to Raheem, but to herself—that not all the guys were like that.

As much as she loved Raheem, sometimes his all-about-him attitude drove her crazy. But she let his comment slide. The last thing she needed was to be arguing with him. She was lonely enough.

JZ's invitation to the Ria was the lifeline she needed and she knew it.

Zoned in on the pizza slice in Mina's hand, Jacinta's brain started its campaign. It wouldn't kill her to go with the flow. No one was asking her to be phony. And it was only for a year, then she could head back to The Cove and go to Sam-Well High next year.

I can do that, she thought, satisfied that her ghetto pass was safe as long as she kept it real.

She looked around the table at the strange faces. She locked on Mina's for a brief second. That little "Princess" comment was the reason Jacinta didn't feel like messing with girls like her. But was that warmth in Mina's eyes or was she being phony, trying to show off for her friends?

Jacinta wasn't sure and at that point, didn't care. She and Mina didn't have to become friends, but they didn't have to be enemies either.

She reached for the slice and sank her teeth into it. The warm, tangy taste melted her tough exterior. Mouth full, she said, "You can call me Cinny."

The New Cuteness

"Let's get ignorant. Let's get hectic."
—Black-Eyed Peas, "Let's Get It Started"

The hot September sun dipped behind a cloud. Finally able to see into the stands, Mina took the chance to get the fifty-some odd fans into the game. She gave Kelis a nod and the squad paired off and began stunting. They threw tosses, throwing the flyer nearly ten feet, as they cheered on the Baby Blue Devils.

A round of enthusiastic applause and cheering went up from the crowd. Whether it was because the sun was no longer beating them to a pulp or because they appreciated the complicated stunts, Mina wasn't sure. She was just glad to hear noise from the near-empty bleachers.

It was hard to get your cheer on when hardly anyone was at the game. But the JV games were so early in the afternoon on Fridays, even the players' parents could barely make it in time.

Under Mina's leadership, well co-leadership since Kelis insisted on calling every other cheer. A few times she called the exact same cheer Mina was about to. Don't think there wouldn't be a little heart-to-heart with Miss Kelis over IM later. That's where they seemed to have the least heated exchanges.

Still, the junior varsity cheerleaders made the best of it—dancing, cheering, and chanting—spiriting as if they were on stage in front of hundreds.

JZ gave them plenty to cheer about.

The spectators jumped to their feet when he shot down the field like lightning, weaving through his opponents until there was no one between him and the goalposts. When he scored for the second time, the thin crowd roared.

With the small group of fans into it, the rest of the Baby Blue Devils came alive, pressuring their opponent with tough defense.

Jangled by the Devils's newfound energy, the opposing team threw an interception. JZ came back onto the field after only a few seconds to catch his breath.

Even winded he wouldn't be stopped.

Within a few seconds of hitting the field, he barreled back down, zigzagging in and out of opponents like they were mannequins.

Mina couldn't see much around the sideline of well-padded, hulking players. She piggybacked onto the crowd's reaction and the announcer's constant mention of JZ's name, pumping her fist and yelling when they did. Feeding off the crowd's frenzy, she kept the cheerleaders' momentum going. They made their tosses higher, their stunts harder, their crowd-participation cheers louder.

JZ intercepted an Eagles pass and scored a touchdown and the noise level from the sprinkle of fans tripled. When he intercepted the next pass, the Eagles benched their quarterback and the Baby Blue Devils had a bona fide rising star in JZ. The crowd stomped on the bleachers and chanted JZ's name.

The fence surrounding the field became more crowded than the stands when curious onlookers, teachers leaving for the day and athletes finished with practice, wandered over to the stadium to check out the action.

By the end of the game, JZ's name, on the tip of everyone's tongue, spread like the flu. The junior varsity football team walked off the field as the school's new hot ticket.

High on the win, Mina threw on a pair of Blue Devil spirit shorts and tee and joined Lizzie and Michael at a bench in front of the school.

"Was Jay on his game or what?!" She planted herself between Michael and Lizzie.

"Oh he got his game on," Michael agreed.

"I wonder if his dad is having second thoughts about making him play on JV?" Lizzie asked.

"You know Mr. Zimms. When he put his foot down . . ." Mina shrugged. They knew the rest.

"He's really amazing to watch. At least all that energy he usually uses to tease us gets used up," Lizzie laughed.

Mina held her hand up for some dap. "I know that's right."

JZ crept up behind Mina and grabbed her in a bear hug as he chanted, "We bad, we know it. We're here to show it."

"Jay, you 'da man, Boo!" Mina squealed, kicking her feet as he swirled her around.

He landed her lightly then gave Michael a pound and a tight grip.

JZ's whole face was a huge cat-ate-the-canary grin. He tapped Lizzie's outstretched hand, giving her five. "I can't lie. We ripped it today."

As if he needed reinforcement, one of the first-string varsity players came up and gave him a pound. "Son, I heard you killed 'em today."

A crowd grew around them, pushing Mina, Michael, and Lizzie farther away.

JZ bathed in the praise. "We stomped 'em good. Ya'll shouldn't have no problem whipping that ass tomorrow."

Mina and Lizzie stepped onto a bench to avoid getting knocked over by more players pushing in to talk to him. Michael stood his ground, for a few seconds, talking to a few people here and there as they made their way to JZ before joining Mina and Lizzie on the bench. He stepped up on the bench's edge.

"Alright, ya'll, I'm out," Michael said.

"Aren't you riding home with us?" Mina asked.

He nodded. "Just call me when your mom gets here."

Michael hopped down and lost himself in the growing crowd without giving Mina a chance to ask again where he was going.

From her perch, Mina laughed. "Dag, so that's how it is when you become the man?"

"Apparently," Lizzie answered. She grabbed onto Mina's elbow as a burly player pushed his way in, nearly knocking her over. "The good news? Looks like more people might be coming out to the games now."

Mina nodded. She scanned the sea of faces, shouting out the cute players.

"Ooh there's Kenny. The new cuteness!"

"Kenny Jackson?" Lizzie wrinkled her nose. "I don't get your taste sometimes. His eyebrows are too bushy."

Mina poked her playfully. "Alright. Your turn. Who meets your approval, Miss Picky?"

"Okay, Kenny almost has a unibrow. So not him."

Mina howled. "That's wrong. His body is hella ripped, though."

Lizzie nodded absently as she shopped for her choice.

She pointed to a blond, freckle-faced guy standing on the outer edges. "Jeff. I think he's adorable. I have Science with him."

Mina squinted to bring him into better focus. "He's . . . plain looking, Liz. He's like the smallest player on the team!"

"He's nice and funny, though," Lizzie defended her choice.

"Alright, I'm not buggin' over your selection. I guess he does look like your type . . . a thinker," Mina teased. "He's probably the one everyone on the team asks to do their papers."

Lizzie hip-bumped her and they laughed, giggling harder when a few people looked up at them.

Giggling behind her hand, Mina whispered. "Okay, remember these numbers, twenty-five, ten, and sixteen."

"Twenty-five, ten, and sixteen," Lizzie repeated then scowled. "Why am I remembering these?"

"Those are my gold-star selections on Varsity. I need JZ to get me a personal intro later. I'm playing one of his numbers on him. Doing him like he does us." She shouted out. "Get me the hookup, Jay!"

Lizzie hid her face behind Mina's shoulder. "Oh my God! You're embarrassing me."

Mina laughed. "He not even paying attention, Girl. Nobody is. They're all up in JZ's grill. Oh my God! There's Craig!"

"Should I call him over?" Lizzie teased.

"Girl, stop playing!"

Mina kept her eyes glued on Craig as he walked up to give JZ a pound. She stared at his lips, trying to read what he was saying.

"I love his slanty eyes. They're sexy as hell."

Lizzie snorted a goofy laugh. "You will find the smallest thing to be attracted to."

Mina grinned. "They are sexy, though. Look at 'em. All narrow, making his face look all exotic. Mmmm!"

"Here he comes!" Lizzie yelled.

Mina jumped, startled, even though she was staring Craig dead in the face and could see he was no closer to walking over than the sun was to falling out of the sky. She pushed Lizzie. "Not funny!"

She was disappointed when he sauntered off toward the football field instead of circling her way. She watched him until he was just a spec on the field throwing a ball and was surprised to see the crowd of mostly varsity players had swollen in the few minutes she had been Craig-watching. She nudged Lizzie with her leg. "Hey, did you know Lila messed with a football player? I'm majorly impressed."

Lizzie had no time to answer. As soon as the words were out of Mina's mouth, Lila was standing next to her. She announced her presence with a simple, "Hey, Lizzie."

Lizzie poked Mina's side. She hoped Mina would stifle her normal flow of commentary or at least not say anything else about Lila. It was safe. Mina was flirting with one of the players, totally occupied. Lizzie chuckled to herself when she saw it was number ten. Guess Mina could check that one off her list.

"So, I've seen you around with Jason Zimms. You guys good friends?" Lila asked.

"Yeah, we've been friends for a while." Lizzie stepped off the bench into the wave of bodies.

Lila nodded her approval. "Cool. Joel, the varsity captain, is my boyfriend."

Lizzie didn't respond and was sure Lila didn't expect one, because her words flowed like someone used to dominating the conversation. "Look, we have this little thing called Lines for Lunch. We hold one every lunch period the two weeks leading to auditions. Wondering if you're interested in joining?"

Lizzie perked up at mention of the troupe. "What's that?"

"Some of the senior members of Bay Dra-da get together and help the new fish run lines. It's like a clinic almost. We give you feedback on your performance." She shrugged. "Help you get better."

Lizzie's face registered complete surprise. Not a lot of the serious Chamils were about helping someone win a role.

Lila burst out laughing, as if reading her mind. "Oh, it's still cutthroat. We don't help you too much. But the last president started it." She waved her hand dismissively, "Some kind of help the needy act of charity. But Mr. Collins likes it . . . something about nurturing new talent."

"Can anyone come?" Lizzie asked.

Lila's lips curled into a sly smile. "No. You have to be invited to LFL. It's for the candidates we think have real *potential*," she said meaningfully. "If you don't mind giving up your lunch period, it can be worth your while."

"Where do you meet?"

"The auditorium, every lunch period. Just let them know I invited you," Lila said. She walked away, conversation over, close curtain.

Lizzie blew a low whistle. She sat down on the bench and tugged at Mina's sock.

"You're a trip, boy," Mina was saying, doing her flirty laugh—soft and feminine accompanied by a light tap of the person's shoulder she was flirting with.

Lizzie snorted and tugged again.

Mina swatted at her without breaking conversation. "So I'm saying, Ms. Claire's class is mad hard. You had her last year?"

"Yeah. I ended up with a B."

Mina nodded, eyes fixed on the guy in an understanding gaze, like this was the most interesting conversation ever. "Well if I ever need help I know who to call, huh?"

"What's your screen name. I'll hit you up sometimes."

Mina broke her neck scrambling for a pen. She kicked slightly at Lizzie's thigh and reached her hand out for a pen.

Lizzie shook her head as she reached in her purse and flicked out a pen.

Mina snatched it up, held her hand out, and the guy put his hand in hers. "Now don't wash this off in the shower till you write it down," she lectured gently, writing her screen name on his hand.

He smiled and winked at her. "I got you, shorty. I be talking to you."

"Okay then. See you, Bo."

Mina grinned, stepped down, and plopped next to Lizzie.

"Hot to death!" She fanned herself.

"Number ten, huh?" Lizzie asked.

"Number ten," Mina sighed happily.

"Okay. Can we talk about me for a sec," Lizzie asked.

Mina took a deep breath and turned her attention to Lizzie. "What's up? Did I see you talking to Queen Bee?"

"Yeah. Act III of this strange drama with her," Lizzie said, voice low. The crowd was thinning out, but they were far from alone near the bench.

"What happened?" Mina turned to sit cross-legged.

"What do you think this is all about? She just invited me to some exclusive lunch." Lizzie paused, concentrated on how to describe it to Mina. "Line tutoring is the only way I can think to describe what it must be."

"Tutoring? For what?"

"Drama. Lines for Lunch."

"Cute name. I think she just knows you're her competition, Liz. She probably wants to keep you close. Know what I mean?" Mina reasoned.

Lizzie chewed at the inside of her lip. That sounded reasonable enough and yet it didn't.

"I don't know. It's scary being her new . . ." she paused, again seemingly at a loss for words when it came to describe the whole bizarre situation, ". . . project. I'm like her charity case or something."

"Girl, stop. She's seen you enough to know you don't need her charity. She's just trying to check you out, up close."

Mina turned, looking toward the curb. "Hey my mother is here." She raised up and called over to JZ. "Jay! You rolling with me, right?!"

He nodded, wrapped up his conversation, and headed toward Mina's mother's silver BMW 7 Series.

"Come on, Chick," Mina said. She slipped her phone out of her purse to call Michael. Lizzie was deep in thought. "You alright?" she asked, dialing Michael's cell.

"Um-hmm." Lizzie rose slowly.

"Mike, where are you? My mom is here, hurry up," Mina ordered. She wrapped her arm in Lizzie's, pulling her along toward the car. "Stop worrying. You're in with Lila. What difference does it make why?"

Lizzie nodded, wanting to agree with Mina. Since the café invite she'd been waiting for hazing . . . having to do Lila's laundry or bring her breakfast at six A.M. But so far the popular redhead's interest was legitimate. She guessed. She hoped.

Having Lila help her was scary enough. She wasn't about to risk jinxing herself by questioning it.

It's Not Stalking If He Doesn't Have a Restraining Order

"You be talking like you like what I got (gimme that)."
—Chris Brown, "Gimme That"

The clique's excited banter about JZ's performance filled Mariah Mooney's car. Lizzie pushed thoughts of Lila and Bay Dra-da far away. She melted into the comfort of the Beemer's leather seats and let herself get drawn into the discussion.

"Ma, can you bring us back to the Ria tonight?" Mina asked.

"I tell you what, you and Lizzie aren't going to drive me crazy this weekend making me play chauffeur." Her mom checked the rearview to make sure Lizzie had heard.

Lizzie grinned innocently.

"Please, Ma?" Mina said.

"Nope. I said you two could have a sleepover this weekend. I didn't say anything about taking you anywhere," Mariah said.

"The Ria isn't really considered going somewhere. Right ya'll?" Mina turned in her seat waiting for backup. But the clique was mum.

"I can't anyway," her mom said. "Daddy's working late tonight and I have a client function that I'm jetting off to as soon as I drop you all home."

Mina's mom owned her own urban marketing communications

firm. Her daytime schedule was flexible but she worked lots of evening and weekends, launching events and promotional campaigns for clients.

"Can JZ and Michael hang out at our house then?" Mina asked. The varsity football team played an away game later that evening, so the Ria would likely be a ghost town until late anyway. Later than Mina's mother would let her head out for the night.

"Of course," her mom said. "JZ am I dropping you off home first?" She steered the car into The Woods.

"Yes, ma'am," JZ said.

"Michael?" Mariah asked.

"No, I can head right to your house. My grandmother isn't home, yet," he answered.

"I'll see ya'll after I change up," JZ said, as the car made the circle in front of his house.

"See you, Jay," Mina said. "So what we gonna do tonight, ya'll?"

"Whatever we do make it include food." Lizzie patted her stomach.

When they pulled up to the Mooneys', Mina's mom pulled out her purse and handed Mina thirty dollars. "Here you guys order something. I won't be home until late."

Mina leaned over and threw a smooch on her mom's cheek. "Thanks, Ma."

"Thanks, Ma," Lizzie mocked, cheesing.

"Don't tear my house down," Mariah warned, jokingly. "Michael, I know you're the reasonable one. Keep your eyes on those girls."

"Always," he said.

When the car pulled off, the three made their way into the house. Michael and Lizzie made themselves at home in Mina's spacious sunroom.

"I'ma hit the shower," Mina said.

Lizzie handed Mina her bag. "Can you take this upstairs for me, best friend?"

Mina slung it over her shoulder. "Never . . ."

"Say you didn't do anything for me," Lizzie finished and they both laughed. "Got it."

Mina disappeared up the stairs.

Lizzie fished her iPod out of her purse and hooked it up to the portable speakers. The theme from *The Wiz,* "Home," blasted from the tiny platinum towers.

"Ass, I forget how strong those things are," Michael said. His head swayed to the slow melody. "I know this song. I forgot who sings it though."

"It's 'Home' by Stephanie Mills. I'm trying to learn it for my audition," Lizzie said. She hummed along.

"Right. Okay, from *The Wiz,*" Michael said.

"Yup. It's this year's winter production."

Michael took out a sketch pad and pencil then settled himself on the coach.

Lizzie plunked beside him, watching Michael's fingers move gracefully over the page. Quickly, nothingness on the page turned into a slim figure wearing a miniskirt, fencing boots, and a beret. The music blared around them as the sketch became more and more detailed—plaid design on the skirt, ruffles on the shirt, the beret angled to cover what would have been an eye if the penciled-in model had a face.

"I've never seen you sketch designs. These are cool," Lizzie said.

"Thanks. I've been doing these for a few years. But . . ." He put the pad down and met Lizzie's questioning gaze.

"What?"

He drew the words out slowly. "I'm . . . trying . . . to get put on as assistant designer." Michael looked toward the stairs, saw no signs of Mina then blurted. "With Bay Dra-da."

"Mike, that's great! Wow, I didn't even know you had skill like this." Lizzie plucked the pad from his hand, admiring the detail of his sketch. "I mean I've seen your caricatures and stuff. But this is . . ." She shook her head. "These are great."

Michael pulled his binder out. Since he'd shown his sketches to Mr. Collins he was anxious to share the news. "I showed these to Mr. Collins yesterday and he liked them." Pride brightened his face, showcasing deep dimples in his right cheek.

Lizzie thumbed through the fat portfolio of drawings.

"I haven't told Mina yet. I'm waiting to see if I actually get the gig, first," Michael said. "So don't say anything. Or is that against ya'll girl code?"

Lizzie laughed. "Mina'll probably kill me. You know she has a million rituals and rules for friendship."

Michael nodded. "Remember how she made ya'll eat Cap'n Crunch with Crunch Berries every day for lunch, 'cause that's what she had for breakfast the day she met you."

Lizzie groaned. "Yes! Every day for like two years! I hate Cap'n Crunch to this day."

They howled together.

"Are you auditioning for the part of Dorothy?" Michael asked, changing subjects abruptly.

"Haven't made up my mind, yet," Lizzie said. She'd thought about going for the Dorothy role but was too nervous to admit it aloud. Going for a lead role as a freshman against senior members of the drama troupe was ballsy. She wasn't sure if she'd grown a set yet.

"Well, you know Dorothy of Detroit isn't like the Kansas chick from the *Wizard of Oz*. You need to come more fly when you audition," Michael said.

Lizzie was impressed with his knowledge of *The Wiz*. The only reason she knew about the production was because it came on TV during her very first sleepover with Mina when they were nine years old. It felt like a million years ago. But Lizzie remembered that Mina's mom had been really excited about *The Wiz* coming on and insisted they watch.

"Oh my God, they never show this anymore," Miss Mariah had

gushed. She sat the girls down with popcorn and watched the whole thing with them.

It was the first time Lizzie was aware there was a "black" version of *The Wizard of Oz*. She loved the music. But the dreary, city land-scape set of *The Wiz* looked low-budget, nothing like the glamorous portrayal of the *Oz* version. Seeing how excited Mina's mom was, Lizzie kept that to herself. She spent weeks, afterward, wondering how she'd never heard of or seen *The Wiz* but saw *The Wizard of Oz* on TV every year. She figured it was a Maryland thing. Since Lizzie was from Kansas they obviously only showed the version that cen-tered around Kansas. It made as much sense as anything else to a nine-year-old.

Staring at Michael's drawing she tried to picture herself in such a trendy outfit.

She wrinkled her nose. "You know, I'm not really into miniskirts."

Michael rolled his eyes. "Well, a hip-hop Dorothy would be. We talking about for the role, Miss Liz."

Lizzie looked at the design again then handed it back. "Ghetto fab, huh?"

She'd been around Michael and Mina and heard them talk fash-ion enough to pick up on some of the style nuances. They thought she didn't pay attention. She did. She was an actress. It was her job to. She just chose not to take any of the style tips for herself.

"Yup." Michael reached for colored pencils and began shading in the plaid in purple and green. "It's about how you hook up stuff. Ghetto fab isn't negative." He chuckled. "Not always. You'd look cute in this and definitely like the person who could carry off a role meant for a black chick."

It occurred to Lizzie that Drusilla Pinkney, another frosh, Kayla Watkins, a senior, or any other black girls that might audition could easily win the Dorothy role if Bay Dra-da was going for authentic. Then again, Drusilla had once played Sarah Brown, the lead in the theater camp's production of *Guys and Dolls*. And *Guys and Dolls* was usually a white cast. As a matter-of-fact, Dru was the only black person in the production that year.

So, all things were possible when it came to casting.

Weren't they?

Michael's fingers flew as he talked. "Shoot, you should have this role on lock from hanging with us, anyway." He squinted at the design then added more purple to the skirt. "I can hook you up with the beret. And Mina has some stuff similar to this in her closet. But you don't have to follow my advice, it was just a suggestion."

"I know. But I'm not sure I'm even going for Dorothy," Lizzie said, unsure why she couldn't admit her fears. Of course, now thanks to this conversation she had a new one. She wasn't black, and she certainly couldn't change that.

"Just let me know, if you change your mind," Michael said. He looked to the stairway then lowered his voice. "Look, Mina knows about my drawings. But she doesn't know about the Bay Dra-da thing. Can we keep it B/U?"

Lizzie nodded. "Just between us," she echoed, secretly pleased. As long as she'd been friends with Michael he'd never asked her to keep a secret between them. It was kind of cool.

Long after Michael made his departure (and JZ never made an appearance) the girls blew up the cyberworld IM'ing anyone who hadn't gone to the varsity's away game or the Ria. At one point, twenty IM chat boxes were open. They took turns on the PC. While one of them typed away conversing, the other read aloud from *A Tale of Two Cities*. Neither was sure if it was the best way to get the book read, but it was more fun than reading it alone.

By the time their IM boxes dwindled to one, they were one hundred fifty pages into the book. Their eyes, tired from the screen-burn and book print, ached until they were forced to shut them. Even

Lizzie, normally night-owling until two A.M., was unable to keep her eyes open by midnight.

The shrill tweet of Mina's phone roused her. Thinking it was the middle of the night and fearing her mother would burn up the hallway to snatch up the phone, Mina answered it on the second ring.

"Ay, girl! What up?" JZ blared. "Ya'll still sleep? I've been up, ran three miles, and swam a few laps."

"Boy what time is it?" Mina whispered.

"It's almost eight o' clock."

Mina squinted, looking around the room, confused. "In the morning?"

"Naw at night. Yes the morning, Mina," JZ said.

"Oh shoot. I don't even remember going to sleep." Mina moved out from under Lizzie's feet and sat up. "Wait. What happened to you last night?! You never came over."

JZ laughed. "Rachel called. I met her over at the Ria."

"That's foul on so many levels, Jay."

"I got caught up. My bad. I forgot to call and let ya'll know I wasn't rolling through."

He sounded sincere.

"Just gonna leave us hanging like that for some chick. Who has a boyfriend, by the way."

"Shoot that's his problem, not mine. Besides I'm not trying marry her. We just had pizza together."

Mina yawned as she fussed. "Still, you're trife."

"Didn't call for a lecture, baby girl. Come on over, later, alright?"

"Nope. I'm gonna ditch you like you did us," Mina said.

"Alright cool. I'll just tell Craig you were busy."

"What, Craig's coming over?" Mina's morning fog dried up at the mention of her crush. "Did he mention me?"

"He notices you, 'cause you be staring at him mad hard every time he sees you," JZ said.

"Well it's not a bad, stalker-type staring," Mina said.

"That's between you and him. But last night he asked where my clique was and he mentioned you, 'the chick on JV I see you with' is what he called you."

"Everybody gotta start somewhere," Mina said, entirely serious.

"Alrightie then, you're tripping hard over dude. But I invited some people over to cook out. He was one of 'em."

"I'm coming back as a boy in my next life. Ya'll get to do whatever you want," Mina groused. "I can't believe your parents letting you do back-to-back cookouts."

"So you and Lizzie coming or what?" JZ said.

"Yeah. We're coming early though. I need to be there before Craig gets there," Mina said.

"Somehow I knew that. Alright I holler." JZ clicked off.

Mina pushed herself up to an unsteady standing position and jumped up and down on the bed. "Lizzie, come on, Girl! Today might be the day Craig Simpson asks me out."

Lizzie grumbled and pulled a sheet over her eyes. But the yellow radiating from Mina's walls poked through the thin cotton layer.

"It's too early," she argued, her body popping slightly off the bed as Mina bounced.

"Jay doing another pool jammy jam. Let's get rolling early."

"What time is it?" Lizzie asked in alarm.

"Eight."

"What?! No! No, Mina. Go away until at least ten." Lizzie rolled away to the wall.

"Nine. You have until nine." Mina stepped down from the bed and went to shower.

Lizzie was asleep before Mina hit the door.

Two hours later they were at JZ's poolside, Lizzie groggy, Mina excited.

Lizzie spread her towel out on a stone-colored chaise lounge chair, sank her shades down on her face, and lay out.

"Don't go to sleep, Liz," Mina whined from beside her. Her chair stood inches apart from Lizzie's but out of the sun.

"I'm not," Lizzie mumbled. "Just tanning. I can still hear you guys."

JZ came over and sat on the ground between their chairs.

"So, what happened at the Ria last night?" Mina adjusted her chair to sit upright.

"Nothing. It was packed though. A lot of people headed there right after the game," JZ said.

"I need to work on getting my curfew extended, for real," Mina said. "Eleven is not gonna cut it."

"Good luck with all that," Lizzie mumbled, her face slack as she drifted closer and closer to sleep.

"I know, right," Mina said. The guys didn't have a curfew. She was so jealous. Most times they'd come hang out at her house knowing she couldn't go out beyond eleven. But now and then they left her behind.

Michael arrived, appearing from the corner of the pool house. His brown suede thong flip flops were color coordinated with his multishaded brown trunks, making for a handsome combo against his skin. He strolled over to the clique.

"Girls, ladies, women's . . . what's up?" Michael teased.

"What's up Surfer boy, M?" Mina teased. "You look cute."

"I know." Michael reached down and gave JZ a pound. "What happened to you last night, son? You get that call?"

"You know it."

"You knew he had a Plan B last night?" Mina pursed her lips.

"Kind of. I tried calling you, kid," Michael said.

"It was too loud. I never even heard my phone," JZ said.

"Yeah, yeah. Yadda, yadda, yadda," Mina interrupted. "What time is Craig coming?"

"Diva, stalking is not a good look." Michael shook his head at her. He chucked his shoes in a corner and walked over to the diving board.

"Okay, it's not stalking if he doesn't have a restraining order out on me," Mina shouted after him.

JZ stood up. "You getting in?"

"I can't get my hair all booked, yet." Mina scowled.

"Girl, you are mad tripping." JZ dove into the water from the side.

"Liz, I'm going over to the wading pool," Mina said.

A muffled "Mrrff . . ." was Lizzie's only answer.

Mina staged herself on the edge at the wading pool, between the shallow and deep ends. Her legs dangled and she waved heartily as people began arriving. By the time Craig sauntered in, his caramel complexion looking rich next to his white trunks, Mina was holding court with Bo, the varsity cutie who claimed he could tutor her in world history, Cassidy, a squad mate, and Sarah, Jessica's twin.

Lucky for Mina, Jessica ran with the rich clique. They were probably country clubbing it today.

Mina let Bo go on about how often he worked out and how Mina could have a six-pack if she did five hundred super mini-crunches a day.

She was fine with her flat, but no-pack, abs, thanks very much, Bo. She mentally deducted five flirt points from him for that.

At least twenty people were there already, swimming, hanging out at the juice bar, and chilling while music pumped out of the speakers that looked like rocks to match the pool's landscape. Mina kept the conversation going with Bo but never took her eyes off Craig as he walked by the diving board and greeted JZ. Mr. Zimms, on his way to replenish the bar with juices, sodas, and water, joined the two boys in a short conversation. Mina could read a few words from their lips. They were talking about football, of course. She was relieved when Bo yelled across the pool. "What up, Craig?!"

"Swazy!" Craig threw up a fist.

"I be back," Bo said, dripping water as he stood up to join Craig's conversation.

Yay, Mina thought.

"Mina, do you guys have the pep rally stuff under control?" Sarah asked.

"Yeah, I think so."

"I thought you guys' themes were cute." Sarah fluffed up her thick curls and pulled them into a high pony. "We voted last night before our game. The Light's Out theme won all of our votes."

"It did?" Mina said, actually forgetting about Craig for a second.

"Yup. Kim will probably tell you if she comes today. Act surprised," Sarah said.

The Light's Out theme had been Mina's idea. The whole pep rally was going to be done in the dark. They would hand out glow sticks and glow necklaces the class period before the rally. Then the cheerleaders were going to wear special glow-in-the-dark tees and put glowing devil horns all over their skirts. They were going to do their whole routine in a darkened gym.

In hopes that varsity liked the theme as much as they did, JV was already hunting for the materials to create "Light's Out Saints" signs, which would dot the gym in, of course, glow-in-the-dark gel pens and paint.

"I'm glad you guys picked that one, it was our favorite, too," Cassidy said.

Mina beamed. She knew she liked Cassidy for a reason.

Craig came and sat on the edge of the pool beside Mina. He stripped off his shirt and threw it on top of the rock speaker. "How come ya'll not in the water?"

"I'm ready to hit the juice bar," Sarah said, pushing herself out of the water. "Wanna come, Mina?"

Mina shook her head.

"I'll go," Cassidy said.

"You getting in?" Craig asked.

"You first," Mina dared.

Craig dropped into the pool, on the deep side of the wading area, and plunged to the bottom. While he was under, Mina did a quick breath check to make sure she was still minty fresh. He popped back up right in front of her, tugging gently at her legs. "Your turn. Or you one of those chicks too cute to get her hair wet?"

"Naw, I'll get in. Did ya'll win last night?" Mina asked. She wanted to stretch the conversation. It was the first time they'd had a real one. She leaned back on her palms and kept her smile to herself when she saw Craig give her curves a quick up and down once-over. A quiver of satisfaction went down to her toes. Who needed a six pack? Craig was enjoying the view.

Mina was certain she'd just set women's rights back, at least by a few minutes, by being so happy about that.

"Yup, fourteen to seven," Craig said, not shy about letting his eyes linger on her thick thighs. "How come you didn't come out?"

Mina shrugged it off. Until somebody in the clique got a license (*or I get a boyfriend with license . . . Craig!*) away games far into the county were either off-limits or better be worthy of her begging the 'rents to drive her.

"I couldn't get a ride out that far," she said.

"Oh, right. North County High is deep," Craig agreed.

Mina peered down at him. "Do you know my name?"

"Mina, right?"

She grinned. "Yeah. I wasn't sure you knew."

"I see you hanging out with Jason at the Ria. Plus, I saw you at the JV game yesterday, getting your cheer on." He mocked a shoulder shimmy. "Were you here last Saturday when Jason had that cookout?"

"No. I had plans." Mina omitted the fact that they included hanging out at the local discount havens.

"So how long you plan to stall?" Craig said.

"Huh?" Mina looked to the pool house. Lizzie was awake and talking to Michael. Mina wanted to wave so Lizzie could see her, but she and Michael had their heads together, deep in conversation.

"Stalling," Craig repeated. "You getting in? Or should I pull you in?"

Mina threw her hands up in surrender. "Nope. I'll go quietly."

She waded into the pool then dove in. Craig's voice came through muffled as she headed up to the surface.

"You down with some chicken?"

"Anytime," Mina said, game for more body aches if it meant sitting on Craig's shoulders.

"Hey, Jason, it's on!" Craig yelled. He motioned to JZ near the juice bar. "Hop on," he said to Mina. He waded to the shallow end and squatted so she could climb on.

Mina's face lit up as she took her place on his shoulders.

JZ grabbed Sarah's hand. "Come on."

They plunged in and met Mina and Craig in the middle of the pool. "Cheerleader chicken, JV versus varsity!" JZ whooped.

"No disrespect, Sarah, but I have a title to protect," Mina said.

"I think JZ can handle this. We ain't scared," Sarah said, very un-Jessica like.

"Lizzie, who's the Chicken Champion Queen?" Mina crowed.

Lizzie gave her a thumbs-up from the sideline. "You, Mina!"

"Shorty, you got this?" Craig asked.

"Mos' def," Mina said. "Watch. We'll make a good couple."

She loved the sound of that.

It's Like Cliques 'R' Us

"What happened to Miss Independent?"
—Kelly Clarkson, "Miss Independent"

Mina's legs pumped furiously. She willed them to get her to soc on time.

"Hello, Miss Mooney," Mrs. Simms chirped as Mina threw herself into her seat two seconds after the second bell.

Mina sang back, "Hi, Mrs. Simms. Sorry I'm late."

"No harm, no foul. But let's not make it a habit." She patiently waited for the morning chatter to wind down before directing the students' attention to a mound of red and blue T-shirts. "For the rest of the day this will be part of your uniform."

With hopes that they chose their own, Mina mentally checked off her choice, definitely the dark crimson, Valentine's Day red tee. The electric neon blue (*turquoise on steroids*) made Mina see spots. It was just her opinion, but whoever had the nerve to sell such a bright, shocking-colored shirt should be put out of business. Fashion clearly wasn't their thing.

Mrs. Simms walked the aisle, handing out the tees, dashing Mina's hope of getting a choice.

"Last Thursday we began discussing societies with caste systems," Mrs. Simms explained. "Some caste systems, like India's are so severe that someone of a higher caste will go wash themselves if someone in a lower caste touches them."

A girl with strawberry-blond hair raised her hand. Mina hoped for the girl's sake she received a red tee. The combination of the girls reddish hair and pale skin against the electric blue tee would make her a fashion mistake on so many levels.

"Yes, Rita," Mrs. Simms said, handing her a red shirt. Mrs. Simms rarely discouraged questions or frank discussion, even if it disrupted her flow.

"I had that happen to me, one time," Rita said. "I brushed against one of the glams and she ran to the water fountain and started washing off her shoulder."

"And what is a glam?" Mrs. Simms asked. A smile in her eyes hinted that she knew but, as always, wanted to hear the students' take on DRB High's mix of social circles.

There was snickering and a few people turned to Jessica, wondering if she'd claim her species. No doubt the girl was talking about Mari-Beth, Jessica, or someone else from their clique.

Jessica had a snide smile on her face, but said nothing.

Rita's eyes popped. One of two things just hit her: (1) that Jessica was in the class or (2) Jessica was a glam. Mina watched as Rita squirmed in her seat, hesitating. But Mrs. Simms was waiting.

"It's . . . just . . . a clique," Rita said carefully.

Grace whispered something in Jessica's ear and Jessica nodded. She kept her eye on the now-nervous Rita and discreetly mimed a throat slit.

"I sense an inside joke of some sort," Mrs. Simms said. "But it proves my point. In true caste systems you are not allowed to marry or work outside of your caste. It rules your life. There are some individuals who believe some are just naturally beneath them. Some of you found the idea ridiculous. Others of you thought it was a great idea. Well, you know me. I say let's see how you like it."

Mina snorted. "Mrs. Simms, I don't mean any harm, but high school is a huge caste system. It's like Cliques 'R' Us. We deal with it every day. And even people who claim to be above cliques are a clique!"

A few people yeah-ed in agreement.

The Guru handed Mina a blue shirt and winked. "No argument there, Mina. But so-called cliques are entered into voluntarily. It's always easy when you choose your own societal standing." She walked on, handing out more shirts. "All right, those of you with red shirts are the elite caste. You have the power to go where you'd like, sit with whom you want, and speak when you please. For today, Del Rio Bay High School is your royal territory."

Mina's jaw fell. She dropped the neon blue tee like it was a poisonous snake. Mrs. Simms had set her up.

"The caste assignment is not voluntary. But you are on the honor system, as with other things in this class." She stopped to fix the class with a meaningful stare. "I trust we are getting our prejudice assignments complete?"

Mumbles of assurance rippled through the rows.

"Good. Well this is no different," Mrs. Simms said. "I can't be in the hallway or your classrooms. But I trust you to follow the rules. Assignments in my class are only as effective as your participation. You are among the lucky few who were placed in this Life Lessons course. Don't cheat yourselves out of the experience."

Mrs. Simms went back to the front of the class, let her clogs drop to the floor and sat upon her desk cross-legged.

"I'm certain that the Reds will help enforce the rules. They always do," Mrs. Simms said, a hint of a laugh in her words.

Mina caught the unsaid in the Guru's words. Of course the Reds help enforce the rules, they were in charge. She slumped in her seat, depression growing as she learned more.

Blue shirts were the lower caste. If they saw a red shirt in the hall they had to carry their books to class and still manage to get to their own class on time. Blue shirts could only socialize with other blue shirts the whole day and weren't allowed to speak to a Red unless the red shirt addressed them first.

Basically, red shirts had the run of things, speaking to anyone they wanted, doing whatever they wanted.

Mina took inventory: Jacinta was a Red; she, Jessica, and Kelly, Blue. The satisfaction of Jessica being a blue did nothing for her spirits.

Mrs. Simms took in the mixed reactions. There was equal celebration as there was groaning. Satisfied with the extremes, she continued. "Fair warning, Blues: do not try to use your vow of subservient silence as an excuse for not participating in class!"

Some Blues laughed aloud.

Mrs. Simms warned the other half. "Conversely, Reds, do not attempt to get out of homework assignments due to your superior status. These positions are temporary, for today only. They also apply only to your interaction with other students. Not teachers!"

"Mrs. Simms, we can't talk to anyone?" Mina whined, already hating the assignment.

"You may speak to others freely only during class time, as part of your usual class participation. But in the hallways and during lunch, you may speak only with Blues or to a Red if they address you," Mrs. Simms answered. "So I suggest you take a good look around to see those with whom you may and may not interact. The assignment starts now and ends after the last bell."

Excited talk coursed through the classroom. The Blues shot envious glances at their red-shirted peers. No matter their status, Mrs. Simms had altered it with one simple wardrobe change.

"Okay, today we move on to tribal rituals. Before we jump into the lesson—Kevin and Charles, take seven chairs and stack them against the wall. Reds, please sit where you like. Blues, fill in any of the remaining chairs."

"But, Mrs. Simms, that means some of us will have to stand!"

Mina cried out in alarm as her chair was snatched from underneath her.

"Yes. That's correct," Mrs. Simms moved on to the day's lecture.

Kelly and Jessica had managed to get seats. Unable to do the same, Mina joined the rest of the seatless Blues in the back. She took one second of satisfaction when she saw Grace was also blue-shirted and standing. With nowhere else to stand, she took a spot next to Grace.

"How painful will this be today?" Mina whispered to her, unable to keep silent much longer. She wanted to make sure she wasn't the only one hating this already.

"I had a friend take this class last year. She said some of the Reds can be obnoxious. But just go with the flow," Grace said. "Mrs. Simms does it every year. You'll survive."

Mina nodded. Survival sounded like a good plan.

As expected, the morning spiraled downward, starting with Jacinta shoving her backpack at Mina as they left class.

"Here you go."

"Serious?" Mina asked, fumbling to grip Jacinta's backpack and her own.

"Very," Jacinta said.

"I think ya'll enjoying this too much, already," Mina grumbled.

Jacinta got loud on her. "Yup. You might be the Princess, but I'm the Queen today." She pivoted on her heels and headed down the hall, Mina trailing behind, trying to shrink into the scenery.

For only having twenty-four people in the soc class, the hall swam in a sea of cheap, tacky shirts. Mina wandered past two Reds high-fiving and pounding each other on the back, enjoying their new status. They spoke to Jacinta and Jacinta called back a breezy "Hey," like they were old friends.

When they arrived at Jacinta's class, Mina handed the backpack over, ignoring the smug grin on Jacinta's face. She was surprised when Jacinta said, "So I missed Jason's party on Saturday, huh?"

Mina looked off to the sides as if double-checking Jacinta was talking to her. "Is this a trick?"

"No. You can talk back to me if I talk to you, remember? Besides, you mentioned his party on the bus, this morning."

"Yeah. It was nice," Mina said. The warm and fuzzy image of her and Craig besting JZ and Sarah in chicken made her long for the weekend.

"I went home for the weekend," Jacinta said. "Does he have parties like that a lot?"

Mina nodded. "Yeah. His parents are probably ready to shut the pool down soon, though."

Jacinta shrugged. "I can't swim well, anyway. I get by but you know. . . . So when are you going to tell me what the deal is with Swirl?"

"Who's that?" Mina asked.

"Jessica 'I'm mixed' Johnson." Jacinta laughed.

"It's a long story, but for what it's worth, I think you're taking the right approach with her," Mina said.

"Yeah. Why you let her punk you? She talk to you like you owe her money."

Mina snorted. It reminded her that Jacinta probably had no idea how deep the cliques in DRH ran. "We have a little history. I just ignore her."

"She's foul. All that fake hair and those fake hazel eyes." Jacinta's shoulders shuddered like she'd just seen a creepy crawly or slime oozing out of the walls.

Mina glanced up at the hall clock. As much as she was enjoying this little diversion, she had to get to class. "I've gotta go, Cinny."

Jacinta waved her off. "Go then," she said, then barked, "Oh, Mina!"

Mina swallowed a sigh and pivoted back around. "Yeah?"

"Meet me by my locker at fourth period. I'll need more help," Jacinta chuckled as she dipped into her class.

Anger squeezed Mina's lungs. The effort to keep her face blank made her eyes sting.

At the end of second period, JZ and Lizzie fell in step beside her.

"We just had two people with these shirts on in our Algebra class. So we know you can't talk," Lizzie said.

Mina tugged at her blue tee and made hand gestures, asking Lizzie whether her classmates were Blues or Reds.

JZ picked up on the sign language. "One of each."

Mina rolled her eyes.

"Girl, I know this killing you." JZ snickered. "But a silent Mina is kind of nice."

With no other way to express herself, Mina stuck out her tongue at him.

"I have Lines for Lunch all week. So I won't be at lunch, today. But good luck," Lizzie said. She gave Mina's shoulder a squeeze, then veered off into her class.

"Alright, Mi. For real, I'm kind of liking the new, quiet you," JZ said.

Mina smacked him and kept going.

"Just jokes, Girl," he said before racing down the hall in the opposite direction.

By the end of second period, Mina had traveled the full area of the school. She had gone out of her way to avoid the Reds, backtracking more than once in the opposite direction to race on to class.

The constant gallop was bad. Wearing the ugly blue shirt was worse. Passing by friends, teammates, and a few of her crushes without as much as a "hello" or flirty head pop was torture.

Worn from the grind, by third period—her last before lunch—her legs ached from pounding the hallways. She dragged, stopping at her locker to slam all but her math book inside. Hatred for the soc assignment nipped at her. To say this was her worst nightmare was an understatement.

Hugging the book to her, she slumped against the locker to catch her breath. People flowed by talking and laughing. Mina envied them. She felt like she was in an alternate world, unseen by anyone who wasn't in the soc class.

The hall, thank God, was Red-free. With an exhausted sigh that came from deep inside, she gathered the strength to swallow the humiliation. It's only for a day, she reasoned. Being a Blue wasn't her life. She could do this.

From half-closed lids she went on Red alert and froze at the sight of Craig heading her way. She flirted with Bo Saturday to pass the time and enjoyed it until the whole bizarre abs conversation, but Craig was still her number one crush.

Deep in conversation, with Jake, Craig's almond-shaped eyes narrowed even more when he laughed at something Jake said. He was adorable. The thought of him seeing her in the fashion no-no tee set Mina's cheeks on fire. Caught between her crush and a hallway that stretched for days, she counted up her options: (1) run, (2) ease into the bathroom across the hall, or (3) be caught in the sbummy shirt, ruining the whole diva doll image she had worked so hard to portray to Craig.

She pushed herself off the locker and bolted toward the girls bathroom, head down. Glancing from the corner of her eye, she could see Craig closing in. On command, her legs scurried across the corridor.

Just as her fingers pushed the bathroom door open, his voice boomed. "Good look, Mina!"

His laughter squeezed past the closing door before being abruptly cut off.

Mina ran into a stall, shaking. Her stomach was in knots. She sucked in huge gulps of air until her chest burned. She wanted to go home and bury herself deep into the covers. Her stomach clinched tighter as she convinced herself she wasn't feeling well.

She sat on the edge of the toilet and searched her pack. Silent for a second, double-checking she was alone, she slipped her cell phone out and dialed frantically.

A cool second of calm returned to her until her mother's voice squawked from the other end, "Mooney-Addison Urban Marketing, Mariah Mooney speaking."

"Mom, I want to come home!" Hot tears streamed down Mina's face. "I don't feel well."

Her mom clicked from professional to parent instantly. "Honey, what's wrong?"

Mina sniffled, locked in her despair. "I just don't feel well!" she wailed. "My stomach is crampy and I feel like I'm going to throw up!"

"Okay. Are you in the health room?"

"No, the bathroom."

"Go the health room and I'll be by in fifteen minutes."

"I can't!" Mina whined.

There was a silent beat as Mina's mom processed "can't," before she jumped back into the questions. "You're not well enough to make it to the health room? Was it something you ate this morning?"

"No. It's this stupid soc assignment. I have to wear this disgusting neon blue, turquoise, aqua, or whatever color it is T-shirt looking like a style reject from the 80s. I have to wear it all day!!! I hate it!! I'm sick. I need to come home, Ma."

"Mina," her mother cut in. "What's going on? Are you sick or . . ."

"The guy I have a crush on just laughed at me. Well, laughed at this shirt . . . I don't know. I can't even show my face, right now. God, he's probably in class laughing it up with people talking about how stupid the fresh fish looks in her sbummy T-shirt."

"Slow down, honey," her mother directed, piecing together a picture. Mina's Drama Queen tendencies were endearing, if not a little over the top. She let her voice dip low, but kept a firm edge to lure her daughter in from the brink. "You're overreacting, Boo. Don't you think people probably know the T-shirt is part of a project? Are you the only one with one on?"

"No," Mina sniffled, head pounding. She stood up and lay her head up against the coolness of the stall, letting her mother's voice unjangle her nerves.

"Okay. So you're not alone. Right?"

"I guess," Mina agreed, begrudgingly.

"Sweetie, head to the health room. Get a cool compress then jump back out there. The day is almost over."

Mina's tears trickled. She wiped them away as she nodded to her mother's words.

"Okay?" her mother called out, softly prodding.

"Alright." Mina inhaled then blew her lungs clear.

"We'll talk about it later, if you want."

"I won't want," Mina said, dejected.

Her mother laughed softly. "Okay. Call me back if you need to. Okay sweetie?"

"Okay," Mina said, five years old again, unwilling to hang up and cut off her safety net.

"Love you," her mom sang.

"Love you."

Mina pushed END, reluctantly.

She didn't want to waste the little bit of strength she'd gained from calling her mom. She burst out of the stall, ran cold water over her face, and sped to the health room where she hid out the remainder of the period.

She used the forty minutes to both talk herself down and chide herself for the breakdown. Her game face was intact when the bell for lunch rang.

She sauntered in, scoping out the lunchroom from the landing for Kelly and other blue shirts.

"Hey, Mi. It's just me and you today," Michael said, popping up beside her. "Lizzie's prepping for auditions and JZ had to meet with his coach."

She fluttered her eyes like mad to get Michael's attention. She wanted to mouth to him that she couldn't talk. But he tugged her toward their regular spot, "Come on."

Mina resisted but she was unable to interrupt Michael's flow. "That blue shirt is not the move, Diva. Sbummy times ten. I've seen a few other people with it on. What's up with it?"

A voice behind them called out, "Hey, Blue, carry these books. They're getting heavy."

Mina turned to face Joey Malone, a snotty, rich dude who had sweet-talked (or bribed) teachers into good grades all through middle school. The life of a Red was his real life. Mina's stomach lurched at the thought of carrying his books.

"Joey, why you tripping?" Michael growled, blocking him from Mina. "She not carrying your damn books."

Joey put his palms up. "Ay man, it's for a class project. She's not even allowed to talk to you right now."

Michael peered at Mina. She nodded and sighed in confirmation.

"Let's go, Blue. I'm starved!" Joey ordered.

Mina snatched his books and sulked behind him, leaving Michael standing on the landing, as Joey led her to his table. She cringed, wanting to smack him when he announced, "Hey, everybody, this is my slave!"

Unable to check herself, she raised her voice, "Boy, you—"

"Ah, ah, ah," Joey clucked. He waved his finger in her face. "Don't speak unless spoken to."

Mina threw his books on the table and turned to walk away.

Joey teased, "Now, is that any way to treat the books of your superior?"

His lunch mates gawked in surprise.

Mina took a deep breath, drawing on her mother's words for patience. She turned around to face the table once again. The eyes of Joey's friends absorbed her every move as she picked up the scattered books, put them neatly in a stack, and then stood back and waited for him to say something. She wanted to respond so bad her tongue itched. But she kept her eyes down, kept her breathing calm.

Joey shooed her away. "Thanks girl. You can go now."

The unspoken venom she wanted to spew at Joey was burning a hole in her gut. She stomped away. "I can do this. I can do this," she chanted through clinched teeth.

Kelly and four other blue shirts scooted down the bench to make room when she approached the table. They all shared sympathetic looks of understanding.

Mina dropped hard into the seat, exhaling long and hard before she shouted. "Okay, it's official—I hate this assignment!!"

The release felt so sweet, she felt ten pounds lighter.

"It sucks," another Blue chimed in.

"It blows," somebody else added.

In spite of the anger bubbling in her chest, Mina laughed. They were a pitiful, broken crew of souls. Her frustration began to subside as the conversation flowed. She was embarrassed to learn that two of the Blues were freshmen that she'd had classes with last year at Del Rio Bay Middle.

Awkward pause when Mina drew a complete blank as the one girl described a conversation the two had shared. Better bone up on rule of engagement number three, Mina thought.

Just as the camaraderie got going, Jessica slammed her backpack onto the table. Startled out of their banter, the Blues looked up at her.

"I'm only sitting here because some stupid Red threatened to tell Mrs. Simms I was talking outside of the assignment," Jessica announced. She cut her eyes at everyone, daring anyone to say a word about her joining them, before sitting with a resigned thud.

The table grew quiet except for Mina. She hadn't been able to talk freely all day. Jessica or not, she was enjoying this brief slice of social time.

"I can't believe how much I hate the Reds. I'm totally jealous," Mina admitted. "Dag, has it really only been a day?"

Kelly patted her shoulder. "Just one day. The thing is, except for having to carry other people's books, it's a pretty regular day."

Mina eyed her curiously. Nothing about this day was regular. "What do you mean?"

As the other Blues peered at her, Kelly grew self-conscious. Her voice lowered as she answered with a tiny shoulder hiccup. "I've never had a lot of friends. Going a whole day not talking to anyone isn't new to me."

Mina started to comment but Jessica cut in, her voice thick with loathing. "I thought people this pathetic were extinct." She waved her hand in front of her nose. "God, it even smells like loser over here."

"Jess, you didn't have to sit here," Mina said.

Jessica waved Mina off. "Yeah, I have a choice where to sit. But you guys obviously are pathetic by nature."

Mina was normally afraid to respond to Jessica's biting comments because saying the wrong thing could hurt her reputation. But Jessica hated her. Shoot, maybe she'd already put Mina on some sort of café Never-Admit list.

She was too tired today to care. Mina probably would never tell her so, but Jacinta had been right. Just because Jessica was nasty didn't mean Mina had to take it without rebuttal.

"Why can't you just admit that you'd rather sit here with people you can talk to than by yourself?" Mina asked.

"Dream on, Mina." Jessica stood up and grabbed her backpack. "You wish I *needed* to talk to you."

She stalked out of the cafeteria, but not before a Red stopped her and made Jessica throw away his lunch tray.

The table of Blues cracked up.

"Checkmate," one of them said.

Another Blue spoke up. "We should get a Red alone and make him carry all our backpacks. The Blues strike back!"

"You know what's kind of scary?" Mina stared after Jessica. "I probably wouldn't treat people any better if I had that stupid, ugly red T-shirt on."

"I think you would," Kelly said. "Some people can't be mean."

Mina nodded, playing along. She hated how the Reds were gloating in their status. But she knew, without a doubt, she would enjoy the power of the hideous crimson tee just like anybody else. Maybe she wouldn't turn into Jessica. But then, you never know.

People Might Take It Wrong

"Ay-yo Swizz, I don't think they ready for this s*&%."
—Busta Rhymes, "Touch It"

Friday night was a double-header, a rare treat when both the JV and varsity games were home. Thanks to their win the week before, the Baby Blue Devils were performing in front of a packed stadium of fans hungry to see a repeat bruising. Varsity football players, dressed in their jerseys, lined the fence around the field.

Mina surveyed the swollen crowd. Spying Michael and Lizzie with their heads together, she waved to them. Michael winked and gave her the thumbs-up then dove back into conversation.

Before she could wonder what Lizzie and Michael were so deep in convo about, the crowd broke out with the "Hey Cheerleaders, let me see you get down" chant. Mina led the squad in a lusty response of "D-O-W-N and that's the way we get down." She popped her shoulders in sync to the chant, rocking her body to the ground.

Racing in from the goal posts nearest the gym, the football team hit the field, igniting the crowd into a chorus of hoots and screams. The cheerleaders fed off their fire and launched into a cheer.

Forty-five seconds melted off the clock before JZ blasted down the field for the first time and made the crowd lose their mind. The second time he raced down the sideline, JZ pushed the score to 14–3.

"Jay-sooonnnn Zimmmmmmmmmmsssssss!" blared from the PA system, fueling the crowd's cheers.

Mina's head snapped as she chanted, her cheer pony bouncing from the force. With a single hand motion to the broadcast tower, she took the energy up a notch, turning the crowd's hunger for action into a full-blown party. PussyCat Dolls' "Dontcha" blasted out over the field, sending the cheerleaders into well-rehearsed spontaneity, a bumping, hip-hop routine and a chant of "Get it hot, Devils" in place of the song's hook. The spectators rocked the stands and sang along, adding to the mania.

Sweat dripping, Mina soaked in the crowd energy like oxygen. When the quarter ended, she turned to Kelis. "Water break?"

Kelis nodded, her face glistening with sweat as much as Mina's. She sent a whispered message down the cheer line and the squad walked toward the fence for a water break.

Mina fiddled with her cheer pony, tightening the rubber band, as she turned to consult with Kelis on their halftime routine. Her eyebrows hiccupped in surprise. Craig was standing at the fence, only a few feet away.

"What?" Kelis asked.

"There goes my Boo!" Mina's smile spread.

"Who?" Kelis instinctively turned to see whom Mina was gaping at.

Mina tugged her arm, hard, in alarm. "Don't look!" her voice screamed in a hoarse whisper. "It's Craig Simpson."

Kelis's mouth dropped. "I didn't know ya'll were talking. Yeah, he's definitely a hottie."

"We're not. I'm just working my way up to that point," Mina said, talking from the side of her mouth so no one else could hear.

She smiled shyly and waved at Craig, embarrassment of the soc tee project a distant haze. Craig threw a head nod her way, sending her smile into a straight-up grin.

Her stomach fizzed with excitement over all the things the gesture could mean. Was it a head nod, like, yeah Girl, I'm feeling you? Or, hey, what's up from a distance? The scoreboard's rusty blare signaled the start of the new quarter, disrupting Mina's analysis.

"Alright ya'll, let's get back!" she instructed, sideways glancing at Craig. In a reckless moment of bold, she winked at him. He winked back, making her entire weekend.

Let a meteor hit Del Rio Bay High's stadium right now and Mina wouldn't feel the blast. She was already miles away.

She stood on the sideline grinning, clapping, and rooting on the team. Giddy, she pumped her fist into the air before going into a perfect toe-touch, nearly three feet off the ground. Nervous energy fueled her chants, making her voice louder than usual. Every few seconds she stole a glance at Craig, who was doing a good job of looking really into the game. But Mina caught him checking her out on the low more than once.

When he finally walked away at halftime, she was exhausted from being on hyperdrive. She had never cheered so hard in her life.

As the halftime whistle blew, the JV squad performed a quickie thirty-second dance routine and a rowdy cheer, catching the fans before they scattered to mingle or wandered to the Devil's Lair for food. Mina was glad to spend the few minutes of halftime sipping water, getting a few instructions from Coach Embry and gossiping with the squad.

But come the second half, Mina kicked it right back into gear when the team continued to outpace the Bruins. This time she actually focused on the team.

Anytime the announcer's excited commentary floated from the speakers, setting the crowd off, Mina yelled along, growing hoarse as the Blue Devils stomped any hope of a Bruins comeback.

The game ended with a final score Blue Devils 42, Bruins 17.

Excitement rippled through the stands as fans filtered out, boisterous and juiced up from the win.

Mina didn't bother to change out of her uniform. She grabbed her duffle, stuffed with her clothes and amenities for the weekend, and met Michael and Lizzie near the field's entrance to wait for JZ. When he finally exited the locker room, a small throng of students waited. They surrounded him, congratulating him.

The clique waited patiently until he slipped away and sauntered over to them. Smiling, JZ gave Michael a pound. "Ya'll staying for the big game?"

Mina gripped JZ in a tight hug. "You were on again, Jay!"

He shrugged her off, gently, his grin saying it all.

Michael slapped him on the back. "I can't stay, playuh." He bowed deep at the waist and announced formally. "Introducing, the new assistant costume designer for Bay Drama and Dance Troupe, Mr. Michael James."

"Oh, my God! Why didn't you tell us, Mike?!" Mina exploded, happily.

Michael's smile nearly reached around the back of his head. "I just wanted to make sure it was solid before I told anybody. But production moving fast, so I need to meet with them tonight."

Lizzie raised her hand classroom style. "I knew! But he swore me to secrecy."

"What's up with the secrets?" Mina frowned. She looked from Michael to Lizzie, waiting for an explanation.

Lizzie gave Michael the told-you-so eyes.

"It wasn't like that, Mina. I just wanted it to be definite first." Michael pleaded with his eyes for understanding. "Like you and Lizzie don't keep secrets from me and Jay."

He had her there. Mina twisted her mouth, pretending to think about it. She was hurt but guessed it wasn't a big deal. She didn't want to go diva on him when he was so obviously happy, happier than she'd seen him in a long time.

Mina wagged her finger at both Michael and Lizzie. "We'll talk."

"Enough with the drama, Deev," Michael said.

"Okay, okay." Mina wrapped her arms around his arm and squeezed. "You are gonna rock those costumes out!"

"That's cool, B," JZ said, his voice flat.

"I stayed for the game. Had to see you mash them busters up, Son." Michael gave JZ another congratulatory pound. "But I gotta bounce to a meeting with the head designer."

"I gotta go, too. Audition sign-ups," Lizzie mocked, pushing her sleeves up. "Time to get to work."

"Going for the big dog role?" Mina asked.

Lizzie shrugged. "Honestly, I'm still not sure."

"Go for it, Girl." Mina gave her a hug. "You've got it on lock. I can feel it."

Lizzie let the vibes from the hug spread. She needed the boost no matter how biased the source was. "Thanks, Mi. See you tomorrow."

Michael flipped his phone open to check on the time. "Come on Liz-O. We gotta roll." He turned heel and let his long stride take him into the evening, Lizzie beside him.

Mina watched them disappear into the school. She picked up her overstuffed duffle packed for the game, the sleepover at Kelly's, and a sleepover at Lizzie's and crisscrossed it over her shoulder, messenger-bag style. "Mike's designs are like fi-ya! I bet he'll blow uuup!"

"I guess," JZ mumbled. He threw on a Blue Devil Football sweat-shirt and sank into the cover of its hoodie.

"Aren't you hot in that thing?" Mina said. The sun was setting but the humidity lingered. The strap of the duffle, scratching against her neck, was making her warm and here JZ had on a sweatshirt. She squinted up into the low-hanging hood of the sweatshirt, trying to read JZ's eyes. But the hoodie cast a shadow on his face.

"Naw, I'm cool," was JZ's only answer. He leaned against the fence circling the field.

Mina stood in front of him, chattering on. "I'm glad Mike is fi-nally putting some shine on his designs," Mina said. "He's drawn some really tight stuff. You should see it."

JZ didn't answer.

Activity buzzed throughout the campus as more people arrived for the varsity game. The parking lot was already packed. Some people filtered into the school; others stood in a line at the Devil's Lair, a white-bricked oversized shack, which served as the ticket window and concession stand.

"Okay, what?" Mina said, confused by JZ's silence. Normally he talked nonstop after a win.

"What, what?" He looked toward the school.

"We won. Why are you so quiet?" she paused, considered his silence, then scowled. "Are you tripping because of Mike's good news?"

JZ frowned back. Irritation crawled into his voice. "No. It's just . . ."

Mina pushed the duffle to her back and put her hands on her hips. "Just what?"

JZ blurted, "Sewing and shit? What's up with Mike? He want people think he gay or something?!" A few people in the ticket line looked Mina's and JZ's way. JZ stuttered, his voice going lower in its fury. "It . . . It . . . it just seem like a strange thing for him to get into, that's all. He got mad drawing skills. I give him that. But costume designing?!"

Mina's eyes popped wide. "JZ, that's so wrong. Michael is your boy!!"

"I know. Ain't nothin' changed! All I'm saying is he need keep that stuff under wraps. People might take it wrong." He dangled his wrist for emphasis.

Mina rolled her eyes. "Jay, this isn't something new. Michael's always had the skill. You should see the tons of designs he's sketched . . ."

The stubborn look on his face stopped her short. She fussed him out. "Based on your funky attitude, I can see why he never bothered to show them to you."

JZ's face, pinched, stared at Mina blankly.

"Come on, Jay," she pleaded. "Puffy is a male designer. So are

Tommy Hill and Ralph Lauren." She pulled on the pocket of his Rock-a-fella jeans. "Every rapper and their momma has a clothing line and you be sporting half of 'em!"

JZ put the edge in his voice that he knew would cut her cold. "Look, Mi, I know all that! But, if Michael starts getting all punk on me, snapping his fingers and calling you girlfriend, I'm gon' have to check him. Know what I'm saying?"

She shook her head. "No, I don't. Number one, you should be happy he's doing something that he's obviously good at. What? It's only swazy when you're the star?"

JZ sucked his teeth. He pulled the hoodie off. "There you go. Ain't nobody saying all that."

"But you're acting like that. How many of your games has Michael missed?"

"I don't know." JZ rolled his eyes skyward.

"You know what I'm saying, Jay." Mina wouldn't give in. She stood right under his nose, arguing up in his face. The duffle banged up against her butt as she fussed. "Even when Michael stopped playing rec league ball himself, he still came to all of your games. Now you can't even *pretend* you're happy over something he's doing?"

JZ clapped his hands and hopped up and down. He made his voice prissy. "Oooohh Michael, boy those designs are sweeter than candy." His face serious once more, he looked down at Mina. "Support like that?"

"Okay, you're acting mad ignorant." Mina gave him the hand. "But I'm sure Michael, your FRIEND, would let that roll."

"Yup. Just like me and Michael, YOUR friends, let all your nagging roll."

"Whatever, Jay. Nagging is better then cold dissing a friend 'cause they're into something you're not," Mina fired back.

JZ threw up his hands.

"I'm saying . . ." He backed up a few paces, seemed to choose his words carefully before being blunt. "I can't stand here and tell you that I wouldn't feel uncomfortable if he started acting like a fag." JZ walked away, calling over his shoulder, "Come on. Let's go get a seat."

Mina stared, stunned, but followed reluctantly. They walked past the Devil's Lair and toward the player's entrance. Blue Devil athletes in uniform—even an official team sweatshirt like JZ's—got into varsity games free.

"Hey ya'll," a familiar voice called out from behind. "Hold up."

Mina peered into the darkening evening toward the parking lot, unsure if the person was talking to her and JZ. Jacinta stepped out of a black Navigator at the curb and trotted their way.

As they waited for her to catch up, JZ avoided Mina's questioning gaze. She shook her head and sent a few telepathic frowns his way.

"I'm glad I caught ya'll before you went into the game," Jacinta said, winded. She hefted a Gucci tote bag onto her shoulder.

"What's up, Cinny?" JZ said.

"Hey," Jacinta said. "I would have felt stupid carrying this big old bag trying to find you in the stands."

"I know right. At least I won't look like I'm going camping by myself," Mina said, wobbling under her overstuffed duffle bag.

"But at least you using your cheerleading bag for your stuff," Jacinta said. She poked at Mina's fat bag. "People probably just think you carrying way more than you need for the game."

"I'll wait for ya'll inside," JZ said.

Mina frowned. "We're right behind you."

He pointed to the line. "Cinny has to get a ticket."

"Oh, yeah." Mina looked at the long line snaking around the fenced field. She wasn't thrilled about giving up her "VIP" entrance. But . . . "I'll stand with you, Cinny. Jay, we'll catch up."

She followed Jacinta, greeting people—*looking for someone who would let them cut*—as they headed to the end of the line.

"I started to just get my father to drop me off at Kelly's after the game," Jacinta said. "I didn't feel like having to bring the bag with me."

"It's a cute bag, though. It just looks like an oversized purse." Mina wondered if it was real Gucci. "Oh there's Kelly . . . come on. Good, now we won't have to go the outer limits."

Mina picked up the pace, steamrolling toward Kelly.

"Where's Swirl?" Jacinta asked, keeping pace.

"Not sure. I sent her an e-mail about meeting at the game," Mina said. "Kelly!"

Kelly looked over. Mina waved. She spoke loudly, still a few feet away from where Kelly stood in the line. "Girl, thanks for getting in line for us!"

Kelly's brows crinkled in confusion.

Mina and Jacinta swooped in, taking their place next to Kelly.

"Okay, I'll be the line-saver next time," Mina said, louder.

"What are you talking about?" Jacinta frowned.

Mina moved in close to Kelly and Jacinta and lowered her voice. "I just said it so people wouldn't think we were cutting."

Jacinta laughed. "It's not like we're in the front of the line. I doubt anyone cares."

Mina shrugged. "Just trying to cut out the drama, just in case."

"I'm glad you guys found me," Kelly said, relief on her face. "I didn't want to walk every single bleacher looking for you."

"I'm surprised you didn't see our bags." Jacinta poked at Mina's bag. "Mina, just how long you plan on staying over Kelly's anyway?"

Mina laughed. "Double SO this weekend. Me and Lizzie are hooking up at the mall tomorrow, and I'm staying with her." She craned her neck, trying to see toward the bleachers around the Devil's Lair. They were still too far away to make out faces. She wished aloud. "I hope JZ gets us a good seat near the spirit section."

"Not the spirit section," Jacinta groaned. "Look, I'm still a Sam-Well Trojan at heart. I can't be sitting right in the middle of the die-hard blue and gold fans."

Mina snickered. "Uh, I'm a cheerleader. As long as you're sitting with *me* that's gonna happen."

"If you cheer for Del Rio Bay, we promise not to tell on you when we go to your house for the project," Kelly said.

"Thanks," Jacinta grunted.

As they made it up to the ticket window, Kelly looked back at the parking lot, then over to the field.

"So where's Jessica?" Kelly said after getting her hand stamp.

"Would anybody be mad if she didn't show?" Jacinta asked, only half-joking. She handed over her two dollars and placed her left hand on the counter for a stamp.

"No comment," Mina said.

The woman behind the window nodded Mina through.

"Shoot, that says more than if you hadn't said nothing," Jacinta said.

The three shared a laugh as they finally made their way onto the sidewalk leading to the bleachers.

"Spoke too soon." Jacinta pulled on Mina's shoulder and pointed toward Jessica, huddled with Mari-Beth and three other glams at the far end of the bleachers, near the fence surrounding the field. "There she go."

"Can we pretend we don't see her?" Mina joked.

"I think we should at least ask her if she plans on walking back with us," Kelly said.

"Okay, you go," Mina pulled Kelly in front of her.

Kelly dug her heels in. "Un-ah. The heat from her eyes makes me dizzy."

Jacinta and Mina fell out laughing.

"Did you just crack on somebody, Kelly?" Jacinta asked, still tripping.

Kelly tucked at her hair and smiled. She felt kind of bad making jokes, but couldn't help getting in on Mina and Jacinta's playful digs. Jessica practically begged for it, the way she treated the three of them.

Mina led the way, trudging through the crowd until they reached the glam's circle. She bit back a fit of giggles when Jessica turned her hazel eyes their way. Choking back laughter, she smacked at Jacinta who was poking her in the back.

"Jessica, are you walking back to Kelly's with us after the game?" Mina managed with only a smattering of giggle in her voice.

Mari-Beth stopped midconversation and frowned in Mina's general direction. "Is she talking to one of us?" she asked her clique.

Jessica rolled her eyes. "Unfortunately, yes."

"Oh, right. The soooccc class." Mari-Beth swished her hair. "Why don't you guys go back to the bleachers, where the nobodies sit?"

The three glams and Jessica laughed, a weird hybrid of dainty teeter and disdainful guffaw. Mari-Beth basked in it.

Mina's arm broke out in gooseflesh. Their Stepford giggle was freaky. She was glad when Jacinta spoke up.

"Look, Swirl, we just want to know if you walking with us or what?" Jacinta said.

"Yeah, as if," Jessica said. "I'll meet you all there . . . if I bother to come."

"Well, the dude in charge of security in Kelly's nabe needs your name if you not walking in with us. Do you spell Bitch with one 'T' or two?" Jacinta asked, her face straight.

"Hey guys," Jessica announced to the glams. "This is Jacinta. I was tutoring her in English. But her parents couldn't afford it anymore, so we never got past the A's in our spelling session."

Jacinta broke through the small crowd and stood inches from Jessica's face. Jessica flinched but stood her ground. Mari-Beth and the clique withdrew a step, leaving Jessica on her own.

"Now, how many people in your clique bad enough to have your back if I smack those hazel contacts out your head?" Jacinta seethed.

Mina tugged on Jacinta's shirt. "Come on, Cinny."

Jacinta stayed put a few more seconds, unworried since none of Jessica's friends were a threat.

"Look, Jess, just meet us at the gates of Folger's after the game," Mina said, adding, "About 9:30."

Mina looked from Jessica to Kelly and Jacinta for confirmation, but got nothing.

Jacinta backed out of Jessica's face, glaring.

"Whatev, Mina." Jessica tossed her fake locks once Jacinta had backed away. Her voice shook slightly as she asked her friends, "Can you believe that?"

Jacinta stalked off. Kelly followed her.

"We'll be there at 9:30," Mina said once more, before racing to catch up with Jacinta and Kelly.

"Hold up," Mina called out to Jacinta.

Jacinta stopped abruptly and waited for Mina to step beside her.

The sidewalk lining the fence was now packed with people. Mina stood on tiptoe, peering toward the stands, looking for JZ. "Come on." She gambled and headed to the spirit section, the first ten rows of the middle segment of bleachers.

JZ was four rows up. The bleacher was full, but Mina, Jacinta, and Kelly made their way over to him, wide-stepping over people, and squeezed in.

"What was going on down there?" JZ asked. "I thought I saw Cinny buck up in Jess's face."

"You did," Mina said, still shaken.

"She has one more time to mention my parents out her mouth," Jacinta warned, throwing the evil eye toward the glams, who had closed ranks around Jessica.

JZ nudged Mina. "It's gonna be a rough night for ya'll."

Mina could only shake her head. Who was he telling?

You're in With Lila... What Difference Does It Make Why?

"If you believe within your heart you'll know."
—"Believe in Yourself," from The Wiz

Lila waxed on about auditions managing to make a ten-minute speech into a twenty-minute soliloquy on the high standards of the Del Rio Bay Drama and Dance Troupe. Bored and anxious, Lizzie squirmed.

In a loud whisper, Michael groaned, "Dag, she loves the sound of her own voice."

Lizzie nodded vigorously. Lila obviously loved not only how her prim, clear, perfectly articulated words echoed off the high ceilings of the darkened theater, but also the power she held over the people who sat in the audience.

Who didn't know the theater president had a "silent" vote in choosing cast members?

Lila had every prospective cast member in the palm of her hand. And the long, drawn out speech was just another way of letting them know she knew it.

Lizzie peeked at her fellow thespians, overwhelmed by the turnout. There were nearly one hundred people in the auditorium, fierce competition.

Why was Lila convinced she, of all the people in here, could win a lead role?

Uncertainty crept into Lizzie's stomach and settled in for a long visit. Her foot tapped furiously. She wanted to run from the theater and join Mina at the football game.

The stage was the only world where Lizzie felt no fear. Too bad it took an audition to get her there. Auditions turned her into a self-doubting, nervous wreck and made her wonder why she loved acting in the first place. It was stressful.

Michael clamped his hand on her knee. "Chill, you'll be alright."

Lizzie gripped his hand, glad to have someone familiar there.

Mr. Collins approached them, squinting in the darkness. He whispered in a rushed tone, "Ah, Mr. James. Come on back. I want to introduce you to the costume designer. She's very excited about your ideas and designs."

Michael grinned. He looked over at Lizzie, hating to leave her, but secretly pleased that, for once, he was not the one being left behind. "You gon' be okay, right?"

Lizzie's weak smile shone in the dim auditorium.

Michael gave her leg a quick squeeze before walking off.

Stricken with a terrible sense of loneliness, Lizzie turned her attention back to the stage. Lila ended her long-winded introductions by directing the students to group themselves based upon the parts they were interested in auditioning for.

Glad for a reason to move, Lizzie sprang up. She hung back, waiting to see where people were going to disperse. Her heart sank when a large herd of people migrated toward the section reserved for Dorothy's role. *I knew it!*

There were at least fifteen people including Drusilla Pinkney and Kayla Watkins—as she'd expected.

Doubt rang in her head like a fire alarm. She stood near her seat and pulled confidence from that first lunch with Lila. None of the other Dorothy wannabes had been invited to lunch in the café. That had to count for something.

In a dose of Best Friend ESP, Mina's assuring voice whispered in her head, "Stop worrying. You're in with Lila. What difference does it make why?"

Lizzie nodded, agreeing with the voice. She eyed the Dorothy section again. Bad idea. Her doubts multiplied, killing the split second of confidence.

Even though Lila seemed sure that Lizzie could be the first freshman to follow in her footsteps Lizzie wasn't able to muster Lila's certainty. She let her feet take her toward the Glinda the Good Witch section, where only ten people stood. So far, none, Lizzie recognized as Queens of the stage.

She penned her name on the sign-up sheets for the Good Witch and her safe choice, the Munchkins. Practically everyone would get chosen for the Munchkins or Emerald City people; neither part warranted an audition.

She stole one last hopeful glance backward toward the Dorothy section and nearly laughed at the handful of freshman hopefuls. It wasn't like any of them, her included, had a prayer.

Damn what Lila says.

Lizzie was familiar with theater politics. Seniority was important. Even raw talent rarely won out over a veteran actor.

As badly as she wanted to try out for Dorothy, it would be a waste of time. She let the old actors' mantra—a small role is better than none—be her guide. With so many people auditioning, she wanted to stick with a role she was sure she could win.

Just because Lila kept hinting she had what it took to get a lead, didn't mean she'd get it. Did it?

Lizzie's head spun. Her heart tugged, pushing her legs toward the Dorothy section. But her brain took over, reminding the heart who was in charge. Glinda was in several key scenes, had a handful of lines in each and was a good, solid role. She could score it easily as long as someone like Dru didn't audition.

Lizzie's heart picked up the pace again.

Of course Dru would audition for Glinda. No one tried out for only one role. It was crazy for Lizzie not to sign up for Dorothy auditions, as well.

She pointed her body toward the Dorothy list. Stopped. Took a step. Stopped again.

What was wrong with her?

Glinda. That was it. Nothing else.

Lizzie beelined it to her seat, to wait for Michael, before her sappy, hopeful heart could change her mind. She sat down, huffing heavily like the battle between her heart and mind was a physical one.

Lizzie crossed her hands over her chest to calm the aggressive thumping against her ribcage. She grabbed her backpack and dashed out of the auditorium before the theater's darkness closed in on her anymore.

Crisp, cool air hit her in the face when she burst outside. The heat that plagued the JV game was gone, whisked away once the sun set. She eagerly gulped in the night's fresh air even as a voice inside scolded her for chickening out.

The thought took hold. She was a coward.

She chastised herself for taking the easy way out.

Lizzie looked toward the football field. The bright stadium lights showcased people pouring from the stands. The game had ended. She couldn't run to Mina for advice.

She closed her eyes and stood, one arm holding the door open, her body half in and half out of the school. With a quick breath, she silenced the bickering voices inside her head and retreated back inside.

Popularity Ain't Easy

"If I were a rich girl (na, na, na, na, na, na, na, na, na, na)."
—Gwen Stefani, "Rich Girl"

Like at least two dozen other communities, Folgers Way was a short walk from the high school. The similarities ended there. An exclusive country club, private park, and golf course lay well hidden in the enclave of rambling estates and mansions of Folgers. You didn't just walk into Folgers. No invite? No entrance.

The main road stretched ahead, wide and black. Street lights twinkled overhead giving the illusion that it was earlier than it was. But no cars passed by, making it feel later.

Just as the girls stepped to the neighborhood's gate, Jessica and Mari-Beth, swaying and sashaying to the same silent rhythm like contestants on America's Next Top Model, rounded the corner.

Jessica stopped in front of Kelly, ignoring Mina and Jacinta.

"Which house is yours?"

"I'm 1489," Kelly said.

Mari-Beth nodded. "That's what I thought. She's just one street down from me."

"Fine. We have to walk Mari home first," Jessica announced.

"No, WE don't. You meet us over Kelly's," Jacinta said, tired of Jessica already.

Jessica and Mari-Beth looked through Jacinta with their best blank mannequin stare.

"It's not a big deal." Kelly slipped a thin plastic card from her pocket and waved it in front of a blinking red console. "Cinny, really, I'm okay with it."

A steel gate whirred softly disappearing behind a high-bricked wall that ran the perimeter of the neighborhood.

"Very James Bond," Mina cooed.

Jessica and Mari-Beth sped up, keeping themselves a few paces ahead of the group.

Jake, Mari-Beth, Conner, Laura . . . Mina ticked off the names of the people she knew who lived in Folgers Way. Laura's mom had hosted several cheer pool parties, years ago. But Laura was going on her second year as a soccer chick. It had been a minute since Mina walked the neighborhood's roads. They were still quiet as ever.

Padding along thoughtfully, Mina listened to the mix their footsteps made on the blacktop. Her cheer shoes, Kelly's flats, and Jacinta's made soft thuds, while Jessica's and Mari-Beth's matching open-toed heel sandals scratched against the road, echoing loudly off the trees.

There were more houses, near the neighborhood's entrance, than Mina remembered. She passed a wide, spacious gap where she was positive there were once trees. Only the dim shine of house lights proved that something, no doubt, another of Folger's mini mansions, was there beyond the darkness.

Jacinta threw Mina a look of disapproval. But Mina's head was turned away looking off into the blackness. Jacinta silently cursed the assignment that trapped her in the lush landscape of Folgers Way on a Friday night with two girls too scared to stand up to someone who talked to them like they were dirt under her nails.

She peered past the well-lit street, lined with tall, full trees, into the darkness beyond, knowing by instinct, but not seeing for herself the homes set back off the road. Not even a breeze blew to rustle the trees. She felt like they had walked out of the world and into a sealed bubble.

The quiet was spooky.

Just as Jacinta was beginning to wonder if there was a world beyond the sidewalk, a three-story house came into view, lit up by half
a dozen spotlights shining from the yard. The house, sitting on a
small hill, shone bright against the blackness. You couldn't miss it.

Yeah, that's the point of all those "look-at-me" lights, Jacinta
thought, suppressing a snort.

Her eyes bugged as the house came into full view. *One, two, three . . .
seven, eight . . .* she counted the endless number of windows along
the front of the red-bricked house (*building?*). Twenty-four in all—
twelve along the top level, six in the middle, and six on the bottom
half. *Twenty-four windows?* No way only one family lived there. Three
windows across was the same width as her entire house in Pirate's
Cove.

It was insane. Seeing the crazy cribs on a show like *The Fabulous
Life of . . .* was one thing. Seeing one up close was like, whoa!

She frowned, shaken out of her stupor by Jessica and Mari-Beth,
who had suddenly slowed down enough so that Jacinta nearly heeled
Jessica. Jessica placed herself on one side of Kelly and Mari-Beth on
the other, forcing Jacinta and Mina off the concrete sidewalk and
onto the grass.

"So, Kelly," Mari-Beth paused dramatically. "I'm dying to know
why you transferred from McStew to public school." Mari-Beth said
public school like the word tasted bitter. She continued, before Kelly
had a chance to answer. "I went to McStew until sixth grade. I *know*
you remember that we both had Ms. Cornwell in fifth-grade language arts."

"Yes, I remember," Kelly said.

"Thought so," Mari-Beth said, smug satisfaction on her lips.

Jessica nodded, as if something needed confirmation.

Kelly regretted not backing Jacinta now. They should have said
no to walking Mari-Beth's home.

Mari-Beth hadn't changed since fifth grade. She was still shallow, ditzy, and mean. Well, one thing had changed. She was now, obviously, the Alpha dog in her clique. But Mari-Beth hadn't been anywhere close to that at McStew, more like a flunky of Maisy Whitmore, their class's popular girl.

Kelly wondered if Mari-Beth's public school clique knew that at McStew, Mari-Beth would have never risen to Queen Bee. Pecking order was all about the number of zeros in your family's bank account, who had a bigger trust fund, who had hallways, auditoriums, and new wings named after their family thanks to fat donations.

Mari-Beth's dad was a successful executive at a company. That was it. He didn't own the company, wasn't the founder or even the president of a division. He just worked there. Mari-Beth certainly didn't go without the usual rich kid spoils. But whatever her dad's salary, it wasn't enough to earn Mari-Beth a place among the ruling class at McStew.

"You're Latino, right?" Mari-Beth asked. "Puerto Rican?"

Kelly eyed her wearily. "Yeah."

"I always figured you were on some kind of scholarship. You know some kind of getting more minority students in McStew kind of thing." Mari-Beth shrugged. "Why leave a free ride?"

"I wasn't on scholarship," Kelly said. Her lips, pinched in anger, disappeared into a thin line.

Mari-Beth shrugged again.

"Okay, so, why did you leave?" Jessica asked again. Her lips turned down into an ugly frown. "People would kill to get into McStew."

"I've been wanting to attend public school for a while," Kelly said. "Del Rio Bay High is one of the best public schools in the state. It's not like I went from McStew to a bad school."

Caught up in her own curiosity, Mina didn't think twice as she peered around Jacinta and asked, "Why did you leave, Mari-Beth?"

Mari-Beth stopped abruptly, tossed her hair, and glared at Mina.

Mina's feet skittered to a stop and she took a step back to realign herself with the group.

Mari-Beth drew out her words slowly, as if Mina were stupid or deaf.

"I *only* transferred because my parents made me," Mari-Beth said. She rolled her eyes. "They said I needed a more well-rounded educational experience. Like, isn't that what college is for?"

Mari-Beth rattled on, dropping her special brand of knowledge. "Outside of having parents like mine who actually believe public school can be a good thing, there are only two reasons to transfer from a school like McStew. Scandal or . . ."

"Stupidity," Jessica finished.

"I told you she was weird," Mari-Beth said. She and Jessica walked off, picking up their pace, leaving Kelly behind. Their identical pod friend cackle echoed in the quiet night.

Mina immediately closed in, joining Kelly on the sidewalk. "I don't blame you. McStew preppies are a whole new breed of snobby."

"I always felt like I was under a microscope there," Kelly said.

"That's anywhere," Jacinta said.

"No, it's different at McStew." Kelly talked so only Mina and Jacinta could hear. "Except for a couple of SKs, most everybody there comes from well-to-do, wealthy, or just plain filthy rich families."

"What's an SK?" Jacinta frowned.

"Scholarship kids," Kelly said. "I'm not surprised that Mari-Beth thought I was one." She didn't bother to admit that it shocked her that Mari-Beth had said it so bluntly. It shouldn't have. Mari-Beth was as clueless and insensitive as ever. But it did. Kelly shook her head. "The few black or Latino kids at McStew usually are on scholarship. There are only a handful . . ."

"Of black and Latino kids or people on scholarship?" Mina asked.

Kelly grinned. "Both. But only a handful of SKs get in each year, black, white, whatever. They're the kids who have the grades but not the tuition."

"I guess you had both," Jacinta said. Her eyes swept the immaculate grounds of Folgers Way. "No SKs are coming from this part of town."

"Nope. But trust me, there are no wings named after Raoul Lopez at McStew, either," Kelly said.

"Who is that? Your father?" Mina asked.

"My grandfather. He was a president at Honeywell, which means I was just one of hundreds from a family that . . ." Kelly struggled to find a word. She shrugged. "Some people go to McStew . . . like I did. Other people *own* McStew."

"Daddy gotta be Bill Gates to get the real love, huh?" Jacinta said, chuckling.

"Something like that," Kelly said.

"Well, DRB High has some clique issues but nothing like that," Mina said. "Hey, JZ asked Jake if he knew you." She laughed, tripping before she got the words out. "Jake was like, 'who that black-looking chick?' Now, what is black-looking?"

Kelly raised her hand. "I'm called that all the time."

Mina hooted again and her uncontrollable giggle spread to Kelly. Even Jacinta smiled.

"But he thinks you're cute," Mina said. "That's something."

Kelly's shoulders shook as she laughed. Mina's constant, ordinary chatter made her feel at ease. She loved how Mina pulled you into the conversation with question after question then set her large, deep eyes on you until you answered.

If Kelly closed her eyes they could easily just be three friends hanging out on a Friday night.

They stopped at the end of Mari-Beth's driveway. Mari-Beth and Jessica stood, waiting, arms crossed. A nod passed between them as Mari-Beth said, "So, Kelly, Jessica and I were talking . . ."

"Umph, somebody call MTV News," Jacinta said.

Mina clinched her toes together to stop herself from laughing.

"Even though you're kind of . . . odd." Mari-Beth tilted her head, a small frown turned down her lips.

Mina couldn't believe her ears. Odd was a putdown no matter how you turned it. But Mari-Beth said it as if she felt sorry for Kelly's condition. Mina waited for Mari-Beth to pat Kelly on the head like a lost dog. Instead, Mari-Beth said, "We were wondering if you wanted to hang out with us tomorrow?"

"Dag, I've never seen somebody insult and invite somebody to kick it in the same sentence," Jacinta said.

This time Mina did laugh.

"Jess, can handle the details," Mari-Beth said. She turned and sashayed down her driveway, throwing a backward hand wave. "See you tomorrow, Jess."

"Your girl is wack," Jacinta said to Jessica.

"Jessica, no harm or anything," Kelly said. Mina noticed it was the same lost-dog tone that Mari-Beth had just used. "But I'm not into cliques and secret societies or any other group that excludes people."

"We didn't say anything about inviting you into the Glams," Jessica sniffed. "Mari-Beth just wants to know if you want to hang out one day, just us three. Give it some thought."

Jessica turned on her heels and headed the way they had come.

Sensing there was no way to say no politely, Kelly opted for her usual answer, silence. She fell into step beside Mina and Jacinta, wondering if Jessica, five steps in front of them, would head to the right house. She didn't have to wonder long.

A few long strides later, Jessica turned to the right down a brick-paved driveway lined by fat flowery bushes. A motion sensor clicked and bright white light illuminated the driveway as a contemporary, brick mansion came into view.

"Here we go. Time to knock out prejudice over popcorn and pop tunes," Mina said.

Jessica's steps slowed enough to let the girls catch up. Together, they approached a porch that ran the length of the house. Six double windows bathed the porch with light from inside the house.

Kelly pressed her hand against a panel on the frame and there was a loud metal click. The finely carved wooden door swung gently open, revealing a huge foyer with walls draped in art. A shiny oak floor laid out like the yellow brick road.

Mina swallowed her gasp. She didn't want to be the first one to come off like she wasn't used to anything. Her father was a techie but even she was impressed by all of the Mission Impossible–like security. And Kelly's house was *huge*.

She gaped in spite of her resolve. She tried to play it cool and snuck a sideways glance to see if Jacinta was holding up any better.

Jacinta's eyes, locked on the spiral stairs next to an elevator, were wide as saucers.

The celebrities on *Cribs* didn't have anything on Kelly's digs. Her house ran high and deep. And that was just the view from the porch.

Mina stepped inside. A tangy spice that smelled out of place tickled her nose. Houses like this usually only had one smell, clean. But the pleasant, lingering scent—Mina couldn't place it, but it was something hot—made the enormous house feel close and cozy. Her mouth watered, reminding her that she hadn't eaten since before the football game.

Kelly's voice bounced off the twenty-foot ceilings. "Abuela, yo estoy en casa!"

Jessica nudged Mina, "What did she say?"

Still gazing at the stairs design, Jacinta responded vacantly, "She said, 'Grandma, I'm home.' "

Mina couldn't have been more surprised if Jacinta had grown a third arm right in front of her face. She elbowed her. "How did you know that?"

"My boyfriend's best friend is Puerto Rican. He speaks in Spanish all the time. I've picked up on a lot of it."

Kelly's grandmother, a dark brown, petite woman with her hair cut in a short pixie style, appeared at the top of the staircase. Stylish in a pair of orange capri pants, matching mules, and a white blouse with ballerina sleeves, she made her way down. She embraced Kelly tight, like they hadn't seen each other in a long time. "Hola, Nena. Estos son tús amigas de la escuela?"

"Hi, Grand. Yeah, these are my friends from school," Kelly translated.

Mina wondered how she could use that word with a straight face about Jessica. But then how rude is it to say, "These are my two friends and this one chick I hate."

Mrs. Lopez beamed at the group. "Hi, girls, I'm Kellita's grandmother. Are you girls hungry?"

Never shy, Mina spoke up for all of them. "Yes, Ma'am."

Kelly teased her grandmother. "Like you're going to cook this late. She's showing off for you guys. She's the main one always telling me and my brother that this isn't a twenty-four-hour kitchen."

"Well, it's not," Mrs. Lopez lectured. "But Cita made empanadas, earlier. There's plenty."

"Thanks, Grand."

"Okay. Well, I sent Kevin to stay with a friend. I knew you wouldn't want him breaking up your party."

"Ooh, thank you," Kelly gushed, glad her grandmother read her mind.

Jacinta murmured to herself, "Not like we'd ever know he was here. This big ass house."

Mina poked her, even though she agreed. They exchanged a tiny smile until Jessica groaned. "You guys act like you're country cousins visiting the big city," she whispered, annoyed. Knowing that she'd felt the same way, years ago the first time she was welcomed into Del Rio's glam side. But that was then. The girls' slack-jawed irritation annoyed her.

"You girls enjoy yourselves. I'm heading up for the night." Mrs. Lopez winked playfully. "If I'm up to it, I may make breakfast for you tomorrow morning."

"Dinner and breakfast? You're spoiling me." Kelly laughed.

"Divertite, Nena." Her grandmother blew her a kiss as she made her way back up the long staircase.

"I will," Kelly answered. "She told me to have fun," she informed the girls.

"So you speak Spanish fluently?" Mina asked. "That must be cool knowing two languages." She rolled her eyes. "I take Spanish and still know jack. I swear, two years from now, you just know all I'll be able to say is Como esta."

"Apparently, she speaks some, too." Jessica nodded to Jacinta.

Mina swore that was admiration and not sarcasm she heard in Jessica's voice.

"¿Cuánto?" Kelly asked Jacinta.

Jacinta's answer was slow and broken. "Habla un poco. Yo lo entiendo mejor que hablo."

Mina peered at Jacinta, fascinated. She turned to Kelly. "What? What did ya'll say?"

"I just asked her how well she knew the language. And she said, a little. But she understands it better than she can actually speak it," Kelly explained.

"Okay, it's official—that is cool!" Mina declared, laughing at herself. She knew she sounded awestruck. But she didn't know anyone, personally, that was fluent in two languages. It was odd in a fascinating way.

Jessica laughed but quickly turned her attitude back on. "Somebody is sure easy to impress."

"No shame in my game," Mina said. "I'm totally impressed."

Kelly led them upstairs in the opposite direction her grandmother had gone, to the wing of the house she shared with her brother.

As they twisted and turned up the grand stairway, Mina got down to business, venturing bravely, "I feel totally nosy, but where is your mom?"

"She travels a lot," Kelly said. She threw open the double doors to an assortment of rooms, stopping the conversation dead.

"Nice suite," Jessica sniffed, more in awe than she let on and even more convinced that Kelly should be hanging with the glam squad. If nothing else, she'd make a great do-this girl, Mari-Beth's term for the newbies they allowed to hang out with them, specifically the girl they thought would do this, do that, do anything the clique asked of her.

As Jessica inhaled every detail of Kelly's room it crossed her mind that she and Kelly, *sorry Mari-Beth*, could be an awesome pair, she as the Alpha friend and Kelly as the do-this.

The thought marinated as Jessica followed the group into a sitting area completely girled-out in pink and green, a wide, flat-screen television in the center of one salmon-colored wall. A long pink lounger and overstuffed retro rocker sat in a semicircle by a striped love seat. It invited them over for a hen session. Mina accepted, plopping down into the love seat while Jessica moved into Kelly's bedroom, taking the full inventory.

Kelly slid her shoes off onto a small platform near the wall.

Standing next to her, Jacinta followed suit, sheepishly, suddenly aware that the carpet begged to be walked on barefoot. She jumped and let out a startled, "Oh my God," as a small opening in the wall pulled Kelly's shoes away.

"Sorry," Kelly said. "It's my shoe organizer. It shuttles them into my closet."

Jacinta's heart skipped. She still wasn't sure it hadn't been magic. She had seen it all, now. A shoe organizer!

"Kelly, you have like the Inspector Gadget house, Girl." Mina broke out the theme song. "Dun-na-na-na-na-na-na-na-na. Dun-na-na-na-na-na-naaaa." She wiggled out of her shoes and carried them to Kelly. "Can I try it? What do I do?"

Kelly showed her where to place the shoes and watched, amused, as Mina clapped when the shoes disappeared.

"That's cool, Girl!" Mina headed to check out a door to her right. "Nice office," her voice called from the room. "Only some-body who busts straight A's could have it this organized."

Jessica walked up to the bedroom's centerpiece, a Queen-sized, princess bed standing on an island in the middle of the room, flanked by several large, well-stocked bookshelves. She fingered the books, cocking her head to read the titles. "Have you read any of these?" she asked.

"I've read them all," Kelly admitted without boasting.

Jessica whipped her head around. She didn't try to hide the skep-ticism in her voice. "All of them?"

Mina stood beside Jessica on one of the steps leading up to the bed. "Kell, there must be . . ." she frowned, doing the math.

Kelly answered for her. "Three hundred twenty-eight books." Of course she knew. She'd had plenty of time to collect, read, and reread them.

"Dag," Jacinta exclaimed. She sank her toes into the deep, pink carpet. "Does your mother travel for work?"

There was a long pause before Kelly said, "Well, for my stepdad's job. She doesn't have a job. She just . . . helps him with his."

Mina was about to ask what Kelly's dad did to afford such a mon-strous house, but Jacinta's loud exclamation of, "Dag, look at this bathroom!" interrupted her.

Mina jogged over to investigate. Jessica plodded behind.

A waterfall shower trickled from one wall. A huge whirlpool tub dominated another.

Mina couldn't resist. She jumped inside. Too curious to play cool, Jacinta scrambled in behind her, fitting comfortably.

"Be real, do you ever really use this thing?" Jacinta scolded, scrunching her legs to her chest to make room for Kelly.

If they didn't think she was a spoiled princess before, they had to now, Kelly thought, hitching her leg over the side and dropping down into the tub.

"It's like being in a boat. Come on ya'll row." Mina mimed stroking with oars.

Jessica leaned against the wall near the shower, frowning disapproval on the silliness.

"So, let's see," Mina said, ready to gab. "Kelly what are your . . ." She tried to remember the exact words of Mrs. Simms on what data they were to collect. Unable to recall them, she settled on. "So, what's your story, Kell?"

Kelly pushed herself back up and propped on the rim of the tub. She wondered how you told three strangers that you'd never had a true friend, had no bond with your mother, and cried at least once a week because you still missed the only father you'd ever known without sounding like a candidate for the Losers' Club.

Her moist palms squeaked on the tub's surface as she fidgeted.

Seeing she needed more specific prompting, Mina said, "So, you have a brother?"

Kelly rolled her eyes in exasperation. "Yeah, he's ten and a total pest."

Jacinta nodded in understanding. "I have two brothers and a sister, all younger than me. I can relate."

"Well you met my grandmother. She and my grandfather basically raised us," Kelly explained. "This is their house." Her face drooped for a second. "Well, was. He died four years ago."

Mina's face looked truly pained for her and Kelly felt a huge burst of love for that. She wanted to hug Mina and almost did when Mina patted her leg and said, "I'm sorry. I'm really close to my grandparents, too."

Kelly slid back down into the tub, hugging her knees as she remembered her grandfather. "Like I was saying earlier, he was the President of Honeywell's Research and Development division and was the highest-ranked Latino in the company."

"Does your grandmother work?" Jacinta asked.

"She used to be a teacher in D.C. But she retired a few years ago, when my mom started traveling full time with Phil," Kelly said.

"Why did she work?" Jessica's voice came from the corner. "Obviously your grandfather was making a lot of money."

Kelly chuckled. "I can't see my grandmother not working."

"I don't get people who work when they don't have to," Jessica said.

"I guess you'd have to know my grandfather then," Kelly said. "Work, Latino pride, and family were his three biggest priorities. Not necessarily in that order." Her face and voice grew animated. "He was the one who insisted me and Kevin learn fluent Spanish and English. He'd always go, Kellita . . ." She paused to laugh at her impression of his voice. "He never called me Kelly, always Kellita. But whenever I'd come home sad because of what some jerk at school said or didn't say to me, he'd say, 'Kellita, you can't wait on people to accept you. Eventually, you will find exactly where you fit.' "

Jessica snorted.

Kelly pushed against the tub until she stood and could see Jessica better. "What was that for?"

"So is that why you spent most of your life hiding in your room reading all those books instead of making friends with people . . . I mean at least people here in Folgers," Jessica asked.

"I wasn't hiding," Kelly said, without a trace of defensiveness. "I'm not like you guys. I don't care if Johnny Eagle, varsity quarterback, likes me or not."

"Jake Phoenix, you mean?" Mina asked.

"It was just an example," Kelly said. "I'm just saying that it doesn't matter to me who likes me. It used to, but it hasn't for a long time.

To be honest . . ." Kelly stopped to consider if she wanted to tell the truth and decided she did. "I remember Mari from McStew. She was one of the meanest girls in my class and a gopher for the girl who ruled fifth grade."

Jessica blanched. The comment pierced Jessica as if Kelly were talking about her directly.

"Obviously you guys like something about each other and that's great. But I'm glad that my grandfather taught me that you don't have to go around announcing yourself," Kelly said.

"What does that mean?" Jessica rolled her eyes.

"If a person is smart or rich, they don't have to go around shouting, I'm so smart, I'm so rich. People around them will figure it out," Kelly said.

"True 'dat," Jacinta said.

"Please don't take this the wrong way," Kelly said. She figured Jessica would. But Kelly said it anyway. "You and Mari flaunt your popularity, like you're trying to convince yourselves you're popular. If I ever acted like that, my grandfather would have put me in my place."

"Whatever," Jessica grumbled.

"Where's your real father, Kell?" Mina asked.

"See, now to me that's nosy," Jacinta said, adding quickly, "Look, I'm not being mean. But I think . . . I mean is there anything that's off-limits? Kelly already said she has a stepfather, so obviously her real father's not around. Why ask?"

"I, I mean I wasn't trying to be nosy," Mina said. "If you're not comfortable, just don't answer. I mean, how else are we supposed to know what's off-limits?"

"I can tell you now, if we're allowed to answer what we want, I'm not answering anything," Jessica said from the corner.

"Is that a promise?" Jacinta asked.

"I never knew my real father. He died when I was younger," Kelly said, heading off another round of bickering.

"Sorry," Mina said. She shot an accusatory glance at Jacinta and back at Jessica. "Am I the only one who's going to be asking productive questions?"

Jessica sucked her teeth. She walked over to the tub and stood beside it, arms folded. "So, where are your mother and stepfather all the time? Why did your grandparents raise you anyway?" She popped her eyebrows at Mina.

Kelly fiddled with her ponytail as she answered. "They're on the road. My grandparents insisted on keeping us in regular school instead of having a road tutor. Now and then Kevin and I fly out with them . . . mainly during the summer."

"Fly you out where?" Mina asked, thinking being Kelly's friend could have its perks.

"Atlanta, L.A., New York. Wherever they happen to be at the time." Kelly said. "My stepdad is in the music business."

"Really? What does he do?" Jacinta asked, her curiosity now piqued.

"How dumb are you guys?" Jessica smirked.

Mina gazed from Jessica to Kelly. "What?"

"You seriously don't know who her stepfather is?" Jessica asked. She mocked them with pretend pity. "I forgot. You all don't run in the same circles as I do. Of course you have no idea."

"Well, are one of you gonna tell us?" Mina asked, ping-ponging between Jessica and Kelly.

Jessica thrust her palms toward Kelly. "Quiet Girl, do we need a drum roll or what?"

"Don't call me that anymore, please," Kelly said, refusing to meet Jessica's gaze. She pulled her ponytail once more, cleared her throat, and looked up at Jessica. They locked eyes for a second before Kelly broke contact first.

"Umph, go Kelly," Jacinta said under her breath.

Jessica shrugged and moved back to lean against the shower.

Kelly sat a little taller in the tub. "Have you guys ever heard of Phil Narcone?"

"Of course, Girl. Super producer! That song he did for Beyonce last year was the joint," Mina replied, sitting up, her voice incredulous. "Why, is that your stepfather?"

Whenever an artist won any type of music award, Phil Narcone's name was usually uttered somewhere in their thank-yous. If a group had been number one on the charts in the last five years, more than likely it was thanks to Phil.

"Yeah, he is," Kelly said. "My mother married him when I was five. So besides my grandfather, he's the only father I've ever known. But they're hardly ever around, so it's still like not having a father." She paused, then added, bitterly, "Or a mother either, for that matter."

Jessica pretended to wipe her eyes. "So sad."

Mina shushed her. She had to know more about someone with celeb connections.

Kelly talked over them. "Okay, here's my story, the uncut short version. I used to stutter, really bad. Like could barely get one word out. It was because we pretty much only spoke Spanish at home. So I was more comfortable with that. I'd get into school and trip over the English words or couldn't remember the proper word I wanted. I got teased a lot and for my first two years at McStew people treated me like I was stupid."

"You barely have an accent," Mina said in surprise.

"That's because I spent two years sitting in my closet, every single night, teaching myself to talk like all the other kids. I didn't want my grandfather to hear me. He would have said I was trying to hide my Puerto Rican roots. But I just wanted to fit in."

She frowned. "At least then I did. So I'd practice words and just say them over and over. I started the fourth grade with no accent at all." Kelly threw her hands up. "Not that it mattered because by then everyone thought I was dumb. In the fifth grade, Maisy Whitmore found out Phil was a producer and decided I was the new 'It' girl."

Kelly laughed. Her moment in popularity felt like wisps of a dream; flashes of it were so clear, while other parts not so much.

Kelly turned to Jessica. "I'm sure Mari would never tell you this. But Maisy dumped her as a friend to be friends with me." Kelly squirmed at the thought. "If you ask me, Mari got the good end of that deal."

Mina and Jacinta laughed.

"Go, Kell," Mina said.

Jessica managed to look bored with the whole discussion.

"So what happened?" Mina asked. "I mean, after everybody was jocking you?"

Kelly's brows furrowed. "Let me put it this way, popularity ain't easy." She shrugged and chuckled bitterly. "Once a few people turned on me because I wouldn't give them the hookup, an autograph, a personal meeting with some rapper or singer, whatever, I just stopped pretending. I chose to be a loner and they said I thought I was cute. Then I became a big, fat, loner loser."

"Okay, losers don't know famous people," Mina said. "Some people gon' hate no matter what."

Kelly stepped off the tub's rim. "Come on. I want to show you guys something."

Mina and Jacinta climbed out of the tub. All of them followed Kelly through the house. They stepped into the backyard and floated past a tennis court to a small cottage.

"Don't tell me this is part of your room?" Jacinta groaned.

Kelly flipped the lights. Gold and platinum albums shone from some of the walls. Scores of photos with Phil Narcone and the hottest Pop, Hip-Hop, and R&B stars dotted the other walls. Kelly, Kevin, and their mom were in a few of the pictures.

Mina and Jacinta crept around the studio, in awe. They pointed out the pictures with Kelly and people they'd only ever seen on a video.

Jessica started on the opposite wall, soaking in the photos. Most of the artists in the pictures had a gold or platinum record thanks to Kelly's stepfather. Kelly was only a phone call away from hot parties, backstage passes, and who knew what else. Not that Kelly would ever "flaunt" her connections. Fool, Jessica thought.

Expressionless, Kelly stood as far away from the wall as the small studio allowed. She eased into Phil's big executive chair and fiddled with the sound equipment.

"Kelly," Mina called, running her hand over a photo with Kelly and Ne-yo. Flashes of watching him on the American Music Awards made her skin pimple. "You have to admit, isn't it off the hook to meet these people?"

Kelly wrinkled her nose. "Nope, meeting them isn't really that big a deal to me. If a celeb is here it just means my parents are actually home."

"What's your mom like?" Mina asked, staring at an image of a thin, busty woman with full, chestnut hair just like Kelly's. Her white teeth gleamed at the camera as she laughed and winked at the camera. "You look like her."

Mina came and sat cross-legged on the small brown leather sofa near the sound equipment.

"My mom? Hmm . . . let me think. It's been so long since I've seen her," Kelly deadpanned. "The best way to describe my mom is . . . nervous energy."

"Is that where you get that tucking the hair thing?" Jacinta took a seat next to Mina.

Kelly frowned. "What tucking the hair thing?"

"Seriously, you don't know you do that?" Jessica asked.

"Kell, you're always pushing the hair on your right side behind your ear . . . even tonight you did it and you have your hair up," Mina said.

Kelly reached to tuck, realized it, and drummed her fingers on the soundboard instead. "Then yeah, that's my mom. She's always in motion. Always going somewhere, off to do something, meet someone. Her hands move a mile a minute and so does her mouth."

"Oh well, naw, that's not like you," Jacinta said.

"I used to get all excited when my mom came home, thinking we'd do a mother-daughter thing. But something always came up and she'd have to be in a meeting or recording session with Phil. Any dates my mom makes with me are totally in pencil . . . erasable," Kelly said.

"That's messed up," Jacinta said.

"Yeah it is," Kelly whispered. "My mom and I aren't very close." She swallowed over the lump growing in her throat and ended the Kelly History Lesson. "Anyway. So the music business is my parents' life. The artists, the music, the awards shows, everything. But it's not mine."

She turned one of the mics on and announced, "So, just FYI, if you're thinking about asking for concert tickets, backstage passes, or autographs or to have someone famous call you on your birthday, don't."

"I guess we've been told," Jacinta said quietly.

"Where'd that come from?" Jessica muttered.

"Okay, well hookup or not, I assume that rich chicks still gotta eat," Mina said. "What's up with those empanadas, mami?"

Kelly dimmed the lights in the studio. "Bien, las hermanas, coman."

"I'm with that," Jacinta said, first to the door.

"Hola, English por favor, for those of us still in Spanish for dummies," Mina said.

"I said, alright, sisters, let's eat," Kelly said. She shivered involuntarily when Mina hooked her arm in hers, pulling her along.

"To the kitchen!" Mina shouted.

Jessica lagged behind them like a forgotten *Lost* castaway.

★   ★   ★

Near midnight, bellies full of ground beef and fried dough, the girls settled down in Kelly's theater room. The brown walls and the eight rows of chocolate leather recliners wrapped the screening room in perfect movie theater darkness. Pajama-clad and armed with their observation journals, the girls spread out, each claiming a recliner in a different row.

Kelly turned the canned lights as high as they would go. "Can you guys see enough to write?"

"Yeah, this is cool," Mina said through a yawn. "Turn the movie on for background."

Kelly held up two DVDs.

"*You Got Served* or *Mean Girls*?"

"Nobody feels like watching Jessica on the big screen," Jacinta said.

"Ooh you are so funny. NOT!" Jessica said with far less venom in her words than usual.

"Guess that means *You Got Served*, huh?" Kelly said, sliding the movie into the machine.

Mina yawned again. "Seriously, I don't know if I'll make it through either one."

"Ice down the back of whoever goes to sleep first," Kelly said.

Mina fought another yawn. "Shoot, just go ahead and ice me down then. I'll just fall to sleep dreaming about being Marques Houston's chick."

She moved from the recliner to the floor. Stretched out, she laid her head down.

"Un-ah, no you don't," Jacinta yelled. "These journals were your idea. You can't go to sleep yet."

"Writing them at the end of the night was Jessica's," Mina mumbled. "I'll do mine tomorrow."

Jacinta put her recliner down with a thump, hopped out of the chair, and joined Mina on the floor. She placed a pencil in Mina's slack hand. "Here we go. Dear Diary, Jacinta is the baddest chick on the planet. I don't know why I couldn't just admit that on day one."

Mina laughed. "Alright, alright. I can't be turning in my observations with all those lies."

Jacinta stretched out beside Mina and tapped her pen on the notebook, waiting for the words to make their way onto the paper.

"I'm almost done," Jessica announced.

"I would be too if I spent half the night barely saying a word," Mina said. "You probably already knew what you were going to say anyway."

"Jealous?" Jessica taunted.

"Yes. Can you do mine, too?" Mina propped herself up on her elbows.

Jessica pretended to go back to writing to hide the little smile playing on her lips. Her head popped up. "Oh, whose house is next?"

The girls grew quiet, waiting for someone to volunteer.

"I volunteer, Cinny," Mina said, scribbling away.

"Thanks, Princess," Jacinta said. She shrugged. "Fine with me."

"I can't do it this coming Friday," Jessica warned. "I told you guys, I have a life outside of this soc class."

"Well, if we do it in two weeks it's a weekend my aunt will be away. We'd have to do it at my father's house," Jacinta said.

Jessica's snotty voice returned to action. "I heard you lived in The Cove?"

"Yeah . . . and?" Jacinta raised an eyebrow.

"Okay, ew, I'm not spending the night in the projects," Jessica said.

"Okay, ew, the projects wouldn't want your fake-eye, fake-hair wearing ass there anyway," Jacinta said.

"Guys, come on," Kelly said. "Why does it matter?"

"Hola, seniorita, maybe you don't know much about The Cove seeing as how you don't get out much," Jessica said. "It's not the safest neighborhood in Del Rio."

Jacinta sat up. "Ay, Swirl, don't go there. I have no problem jump-ing off this floor and . . ."

"Ya'll look. It's too late for me to be breaking up a fight," Mina said. "Jacinta host the next SO wherever you want. We'll all be there."

"Maybe!" Jessica said.

Jacinta rolled her eyes and went back to writing.

Freshman Sociology
Project Prejudice
September 9, 2005
Observations by Kelly Lopez

I haven't had a sleepover since fifth grade when Maisy Whitmore came over.

I remember almost getting sick all over the leather seats in my mom's new Bentley. My mom nearly wrecked trying to pull over. That's how excited I was when we went to pick up Maisy. Maisy was barely in the car be-fore her mouth ran a mile a minute asking a million questions about Phil. What singers had I met? Could I get Diddy to perform at her confirmation party? That's how obvious it was why she was suddenly being so nice to me. We were friends for a year and then I finally told her I couldn't get Diddy or anyone else to perform for her party. Friendship finito.

So, I know that I'm getting my hopes up—one night does not equal a friendship.

Still, I loved how Mina acted like she was just here to visit (for more than a project). I really like her. Jac-inta wasn't as defensive as normal . . . well, not with me, anyway. Friendship wouldn't be out of the question,

I guess. She and Jessica are another story. They're like two grizzly bears circling one another before charging. Yikes.

I'm still lost about that weird invitation to hang out with Mari-Beth and Jessica. I've never been interested in being friends with Mari-Beth. And I doubt Jessica and I would ever become friends, because . . . well, Mari-Beth.

This group of girls knows more about me than most people! I don't know what they think of me. But I'm off the hot seat and it feels so good!

Freshman Sociology
September 9, 2005
Jacinta Phillips

So Kelly isn't as boogee as I thought. The thing is, I have crazy respect for her—the love she shows for her grandparents, how she's down to earth instead of being all Paris Hilton.

She has this <u>Cribs</u>-sized mansion, a friggin' shoe organizer, and a bathroom the size of my living room. Seriously, I think Kelly's house could probably fit—and I'm not joking—six garden homes from The Cove in it. Maybe eight! But she's not flossing any of it.

I'm still tripping that me and her have a few things in common. I'm not saying we'd ever bump into each other out in the streets—my father's a mechanic and hers is a music producer—shoot, we don't even walk the same streets. But I can kick a little Spanish with her (more than I even knew I knew), and thanks to Angel I'm down with the Puerto Rican culture.

Second thing, neither Kelly's mother nor my mom is winning any Mother of the Year Awards. Kelly had that "it ain't a big deal" tone in her voice when she said she and her mother aren't close. I've said it the same way about my own, a million times.

I've got to give props to her for being straight up with us about the tickets and stuff. Don't ask 'cause ya' not getting. All in all I gotta admit that I'm feeling shady for assuming Kelly would come off as the snobby one. Mina had that on lock with that whole Princess comment at the pizza place. Yeah, yeah, I swore to let it go . . . but she said it. I refuse to let her live it down!

I get to see what they're all made of when they come to my block. My house is too small to sit up in all night long. So trust, I will give them the whole experience.

Project Prejudice
9-9-05
Jessica Johnson

Two words to sum up tonight: Wasted Potential!

The only reason I wasn't dreading this first sleepover was because it was on my turf. Well, Mari-Beth's turf. But I'm over here so much this neighborhood feels more like home than my own. First, I was going to bring up Kelly hanging with the glams again. Obviously, Mari-Beth thinks she has something to add. But Kelly's a lost cause. Here's why:

1. Transferring from McStew to public school in the ninth grade. Big loser move. That's like dropping out of college to attend high school. 2. Being so googly eyed friendly with Mina. Hello, is she too blind to see Mina has no pull? At least not outside of the fresh fish pond. 3. Not seeing a problem with having the next sleepover in Pirate's Cove aka Hustler's Heaven. Kelly, wake up. You were born into the elite. Never waste it by slumming. Even for a class project.

Maybe she and I were switched at birth. I swear! I wouldn't have a problem living in a big old house like this overlooking a tennis court, studio, and pool. No doubt in my mind that Kelly would fit in wonderfully in my we're-poor-but-proud-household. Gross!

The only thing Kelly said tonight that I can really relate to was Popularity's a bitch. Well she said it much nicer (it figures).

What? Do they think it's easy being a glam (ha, ha). Seriously, you've got to work hard to stay on top. And as far as I'm concerned, all Kelly did, with all her "you don't have to announce yourself," was prove that she's too weak to handle the world she was born into.

Freshman Soc
9/9/2005
Observations by Amina Mooney
Grrr . . . I'm tired. Whose idea was this to write these things? Oh, wait . . . mine!
Okay let me think . . . Kelly is a total sweetheart.

Bad, bad Mina for joking on her with Lizzie saying that she was odd and weird. Sorry, Kell, I didn't know you.

Then again, that's why she's such a sweetheart. I'll admit it's hard to swallow that someone who could get a celeb to show up at her doorstep with one simple phone call from Papa Producer is basically like, yeah, whatever. I mean, at first, I thought it was an act. I was waiting for her to go diva at least once. She never did. Well, except when she said not to ask for any tickets . . . but if people only ever liked me because of that, I would be the same way. So I'm not mad at ya, Kell-Kell. BUT, it's hard to believe there are people who don't care about status and power and cliquin'. Still, I can tell Kelly's a big old marshmallow; no diva in that little body.

I have to admit, I had to really keep myself in check in the studio. I wanted to go totally fan crazy and get stupid. I was this close to asking for Chris Brown's autograph. Chris, love you! But, I respect that it's a sore spot for Kelly.

Next to Kelly, I must look like Jessica, with my clique and café dreams. And trust, if I were Kelly I'd be holding my connections over people's head something terrible until they bowed and called me Your Highness. Hee, hee! I can't help it. Popularity is add-ic-tive!

Alright, I am tired, people. Kelly, you're a real sweetie and you know what, you can roll with me and my clique anytime. Can you bring Chris, though? Jokes. Just jokes!

I Thought He Was Going to Hit You!

"Throw 'dem bows."
—Ludacris, "Southern Hospitality"

Mina silently rated who was hot and who was not among passing guys in the mall's food court as Lizzie caught her up on her audition worries. Still groggy from the sleepover, she found it hard to concentrate on both the eye candy and Lizzie's stream of conversation.

"Is it crazy for me to think I could get a lead my first year out?" Lizzie winced in anticipation of a negative answer.

"Is it impossible for a frosh to get a lead role, or just unlikely?" Mina quizzed. She waved at one of the varsity soccer players, a cutie from her biology class.

Lizzie kicked at her, wanting Mina's full attention. "Unlikely."

Mina had never seen Lizzie this keyed up over an audition before. She focused on the desperation in her voice and forced herself to be alert. "Okay, seriously. I think you should just go for Dorothy. I know you're good enough to snag the role. If you don't get it, we'll know it's all about politics." Her voice distorted as she yawned. "But they'll still have to give you a good role. Your skills are too phat for them to ignore."

The worried look in Lizzie's eyes softened. The vote of confidence from Mina soothed her ego. Feeling guilty for dominating the conversation with her obsessing, she switched the subject. "Your turn. How was the sleepover? Break any new ground?"

"Oh my God, Liz, Kelly's stepfather is Phil Narcone!"

"Phil Narcone, the music producer?"

Mina gushed, "Yup. They live in this huge house in Folgers Way, with a tennis court and a theater room . . . just crazy big. Kelly even has this automated shoe organizer thing. Now how rich do you have to be to have a thingamijig to organize your shoes?"

Lizzie chuckled. "No, you mean how rich do you have to be to need one. The machine would die of loneliness trying to sort through my three pairs of shoes."

They cracked up. "I know that's right," Mina said. "Well the answer is very. Because they're rolling in it." Her words tumbled quickly. "Girl, Phil even has a studio there, and we saw him with all of these celebs."

"What?" Lizzie frowned unable to decipher Mina's rambling. "He was there last night? With what celebs?"

Mina explained. "No, I mean we saw pictures of him with different groups he's worked with."

Lizzie dug for the scoop. She hated to admit it, but she was curious about the girls Mina had to spend an entire semester with. "So, is Kelly a total snob?"

Mina shook her head. "Not really."

"Jacinta still hating us burbalicious girls?"

"Burbalicious. I likey." Mina grinned. She shrugged. "She's getting better, I guess. Not so much hatin' as willing to breathe the same air as us."

"Ugh, how was life with Her Majesty Queen Be-yatch?" Lizzie prodded.

Mina rolled her eyes. "Umph, not good. She and Mari actually tried to recruit Kelly to the glamour girls or whatever they're calling themselves."

"Ha! Were you jealous?" Lizzie teased.

"Yup. About as jealous as I am of people on *Fear Factor* eating cow balls."

People stared as they howled again.

Mina stood up and stretched lazily. "Come on, let's walk before I nod off. I'm mad tired."

They took all of ten steps before Mina came to a screeching halt.

"Oh my God, look! Aren't they cute?" She ran over to Macy's and picked up a pair of crocheted multicolored boots from the store-front display. The colorful mitton boots screamed for attention among the sedate brown and black leather knee boots.

Lizzie came over and looked over her shoulders, only mildly interested.

"Lizzie, these are adorable." Mina read the tag. "Ooh they're NYLA mitton boots. I've gotta have 'em. Let's ask your mom tonight if she can get us the hookup."

"Us?" Lizzie held up one boot by a corner far from her face like it would bite. "Uh-uh. You are most definitely on your own. It's like a sweater for your feet."

"Look, they come in brown and white. Those aren't as wild as the orange, red, blue, and green ones. They're so different."

"Wasn't the word I would use but . . . okay, different," Lizzie said.

"These would go so good with my cropped flare pants . . ." Mina trailed off, noticing Jacinta and a tall, dark-brown guy with cornrows on the other side of the corridor. She called out over the mall's noise, stopping Jacinta in her tracks.

Jacinta tapped the guy's arm and headed over. "Hey, Mina, I didn't see you. Hi, Lizzie."

Lizzie waved. The sleepover must be working miracles, she thought. Jacinta was . . . friendly.

"You recouped from last night yet?" Mina asked.

Jacinta's mouth opened wide in a yawn as she shook her head. "My bad," she apologized. "Raheem, this is Mina and her girl, Lizzie."

"Wassup?" he asked in a low, deep voice. He eyed the girls up and down, seemed bored with the view and sauntered away.

The three girls stood in place, unsure what to say next.

"Ya'll shopping?" Jacinta asked, one eye on Raheem.

"Nah. Lizzie wouldn't allow that," Mina said. "She puts up with the mall under strict orders that it won't involve shopping."

Jacinta nodded as she edged away to keep up with Raheem.

"I just don't enjoy shopping as much as Mina," Lizzie explained, trailing behind as Mina instinctively walked along with Jacinta.

Raheem remained slightly ahead of them.

"Do you have any sibs, Jacinta? Or are you an Only like me and Mina?" Lizzie asked.

"Two brothers and a sister, both younger than her," Mina cheesed.

"Gold star for the Princess," Jacinta said.

Lizzie's skeptical eyebrows were working overtime. Jacinta was one hundred and eighty degrees different from the first day. It wasn't what Lizzie expected from someone who was only "willing" to breathe the same air as them. Either Mina was a good actress or that relaxed, familiar tone she used with Jacinta was sincere. It was surreal.

The girls walked along in silence until Mina raised her voice to be heard over the mall's steady hum of traffic and noise. "Raheem, you should come out to our JV games sometimes!"

He turned his head slightly to be heard, but kept walking. "I ain't really into JV. Besides, ya'll ain't no kind of competition for Sam-Well. We got the championships on lock already."

Raheem was like everybody else who went to Sam-Well, assuming their school's athletes had more skill. No matter how much competition Del Rio High gave Sam-Well in football and basketball, their athletes would never be more than a bunch of "lucky" white boys and a few gray boys that had a little skill.

"Shoot, ya'll bamas not all that! Our boys can ball!" Mina yelled back.

Raheem stopped short and Jacinta stumbled on his heels, smashing her face into his back. She shoved him lightly, embarrassed. "Boy!"

Raheem turned around, his eyes were slits locked on Mina. A

sneer played at the corners of his mouth. After a few seconds, he chuckled soft and sarcastic, shaking his head. "Shhhit. Either you blind or crazy. Ya'll gray boys can't hang with us. We state champs two years running, Girl."

"It won't be a third!" Mina sped up to walk beside him, leaving Jacinta and Lizzie a step behind.

Raheem let Mina catch up. "I heard ya'll got this one dude, Jason something, supposed to be all that," Raheem continued in a raspy sulk. He added, with a touch of admiration. "I heard kid is bad."

"Exactly. That's why ya'll going down this year. He is bad. His name Jason Zimms, and that's my boy," Mina bragged.

"Oh, that's you?" Raheem asked, assuming JZ was Mina's boyfriend.

"Oh, no, not like that. I'm saying, we go back . . . you know, grew up together. We're tight . . ." Mina rambled as he walked into the FYE without another word. Well at least I stood up for my Blue Devils, she thought, a satisfied grin on her face.

Mina's smile faded when she turned around and saw how pale Lizzie's face was.

"What?" Mina asked, concerned.

"Oh, my God, Mina, I thought he was going to hit you!" Lizzie blurted, clutching her chest.

"Why would he hit her?" Jacinta snapped, her mouth fixed in an annoyed snarl.

"Well . . ." Lizzie cut her eyes toward Mina. She licked her lips nervously. She chose her words carefully. "It was the way he stopped so . . . suddenly. I thought Mina said something wrong."

Jacinta rolled her eyes while Lizzie's pleaded for Mina's help.

Mina picked up on the cue and played it off. "Liz didn't mean any harm. Shoot, I thought he was gonna hit me too for challenging his mans and 'nem."

Jacinta's wave was dismissive. "Girl, please. He's on both varsity football and basketball teams, so he could probably go on and on about those things. He not a big talker, but you hit on something he don't mind talking about." She backed toward the music store. "Are ya'll coming in?"

Lizzie wasn't making any moves toward the music store.

"We might catch up," Mina lied.

Lizzie was glad Mina had begged out of heading into FYE. Score a point for the best friend radar. There was something about Raheem she didn't like. Lizzie found herself comparing him to JZ and Michael. But found no comfort there. He wasn't like her friends. She couldn't say why. He just wasn't.

Once Jacinta had disappeared into the bright, noisy music store, she exhaled, shaking her head. "I didn't mean to offend her, but her boyfriend looks mean."

"Not really," Mina frowned. She glanced back to make sure no one was behind them. It would be just her luck that she'd end up messing up the soc project by talking about Jacinta behind her back and getting caught . . . again. But mall traffic had filled in behind her. There was no sign of Jacinta.

"Uh, yeah, he was," Lizzie insisted with a roll of her eyes.

Mina's voice rose in irritation. "Whatever, Liz. He seems cool to me."

"Whatever, Mina. Any other time you'd agree that someone like that . . ."

Mina stopped short. She folded her arms and rooted herself in the middle of the corridor, causing a minor ripple in traffic. People behind them quickly readjusted and filed around. A few people shot them dirty looks.

"Like what?" Mina said.

"The thugged out, cornrows, baggy clothes, and fake gangster wannabe that, that's what," Lizzie hissed, trying to keep her voice down. She kept her arms at her sides, refusing to match Mina's argumentative body language.

"You mean someone black who not all prepped out like some of these other Del Rio Bay boys?"

"Prepped out?!" Lizzie shouted, her arms folding on cue at the high pitch of her voice. Two girls, about ten, passing by snickered and Lizzie turned down her volume. She took a few steps back and out of the middle of the walkway, refusing to talk until Mina moved toward her. When Mina did, Lizzie spoke in a normal tone. "Just yesterday you were crushing on one of those Del Rio Bay boys. Last I heard you still were! Or is Craig not gangsta enough for you?"

Mina rolled her eyes. "All I'm saying is, you're acting like Raheem was gonna pull out a gat and shoot you in the middle of a crowded mall. He was just tripping 'cause I called them bamas and said his team wasn't all that."

Lizzie's voice rose, once more, with agitation. "And all I'm saying is he looks mean to me! Why are you taking it personally? Am I mistaken or didn't you meet him today just like me?"

She started walking again, forcing Mina to follow and talk to the back of her head.

"Calm down, Lizzie. Dag, he didn't actually threaten me."

Lizzie whirled around. Her eyebrows were arched practically to her hairline. Her head wagged as she talked. "I know he didn't threaten you. But I wouldn't put it past him."

Mina challenged her. "Why? Because he's black and not from the rolling hills of your nabe?"

"No, because he just looks like the type," Lizzie retorted, her eyes brimming with hurt.

She was invoking the unspoken rule of best friends—side with me in public, disagree later. But Mina was too agitated. So many times they had been at the mall or the beach or wherever with the roles reversed, meeting someone that Lizzie knew, Mina tagging along. No matter how strangely dressed they were or weird the person acted, and some of Lizzie's theater friends were seriously from another planet in Mina's opinion, still, she went along, acting as if any friend of Lizzie was a friend of hers.

Her mind was mush from lack of sleep, but it picked up one thing; Lizzie was stereotyping Raheem and she wanted Mina to go along with her. *Sorry, Liz, brain too tired to mind the friendship rules,* Mina thought before ordering, "Liz, let's drop it!"

Mina walked faster, passing Lizzie by a step, and headed toward the food court exit, where Lizzie's mom dropped them only two hours before. She leaned against the fake marble wall near the exit, glaring. "You're walking right on the edge of saying something ignorant. I don't feel like talking about it anymore."

Lizzie stared at her for a second. Mina's face was twisted, her arms folded; she was seriously upset. Lizzie shook her head and tucked away the need to nag.

They'd said these types of things before about people, sometimes joking, sometimes not. But for some reason, Mina's mind was made up. Lizzie knew they wouldn't get anywhere now. Mina had decided she was through talking.

Lizzie took out her cell phone and called her mom to come get them.

So What can We Talk About?

"Let me know that I've done wrong. When I've known this all along."
—All-American Rejects, "Dirty Little Secret"

After a wordless ride home, unless you counted Mrs. O'Reilly forcing the girls to talk by asking them question after question about life as freshmen, the girls retreated to Lizzie's room.

Mina pulled out *A Tale of Two Cities* and sat in the window seat. Lizzie popped in *The Wiz* DVD, stretched out on her bed, and pretended to watch. Neither knew how to breach the tension that mounted with every second they didn't speak.

Going to their separate corners during sleepovers was part of the only child syndrome. It wasn't anything for Lizzie to clamp on headphones to take a break from Mina's wonderings, ponderings, and fashion what-ifs, peppering the convo with a few "yeah, I know" and "hmmm, really" as necessary. Not that headphones stopped Mina. If it was something she really wanted more than an "uh-huh" on, she'd just shake Lizzie's toe or poke her arm to get her attention.

But the freeze between them, now, had nothing to do with wanting time out from each other.

Ten minutes into the movie, Lizzie relaxed. The argument seemed silly. Obviously she had underestimated how serious Mina was taking the LL course. Lizzie was still baffled over how Raheem fit into the whole thing, but going all night without talking because of some hip-hop imitator was stupid.

She caught Mina daydreaming, staring out of the window, and dove in. "So Lines for Lunch starts tomorrow. You gonna survive lunch period with just the guys until after auditions?"

Mina's answer came from far away. She kept her gaze out of the window as she talked. "Yeah, I guess. The streak's officially dead now, huh?"

"Yeah," Lizzie said. She sat upright. "I'm sorry I broke it."

"Nah, I would have done the same thing for cheerleading," Mina said, in a strangely wooden monotone. "I guess Kelly will keep me company at lunch."

"What's out there?" Lizzie said, hoping her teasing tone hid her annoyance. She wanted to believe she was only annoyed at Mina's zombie answers. But it was really Mina saying Kelly would keep her company. *Am I really that easily replaced?* Lizzie wondered.

Mina blinked hard and shook her head. "My bad. I was just thinking."

"What about?" Lizzie said, letting her momentary jealousy dissolve. She turned the volume down on the movie.

Mina chuckled. "Kelly went a little diva last night. Telling us not to ask her for tickets, autographs, and stuff. It was just funny. She's not as shy as I thought."

Lizzie wrinkled her nose. "I didn't know the girl ever spoke above a whisper."

"Yeah. But I wouldn't call it shy. She's . . . quiet," Mina said. She laughed. "You know, the opposite of me."

Lizzie nodded, not caring. She didn't feel like talking about Kelly, Jacinta, or anyone else associated with the soc project. Any other time she could say so to Mina. But after the whole Raheem episode, she decided to hold her tongue.

"Of course, Jessica already knew that Phil Narcone was Kelly's stepfather. You know she always has to know everything," Mina said.

"Uh-huh," Lizzie quickly changed the subject. "Hey, Michael volunteered to help outfit me for my audition."

Mina closed her book and turned away from the window completely. She pushed thoughts of the mall argument away. She had been tired (*still was*). Not like it was the first time she let cranky get the best of her. And maybe (*maybe!*) Lizzie had a right to be annoyed. This was supposed to be a best friend day out. Mina should have waved to Jacinta and let her and Raheem keep rolling.

"That's cool," Mina said. She walked over and sat beside Lizzie on the bed. "I love how he hooks stuff up. I bet he'd like those mitton boots."

Lizzie groaned. "Ugh. Well, as long as that's not part of the outfit he wants me to wear."

"You know what I wonder? How is it that Jessica be wearing more name brands than me?" Mina said.

Lizzie held back another groan as the conversation went right back to somebody involved with the project.

"You know, last night she had on this cute American Eagle Henley hoodie," Mina said. "The same one my mother refuses to buy me until it goes on sale. When it does they won't have the color I want."

Lizzie shrugged, hoping Mina would pick up on her lack of feedback. But Mina rattled on with her analysis.

"I'm saying, Jess's mom doesn't even work. Now, how both my parents work and my mother is bickering over paying full price when Jessica has the thing hot off the rack with one working parent?"

"Maybe she's just spoiled," Lizzie said. She stretched back out and turned her attention to *The Wiz*.

"Well, yeah. But I am, too," Mina said. She laughed, noticed Lizzie didn't, and nudged her. "That was a joke."

Lizzie contemplated for a second. She didn't want to argue anymore. But it seemed stupid to start tiptoeing around things she'd always been able to be up front about. She sat up, bringing her and Mina face-to-face. "Can we change the channel?"

Hurt flashed across Mina's face and Lizzie's stomach fell. Honesty wasn't popular today.

"My bad." Mina flopped onto her stomach and propped herself up by the elbows. "What *can* we talk about today?"

"Anything. I just don't feel like talking about . . . Jessica," Lizzie said carefully.

"Well we weren't. We were talking about clothes, but whatever," Mina said. She turned her eyes to the television and fell silent.

The tension settled back over them.

Lizzie rolled her eyes to the ceiling. She flopped onto her back and listened to the movie. She didn't need to see *The Wiz*, just hear it. She listened for the emotions of each character.

Usually Mina commented on dialogue, scenery, and the cast's wardrobe whenever they watched a movie, annoying Lizzie to no end. But for the first time, ever, they watched without her uttering a word of commentary. Instead of enjoying the silent bliss, Lizzie found the movie boring without Mina's colorful analysis.

She glanced over at Mina, whose lids were partially closed, and shattered the silence once more. "So will you help Mike hook me up?"

"If you want me to," Mina said through a yawn.

"He said you have a skirt like the one he has in mind."

"Uh-huh," Mina said. Her eyes drooped more.

"Do you still have those black fencing boots? Those were the kind he had in his sketch," Lizzie said.

"Ummm . . . yeah, I do. I just got 'em last year," Mina said. Her elbows relaxed and she laid her head across her arms, turned away from the television. "How many times have you seen this movie?" her muffled voice asked.

Lizzie chuckled.

When she first found out that *The Wiz* was going to be this year's production, she ran out and bought the DVD and watched Diana Ross and Michael Jackson ease on down the road ten times until she got a feel for the movie's tone.

"A lot. And mostly in the last few days," she admitted. "You know, I'm bummed about missing lunch. But I'm excited about Lines for lunch." Her voice drowned out Mina's soft snoozing. "You're the one all into signs. Isn't it a big one that the president of the drama club thinks I could win a lead role?" Lizzie flipped over onto her stomach. "That's like a humongo neon flashing sign, right? I shouldn't be so freaked about it. But I am."

Lizzie frowned. "Mi . . . Mina." She elbowed her. "Did you hear me?"

A drowsy "uh–huh" was Mina's only response.

"I'm going to try and not be totally offended that you're falling asleep on me after hanging out all night with a bunch of strangers," Lizzie said, miffed.

"I'm just sleepy, nothing personal," Mina mumbled.

"Yeah, right," Lizzie said under her breath. She rolled onto her back and let *The Wiz* do the rest of the talking.

The next afternoon, Lizzie sat at her desk. The computer screen stared at her vacantly.

The cyberworld was a ghost town.

It was almost as quiet as Mina had been in person last night.

Lizzie's left hand reached for the phone and her right clicked the mouse to refresh her inbox, in case Mina had e-mailed her in the last sixty seconds. Her mind pored over their sullen weekend.

By the time Mina awoke from her nap, it was late and Lizzie couldn't resist giving her the cold shoulder. When Mina asked if Lizzie wanted to do the read-aloud thing for their Lit class, Lizzie pretended not to hear her over the blaring iPod. Mina ended up reading on her own and falling back to sleep within the hour.

Last thing Lizzie remembered was Mina tapping her, announcing her mom was there to pick her up. It took Lizzie several minutes to figure out it was Sunday morning and by then Mina's footsteps were echoing down the stairs. Lizzie was ready to stew in pity all day until her mother asked her outright. "So, you guys were awfully quiet last night. Having a tiff?"

Lizzie suppressed an eye roll. "Mom, we're fourteen not four. We had a disagreement."

Marybeth O'Reilly combed through Lizzie's bedhead with her fingers. "Sorry. Is everything okay? Mariah came earlier than I thought we had originally talked about."

Lizzie shook her head. She truly didn't know the answer. "Everything's okay," she said finally. "Mina's a grump when she's tired."

After she'd said it, Lizzie realized that's what it was. Mina was an early-to-bed chick. The double SO could be brutal, two days in a row of late-night talk. That had to be why she was so touchy.

Lizzie was phoning the same time an IM from Mina popped on her screen. Lizzie hung up the phone before anyone at Mina's could answer. She typed eagerly in response.

BubbliMi: Hey Liz-O!!

Lizzie grinned, relieved. So everything was cool.

Liz-e-O: Omigod . . . look what the cat dragged in. I was just calling u.
BubbliMi: It's Mi, It's Mi . . . it's Bubbli-Mi.
Liz-e-O: U totally left me hanging this morning. i was still wiping crud out of my eyes when I heard the door slam.
BubbliMi: Ok ewww . . . I had to get home.
Liz-e-O: Y?
BubbliMi: hello, 813 pages of Lit! Plus, need to do some stuff

for our first cheer fund-raiser that I've gotta have ready to
show Kelis in the A.M. blah, blah, blah

Liz-e-O: Gotcha. so u sorry yet?☺

BubbliMi: 4 what?

Liz-e-O: 4 wigging out on me yesterday. U R a total grinch
when ur tired

BubbliMi: what r u talking about?

Liz-e-O: The whole Jacinta's BF thing.

BubbliMi: What about him?

Liz-e-O: Mi, normally you would agree with me that he's scary
Grrr . . . like DMX where my dogs at scary.

BubbliMi: Why Liz cause he black?!

Liz-e-O: R U serious? No, because he's the type of guy we joke
on all the time w/his hip-hop, I'm bad, my team is bad talk . . .
and because I thought he was going to smack you into next
week. ☺

BubbliMi: u know what? For real, let's drop it. B/c I don't see it
like u do

Liz-e-O: Fine . . . sorry I brought it up. Thought we could joke
about it . . . was wrong! ☹

BubbliMi: u know, the one time it's your turn to give my friends
the benefit of the doubt u don't!

Liz-e-O: FRIENDS?! My fault I didn't know u and Raheem
ROLLED in the same circles

BubbliMi: Careful Liz-O ur color is showing!

Liz-e-O: This is so NOT about race!!

BubbliMi: It SO is!!

Liz-e-O: This is stupid

BubbliMi: Let's agree to disagree then

Liz-e-O: Fine by me

BubbliMi: Alright TTYL

Liz-e-O: What, no juice? No gossip?

BubbliMi: Nah—I'm still kind of dragging azz from the double
S.O. I just jumped on 4 a hot minute
Liz-e-O: OK TTYL
BubbliMi: C U

Lizzie was dumbfounded. She sat back heavily in the chair, whacking her shoulder bone against the wooden edge. It brought tears to her eyes. She tried but couldn't convince herself her sore shoulder was the reason the tears kept flowing.

Sometimes, a Few Knuckleheads Ruin It for Everybody

"Back in the day when things were cool."
—Erykah Badu, "Back in the Day (Puff)"

Mina wasn't faring much better than Lizzie in the aftermath of their argument. Late Sunday evening, she sat on her bed, across from her computer, hearing the creaks, whistles, and horns of her friends coming and going online. Mina didn't feel like talking to anyone . . . except . . . Lizzie's screen name still glowed on the screen.

Mina stared at it, expecting it to go gray at any moment, indicating Lizzie was gone. She told herself that if Lizzie stayed online for another *ten, nine, eight* seconds she'd get off the bed and IM her.

Lizzie's darkened screen name lured Mina over to the desk. Lizzie would probably log off before she could get there, Mina told herself.

But Lizzie didn't.

Mina walked over, sat cross-legged in the chair, and lifted her fingers to the keyboard.

"Miii-na! Come here for a second, please," Mina's mom called from downstairs.

Well, that settled that.

Mina pulled herself away from the computer, walked out of her room and stood at the top landing. Her parents were standing in the middle of the sunroom, her father on the phone, her mom beside him watching him talk. Her mother turned away long enough to beckon to Mina.

Jackson Mooney never talked on the phone unless it was his cell phone and that was normally business-related. When the house phone rang he ignored it. "It's never for me," was his reply if Mina's mom ever launched into a lecture about him walking past a ringing phone.

Mina took each step slowly, nosing in on her dad's conversation from a distance, and padded across the dining room and into the sunroom. She took a seat on the sofa as her father said, "Okay. Well I appreciate the call."

Jackson Mooney nodded as he answered the person on the other end with an "um-hmm," then a laugh. "Yeah, I know exactly how that is. I tell you, having these girls is either going to keep us young or kill us," her dad said, his laughter a velvety baritone.

Mina whispered up to her mother. "Who's that?"

Mina's mom placed a finger on her lips and waited for her husband to finish.

"Okay, Jamal," Mina's dad said. "Good to meet you, man. Thanks a lot. Good-bye."

"Who was that?" Mina asked, looking first at her dad then mom.

"What did he say, Jack?" Mina's mother asked, as curiously as Mina.

"That was your friend Jacinta's father," Mina's dad said. He sat in the overstuffed chair next to the couch. "Apparently, you all are staying at his townhouse in The Cove next Friday for your class project?"

"Oh, yeah," Mina said. "Dag, Cinny already told her father? I need to remember to tease her about being pressed."

Mina laughed.

"I thought Jacinta lived down the street on Lakeview?" Mina's mom asked. She sat down beside Mina.

"Her aunt does," Mina said. "I was going to tell you tonight about our next sleepover plans."

"So what did he say, Jackson?" Mina's mom asked.

"That he wanted to introduce himself, he'd definitely keep an eye on the girls while they're there, and they'd be okay," Mina's dad said. "Just touching base with all of the parents."

Hearing her dad say the words "they'd be okay" reminded Mina that The Cove had a reputation. The fact that Mr. Phillips already called to say she, Kelly, and Jessica would be "okay" was a sign to Mina. There had to be something to worry about whenever someone emphasized things would be okay. Mina's stomach did a tiny flip flop.

Pirate's Cove was barely ten miles away from her house, but Mina had never been there. All she knew of it was what was in the local newspaper—when she bothered to read it—and bits and pieces she gathered from Michael, whose aunt lived there.

When they were kids, Michael's grandmother would send Michael to stay at her sister, Tess's, whenever she had church business or volunteer work to do. Michael used to love it. He'd come back from his weekends bragging about roaming The Cove's buildings, playing basketball into the evening (The Cove's courts had lighting, The Woods' courts were strictly for daytime), hanging with the friends he made there, and being out on the playground late nights with his older cousins. He always talked about The Cove like it was the most exciting place on earth.

Now that Michael was older, his visits to Aunt Tess were more irregular and had more to do with Michael's grandmother nagging him into a visit than anything else. Michael had lost interest in hanging in The Cove once drawing officially replaced basketball as his favorite hobby a year ago. But when he was going on the regular, he took JZ with him a lot. JZ loved it because it was another excuse to play street ball. He still played ball in The Cove during Del Rio Bay's summer league basketball tournaments.

Mina couldn't remember Michael or JZ ever talking about anything bad happening to them when they hung out in The Cove. She'd asked once, a few years back. But they made her feel so stupid for asking that she never bothered again.

The question was simple enough. What did they do when the shooting started?

But when she asked, a look passed between Michael and JZ before they fell out laughing.

"What shooting?" Michael asked.

"There was an article in the paper that said there's a shooting in The Cove every weekend," Mina said, feeling dumb for bringing up the article. She'd only read it in passing. Maybe she'd read the information wrong.

"Yeah, well it wasn't one this weekend," JZ said.

He and Michael did their stupid "boy" laugh, the one where the inside joke was Mina was a girl and wouldn't get it even if they explained. Mina hated it. Later, she reread the article, thinking maybe she'd misunderstood. But the story about crime in Del Rio Bay said that "on average" there was a shooting or violent assault in The Cove fifty-two times a year. *Now wasn't that once a weekend?*

The reason the number stuck out in her head was because the article was about the relatively low crime in the city—average five murders a year, four hundred robberies, blah, blah. Then it listed the city had more than two hundred aggravated assaults. And that's where The Cove shooting number came in. Even Mina's fuzzy math knew that fifty-two shootings in one neighborhood was a big chunk of the city's total number of assaults.

Still, Mina never brought it back up. Michael and JZ came back from The Cove in one piece each time. That was good enough for her. And she always made sure she had plans with Lizzie when trips to Aunt Tess were on Michael's agenda. It kept her curiosity about what they found so great about The Cove away.

Now Mina's interest, mixed with a smidge of apprehension, was back, all because her dad said, "They'd be okay."

Mina's arms pimpled as she thought about the robberies, drug dealing, and shootings the paper connected to the neighborhood. Michael and JZ had never witnessed any, well never told her, but obviously, those things happened.

The thought of being there overnight chilled her. Mina tucked her feet under her and plucked a nearby throw pillow to hug, anxious to hear more about her dad's conversation.

"Do we know Jacinta's father, Jack?" Mina's mother said. "Did he go to school with us?"

Mina's parents had grown up in the 'burbs of Del Rio Bay, unlike Lizzie's parents (Kansas), or even JZ's, who were from the D.C. area. Let her parents tell it, they knew every other person in the whole city. But not this time.

Jackson Mooney shook his head. "Not sure," he said. "I don't think so. I don't remember any Jamal Phillips. But, apparently he's lived in The Cove for about ten years and is really active on the community board and neighborhood watch. Sounds like he only lives a building away from Tess."

"Oh, okay," Mina's mom said, nodding as her eyebrows scrunched then raised then scrunched again. Mina called it her "thinker" look. Her mom got it whenever she was mulling over details. "So he lives near the front of the neighborhood."

Mina's dad nodded.

Mina's mother sat back against the sofa and crossed her legs. Her eyebrows were at rest.

"So that's good then?" Mina asked. She was unfamiliar with the layout of the community. What difference did it make if they lived in the front or back or whatever?

"I didn't mean it that way," Mina's mom said. "I recall Mae Bell telling me, once, that her sister lived in the second building."

"Are the front buildings safer or something?" Mina asked.

For a second, she regretted asking. Her parents exchanged a look and Mina was sure they were going to laugh at her the way Michael and JZ had that time.

"Well, you know we wouldn't be letting you go if we didn't think you were safe," her dad said. "Jamal assured us he'd keep a close eye on you girls. Plus, we could always get Mae Bell to call her sister and let her know you'll be there."

"You should probably stop in and see Miss Tess anyway," Mina's mother said. "Say hello, while you're there."

Mina groaned. "Ma, I don't even really know her. I mean, well I haven't seen her since I was a little girl."

Mina's mom pulled Mina to her. She held Mina in an affectionate bear hug. "Oh calm down. I was only joking."

"Do you think I should leave my earrings home?" Mina sank into her mom's embrace and rubbed at the pearl and sapphire earrings, a gift for her thirteenth birthday.

Mina saw her father's eyes narrow. She sat up and looked over at her mom, who had a concerned look on her face. Her eyebrows were back in action.

"What?" Mina asked.

"Sweetie, it's really not all *that* bad in Pirate's Cove," her mother said. "No one's just sitting there waiting to harm you. Sometimes a few knuckleheads ruin it for everybody . . . giving the whole community a black eye."

Mina started to bring up the old article but her father jumped in.

"We're not saying we want you hanging around there all the time. But we don't want you going in afraid just because of things you've heard either," her father said. "Jamal has a daughter of his own. I'm sure he has plenty of ground rules he'll expect you girls to follow."

"Just make sure you listen to Mr. Phillips," her mother said. "The Cove isn't *that* much different from any other neighborhood in Del

Rio Bay. I'm sure people know Jacinta's dad and would let him know if you girls were in trouble . . ." She tapped Mina's thigh. "Or if you were out acting a fool."

Mina frowned. "What do you mean?"

Mina's mom laughed. "I remember how mysterious The Cove was to me when I . . ."

"Was your age," Mina chimed in.

Her mother smiled. "Yes, Miss Smarty. The first time I went there with some friends of mine, we acted all grown because being there, felt, so . . . far away." Mina's mom shook her head. "All eight miles from our own neighborhood. We got caught up in our 'freedom' and mouthed off to some woman who thought we had overturned some flowers on her back porch. We didn't do it but got blamed."

Mina's eyes popped. "You used to hang in The Cove?"

Her mother shook her head. "I wouldn't call it hanging. I only went twice. After that second time, it got back to your grandmother that me and these girls were 'making trouble' and she and your grand-father stopped me from hanging with that girl. I forget her name."

"Inez," Mina's dad volunteered.

"Oh yeah, that's it," Mina's mother said, laughing.

"You too, daddy?" Mina said.

He laughed. "I had a few friends from The Cove. But I wasn't a bad ass like your mother, vandalizing folks' yard and whatnot."

Mina's mom rolled her eyes. She dismissed Jackson's comment with a chuckle.

"Anyway," her mom said. "Del Rio Bay is a small city. You never know who knows whom. So don't go showing off."

Mariah Mooney's attempt at regaining her seriousness came off as a half-raised eyebrow and a smirk.

"Remember our rules," Mina's dad said. His voice, stern, had that definite "I mean it" ring to it. "And make sure you listen to Mr. Phillips. You'll probably have fun meeting some of Jacinta's friends."

Mina nodded, still trying to imagine her mom kicking it in the projects.

She couldn't put together the image of her Donna Karan–suited mom, hair always styled, tipping in her high heels with that of some teen chick knocking over someone's flowers and making the dash.

Está Loco

"Everyone knows I'm in over my head."
—The Fray, "Over My Head (Cable Car)"

As the bus rumbled toward DRB High the next morning, Mina was one part excited about the sleepover on Friday (if her mother could roll in The Cove, Mina certainly could) and one and a half parts scared out of her mind (*shootings!*). She let her parents' ease with the sleepover take the lead and tucked the fright away for later thoughts. For now, she had some teasing to do.

She still couldn't believe Jacinta's father was calling people about the sleepover, only one day after the group had met at Kelly's.

Pressed much, Cinny?

JZ and Jacinta sat in the seat in front of Mina and Michael. JZ was talking Jacinta's ear off. Mina waited for a pause in the conversation. When it seemed JZ would talk forever, Mina propped her elbows on the back of their seat and peeked her head over.

"Ahem," she said loudly, pretending to clear her throat.

"Yeah, next time ask him if he remembers when we were balling up at the courts in Meade, that day," JZ said. "We were on the same team."

"He might," Jacinta said. "He's always playing ball all over the place. Seems like he knows anyone who plays on any team in the county."

Mina inched closer to JZ's ear. "AHEM!"

JZ looked back at her. "Yeah?"

Mina's eyes darted toward Jacinta. "I need to tell Cinny something."

Jacinta scooted over to the window and turned in the seat so she could look directly at Mina. "What's up?"

"Your dad called mine yesterday," Mina said, grinning.

"Did he?" Jacinta frowned. "What's so funny about that?"

"You've already started planning for your sleepover," Mina pointed out, still smiling ear-to-ear. "Admit it. You're kind of feeling the bobble head 'burb set . . . just a little." She sang, "Youu, doonn't hate us-sss."

There was a playful glint behind Jacinta's exaggerated eye roll. "Girl, please." Jacinta sucked her teeth. "I had to check his work schedule, make sure he didn't have to work early Saturday. That's the only reason I told him the next morning."

"Uh-huh, sure," Mina teased. "You probably called him up all excited because you finally made some friends here in the 'burbs."

Jacinta waved Mina off. "We not rolling like that, yet."

"So what are ya'll talking about?" JZ said.

"The next sleepover is at Cinny's house," Mina said.

Michael's morning drowse wore off and he joined Mina in talking over the seat.

"What? Mina finally making her first trip to The Cove?" Michael said.

Mina leaned back long enough to elbow him in the side.

"That should be interesting," JZ said.

"Dag. I didn't realize this was your big debut to the projects, Mina," Jacinta said, the sarcasm obvious.

Mina shot JZ then Michael an annoyed glare. Now Jacinta would probably think Mina was going into the sleepover with a closed mind. And it wasn't that her mind was exactly closed, but Mina definitely had some fears. Not that she planned on sharing. She prayed

JZ and Michael didn't bring up the whole "what do you do when they start shooting" incident.

"Yeah, true, I've never been to The Cove," Mina said, then eased into her white lie. "But it's not a big deal. I don't know why Michael and JZ"—she turned and gave Michael a hard look, then nudged JZ's head as she said his name, hoping they got the message to let it go—"are making so much over it."

"I'm not making it a big deal," JZ said. "Just saying it will be interesting. Not like Cinny would be surprised that you mostly stay on your side of the DRB Bridge . . . except when you're hitting the mall."

"Whatever, Jay," Mina sniffed.

"I'm not making a big deal, either," Michael said. He chuckled. "But now I see where Lizzie must have been coming from last night."

Mina whirled around in the seat, The Cove forgotten for a second. What was Michael talking about?

"What do you mean?" Mina said. She sat back. "Where did you and Lizzie go last night?"

"Nowhere. She IM'ed me . . ." Seeing Mina's eyes bug, Michael added quickly, "About costumes for her audition."

For a second Mina thought Lizzie had gone running to Michael to complain about her. But it was just theater stuff. Mina's eyes relaxed. She ignored the quick sprint of her heart.

"Yeah, she mentioned that you wanted her to wear my boots," Mina said. "So what do you mean, where Lizzie was coming from? What did she say?"

Michael tried shrugging it off. "That ya'll had a disagreement."

JZ turned in the seat, facing Michael and Mina. "What? You mean the best, best friends forever beefing?"

Mina groaned, surprised Lizzie had told Michael. Jacinta had now joined JZ and was turned in the seat facing her and Michael. Mina eyed them wearily, unsure how to ask Michael exactly what he knew.

She didn't have to. No surprise, Michael offered his opinion.

"Lizzie was definitely bummed about it," Michael said. "And the whole thing sounds crazy being that ya'll so close."

Irritation and jealousy tore at Mina. Why did Lizzie have to go and vent to Michael?

Now Mina fully regretted not IM'ing Lizzie when she had the chance. Lizzie had already put her spin on the story and Michael was siding with her.

"Anyway, so now you going to The Cove for this sleepover and I kind of see what Lizzie was saying," Michael said. "Has our little boogee princess gone ghetto on us?"

"Well, what are ya'll fussing about?" JZ asked.

"Nothing," Mina said, distracted by JZ's question. She was annoyed that Michael hadn't bothered to IM her last night to get her side. "What are you talking about me going ghetto?"

"Lizzie says you are, and I quote, 'all up Jacinta's butt.'" He chuckled, shaking his head.

Jacinta snorted softly.

"What?! She said that?" Mina's eyes were huge with anger and hurt. "It's not even like that. And really, this wasn't even about Cinny. It was about her boyfriend."

"Wait? Ya'll got into it after me and Raheem left?" Jacinta asked.

Mina nodded.

"Even after I told her how Raheem just a Trojan fan through and through?" Jacinta asked.

Mina nodded again. She didn't want to go into too much detail. But the last thing Mina wanted was Jacinta hating on her best friend from a wack first impression.

"Lizzie was just freaked 'cause Raheem caught her off guard

when he was gritting on me." Mina poked hard at the seat toward JZ, like he was to blame. "I was defending ya'll."

JZ threw his hands up in surrender. "Uh-ah, don't put me in it."

"No, I mean I was just telling Raheem that our team was hot this year," Mina said. "Anyway he gave me this look and Lizzie took it wrong."

Jacinta pursed her lips and shook her head. "I told her he didn't mean any harm."

Even though Mina was already thinking ahead to what she was going to say when she saw Lizzie in Lit class, she scurried to defend her best friend. "Yeah, I told her that. It wasn't a big deal . . . it's not like we beefed about it all night or anything."

"Lizzie wasn't clowning anybody," Michael said, he made it a point to look at Jacinta when he said it, then turned to Mina. "She wrote just kidding when she made that comment about you jocking Jacinta. It seem like ya'll just disagree. It's not like this is the first time you don't see things the same, right?"

Jacinta shrugged. "Your girl need grow a sense of humor."

She sat back down in the seat, interest lost in the conversation.

"I can't believe Lizzie said I was all up Cinny's butt," Mina said, making her voice low so only Michael could hear. She was glad for the bus's usual chatter. "The way she went on about Raheem, you would think I had asked her to commit a drive-by with me instead of just hang out with someone new."

"Okay. Somebody tell me the story, please," JZ said, straining to hear.

"It's *not* a big deal," Mina said, loudly. She made frantic eye motions at the back of Jacinta's head, willing JZ to leave it be.

JZ got the message. He rolled his eyes.

"Must be if ya'll both chewing Mike's ear about it," JZ said before sitting back down.

Mina leaned over to Michael and whispered in his ear. "Lizzie thinks Jacinta's boyfriend looks like a gangster." She leaned back to ensure Michael heard her. He nodded. She leaned back in again, her head close to Michael's, and kept her voice low. "She acted like he was going to jack me right there in the open at the mall Saturday and I called her on it and said she was overreacting."

Taking Mina's cue, Michael kept his voice hushed as he admonished her. "Like you'd hang out with the dude yourself. Come on, Mina."

Mina shot back, "Michael, I don't know anything about the boy."

Mina sat up for a second to see if Jacinta was paying attention. Luckily, JZ had struck up a new conversation with her. Their voices mixed in with the rest of the conversations flowing. Mina hunkered back down, keeping her voice low but above a whisper. "What, because he from the projects, he not the type of person I'd roll with?" In a childish one-up she added, "Since the next sleepover is at Cinny's father's place in The Cove, you and Lizzie are both wrong. I would and will hang out with Raheem!"

She rolled her eyes as she folded her arms.

Michael touched her shoulder. "I'm not trying to choose who was right or wrong between ya'll," he said. "I know that's your girl. And I was just joking, that day, when I said Lizzie would go back to the other side."

Mina's funk robbed her of the joy of Michael admitting he was wrong. Who knew when she'd hear that again?

He gave her shoulder a comforting squeeze, "I think it's cool that ya'll have never let color interfere with your friendship. So just squash this and make up. Because who else will set a good example of how to be the best darn friends in the world?"

Mina tried to let Michael's teasing cheer her up.

"Look, you're not even used to hanging out with anybody from The Cove," Michael said, gently. "So you know Lizzie's not. Cut her a break."

Mina started to object. But Michael was right. Del Rio Bay's projects were mild compared to its counterparts in D.C. or Baltimore, but it was still different from the upper-middle-class subdivisions she kept to. Arguing that would be futile.

"Friends beef, Mi," Michael lectured. "Maybe it's a little harder this time, because it's the first time you all saw things differently because of race . . . but it's still just a difference in opinion."

Tripping!

"What I did was wack, but you don't get your man
back like that."
—Ghostface Killah (ft. Ne-yo), "Back Like That"

Later, during lunch, Mina and Michael rehashed the morning's conversation for JZ, who insisted that Mina owed him big since he'd missed out on the original recount of the mall argument because he was keeping Jacinta occupied.

In the end, JZ agreed with Michael. It was nothing more than a difference in opinion.

"Mike is right, ya'll need to lay this one down and make up," were JZ's last words.

Michael's words made sense. JZ's advice was on point.

Mina knew it.

She promised herself she was going to let it go. And was half convinced that if Lizzie hadn't been at Lines for lunch, they would have had a good laugh over the whole thing. But all of that flew out of her mind the second Lizzie walked into Lit class.

Mina waited until Lizzie sat down. She took a quick look to make sure Ms. Qualls was still in the hallway, ushering students in.

"How was lun . . ." Lizzie got out before Mina lit into her. "Why did you tell Mike that I'm all up Jacinta's butt?"

Lizzie's face froze for a second and Mina took smug satisfaction in her sneak attack. "It wasn't like that," Lizzie said. She took her seat and swiveled to face Mina. "I said it in a joking way . . . kind of."

"Kind of?" Mina said, her voice frosty.

"That part was a joke. But the reason I said it wasn't."

Mina's face fell and hurt replaced the icy tone. "Why would you even joke me like that?"

Lizzie threw her hands up. "I'm sorry. I'm tired of hearing about the soc project. It's worse than your countdown. Whenever we talk it always ends up back at the same conversation."

"You could have just told me that," Mina said.

Lizzie's eyebrows stretched. "I did!"

"When?"

"Saturday night and you got all mad, then went to sleep," Lizzie said.

"I don't remember . . ." The first bell rang over Mina's words, bringing the teacher back into the room. Mina lowered her voice into a fierce whisper. "My bad! I'll just stop talking about the soc class."

Lizzie turned to face the front of the room. She whispered back. "Don't be dramatic, Mi."

"Who me?" Mina said sarcastically. "Never."

Lizzie swiveled back around to face Mina again. Anger and confusion flicked in her green eyes.

"I don't get you," Lizzie said. "How is it after one sleepover with Jacinta, you're defending her boyfriend like you guys are best friends?"

Students filtered in, closing in around Mina and Lizzie.

"This isn't just about Raheem." Mina crossed her arms and laid them on the desk, pushing herself closer to Lizzie. She spoke in a rushed tone. "When was the last time I tripped because one of your weirdo theater peeps popped up at the mall while we were hanging out?"

"Weirdo?!" Lizzie cried.

The boy seated in front of Lizzie turned around and frowned.

Mina rushed on. "How many times do I get hot when conversation tick tocks back and forth to the latest production or costume drama or whatever? Ummmm . . ." She squinted at the ceiling, pretending to think it over before coming back with a strong, "None!" Mina's eyebrows raised in a triumphant take that.

"So you think my friends are weird just because they're not into shopping and cheerleading and being a glam, spam, or hot ham?" Lizzie spat.

Normally, Lizzie's rhyming comeback would send the two into a fit of giggles. Instead, Mina rolled her eyes. She remained on the defensive.

"You know I hate the glams as much as you. And the people I'm talking about aren't weird *because* they're into theater. I'm sure they were weird wayyy before all that."

Lizzie threw her up her hands. "I give up . . ."

The second bell rang, forcing Lizzie to wrap up the bizarre discussion. "I have auditions and other 'weird' stuff to get ready for," she said, then leaned in, so her words weren't lost in the room's growing noise. "You know what? I don't care who you hang with, Mi."

I Bet Her House Has Roaches

Mina dragged into the cafeteria the next day. In a way, she was relieved that Lizzie had Line for Lunch and wouldn't be there. But she'd be lying to pretend the ache in her belly was a yearning for cafeteria food. The ongoing argument with Lizzie had her sick.

Other than getting into back and forth with JZ, which was all the time and never serious, or having Michael get on her nerves always wanting to be right, Mina had never been in a fight with Lizzie, Michael, or JZ.

A fight.

That's definitely what this had become.

Mina's stomach roiled and suddenly the cafeteria's usual stench was ten times worse.

Apparently, her day wasn't going to get any better. Jessica was runway-walking her way toward Mina. Mina was surprised to see she was alone.

Before Mina could make it to the table where Michael was sitting with Kelly, Jessica stopped in front of Mina, legs wide, hands on her hips.

Mina seriously wondered if Jessica thought a herd of photographers were following her. Did the girl never not strike a pose?

"Mina, I need to talk to you," Jessica said.

Mina met Jessica's gaze but said nothing.

"Look, I need you to switch weekends with Jacinta." Jessica tossed her hair. "Just tell her that all along you really wanted your sleepover to be the second one. I'm sure she wouldn't care."

"Jessica, she's already made the plans," Mina said. She glanced beyond Jessica. Michael was looking her way. A smile played on his lips.

Mina fought the urge to roll her eyes.

"Yeah, I know. Her father called and talked to my mom last night," Jessica said. She rolled her eyes. "My mom actually said she thought this would be a great learning experience."

"Well, I think Jacinta might actually be looking forward to it," Mina said. "It's her turn and I'm not going to ask her to switch. Besides it's Tuesday. The plans are made."

"I heard people deal drugs right on the street corners," Jessica sniffed.

Mina thought back to what little JZ and Michael shared with her over the years about The Cove. She had no idea if what Jessica said was true or not. But it sounded like an exaggeration. She came back with a simple, not very convincing, "I doubt it."

"Have you ever been?" Jessica challenged.

"No. But neither have you," Mina said. She shrugged. "I'm just saying, it's not all bad. I know people there."

Mina hoped Jessica wouldn't ask who. It came out sounding like she knew lots of people in The Cove. She'd probably look crazy only naming Michael's great aunt.

But Jessica only turned up her nose. "Whatever," she said. "Remember last year they found that dead body there?"

Mina nodded. Of course, she remembered. It was all she'd thought about since Sunday—the dead body and the article. They sprung to mind no matter how often she tried to insert her parent's assurances in their place. .

"I bet her house has roaches," Jessica said, twisting her mouth in disgust. "You know they could crawl in our bags and we wouldn't even know it."

"Jessica, I'm not thrilled about it, either." Mina winced at the admission. In that instant, it occurred to her that this conversation could get back to Jacinta completely twisted. This was Jessica she was talking to. But it was out there. Mina finished her thought. "But, who knows, we might have a good time."

"Okay, none of these sleepovers are my idea of a good time," Jessica spat. Incredibly, her voice softened. "Just tell Jacinta you want to hold the sleepover this weekend. She'd probably switch, if *you* suggested it."

The thought of using the request—request nothing, Jess was practically begging—as a way to blackmail Jess into inviting her into the café danced across Mina's mind.

Well, well, well, she had something Jessica wanted. Or at least Jessica seemed to think Mina had the power to make Jacinta switch.

In the end, her dislike for Jess won out.

"I'm not going to ask Cinny to switch," Mina said. "I don't know why you think she'd switch just because I ask her to anyway."

Jessica's eyes went flat.

"You're right," she said. "I have no idea why I thought you'd suddenly bother to be useful."

Jessica brushed past Mina. She swung the café door open so violently it made a huge clang against the double-thick plexiglass.

A few people stared, startled by the noise, before going back to their lunch.

Mina stood rooted for a second, a tiny smile curling the edges of her mouth.

She felt a tickle of victory.

It felt soooo good to refuse Jessica.

Thanks to Jessica, surviving lunch had been easier than Mina expected. Instead of spending the lunch period worrying about her fight with Lizzie, Mina gave Michael and Kelly a blow-by-blow account of her convo with Jessica. In truth, retelling the conversation part was pretty short. Mina spent most of the time gushing about how great it felt to chop Jessica's ego down a peg with a simple "not gonna do it."

It didn't escape Mina that Kelly's response was only a low-key chuckle. She didn't join Michael and Mina in making fun of Jessica and her America's Next Top Model flare.

It made Mina feel bad for enjoying it so much. Their assignment was to better understand each other, not add on reasons to dislike.

But Kelly didn't have a history with Jessica. Mina did, thank you very much.

It wasn't until the bell rang and she scooped her books up to head to Lit class that the reality of facing Lizzie hit Mina.

What was she going to say?

Could she drop all the madness if Lizzie acted like everything was cool?

Should she give acting like everything was fine a shot first?

Mina stepped into the classroom, saw Lizzie wasn't there, and headed to her seat.

Just as she sat down, Lizzie came in.

Mina's heart boom-boomed and she took a few quick breaths to expel her anxiety. Still uncertain what she was going to say, Mina opened her mouth to break the ice when Lizzie turned in her chair and said, "Hey, my audition is tomorrow."

Mina smiled. "Right. I almost forgot."

"I'm not surprised," Lizzie said in a flat voice.

Mina's eyebrows furrowed as if to process exactly what she'd heard. But Lizzie talked on, disrupting her thoughts.

"Is it a big deal if I borrow your fencing boots?" Lizzie asked.

Still surprised at Lizzie's snipe, Mina only nodded.

"If you bring them to school tomorrow, just give them to Michael," Lizzie said. "He'll make sure I get them after school."

"Okay, wait . . . what do you mean, you're not surprised?" Mina said when she was finally able to speak.

Lizzie's shoulders fell as she sighed. "You had the soc project on your mind when I told you about the audition outfit Saturday. So I figured you probably had already forgotten." Lizzie shrugged.

"Well . . ."

"Mina, I'm not being a bitch," Lizzie said. "I just wanted to borrow the boots and figured you didn't know my audition was tomorrow."

"Well I didn't . . . I mean I did but forgot," Mina lied. She had no idea auditions were this week. Normally Mina and Lizzie knew each other's schedule inside out. Mina had never felt so far out of the loop on her best friend's life.

"Look, don't worry about the boots," Lizzie said.

"No. You can borrow them. It's not a big deal," Mina said.

"Thanks," Lizzie said. She faced the front of the room without another word.

Go Time!

"I wish I was home. I wish I was back there."
—Stephanie Mills, "Home"

The next morning, Mina chucked the fencing boots at Michael.

"Dag! What's up with you?" Michael said, juggling as the long boots slipped from his grasp.

"Lizzie told me to give you those," Mina snapped.

"Seriously, ya'll still haven't let this mess go?" Michael rolled his eyes.

"There's nothing to let go," Mina sniffed. "She asked to borrow the shoes and I'm letting her."

Michael stuffed the boots in his backpack. He looked up the road and saw Jacinta heading their way. This was her second time walking to their stop to catch the bus. Michael rushed his words. "Mina, I can't sit here and claim to know exactly why you or Lizzie letting this thing get nasty," he said. He head-checked once more. Jacinta was only a few seconds away. His words tumbled together. "But ya'll need to stop the madness. Maybe you should try getting Lizzie together with you and Jacinta or whoever. Did you ever think that maybe she just a little jealous?"

Mina nodded. But the truth was it hadn't occurred to her.

Jealous?

It kind of made sense. Well, Mina could fix that.

As Jacinta approached, Michael switched conversations. "Yeah, I told Lizzie these boots are gonna be hot on her. Hey, Jacinta."

Jacinta joined their huddle. "Hey."

"Hey. Are you down for pizza tomorrow?" Mina asked. She glanced at Michael. He nodded in approval.

"O'Reilly, Elizabeth," the casting director called, eyeing her clipboard. She scanned the auditorium for the owner of the name.

Lizzie stood too quickly at the sound of her name. Her head swam. She took a deep breath to silence the butterflies in her stomach. *Butterflies!* It was such a stupid way to describe the anxiety she felt right now. It was hardly anything as pleasant as butterfly wings fluttering. Instead, her stomach had turned into a dryer, flip-flopping a hot load of laundry over and over. She moved slowly toward the stage, pushing down the urge to be sick.

"You're up next. Go on back," the casting director instructed.

The eyes of the judges were on her as she walked backstage. She could feel them appraising her, taking inventory of her every move, every trait.

Did they have a taller girl in mind? A thinner girl? Or maybe a bigger girl?

To have hips or a little junk in my trunk, Lizzie thought, cursing her thin, long-legged torso.

The heat in her belly intensified.

Thank God auditions were closed. She couldn't take people, other than the judges, gawking at her right now. A record twenty-five girls had auditioned for Dorothy. She was the last to audition thanks to her hasty scribbling of her name on the sign-up sheet seconds before Mr. Collins collected them off the auditorium door Monday morning.

Lizzie wearily eyed the only other girl backstage preparing to go on stage. In full costume, blue gingham dress, long pigtails and all, she really did look like Judy Garland as Dorothy. It's just the totally wrong look for this particular version of the story, Lizzie thought with smug satisfaction.

A quiver of pleasure ran through her. She was so glad Michael talked her into donning the miniskirt, beret, and Mina's boots for auditions. Getting her into a mini for school was out of the question. But for auditions she did what she had to. If nothing else, she looked the part.

Lizzie refused to dwell on the fact that she'd gotten the boots through Michael rather than from Mina directly.

Maybe she had been bitchy yesterday.

Lizzie could have easily asked Mina to bring the boots to Lit class today. She was just sick of arguing. No doubt, something else would have incited another round of bickering if they said more than two words to one another.

Earlier that day in Lit, all she and Mina had said was "hey."

Hey!

Lizzie squeezed her eyes shut on the image.

The Dorothy of Oz–looking girl suddenly broke the silence. "Who are you going for?"

"Dorothy," Lizzie answered.

The girl looked Lizzie's outfit up and down. With a skeptical sniff, she replied stiffly, "Well, good luck."

Lizzie sniffed back, "Yeah, break a leg."

Wannabe! The only thing worse than a wannabe was a wannabe without a clue. Lizzie sent another silent thank you up to the Gods for her own hip-hop fab costuming. A little research goes a long way.

"Karen Wells," the casting director called out, jolting Lizzie from the premature celebration.

The Dorothy of Oz–looking girl walked out smiling broadly and launched into a dramatic rendition of "Somewhere over the Rainbow."

Lizzie watched intently, sizing up her immediate competition. Karen's voice wasn't bad, but she looked robotic. Opera wouldn't have sounded one bit odd coming from her mouth.

"You all ready?" a voice whispered from behind.

Startled, Lizzie whirled around. Lila was grinning at her. She exhaled loudly to blow off the nervousness, "Yeah, ready as I'm going to be."

Lila peeked out at the girl on stage and discounted her quickly. "She's the least of your worries. Knock 'em dead!"

Lizzie smiled weakly. With the weird, sort of creepy approval of Lila in her back pocket, she went back to watching the girl onstage. It was almost time.

She shut her eyes tight and breathed deeply until her heart beat steady and calm.

Drawing on the sounds of *The Wiz* she'd listened to over the last two weeks, Lizzie let her mind melt her into Dorothy, a girl from the projects thrust into a land full of strange people so unlike her that she longed to go home.

Her name was called to take the stage. Go time!

She mumbled a quick prayer, crossed herself and walked onstage under the blinding, but comforting, stage lights. Slowly they melted her doubts and anxiety. Feeling as if she were the only one in the auditorium, she nodded in the direction of the woman on piano, closed her eyes, and let the music float over her head for a second.

She looked out into the space where an audience would be and launched softly into her song, "When I think of home I think of a place, where there's love overflowing."

NeVer Speak to My Enemies

> *"Whatcha doing to me? You're confusing me."*
> —Alicia Keys, "Karma"

Mina stared a hole in the Ria's door, willing Lizzie to walk through it. Michael, JZ, Jacinta, and Kelly talked around her. Mina hoped to show Lizzie that Kelly and Jacinta were fun to be around. She was going to make it work. If she could get two hard-headed nine-year-old boys to become friends with the girl they used to call "vanilla chip" behind her back, she could certainly get Lizzie on board with quiet Kelly and all bark, no bite Jacinta.

Now she waited, anxiety prickling at her, wondering if Lizzie had decided she wasn't up for pizza and cliquing. Not like it would be the first tradition broken since the school year started.

Jessica made her way toward their table, speaking only to JZ as she passed.

"Hi, Jason."

"What's up, Jessica?" JZ said.

Jacinta and Mina gave each other a look. When Jessica was out of earshot, Mina threw a napkin at JZ. "Never speak to my enemies."

He threw it back at her. "I can't keep up with that list."

Jacinta laughed. "Umph, I heard that."

"Be quiet, Cinny. Whether you like it or not, I took you off that list."

"I don't know if that's good or bad," Jacinta said.

"She your enemy too, Kelly?" JZ asked.

Kelly looked at Mina and Jacinta's eager faces, then glanced at Jessica at a corner table with her friends.

"Don't go all diplomatic on us, Kelly," Mina warned.

"I wouldn't say enemy." Kelly shrugged. "That's the best I can do, Mina."

A laugh died in Mina's throat when she saw Lizzie come in. She wasn't sure if she should be looking serious like she wasn't having fun or what. She grew nervous as Lizzie walked to the table. There was definite confusion on Lizzie's face.

Michael patted the seat between him and Mina. "Liz-O, we kept your seat warm."

"Hey," Mina said, shyly at first then louder after hearing the meekness in her voice. "Hey, Liz."

Lizzie threw up a noncommittal wave that could have been for anyone or everyone at the table and sat down.

"So how did the big audish go yesterday?" Mina asked.

"Fine, I guess. I mean, I didn't choke," Lizzie said.

"Mina said you've been singing and acting since you were little," Kelly said.

Mina sent a silent "way to go" across the galaxy, thankful that Kelly started a conversation. *See Lizzie, Kelly isn't freakishly quiet.*

"Yup. I've been acting forever, feels like." With a deliberate swivel of her head, she looked to Mina. "Apparently, I don't act well enough at the right times."

Mina's mouth gaped open.

Michael jumped in. "So when will they post the cast?"

"Tomorrow night," Lizzie said. She eyed Mina wearily, unsure what to say.

It was starting to feel like she was onstage all the time, except when it came to Mina she didn't have the script.

Mina groaned. "They post it tomorrow?"

Whenever Lizzie was waiting for a cast list to be announced or posted, she and Mina came to the Ria to wait it out. It was one of the few times Lizzie let Mina prattle on as long as she kept Lizzie's mind off her fate. But Mina couldn't do it tomorrow. It would be the first time she wouldn't be there to soothe Lizzie's nerves with her overly bright best friend predictions. "You know you've got this," "Girl, this part is all you," and anything else Mina thought Lizzie needed to hear.

Argument or not, Mina would have been there. She knew how nervous Lizzie got when the casting list came out.

"Oh, Liz, I can't be here," Mina said.

"Soc sleepover, right?" Lizzie said dryly.

Mina fidgeted in her chair. "Yeah. It's at Cinny's."

"Don't worry about it," Lizzie said.

"We have an away game tomorrow," JZ said.

"And I'll be with Mr. Collins getting ready for fittings," Michael said.

"It's not a big deal, you guys," Lizzie yelped. "I'll be fine."

A bright red burnish spread across her cheeks. She wasn't sure what was worse. Knowing you were going to be stood up by every one of your friends or having them admit, in front of strangers, they were going to stand you up. She felt like the world's sorriest charity case.

She wasn't in the mood for pizza anymore and was about to call it a day when Mina tugged at her French braid. "It sucks that I can't come tomorrow. I'm sorry. For real."

Lizzie couldn't form her mouth to say it was okay. Mina was the one always banging the friend rituals into all of their heads. Lizzie wasn't going to let her off the hook even though it felt good to have Mina sound sincerely sorry.

"Well, I guess eliminating prejudice is a *little* more important than whether I get the role of Dorothy," Lizzie said.

"Lizzie, I'm sure you're used to it. We all know how busy the Princess of The Woods is," Jacinta said.

"Of course," Lizzie said, going along with the joke.

"See, you're not going to let that go are you, Cinny?" Mina said.

"Nope."

"Alright. Well, shoot, don't hate. Yes, I'm a busy chick," Mina said. She popped her collar. "And as Kelly said . . ."

Mina paused and an invisible signal passed between her, Jacinta, and Kelly before they chorused, "Popularity ain't easy."

Their laughter barely made a dent in the Ria's noise level, but it cracked Lizzie's last ounce of patience. She could take the constant references to the sociology class. She could take Mina bitching about Jessica; that wasn't a new one. She could even take having their friends-only day invaded by the occasional outsider. But now they had inside jokes? That, she couldn't take.

Lizzie snatched her backpack from the back of her chair, knocking it down in the process, and stormed off, leaving the clique staring after her.

Are You Feeling Left Out?

"Don't push me. 'Cause I'm close to the edge."
—Grandmaster Flash, "The Message"

Twenty-four hours later, only a half hour stood in the way of knowing whether she'd join Bay Dra-da as a bit player or a star. Thirty more minutes to nitpick over every single flaw in her auditions and wonder if attending the LFL sessions had been worth skipping her daily midday meal for a week and a half.

Lizzie's stomach grumbled loudly, weighing in: one vote no.

She took a gnat bite from her slice of pizza and tried to shut off her brain. The usual comforting scents and sounds of Rio's Ria weren't doing anything to settle her nerves. She felt naked without the clique or even the comfort of knowing they would burst through the door, eventually.

She was still trying to forget her dramatic exit from yesterday. It hadn't ended the way she planned. Her neighborhood wasn't within walking distance of the Ria. So instead of leaving the table in a flurry of attitude and walking off her steam, all she could do was walk down a block, call her mom, and wait.

Mina had come after her immediately. Lizzie wanted to take comfort in that, but couldn't. She hadn't been in the mood and told Mina so. She just wanted a few minutes alone. But did Mina give her that time?

Yeah, but not before saying, in a voice so sickeningly patronizing it made Lizzie want to scream, "Liz, are you upset because Cinny and Kelly are black? Are you feeling left out?"

The first question Lizzie refused to acknowledge. Was she feeling left out? Uh, yeah and by the way, anyone would under the circumstances.

"If you're feeling left out, I'd understand," Mina had said.

The whole thing made Lizzie's blood boil. She had left Mina standing on the corner hollering after her.

The only reason Lizzie didn't explode was because Mina seemed convinced that this was somehow yet again a part of her sociology class—some sort of case of prejudice.

If it were, let Mina solve it. She was the one on a mission.

Lizzie shook the thoughts out of her head. This was not the time to think about that. She closed her eyes, not caring who might be looking, and tried to shut off her brain. She commanded silently then began chanting it under her breath.

"Shut off, shut off, shut off."

"Shut off what?" a voice asked.

Lizzie's eyes snapped open and focused in on Lila staring down at her. Three of her flunkies stood behind her, ogling Lizzie. Lila's superior stance made her feel like a peasant kneeling at the feet of a queen, but damned if she was going to show it. Still, Lila's raised eyebrow, pressed Lizzie to answer. "Just talking to myself."

"We can see that," Lila said, pausing for the expected giggling from her crew, who obliged.

Lizzie nearly burst a vessel forcing herself not to roll her eyes. Be good, Liz. No sense blowing it now, she thought.

"The audition list is about to go up. Want to walk with us?" Lila asked.

Lizzie looked around. There was not one thing she could use as an excuse. The thought of spending time with Lila and her yes-girls made sitting there alone even worse. Damn Mina for deserting her.

The only rituals Lizzie believed in were her audition rituals. Pep talk from Mina before auditions (didn't happen this time), Mina's chatter to keep her mind off auditions afterward (again, nada).

If she didn't get this part . . .

Lizzie snapped back to Lila staring at her, refusing to think about failure. She stood up. "Yeah, why not."

Lila turned to the flunkies. "Can you guys go ahead? We'll catch up."

They scattered on cue, making Lizzie smile and wonder if they rehearsed the quick move.

Lila waited until the flunkies were at the door before she began to walk, slow and deliberate as she spoke. "I wanted to let you know that, even though I can't reveal what all went on at casting, the judges were impressed with you and felt you had a lot of potential."

Lizzie's brain froze. It was over. She hadn't gotten the part. People with "potential" don't get lead roles.

She stammered, "Thank you."

Lila's mouth was still moving but Lizzie couldn't hear her through the white noise buzzing in her ear. When she tuned back in, Lila was saying, "No matter what happens in this production, they think you're going to be a great addition to theater." Lila frowned. "Are you okay?"

Lizzie nodded mechanically, her needle still stuck on "potential."

They stepped outside onto the sidewalk, waiting for the light signaling them to cross the street. The road in front of Rio's Ria was jammed with rush-hour traffic and Lila raised her voice to be heard.

"We had a great turnout for auditions," Lila said.

Lizzie nodded along. She let the cool evening air refresh her while gazing over at the high school. Against the setting sun and without students streaming from its doors, it loomed across the street like a haunted mansion. Through its doors was the list that would set the tone for the rest of her semester. Had school really only started three weeks ago?

It felt like forever.

Needing to satisfy her curiosity, that this was all really happening, she turned to Lila, suddenly bold. "Why have you been so nice to me?" Her words clung together as she rambled. "I mean, I know we've seen each other around theater camp every year, but you know . . . it's not like we ever hung out. Why have you been encouraging me? Supporting me in going for the lead? Why?"

She made herself look Lila in the face.

Lila flipped her hair theatrically. "You are such a frosh, Lizzie. Don't go getting all sappy on me! The truth is you remind me of me."

Lizzie scrunched her eyebrows. Was that supposed to be a good thing?

"So what, is this some kind of adopt-a-freshman thing?" she asked.

"If I were going for the lead role in this production I wouldn't have been as friendly," Lila admitted, in a clipped, haughty voice, en-suring Lizzie remembered she was the star and Lizzie was just a wannabe. "I thought Bay Dra-da's lead should go to someone else with that hunger for the spotlight. I've seen you in action. I knew you had it."

Lizzie nodded slowly, still uncertain. "Thanks."

Lila whispered, "But friendly advice lasts only as long as the next set of auditions. Watch your back for the spring production."

Just then the light turned red, halting traffic and giving the girls the go to cross.

Lila stepped off the sidewalk and right on cue, the flunkies came out of nowhere, babbling, falling into step.

Lizzie swallowed fresh air in gulps. Her footsteps were tentative as she made her way onto Del Rio High's campus behind Lila and her crew. Drowning out the flunkies chatter, she gave herself the silent version of Mina's traditional pep talk. She could do this. It didn't matter what part she got. This was her first year, she had to be reasonable about the competition.

Lila startled her by stopping abruptly and whispering, "No matter what part you get, just rip it. Trust me, it won't go unnoticed."

Lizzie stood immobile for a second, while Lila and the flunkies whisked inside.

Reluctantly, Lizzie reached for the auditorium door. Her clammy hands slipped on the cold steel handle. She gripped it and stepped into the dimly lit hallway. The rest of the school was darkened to discourage people from wandering through.

People milled around the walls, searching for their names on the posted lists. Some walked away elated; others, dejected.

Lizzie chose a list closest to the door, in case she had to race her tears. She wanted to hit the doors before they hit her face. Squinting up at the list through the hallway's gloom, she started from the bottom—bit parts, munchkins, Emerald City people, all the parts she didn't want.

Her heart did the happy dance. Her name wasn't there. She allowed herself a tiny grin then gathered the courage to peer up again.

Her eyes skidded side to side, frantically roaming the list for her name under Glinda, the Good Witch. Nothing!

Nothing?

Her throat closed and her breath whistled through her nose. Panic set in. She rubbed absently at her chest.

People pushed and shoved their way around her toward the list.

Lost in a sea of fear, she stared at the name under Glinda. Her eyes refused to move any farther up the list. She couldn't take not seeing her name under Dorothy. The thought filled her with steely bitterness.

She was good. She deserved the lead.

Lines for Lunch or not, Lila's pet or not—she ripped that audition and knew it. If her name wasn't under Dorothy . . . she didn't know what she'd do.

Her knees buckled and she locked them tight, straightening up. She would not faint. "It would take all four years of high school to live that one down," she muttered.

A cheerful voice in her head reasoned that if she didn't make it, there was always the spring production. It sounded like Mina.

"Shut up!" Lizzie snapped, out loud, startling the two people standing next to her. They threw her puzzled looks then returned to jockeying for better angles.

This is it, just do it, she commanded herself. Her eyes felt like balls of lead as they rolled slowly upward to the top of the list—the star spot. They remained fixed there as she took a deep breath and wiped away a tear.

What, No Momma Jokes?

"I'm in the hood. It's all good."
—DMX, "Where the Hood At?"

Mina rested her head against the seat. The week weighed heavily on her mind. She and Lizzie were barely talking. She'd gotten a C on her first Lit essay and her parents had promptly swiped her phone and prohibited her from being online for the week. And as much as she wanted to take comfort in her parents' attitude toward The Cove, Jessica had assaulted Mina at the cafeteria door again on Thursday with tidbits about the neighborhood in her campaign to prod Mina to switch weekends with Jacinta.

It felt good to refuse her, once again, until now.

As the black Expedition sailed over the DRB Bridge out of the county's suburbs and into Del Rio Bay's city limits, Mina's nerves buzzed.

The bass from Rihanna's S.O.S. thumped through the speakers.

Jacinta turned it up. "Yeeahhh, this my song!"

"Mine too," Mina said. She bounced her shoulders to the dance track letting go of her nervous energy. "Did Phil produce this, Kell?"

"I don't think, so," Kelly said.

Jacinta sang lustily. "S.O.S. please someone help me."

Mina joined in on the hook, rocking her head. "Y.O. U. are making this hard."

They belted out the last line together.

"Way to have my backup," Jacinta said. She thrust her palm flat toward the back and Mina dapped it up.

Kelly made pitiful eyes at Jacinta's father. "Sorry, Mr. Phillips. This is my fault. Since they stayed at my house they think they have talent."

Jacinta rolled her neck. "Who? I know I got golden tonsils."

"Which need to be removed," Kelly shot back, softly.

Kelly's cracks, more frequent now even though she still spoke like she had been raised in a public library, soothed Mina's uncertainty. Kelly had no anxiety about visiting The Cove. But then again, Kelly didn't know anything about the café either. Mina couldn't count on her sheltered outlook on the DRB. Plus, Kelly refused to judge. Mina admired that, but the soc class hadn't worked that much magic on her.

Jessica, ice-queen rigid near the other window, suddenly spoke up. "Mr. Phillips, does it bother you that you live in the projects?"

The singing died on Mina's lips. She sent a silent apology on behalf of the group with her eyes to Mr. Phillips in the rearview mirror and whispered to Jessica, "That's too personal."

"This project is about getting personal!" Jessica huffed. "Besides, how is it worse than you asking Kelly where her father was?"

"It's okay," Mr. Phillips assured Mina, his eyes friendly. "Now you'll see The Cove is just a neighborhood like your own." He steered them into a turn lane, handling the heavy truck smoothly, before looking back into the rearview mirror. "I know it's cool to glorify ghetto life as something to aspire to. But most people live in the projects because their circumstances haven't allowed them to live anywhere else. Right now, I'm one of those people."

"I hate when rappers talk about how great it is to be poor," Jessica said. "Especially since they only rap about it once they have money."

Mr. Phillips surprised Mina by laughing.

"Yeah, that's an interesting point," he said. He looked directly at

Jessica, his eyes darting back to the road as the truck pulled in and out of traffic. "But to answer your question, no. I don't care what others think of The Cove. The biggest difference between where you live and The Cove is the income made by the people living there."

"No. There's lots of crime there and it's not like that in my neighborhood," Jessica said.

Mina shot Jessica another look.

"Every neighborhood has its issues," Mr. Phillips said.

"Daddy, don't defend our block to her," Jacinta said. "Her mind is made up anyway."

"What have I said about The Cove that isn't true, Jacinta?" Jessica asked.

Mina and Kelly exchanged a nervous glance.

"What do you know about it, though?" Jacinta turned in her seat and glared. "I mean, besides what some newspaper says."

"So the newspaper is lying?"

Jessica's hazel eyes gleamed. Proof enough for Mina that the girl loved spewing evil vibes into the air.

"Anyone can take facts and then put them in any order they want. It doesn't mean the actual story ends up being true," Jacinta said.

"You're both right," Mr. Phillips said.

"Daddy don't try to be nice. Both of us can't be right," Jacinta pouted.

"Okay, wait a second, I'll show you how you're both right," he said.

He turned off the busy main road onto a long, lonely stretch of road surrounded by full, mature trees on either side that smothered what was left of the setting sun. Small pockets of light illuminated from three street lights, one at the entrance, one in the middle and one at the end of the strip.

Mina's stomach clenched when Mr. Phillips stopped the truck abruptly in a patch of darkness well beyond the lonely lamppost that served to "light" the middle section of the road. He turned the radio down and pointed to the heavily forested trees on the left.

"The trees go back four miles. If we walked into the woods . . ."

"But we're not, right?" Jessica asked, in a high-pitched wail.

Mr. Phillips's voice was parentally patient. "No, of course not, sweetie. Sorry if I'm scaring you girls. I just wanted to make a point."

The girls' eyes followed Mr. Phillips's pointing finger into the thick gnarl of trees.

"The Cove's property stops twenty feet into the trees. The other three and three quarters mile of woods belongs to the Del Rio Bay Mall."

"Ohhh," Mina said, recognition dawning. If they'd stayed straight instead of turning into The Cove, they would have been at the mall within minutes. Mina was comforted knowing the mall, a place she'd live at if she could, was on the other side of the woods.

Mr. Phillips nodded. "Last year, when a body was found, the headlines and story said it was found in The Cove. The truth was it was found in these woods about fifty feet from the mall, nearly three miles from The Cove."

The lines in Jessica's face went smooth with relief as Mr. Phillips finally pulled off. Mina eased back onto her seat, equally as glad to be away from the eerie quiet of the The Cove's entrance.

"That's why you're both right," Mr. Phillips said. "Yes, a body was found. But not in The Cove. Still the newspaper kept the focus on The Cove and its crime statistics."

The car emerged from the shady strip onto a sea of blacktop. "Just something to think about," Mr. Phillips said. "Most people who find trouble here are looking for it."

A jungle of building units sprouted from the tar-black streets. Twenty in all. Each had ten, two-level attached row homes, narrow, tall, and identical except for their different colored doors. The Cove was home to more than seven hundred people, some Hispanic but most black, all of them poor, at least by Del Rio Bay standards. And just like the name implied, the neighborhood was its own little inlet, well-hidden from the toney areas of the city. People could drive past the neighborhood a hundred times and never know it was there. But beyond the deserted entrance, the neighborhood vibrated. People walked the sidewalks, television sounds came from cracked windows and open doors, and laughter from nearby kids ebbed then flowed in rhythm, as they sang along to the thumping bass of a passing car.

The girls filed out of the truck then waited for Mr. Phillips to hand them their bags.

Three kids whipped out of a row home with a green front door, screaming Jacinta's name. They overtalked one another, anxious to be the first to get their hello in. Their excited voices drowned out The Cove's other melodies.

"Are you home all weekend?"

"Can you help me build my moat?"

"Metai was talking about me at school."

Jacinta's face glowed. She handed her bag to the tallest boy and addressed the last question, which came from her sister. "I told you stop stutting Metai. She just jealous of you." She waved her classmates in closer. "Hey ya'll, this is my sister Jamila and my brothers JJ and Jeremy."

Her siblings stared, overnight guests obviously a new concept to them.

"This is Mina, Kelly, and Jessica," Jacinta finished up.

A chorus of shy "hi's" went up from the group.

They walked inside the row home. Jacinta's sibs' chatter filled the entire house, which didn't take much. The first floor, living room/ kitchen small enough to fit in Kelly's foyer, was cramped but with a lived-in vibe that Kelly's large, quiet house could never give off. Warm brown faces of black art dotted the walls, a PlayStation spilled out of the entertainment center into the middle of the room, and the

TV's cartoon blather competed with JJ, Jamila, and Jeremy. The tiny room invited people to hang out on the oversized couch and one chair hugging the room's slim curves.

Taking it all in, Mina moved to the side to let Mr. Phillips through and tripped over Kelly's foot then Jessica's bag. She stumbled, trying to find a spot out of the way, but there was nowhere to go. Mina steadied herself against Kelly. Together with Jessica they stood glued at the shoulders, a mutated Siamese triplet blocking the way to the kitchen.

Jacinta peeled Jamila off her arms and led the girls up a narrow staircase. "Mila we'll catch up later," she promised her disappointed sis from the top of the stairs.

"That's so cute that she misses you," Mina said.

"Mila is my heart. She's only eleven. But we outnumbered in the house, so you know . . . us chicks gotta stick together," Jacinta said.

They stepped into Jacinta's room, once again crushed together, competing for space with the bunk bed, dresser, and desk.

Jessica took up residence in the corner next to the window, stock-still, touching nothing. A curtain snaked across her arm and she jumped, smacking herself silly.

"It's the curtain, girl," Jacinta said, not hiding her amusement.

"I thought it was a . . . a roach," Jessica said. She glanced down, double-checking her shoulder.

"Naw, that wasn't . . . but what's THAT?" Jacinta said.

Jessica danced in her spot. "What? Where?!" She brushed wildly at her hair and arms.

"That's wrong on so many levels," Mina said, her face struggling to stay somber.

"But it was funny, right?" Jacinta said. Her body shook with laughter as she piled the girls' bags inside her closet.

Jessica held her hand out. "I want to keep my bag out."

Jacinta threw it over without looking up.

Mina bent in for a closer look at a G-Unit poster behind the desk then stepped back, bumping heads with Kelly as she made her way to sit on the bed.

"My bad," Mina giggled. "I've never seen this one, Jacinta." She looked for somewhere to sit. Finding none, she stood in place in front of the desk. "Where'd you get it?"

"My aunt Jacqi is the Admin Assistant at *Sister2Sister* magazine. She always hooking me up with posters and stuff," Jacinta answered.

"You and your sister must be close," Kelly said from the bed.

"We are. She just started sixth grade. Not having me here every day is hard," Jacinta said, affection softening her usual no-nonsense edge. "Plus JJ is thirteen and Jeremy is eight, so . . . she's kind of stuck putting up with them, alone."

"So . . . well, if I ask this am I being nosy?" Mina said. She leaned against the desk chair.

Jacinta shrugged. She'd had less than a week to get used to the fact that the girls would see her home, meet her family, and ask their questions. On Sunday night, right after Kelly's sleepover, she told herself, "They'll be on my block. I can handle this." The next night, thinking about her tiny room and cramped row house and knowing her neighborhood looked nothing like any of theirs, she almost e-mailed Mina in a panic, asking if they could switch.

Even though, by Tuesday, everything was set to have it in The Cove, she actually wrote the e-mail to Mina and was about to send it when her Aunt Jacqi walked in for their nightly "how was your day" talk.

"Will you be home next weekend?" Jacinta asked.

"Yeah. Why?" Jacqi said.

"Because it's my turn to host this class sleepover and I'd rather do it here."

"Why?" Jacqi's voice had an edge. She was going to fuss if she didn't like Jacinta's answer.

"Because these girls are all so boogee, I don't want them turning up their nose at where I'm from," Jacinta said, the words gushing. "Don't get me wrong. I'm not ashamed . . ."

"Then have the sleepover at your father's."

"But . . ."

"Cinny, if they turn their nose up at it, it's just one obvious sign that ya'll probably aren't friends. Never will be," Jacqi said. "You grew up in The Cove. It's where you're from. Period. What friend would care about that?"

"I don't care what they think," Jacinta said, sounding more assertive than she felt. "We're not trying to be friends anyway. I just don't want to have to sit in class with them, knowing they looking down on me or feeling sorry for me or whatever."

"You can have the project here if you want," Jacqi said, walking to the door. "But that doesn't change where you're from. Now does it? Run . . . but you can't hide."

Every night after that, Jacinta started to feel less frightened. And by Friday morning, she was glad that for once the girls would be the fish out of water.

Aunt Jacqi's words clear in her head, Jacinta answered Mina. "I guess somebody gotta be the first. May as well be you, Princess."

"I never hear you talk about your mom," Mina said.

Before Jacinta could answer, JJ appeared at the front door. "Ya'll wanna play some DDR?"

"JJ, we kind of have homework to do," Jacinta said.

He frowned. "On a Friday? Dag, I'm glad I won't be going to Del Rio High."

"I wouldn't mind playing," Kelly said.

"Me either, really," Mina said.

They all looked at Jessica.

"I didn't come over here to play Dance Dance Revolution with your little brother, Jacinta," Jessica said.

"Maybe we'll play ya'll later, JJ," Jacinta said. She grabbed a jacket and headed for the door. "Come on, we may as well go out for a while."

"Go outside?" Jessica said.

"Yes, outside," Jacinta said, before bounding down the stairs.

Jessica cut her eyes at Mina. "All you had to do was ask her to switch. Now we're stuck rolling through the hood all night. You're useless." She stormed out of the corner past Mina and Kelly.

Mina made a face. She mocked Jessica, under her breath. "Guess I failed that test," she said.

"What test?" Kelly asked.

Mina shrugged. "The one where I should have been willing to do anything to win her approval."

"Good. You don't need her approval," Kelly said.

Mina nodded as they started down the stairs. But she wasn't completely convinced.

"Daddy!" Jacinta called. "Me and the girls rolling out."

Mr. Phillips came out of the kitchen. "It's a little after seven, so be home by nine." An or else lingered in his words.

"Daddy," Jacinta protested, already out the door.

Jamila ran over to him. "Can I go, Daddy?"

"No. Let your sister show her friends around."

Jacinta spoke gently to her sister through the screen door. "We'll do something together tomorrow, okay?"

Eyes moist with tears, Jamila nodded.

"Nine," her father said, once more.

The breeze, hinting at the chill that would sweep in upon full dark, rustled the thick forest of trees surrounding the complex, simultaneously muting the buzz of passing cars from the main road and ushering in the scent of greasy burgers from a nearby fast-food place.

Mina zipped up her yellow fake-fur middie vest, glad she hadn't listened to that voice that called her crazy for wanting to bring a jacket. She sank her hands into her pockets and fell in step beside Jacinta.

Even more people were out now, sitting on front stoops, hanging under street lights, and standing on the sidewalks talking. Jacinta shouted out to nearly everyone they passed, laughing off the ones who ribbed her with comments like, "Oh you back on the block, today, huh?" "Jamal let you come home again?" or "What are you doing home?" It seemed everyone knew Jacinta had defected to "the country."

Mina, Kelly, and Jessica faded to the background when Jacinta stopped to talk to two girls. The girls were loud and animated and kept sneaking peeks at the soc group.

"You meet any fine dudes since you been at DRH?" the short, thick girl asked.

Jacinta pursed her lips. "Like I'm looking."

"Umph, Raheem got your ass trained," the one with big hoop earrings said. "You can still look, Cinny."

"We holler at you when Sam-Well play ya'll," Thick girl said. "Maybe we can stay at your Aunt Jacqi's that night."

"Ooh now who you gon' root for?" Hoops said.

"You know Raheem would trip if I called myself cheering for the Blue Devils," Jacinta said.

The girls cackled, clapping and amen-ing Jacinta's comment.

"Alright. I catch up with ya'll at the court later," Jacinta said, motioning to her classmates to walk on.

"How come you didn't introduce us?" Kelly said. "Embarrassed of the bobble head 'burb girls?"

Jacinta laughed. "Not you putting me on blast, Kelly. Naw, I just don't need them up in my business."

"Seems like everybody already knows it," Jessica said, sour-faced. "What, did they post a sign announcing you were back today?" She pressed her folded arms closer to her chest not wanting anything in The Cove, not even the air, to touch her. Angry at Mina, still, she became testy and more irritable every second they moved deeper into the neighborhood. "I feel like everybody is staring at us."

"Yeah, we have this newsletter called the Ghetto Blaster. Me coming home for the weekend was headline news," Jacinta said with a roll of her eyes.

"Ghetto Blaster. Cute," Mina laughed.

Jessica's eyes darted side to side. She crowded in closer to Kelly. "It's too many people out here. What happens if someone starts shooting?"

Jacinta rolled her eyes. "Duck."

Jessica crouched and threw her arms over her head drawing the stares of four young dudes sitting on a car.

Jacinta laughed. "I didn't mean now. But you asked a stupid question and I gave you a stupid answer. If somebody starts shooting, duck."

Jessica stood stiff-backed and fluffed her hair. "That wasn't funny, Jacinta."

Jacinta pointed to the guys laughing in their direction. "They thought it was." Her pace quickened as she talked. "You think you're better than every single person here, but one thing is for sure, you just another black chick right now. Not mixed, black."

"Why does it kill you to admit that I'm mixed?" Jessica said, hazel eyes blazing.

"I don't care what you call yourself," Jacinta said. "At Del Rio High and in ya'll neighborhoods maybe you do stick out 'cause everybody else is white . . . but tonight, you just another black face in the crowd."

Jessica's face tightened. "I would hope anybody could see I'm *not* from here."

She winced when a couple going by overheard her and did a double-take.

"Okay, well just in case something go down and the cops roll up through here, I hope you have your my mom is white card," Jacinta said.

"Well, I love how many people are still out," Mina said. "By this time on a Friday night, The Woods is like a cemetery compared to here."

"Why did your dad send you to live with your aunt?" Kelly asked.

"The reason he gave or why I think he did it?" Jacinta said.

"Ummm . . . the reason he gave," Mina said.

Jacinta shivered as the breeze momentarily whipped around them. She'd thought a lot about what she was going to reveal to the girls. If someone asked her three weeks ago how much of her business she was going to give up, the answer would have been nothing. She didn't care if she had to make up stuff.

Lying or saying nothing didn't feel like options anymore. A lot had changed in the three weeks since school began. She stopped at the edge of a playground. The girls crowded around her.

"My father doesn't want me to become a hood rat," Jacinta said.

Kelly frowned. "I guess I should know what a hood rat is but . . ."

"Somebody who doesn't care about living anywhere else but the hood," Jacinta said. "My father expects me and my sister and brothers to want more."

"Well you seem pretty proud of your *hood* to me," Jessica said.

"I didn't say all that. Just 'cause I'm not trying to hide that I'm from here don't mean I want live here forever," Jacinta said.

Jessica looked around the rundown neighborhood. "I wouldn't be telling anyone I lived here."

"Good. The less we have in common the better," Jacinta snapped. She addressed Kelly and Mina, echoing Aunt Jacqi's words. "It's not like I can hide where I'm from."

"Good thing you're not ashamed. When your friend with the ghetto hoops shows up at a football game, trust me, everyone will know she's from either here or Del Rio Crossing," Jessica said, mentioning the DRB's only other housing project.

"So," Jacinta said, refusing to let Jessica's snobbery bait her.

"Even you aren't that tacky," Jessica chuckled.

Jessica was mouthing off, *being herself*. Even on Jacinta's turf, she couldn't stop playing the diva. But it didn't escape Mina that Jessica chose to stand near Kelly, the farthest point from Jacinta.

"Do you seriously believe that you all that with those zombie-cat eyes?" Jacinta said. "You skinny like a model. But trust, unless you walking down the runway with a paper bag over your grille nobody is rushing to snap your picture."

"Was that supposed to hurt my feelings?" Jessica said.

"I didn't think you had any." Jacinta scowled.

"Come on, you two," Kelly whispered. "Your voices are getting loud."

"Oh, like a fight in this neighborhood would draw attention," Jessica said. "It's . . ."

Mina cut in. "Cinny, where is your mom?"

"In rehab," Jacinta said. She answered quickly, like tearing off a Band-Aid. She knew someone would ask eventually and she'd decided she'd answer fast and honest. Jacinta let the rest of the details spill, quickly, working to keep her voice even and nonchalant. "She's been on and off drugs . . . mostly on since I was in kindergarten."

"What kind of drugs?" Jessica asked in a skeptical voice.

"What does that matter?" Mina frowned.

"It doesn't. I'm just curious," Jessica said.

"Crack." Jacinta let the word sift through the breeze. It was out there. She felt naked waiting on the girls' reaction, but also a sense of relief. She'd said it and the world was still spinning. Two people standing nearby didn't stop and turn. Birds didn't stop chirping.

"Your mom is a crackhead?" Jessica squinted in disbelief. "Original."

Jacinta knocked Mina to the side as she leapt forward into Jessica's face. Mina regrouped fast and tugged on Jacinta's arm to keep her from striking. Kelly instinctively grabbed Jacinta's other arm. Jessica flinched and reared back.

Jacinta's finger was inches from Jessica's nose. "Let's get something straight. Anything I tell you, I'm saying 'cause I want to. Check your stankin' ass attitude! Because I *will* beat you down if you say the wrong thing."

Jessica pursed her lips.

"That's what I thought," Jacinta said. "Any jokes or smart comments you better keep on the DL. And if we get back to school and somebody make a smart remark about my moms, I'm gon' know it was you that spread it. Trust I'll be on that ass!"

Jacinta eased away from the circle, glaring at Jessica.

Jessica's hands shook as she raked her hair. The fact that she was alone, in a neighborhood foreign to her, with girls she doubted would help her if Jacinta became physical, made her legs rubbery. She tried to regain composure but her voice quaked. "Is . . . the ghetto part of your lecture o-over?"

"Only if you gon' act like you know," Jacinta said. She turned to face the playground.

"You don't scare me, Jacinta," Jessica managed to say without stammering.

"And you don't impress me, with the my-shit-don't-stink act," Jacinta said, over her shoulder. "You not the only one who wasn't thrilled about this project. So, stop acting like we offend you just 'cause we exist." Her voice lost steam. "Just act like a normal person for once."

Jacinta's heart rattled against her rib cage. Hearing the word "crackhead" coming from Jessica's mouth was more than she could stand. She'd been teased about her mother before, all the time in elementary school. She and Raheem became friends when he broke up a fight between her and Charmaine Tolbert in the third grade. It was the last time Charmaine ever said anything about her mother though.

If Jessica wanted her to be "ghetto," Jacinta could show her ghetto. *Let her say something else that sounds even close to crack. Smack, track, wack, rack and I'm going off,* Jacinta thought.

She cut her eyes toward Jessica, who was looking at the woods beyond, and couldn't resist a last taunt. "What, no momma jokes?"

Jessica stared straight ahead.

Mina shuffled, placing herself between Jacinta and Jessica. "So your dad has always raised you and your sibs?"

"Yeah. One of the reasons it seems like everybody knows me is because my father is probably one of the only single fathers on the whole block," Jacinta said.

Kelly smiled. "Mmm, I know the single moms must love that."

A smile crossed Jacinta's lips. "Oh most definitely. Single father, three kids, holds a job . . . streets be talking all the time."

She, Mina, and Kelly laughed.

"We not all just a bunch of ignorant, lazy people . . . Jessica." Jessica hitched an eyebrow but remained mum as Jacinta continued. "My father spent half his time at work and half his time trying to find and bring my mother home off some corner. This is her"—she cocked her head as she calculated—"fifth time in rehab." Jacinta shrugged. "If she ever went straight that would be the shock. My moms is a definite hood rat."

The look of pity on Kelly's face embarrassed her. She hadn't told them so they could feel sorry for her. She was just doing her "part" for the project. Jacinta barely felt sad about it anymore herself, it had been so long. Until she tried to smash Jessica's face she wasn't even aware she could still get angry over it. Her mother being a crackhead was just fact.

"Has she ever been clean?" Mina whispered.

"You don't have to whisper. I've lived here since I was five; most people here probably know more about my mom's wildin' out than I do," Jacinta said. "It feels like she never been clean. But there was a time when I was real young, like five. I barely remember though. Us being over at my aunt's when he went out looking for her, I remember. Her being a mother, at home with us, I don't. Not really."

"I think it's sweet that your father wants you to just have a normal life," Kelly said.

"Shoot being with ya'll not normal," Jacinta said, but there was a laugh in her voice.

She looked beyond the playground packed with young kids playing on swings and monkey bars. Squinting into the far corner, she locked in on a circle of men, teens, and adults stooped over shooting dice under a street light that was just beginning to shimmer.

The wind carried the call of, "Craps!" across the playground. The group of players stood up in a fluid wave and exchanged money before crouching down again.

"Hey, Angel!" Jacinta called.

A young, tall, thin Puerto Rican stood up, said something to the group, and then broke away.

He strode over. "Hey, Mami. I didn't know you was home this weekend." Platinum glinted from his grille as he smiled in the girls' direction. "Who dis?"

"They some friends from DRH," Jacinta answered, then stuttered, "I mean, you know, a few girls I got class with."

"Hey, friends from Del Rio Bay High. Ya'll got names?" Angel asked.

Kelly and Mina announced their names in a shy round.

Jessica stood, tall, icy, and silent.

Angel leaned toward Jessica. "What's your name, Mami?"

She leaned away and answered curtly, "Jes-ica."

Jacinta gave Angel a quick, don't even ask look and head nod toward Jessica. "This Angel, ya'll. You seen Heem?"

Angel's light-brown, almond-shaped eyes lingered on Kelly.

"Don't even think it, Angel," Jacinta said.

"What?" He chuckled. Still side-glancing at Kelly, he addressed Jacinta, "¿Es ella borinqueña? Ella es linda."

Kelly beat Jacinta to answering. "Yes, I'm Puerto Rican. Y gracias."

Angel's straight, white teeth gleamed as he smiled.

Mina listened, fascinated. "I didn't know I was gonna need my Spanish book to help me through this sleepover, Cinny."

"Alright, parada. Stop, ya'll two." Jacinta cut into Angel's flirting. "Where's Heem?"

Angel never took his eyes off Kelly. "Heem at the court. You hanging tonight? Or you got a curfew now?"

"Boy, please." Jacinta prayed none of the girls would be stupid enough to remind her of her father's nine o'clock warning.

"I see ya'll over at the courts." Angel gave Kelly a flirtatious wink before heading back to the dice game.

"He's cute in a thuggish-ruggish, hot Latino way," Mina said. "Kelly, he's definitely feeling you."

Kelly glanced back toward the game. "Yeah. He has pretty eyes."

"Pretty eyes, nice teeth, little caramel cutie boy," Mina said.

"And you got all that just that quick?" Jacinta teased.

"Don't sleep on my skills. I can size up a dude like that," Mina clicked her fingers.

"This is like a low-budget version of Room Raiders," Jessica quipped, her icy attitude down a notch. "Now that you've seen where he's from Kelly, date or no date?"

"Shoot, I say, date," Mina said.

"Please. No date," Jessica said.

Kelly's face flushed. "Do I get a say in this?"

The girls fell in step around Jacinta.

"No. Stick to the gray boys," Jacinta said.

Crowd noises got louder as the girls turned the corner at the last set of row houses and arrived at two partially fenced-in basketball courts, three playgrounds, and a neighborhood recreation center. Every child and teenager who lived in The Cove's two hundred row homes seemed to be here.

The high-pitched squeak of tennis shoes and the hollow bounce of the ball mixed with excited sounds of spectators. Masses of people mingled or watched the shirtless guys running up and down the court.

Jacinta stopped at the fence, caught Raheem's eye as he ran down the court, and signaled with a wave that she was there. She strode through the thick crowd to an empty picnic table and sat on the table top. The girls filled in beside her, Jessica on the far end.

With her back to the girls, Jacinta leaned over, elbows on her thighs, and watched the action on the court in silence.

"Way too many people are here. How can you guys not be un-comfortable?" Jessica asked. "Mina, you even said yourself you weren't comfortable coming here."

Jacinta whipped around. Her steely glare seared through Mina.

Mina leaned up and peered at Jessica. "Why are you trying to start stuff?"

Jessica's eyebrow arched. "What?"

"You know I never said . . ."

Jacinta folded her arms. "Oh, so all that smack you talked on the bus Monday morning about it not being a big deal coming here was all for show?"

Mina rushed to explain. "It wasn't like that." She shot Jessica a nasty look. "Why are you lying, Jess?"

"What was it like, Princess?!" Jacinta asked. Hurt made her eyes into droopy slits.

"Cinny, seriously, I didn't say I was *uncomfortable*," Mina said, taken aback by how much she cared that Jacinta knew the truth. Things were still mad weird between Lizzie and her. The new friendship, if it could be called that, with Jacinta and Kelly mattered to her.

"Whatever, Princess. I kind of figured when it all came down to it, you'd be down with the grays," Jacinta said.

"God, Mina, are you seriously that pressed what she thinks about you?" Jessica flung her head in Jacinta's direction. She crossed her legs and sat primly atop the table. "You're so not café material."

The comment took Mina back for a second. She hadn't been

thinking about how any of this translated to her status at school. The soc project felt so separate from the rest of her life, sometimes.

"This isn't about the café. If you're so hot to keep me out, then do it," Mina said, wincing at her own words. But it was out, so she finished. "If I had gone along with you and voted not to have the sleepover here, it would have been all swazy." She forced herself to meet Jacinta's stony face. "This is all because I wouldn't ask you to switch weekends. Finally, I told her I thought everything would be fine and how . . ." She raced down a mental checklist of best ways to say what she needed to say. Finding none she told the truth. "I said I wasn't thrilled about coming to The Cove. But I was just nervous."

"Like I said, you weren't comfortable coming here," Jessica said.

"No, I didn't say that," Mina insisted. "Cinny, I wasn't trying to disrespect your nabe. But I was nervous about coming here. Jessica wanted me to switch weekends with you because she was uncomfortable. And I wouldn't."

"Alright, well whatever. It's not like you were so into coming here." Jessica shrugged.

"You're just jealous because me, Cinny, and Kelly are getting along," Mina said.

Jessica's laugh was a hoarse bark. "As if, Mina. You can wake up now. Because only in your dreams am *I* jealous of *you*."

"Whatever. I just don't want Cinny thinking me and you are anything alike," Mina said. She sat back, hiding how badly she felt like crying.

"It's cool, Mina," Jacinta said quietly. "I know you're not like her. Nobody is."

"I don't care what you guys think about me," Jessica said. She uncrossed her legs and leaned in, so they could see her face through the darkening evening. "I'm not going to feel bad because I don't think being poor or a criminal is cool."

"And I'm not gonna run around crying and worrying what

everybody and their brother thinks about where I'm from or who I hang with," Jacinta said.

Jessica rolled her eyes. "Maybe you should."

"Why? So I can be like ya'll, changing how I act every time somebody whispers something new about me?"

Mina wasn't sure if she was included in that mix but felt reprimanded anyway.

"At least Kelly can be real and say she'd rather be alone than worry about keeping up with all the crazy rules," Jacinta said.

"Cinny, we're not judging you," Kelly said, giving Mina and Jessica a look.

"Well, I'm not. But what you're saying isn't fair, either, Cinny," Mina said. She didn't want to be on Jessica's side, ever, but she felt attacked. "Just because we don't have to deal with drugs or crime in our nabe doesn't mean all our problems are petty."

"Maybe. But the only things I ever hear ya'll go on about is who likes who and who doing what where." Jacinta hitched her shoulders. "I'm sorry, Mina, it's petty to me."

"And when you're hanging out with Raheem and Angel, ya'll seriously sit there and discuss how you can make The Cove a better place to live?" Mina shook her head. "Come on."

"I'm not saying that."

Jacinta stood up. She stared vacantly at the ugly, plain, worn buildings, some covered in graffiti. Some of the vacant homes had windows busted out. The grass surrounding the units was patchy, burned out, barely there. Broken glass and litter were strewn in the areas nearer the trees. She pointed to the shabby areas. "I know ya'll probably look around and think this place is all tore up. And it is. But it's just home to me. So, naw, we don't sit and talk about making it a better place to live. 'Cause most times it's not that horrible of a place to be."

"So, then when you're with your friends you probably talk about the same type of things as anybody else, right?" Kelly said.

"I guess," Jacinta admitted reluctantly. "The difference is, I'm not all pressed about what other people think of my friends. If you my friend, you my friend no matter what."

"I feel the same way," Mina said.

Jacinta's face was skeptical and Mina's immediately registered hurt.

"No harm, Mina, but . . . I'm not so sure about that," Jacinta said.

Just then Raheem walked over, his game ended. Jacinta's whole demeanor changed. She got up from the table and threw her arms around Raheem's sweaty neck.

"How was your game, Boo? Did ya'll win?"

He pursed his lips. "Now, what you think? Wassup, Mina?"

Mina nodded a hello, surprised he remembered her but pleased to have the inside track, since he didn't acknowledge the other girls.

Angel appeared out of nowhere. Deep into a conversation on his cell, he slid onto the edge of the table, on the end near Jessica. She stood up and stepped away like he was diseased, placing herself on the opposite end of the table, where Jacinta had sat.

Angel paused his conversation long enough to yell, "Ay, Heem, this the Del Rio Bay clique."

Mina stole a glance at Jessica, sure she was horrified that Angel would consider them a clique. She half-expected Jessica to correct Angel. But Jessica stared ahead, stony.

Angel pursed his lips in a suggestive kiss and blew one to Kelly. She tucked at her hair and smiled.

Angel flipped his phone shut and summoned two hulking figures from the shadows to his side. The incredible hulks took the phone and stepped back. Their silhouetted figures blocked Angel from any-one passing by from the courts.

Mina whispered to Kelly. "What's up with the bodyguards?"

Kelly shrugged.

"So, Kelly, you gon' let me holler?" Angel asked, grille blinging in her face.

SO NOT THE DRAMA   273

"He's trying to get with you," Mina whispered, elbowing Kelly's back. "Talk to him."

"Man, she a good girl, so you can squash that," Raheem said.

"Yeah, every girl was at one time," Angel said with a low chuckle. He gave Raheem a conspiratorial hand slap. "Now that you live over in the country, you a good girl again, Cinny?"

Jacinta's voice came back muffled from Raheem's chest. "Go 'head, Angel, with your five-dollar rap."

He snatched a knot of money from his pocket and waved a few dollars at her. "Here you need me bless you?"

Jacinta pushed away from Raheem long enough to smack at Angel's hand. "Boy, go 'head with that."

Angel turned back to Kelly, his dark eyes smiling. "So, Kelly, can I holla at you for a minute?"

Kelly's eyes darted between Angel and the girls.

Raheem rescued her momentarily. "Man, she probably like those old gray busters at DRH. You too ethnic for her."

Angel was persistent. "Look, everybody stop talking for the girl!" he growled before turning the charm back on. "My bad. So Kelly, can I get your number?"

Jacinta let go of Raheem and checked her phone. "No time, Angel. We gotta go."

"Yeah, I knew Jamal finally put that choke hold on you," Angel taunted. He crossed his wrists, miming handcuffs. "Got your ass on lockdown."

"Whatever. I just don't feel like listening to your weak mack all night."

"Go 'head with that, Ma," Angel warned. "Heem, you better get your girl."

Raheem pulled Jacinta back to him and nuzzled her neck, quieting her down.

"Hurry up and do your little mack thing, please," Jacinta said. Her annoyance was unconvincing as she melted into Raheem's arms.

Angel summoned the hulks over and they handed him a back-pack. He took a phone out.

"So how old are you?" Angel asked.

"Fourteen," Kelly said, her voice reverting to its usual low.

"Maybe Cinny can bring you around and we can kick it with her and my boy, Raheem," Angel said.

Mina nudged her, giggling under her breath. Kelly didn't know how to respond. Luckily she didn't have to. Angel kept talking.

"If that's cool, put your number in my cellie." He handed Kelly a slim, silver slide phone.

Kelly held the phone, unsure what to say. Mina was poking her leg to death, a clear vote for yes, key in the number. Jessica was indifferent, staring over at the basketball game in between sly looks back at Kelly. And Jacinta was whispering up in Raheem's face. Kelly keyed in her number and saved it in the directory.

"So it's alright if I call you?" Angel said.

"Sure," Kelly said.

"Tome el cuidado, la nena," Angel said. He kissed Kelly on the cheek and then rolled out. "Heem, meet me at the spot."

"We gotta get ready to roll, anyway," Jacinta said. "My Pops is mother-henning me to death." She rolled her eyes, but her voice was playful as she pointed at her group mates. "He don't want the bobble head 'burb girls to get hurt."

"I catch you tomorrow, right?" Raheem said.

Jacinta pressed her lips against his in answer.

"Come on, ya'll," she said. She hoofed it back to the house, legs kicking as she jog-walked. The girls raced beside her.

When they reached the row, the girls sat on the front stoop while Jacinta stuck her head in the door and hollered they were back.

"Kelly, stop yourself before you end up damaged goods," Jessica whispered.

"What do you mean?" Kelly said.

"I'm saying, if it gets around to the guys at Del Rio High that you're dating someone like that, none of them will want to go out with you."

"Aww, Kelly, you mean Biff and Skip and Josh and Jake won't ask you out?" Jacinta said, pretending to flip hair off her shoulders. She sat on the corner of the stoop.

Kelly hugged her chest to her knees. "I guess she's saying that long line of guys knocking down my door will go away."

She, Jacinta, and Mina shared a giggle and high fives.

Jacinta's father appeared at the door. "Alright, that's it for the night." He stared down at Jacinta and a silent agreement passed between them.

"Yes, Daddy," she answered sweetly.

"Are you in trouble?" Mina whispered.

"No, it's cool," Jacinta said, confidently. "Let's just chill out here for a minute."

Her father laid on the stern Cosby act thick because of the girls. Any other time he was much more lenient. Jacinta was willing to play along.

"Jess, Angel seems nice enough," Mina said. "Hey, Kell, what was that he said to you?"

"Take care, Baby Girl," Kelly said, mimicking Angel.

Mina squealed. "That's so cute. I've gotta get my Spanish straight."

"Okay," Jessica warned. "Date this Angel guy and see just how often you'll be sitting home by yourself." She leaned back on her palms and swished her hair. "Not like I care. I'm just trying to help you out."

"As usual you overhyping," Jacinta said. She turned to Kelly. "But Angel is . . . well, I can't see you dating him."

"See, even Jacinta knows I'm right," Jessica said triumphantly.

"Woah, naw. I didn't say that," Jacinta said. "Angel is my boy, don't get me wrong. But he's in that hustle. Just saying I can't see Kelly going from McStew Preppie to ride-or-die chick."

"What hustle? Drugs?" Jessica sniffed, as if expecting this all along.

"He slings drugs?" Mina said in a loud whisper.

"Okay, that's not really a whisper," Jacinta said. She chuckled. "Yeah, that's what I'm saying."

"Well you're friends with him. He must not be a bad person," Kelly said. She was having a hard time connecting Angel's friendly boyish face with drug dealing.

"I told you, I'm not like ya'll. I'm not all fair weather like some people," Jacinta said.

"How can you be friends with someone that could land you in jail?" Jessica said. "If he ever got caught, how do you know he wouldn't pull you into it?"

"You watch too much TV," Jacinta said. "Me and Angel were friends long before the game. He wasn't always a hustler, you know."

"Well, people grow apart, Jacinta. Maybe you guys should have once he started breaking the law," Jessica said.

Jacinta wondered if Mina's and Kelly's silence meant they agreed. Heat rose in her face. She didn't want to be angry with them. But they were staring and it felt like they were dissecting her. She resented it. She never asked why Mina was friends with a blond-haired white girl. Or why Kelly didn't have any friends.

"Is that how ya'll do?" Jacinta looked at Mina specifically. "Ice a friend when they not doing things you want 'em to do?"

"What? I didn't say anything," Mina said.

"Still, is that how ya'll roll?" Jacinta asked.

"Well, I never had any friends to ice," Kelly joked.

Jacinta kept her unsmiling eyes on Mina. She needed to know. Every step she and Mina took toward being cool, something came up and they took a half-step back. If Mina was sometimy, Jacinta could stop wasting her time now.

"What about you, Mina?" she asked. "You and your girl Lizzie were mad tight that first day at the pizza joint. Last time we were there she left, pissed off. Is that how ya'll do friends over in the 'burbs?"

"Me and Lizzie are fine," Mina lied.

Jacinta popped her eyebrows. "Okay. As far as me and Angel, we're *real* friends. Like, him hustling to make a dollar and me moving to the suburbs won't change nothing kind of friends."

Jessica refused to see it Jacinta's way. "It's not against the law to make new friends," she said.

"I'm able to separate Angel's grind from our friendship."

"And I don't see how," Jessica said.

"Because he always has. Last year, when my moms was mad strung out, Angel wouldn't sell her any drugs specifically 'cause she was my moms. So yeah, he's a hustler." Jacinta waved it off. "But he saw past making a dollar for a friend. Why would I turn around and throw shade on him now?"

"Loyalty is one thing, but you could have stopped Kelly from giving the guy her number," Jessica said.

"Like you care," Jacinta snapped. "Kelly could have said no. And by the way, next time just get his. Always get his so the dude won't be blowing up your phone."

"It's not a big deal. It's just a phone number, not a prom date," Kelly said.

"Until the feds knocking down your door," Jessica mumbled.

Jacinta sucked her teeth. "For real, cut back on episodes of *The Shield*. Angel not hardly big timing it like that."

"If nothing else, he can be your phone boyfriend," Mina suggested.

Jacinta choked out a laugh. "I don't mean no harm, Mina, but Angel not trying to be somebody's phone boyfriend."

"Well maybe she could settle for a distant crush," Mina said.

"Yeah, The Cove is real distant. All eight miles away from Kelly's mansionette." Jacinta clapped her hands and laughed at her own joke. She shook her head. Everything was so innocent and simple for the bobble head 'burb girls, especially Mina.

Phone boyfriends, distant crushes—Angel wouldn't know what those meant if someone spelled it out for him. He was digging Kelly; talking to her over the phone was only part one of the plan.

She wished she could see things their way sometimes, but knew that would be like going back into the womb—impossible.

Still laughing, she stood up. "Kelly, look, if you don't want to talk to Angel, just tell him. Or don't answer when he calls. Not like he'll lose sleep over it."

"I wouldn't answer," Jessica said.

"You got much mouth for someone who doesn't care," Jacinta said.

Jessica clammed up.

"Alright ya'll, that's a wrap. Let's head in and do these daggone observations." Jacinta opened the door. "Then I can whip up on ya'll in some DDR."

"I'm with that," Mina said.

"Can we write our reports outside?" Jessica asked. She trailed behind, not anxious to be back in the stuffy house.

"Everybody in favor of having the next sleepover at Jessica's so she can shut up, say I," Jacinta said.

Two I's rang out strong in the night.

Sociology
September 16, 2005
Jacinta Phillips

Forget all about these girls surviving The Cove. How about I survived them!

Whoever thinks it's easy spending the whole night with people you not that close with have never done it.

Even though I swore I wouldn't take the way they re-
acted or the things they said personally, I did when
Jessica asked about my moms being a crackhead. She
was ready to get knocked the $&@# out!

I'm glad I didn't hit her, though. It would have just
been one more thing for her to feel right about. "Oh
people from the projects are violent." Whatever, man!
Let me talk about her white-bread momma and see if
she don't get pissed.

And with Mina . . . I think she's an alright chick. But I
don't know if I trust her. I think she talks so much that
she don't even know how much of other people's
business she spreading. And I think she may be sometimey. The way her girl Lizzie booked out of the pizza
joint the other day, I know something up between them.
And that's her girl. So . . . I don't know if we could be
friends.

Alright, maybe I should have jumped in and forced
Angel to back up off Kelly. Or I should have told her he
was a hustler. But I wasn't trying to spread his business
right off the top. I don't want her feeling like she has
to talk to him just because he's my friend. Then again,
we've seen her get raw when she needs to. A little of
her must have wanted to give Angel that number. I'll
keep my eye on it. She gets mad respect for being the
only one not to piss me off once tonight.

Soc

9/16/05

Observations by Amina Mooney

That was wild! Flowing through her nabe and being around so many people. You never see that many people in The Woods outside except when there's a game at the park and that's daytime. The only time I felt uncomfortable was when Mr. Phillips stopped the truck on the road leading in. Not on a dare would I walk that road.

Seeing Jacinta with her sibs and with Raheem was like seeing a new person. Even though she's hung out with us a few times, I still had never seen her that laid back. Hi Cinny, I think we're finally meeting for the first time!

What made me mad was Cinny saying our problems are petty. Just because every problem isn't life or death doesn't make it petty. Okay . . . well here I go flip-flopping, but her mom's a drug addict and one of her close friends deals drugs. The toughest issue I deal with each year is keeping my grades up and campaigning for an extra half hour on curfew. So, yeah curfew is a petty issue compared to multiple rehab trips.

I don't think we're different when it comes to friends though. Who is more loyal than me? I'm like the best best friend ever. I can't claim to see things as simply as she does when it comes to Angel (yikes!) but her loyalty? I likey! Eventually she'll see I'm down with the loyalty thing too. The verdict is in. I got nothing but love for you, Cinny. Even though you so cheated on that last round of Dance Dance Revolution—left, left, double up, back, Goldi!!!!

Sociology
September 16, 2005
Observations by Kelly Lopez

I finally get Cinny. Tonight she laughed and got her feelings hurt—bad move, Jessica. And trying to stop her from fighting, Jessica came out of nowhere. I've never been in a fight my entire life! And I'm not anxious to be that close to one again.

Seeing Cinny with her dad and her brothers and sister and being all goo-goo eyed with Raheem (did you win, Boo?) Ha-ha!! Now I feel like I know her. And now, I'm going to need her to help me with Angel. Since they're friends I want to get the real scoop. Would she really be friends with him if he was Nino Brown/Scarface movie drug dealer bad? I'm thinking maybe he's more like Jay-Z/Young Jeezy hip-hop rapper, walking the bad side but one day he'll own part of a basketball team or push record units instead of o-z's. It could happen. Right?

Cinny was right. I should have gotten his number. It was cute how she and Mina were trying to protect me (of course, after I had already given out the number). Little late, guys. Still, would they bother to give their advice if we weren't becoming friends? I don't think so. After two sleepovers and going to Rio's Ria with them . . . it feels like we've friends. I hope we are.

Still, I wish I didn't know what I know about Angel. He

looks like any other seventeen-(??) year-old. I was too nervous to ask him anything. I would be lying if I said I didn't think he was gorgeous (love his eyes) and really liked how much attention he paid to me. Now I'll be playing race to the phone to get it before Grand does. Three weeks ago, I would have never had this problem. I called it by saying this would be interesting. Just didn't think I'd be the one making it that way.

Soc
9-16-05
Observations by Jessica Johnson

Today was my first and LAST time in The Cove and any projects if I can help it. I'm seriously reconsidering ever coming to Del Rio Bay Mall again—it's too close to this place. I don't know what I'd do if we had to live some place like here. The house is so small they're practically tripping over one another. I didn't see any roaches, yet. But I swear, tonight I will call and make my dad come get me if I do. And I'm throwing away every single thing I have on when I get home. If I'm of-fending anyone, GOOD.

The best thing I can say about tonight is, Jacinta's dad seems nice. I respect that he's probably struggling to raise a family on his own. My dad's a teacher and my mom stays at home, we're not rich (hate writing those words). I know that my dad sacrifices so Sarah and I can have the things we want. So Mr. Phillips, smooches to you, you're like dad of the year or some-thing.

But Jacinta—whatev! You can have "kicking" it with your drug-dealing, grille wearing, crap shooting hood rat friend and your boyfriend, Mr. Talkative. Did he say more than five words?! Jacinta can stay on this side of Del Rio Bay and I will stay on mine. The day this soc project ends and we never have to speak to one another again will be the happiest day of my life. Happiest. Day. EVER.

I don't know why Mina kept Jacinta from hitting me. Maybe she realizes that there is life outside of this soc project and in that life, Mina, I'm still "that" chick and you're still that wannabe. Good call, frosh!

I was ready to call home by then. But I wasn't about to give Jacinta the satisfaction of thinking her ghetto intimidation worked. I said I wasn't afraid of her and I meant it.

Now I can see why Mari-Beth has written Kelly off as a lost cause. I've said it all before, wasted potential.

Glad this is almost over. I don't plan on sleeping a wink tonight. Not one wink.

Oh I forgot. Have I eliminated my prejudices against Jacinta now that I've collected and analyzed the data? That would be a NO!

NO! NO! NO!

Replaced

"OH NO! The fight's out . . ."
—Ludacris, "Move B*&%$"

Lizzie floated down the hallway Monday. *I won't care if Kelly's at the table. I won't care* she told herself as she made her way to the cafeteria. *I won't care.* It was her first day at lunch after spending two weeks in the quiet auditorium running lines. Her stomach grumbled at the prospect of eating something besides yogurt and fruit. But the light diet had been well worth it.

Even with the strange tension between Mina and her that hadn't left them since the mall fiasco, Lizzie was walking on sunshine. Sharing the feeling with her BFF would be the icing on her Cloud 9 cake.

She glided into the cafeteria and stopped dead on the stairs. Kelly was at the table. *It's okay, I'm cool with that,* Lizzie told herself. But Kelly was in *her* spot, sitting right across from Mina.

To Lizzie's amazement, the bookworm was engaged in a full conversation with Mina and Michael, not that one-word crap she had subjected them to weeks earlier.

No doubt, soc class hocus pocus, she thought bitterly, watching as Kelly chatted up her friends, laughing and smiling like they'd been buds for thirty years instead of thirty days.

She hammered the word "replaced" out of her head before it could settle in.

Too late.

Irritation itched its way up to her throat. She swallowed it down and rationalized.

The soc project was in full swing, Mina had even invited Kelly to their Thursday Ria date. Of course Kelly and Mina were "friends." Mina thrived on making new friends. It had never bothered Lizzie before. But then Mina had never been so touchy before.

This was new territory. She desperately wanted to conquer the new ground. She made her way to the table and took the seat on the other side of Mina.

"Hey," Lizzie said, a happy chirp in her voice.

Mina was glad to see Lizzie back at lunch. She half-thought Lizzie would go back to the café with Lila and the flunkies once the Lines for Lunch ended. "Hey, look who's back at lunch with the little folks," she said, smiling.

"Not much longer, though." Michael winked at Lizzie. "Your girl gon' be stomping with the big dogs. You are looking at Dorothy of Detroit for the Bay Dra-da production of *The Wiz*," he announced, into an imaginary microphone.

Lizzie smiled, glad Michael had broken the ice. Winning the role of Dorothy felt hollow without a good old-fashioned giggle session with her girl. But it was always better to have someone else toot your horn.

Mina's mouth dropped in surprise. "You got the lead?"

"Yup," Lizzie grinned, mistaking Mina's question for happiness.

"What's up with the secrets lately? Mike finding out everything before me," Mina snapped, arms folded.

Anger pulsed in Lizzie's throat. She put her hands on her hips and glared. "You were gone Friday. The SOC sleepover, remember? I left you three messages and an e-mail, Saturday. You never bothered to call me back."

"Well, I didn't get your messages," Mina said, embarrassed to admit her parents put the smackdown on all of her electronic communication because of that C on her Lit essay. Facts she would have preferred to share with Lizzie in private. Backed into a corner, her anger went up a notch. "What else ya'll keeping from me?"

"Come on ya'll, don't fight," Michael pleaded.

Kelly shrank as far away from the table as she could without standing up and running away. She kept her head down against the storm of words flying.

JZ's "Wassup?!" was lost as the girls' cat fight went up a notch.

"Well, you've been too caught up with your new friends!" Lizzie spat.

"Liz, I asked if you were feeling left out and you told me to let it go."

Exasperated, Lizzie sucked her teeth. "Oh, my God, Mina! No one said anything about black or white!"

"Then why are you bringing the drama?" Mina said.

Lizzie worked to control her temper, rising out of her seat as she answered through clenched teeth. "Me bring the drama?! You're un-believable, Mina."

"Meaning?"

"Meaning, this couldn't possibly be about what I said about Ra-heem," Lizzie said. "Stop treating me like I just burned a cross in front of your house and admit that this is about you, not me. Admit that you're feeling torn between your new friends and me."

Mina gaped, unable to answer and instinctively looked over at Kelly, who was tight-lipped and hunched over a new book that had miraculously appeared when the words turned angry.

"Here, I'll make it easy." Lizzie threw her Best Friends charm on the table. "Consider this a free pass to go on your way without feel-ing guilty that you ditched our friendship."

Mina recoiled from the charm. She stared at it, bug-eyed. She could barely remember why they were fighting until Lizzie said, "Look,

Mina, if you're trying to find yourself and explore new friendships that's fine with me, but—"

"Find myself?!" Mina shouted. People from nearby lunch tables stared.

"Alright ya'll making a scene," Michael said, sternly. But Mina ignored him.

"Just because one day out of the thousand times we've hung out I decide to hang out with another black person doesn't mean I'm lost."

Lizzie threw her hands up in the air. "You are really tripping!!"

Mina picked up the charm bracelet piece, turning it over. "For as far back as I can remember, I've hung out with you and been the only black face in the place. And it's been all good for you. Well now it's my turn to be in the majority. Can you respect that? "

"Yeah, I can respect that." Lizzie gathered her things. She spoke just above a whisper, her fury bottled. "But if you don't mind, I'll respect it from a distance where I won't get trampled from you jumping from clique to clique." She looked at Michael and JZ. "I'll talk to you guys later."

"What the hell was that?" JZ slid down onto the seat. He looked at Mina. "Mi, what's up with that? Why ya'll tripping?"

Still caught up in a vortex of anger, Mina spat, "We not tripping anymore than you are over Michael getting his fashion design on."

Michael frowned. "What?"

JZ pursed his lips, his evil eye shooting a laser at Mina.

"What's up, you got a problem with my grind?" Michael asked.

JZ grunted, shaking his head at Mina, disapprovingly. "Look, I just told Mina that I hope hanging out with some of those theater punks don't rub off on you."

"What does that bullshit mean?"

"Man, it just mean tongues already wagging and you not making it no better running around with a needle and thread, stitching up dresses," JZ said, his anger rising.

Michael looked him square in the eye. "Tongues wagging? Just say your peace, kid. You know how we do."

Helpless to stop what she started, Mina couldn't say a word. Her eyes darted around the cafeteria. Lots of people were watching. She wanted to melt into a puddle.

"I don't feel like defending you every time somebody go calling you a punk or a bitch," JZ said.

"Man, since when you care what people say about me? It ain't no reflection on you and I know that's all you care about!"

Michael's words pushed a button but JZ denied it. "I ain't faded by what people think. But if word get out that you not with the honeys, rumor or not, the shit will get ugly."

Michael's voice was tight and controlled, but it simmered with anger. "Jay we go back to the playground, son. I would have your back no matter what . . ."

"And I got yours, kid, but . . ."

"Naw, let me finish!" Michael snapped. "I roll with you through whatever. Nobody deny you your shine when you do your thing on the field or the court. Nobody jock-block when you try holler at every shortie you see. But now, 'cause I'm doing something that don't fit with your program you gon' throw shade?"

"It's not like that, kid."

"Naw, it's definitely like that. If people think I'm a fag 'cause I design clothes and it don't bother me, why it gotta bother you?"

Michael's stare challenged JZ, daring him to admit it was more than the costume designing making him act shady. But JZ wouldn't.

"It bothers me if it ain't true," he said, his jaw tight, chin up as he threw the challenge back to Michael.

"Whatever, man. You want to roll with a different clique 'cause you don't like where my skills at, that's on you. I'm out." Michael pushed himself away from the table and walked off.

Mina's saucer-sized eyes, glistened. She whispered, "Jay, I'm sorry. I didn't mean to cause that. I swear."

JZ stared after Michael. "Naw, something was gon' pop off either way." He shook his head. "He gotta do what he gotta do and so do I."

Open Session

"Yea, you better do the right thing like Spike Lee."
—Dem Franchise Boyz, "I Think They Like Me."

The next day, Mrs. Simms stood at her post in the doorway. She watched the students' faces as they walked into the classroom stripped of all furniture except her desk and the bookshelves. In the place of the students' desks were throw pillows of every size. Bright swatches of orange, yellow and violet crepe paper decorated the walls. Lamps scattered around the room cast a soft, ivory glow.

The lack of furniture, calm lighting, and dazzling wall décor jolted the students' systems. They milled around the room and did double-takes, as if to make sure they were still in a classroom.

Pleased with the mixed looks of confusion and delight, Mrs. Simms asked, "So, what do you guys think?"

Soft rumblings of approval echoed in the room.

Mrs. Simms's loud laugh spilled into explanation. "This year's winter production will be *The Wiz*. How many of you know the story?"

Nearly everyone raised a hand. Mina's ears perked up at mention of *The Wiz*. She listened, spellbound as the teacher's low voice reeled her in.

"Good, good," she clucked. "Everyone knows *The Wiz* and the original production, *The Wizard of Oz,* are about a girl trying to find her way back home to the place and the people she cherishes the most. What's interesting about the story is, at the beginning, Dorothy is actually running away from home. So a lot of her journey is really about the realization that home is special."

As Mrs. Simms spoke, the students remained standing. "Much like Dorothy felt in Oz, you all seem out of place in this new world I've created. Why are you all still standing?"

The students looked around at one another.

Mrs. Simms nodded toward Mina's raised hand.

"Because we weren't sure what to do," Mina admitted.

"Yes, but the procedure every day is that you're to come in and take your seats. Why should the rules change just because there's no furniture?"

Another student spoke up. "Yeah, but if somebody came and sat on the floor then you announced we were having class somewhere else, that person would have looked stupid."

The students laughed. Confirmation most felt the same.

"You're on the right track." Mrs. Simms nodded. "When we're in unfamiliar surroundings, instead of exploring new possibilities, we often contemplate how to make old traditions and habits fit into our new world. And as we're pondering how to do that, usually our first reaction is not to react at all." She cocked her head as a thought hit her. "But sometimes our reaction is to overreact."

She signaled everyone to sit down.

"Open session!"

Mina eased onto the floor, scooting in close to Kelly so Jacinta could squeeze in.

Jessica sat, near Grace, on the opposite side of the room. She made it a point to never sit near Mina, Kelly, and Jacinta during class.

This was the second open session, an entire period of class discussion. Mina loved them. No matter how often Mrs. Simms discouraged judgment, the sessions still ended up as forceful, heated debates. No matter who felt they were right, in the end the teacher reminded them that these were brainstorm sessions and no idea or opinion would be ignored, another reminder that the sociology class was unlike any other.

Mina grabbed a pillow and relaxed against Kelly. With the soft lighting and everyone lying on big pillows, it was the world's largest sleepover. Surrounded by her group mates she could almost drown out the bitter echo of Lizzie saying she was jumping cliques. As of yesterday, they were officially not speaking.

The realization made her nauseous. A slow pounding started in her temple.

She squeezed her eyes shut, slammed the door on the mess and opened her mind to the session. Sociology was her favorite class. She was learning a lot about herself. And if she ever needed the class's insight, it was now.

Mrs. Simms opened the floor for discussion. "Okay, today's topic: how to deal with being pushed out of your comfort zone. Consider whether or not the rules have to change just because our environment changes." She raised her voice over the excited chatter, "I expect the freshmen to have a lot to say since you're new to the high school environment. Who wants to start?"

Jay, It's Just Me and You

"I really feel that I'm losing my best friend."
—No Doubt, "Don't Speak"

They weren't coming.

Mina had a clear view of the door, despite the sea of bodies crushed into the Ria, and the clique hadn't walked in yet.

They weren't coming.

With no cell phone, Mina couldn't call anyone. But then who would she call? She and Lizzie weren't talking. Michael was back to being moody and JZ had been sulking. It was her fault. She knew it. And this was her punishment. Sit in the Ria alone amidst nearly every single clique walking the earth.

Even Jacinta and Kelly had deserted her, or at least had other plans. Raheem was stopping in to visit Jacinta. So there was no tearing her away from her Aunt Jacqi's today. And Kelly had somewhere to go with her grandmother and brother. Mina took some comfort from the fact that Kelly seemed genuinely disappointed that she wouldn't be able to hang out for pizza.

It wasn't enough comfort to shield Mina from feeling an eerie sense of loneliness inside the crowded restaurant. She groaned at the sight of Jessica and a fellow glam walking through the door.

Mina welcomed the thought of Jessica ignoring her. But had no such luck.

From across the room, the glam with Jessica pointed to a table behind Mina and the two headed Mina's way. Jessica stopped beside Mina's table.

"Oh, now see, this is how I expect to see you more often," she said.

Mina didn't have the fire to fight back.

"Jason finally wised up and stopped hanging around with you?" Jessica said. "Good for him."

Mina's face lit up as JZ came through the door with Craig. She was saved and didn't have time to dwell on the fact that Craig walked over to another table. Seeing JZ walk toward her was the oasis she needed.

"What's up, girl?" he said, taking a seat.

Jessica frowned and walked off. Mina wrinkled her nose in distaste once Jessica was safely behind her.

"Jay, it's just me and you," Mina said, near tears.

He looked around. "Yeah."

"I'm sorry . . ."

"Mina, I know." His voice was gruff. He rubbed at his head, still looking around as if he expected Michael and Lizzie to walk in, too. "Let's just . . . drop it."

"No. We . . . I gotta fix this," Mina said.

"I don't even get what you and Liz beefing about," JZ said.

"Things are just different between us," Mina shrugged. "I mean . . . I guess it's me."

"What are you tripping about?"

"I really like hanging with Kelly and Jacinta," Mina admitted. The soc project was almost over and she'd found herself feeling sad that they wouldn't be together on the weekends. She didn't want to say it out loud. She already felt disloyal enough to Lizzie.

"Nothing wrong with that. What, you think they wouldn't be down with kicking it with Liz?"

"No. I mean, I don't care . . ." Mina shook her head. "What if

Lizzie's tired of hanging around with a whole bunch of black people?"

JZ's eyes popped. "Did she tell you that?"

"No. Of course not." Mina leaned in and lowered her voice. "But what if she is? I'm not ending our friendship because I like Cinny and Kelly. But it's like we can't all get along because I'm with them."

"Ya'll could. But not if you gonna force them on Lizzie. Just ask her if she down," JZ said.

Mina nodded. She knew JZ was right. She had to put it out there and then go from there. If Lizzie wasn't down . . . she'd cross that T when she wrote it.

"Things will work out. Just stop tripping over it," JZ said.

"Oh, now there goes the old JZ advice," Mina said.

Forever Is a Long Time to Be a Shadow

"It can't get much worse."
—Fall Out Boy, "Dance, Dance"

A jellybean mix of kids, Asian, Indian, Middle Eastern, black, white, and in between, rode scooters, skates, and bikes up and down the sidewalks. Their parents called to one another from their yards some with heavy accents, others in clear English.

From high atop a trampoline, Jessica, a princess with a distaste for individuality, surveyed her neighborhood, a world where neighbors wore their unique differences loud and proud. Flags from countries far away hung near people's doorways emphasizing this wasn't another cookie-cutter suburban subdivision.

Jessica closed her eyes. Whenever she found herself hanging around the house, which wasn't often if she could help it, she sat on the trampoline wishing The Great Melting Pot away and plopped ritzy Folgers Way in its place. She imagined that the rinky dink one-story rambler homes were really the wide, spacious, multilevel homes of her friends. In her head, the yards flowed with lush greenery instead of struggling crab grass. Her neighbors weren't Kristopoulos, Semos, and Lenferink but Whitmore, Davis, and Wang (the DRB had a growing Asian population and many of them were nouveaux Folgers Way rich). She and Mari-Beth agreed, the glams needed an Asian member by year's end.

The tramp was the one thing about their house she liked. She and Sarah begged their parents for it one summer. Making promises, like kids do, about how often they would use it and how it would help Sarah's gymnastics and Jessica's coordination. Anything to snag the eighteen-foot, black and yellow "moon bounce for big kids" as their mom called it.

Six days out of seven, Jess and Sarah disagreed on fashion, food, and music. But every now and then their twin chemistry kicked in and they worked like the world's best team. Securing the tramp had been an especially delicious twin victory because for weeks after, the girls had been closer than they had in a long time, practicing jumps and tumbling together, lying atop the tramp gazing into the sky and talking about their crushes and futures, in that order.

If Mari-Beth hadn't called, irritated that Jessica hadn't been to her house in "ages," who knows how close the trampoline would have brought the two sisters. But the phone call ended the honeymoon. Now, Jess did more sitting and thinking on the tramp than jumping.

The trampoline dipped and creaked, announcing a visitor, forcing Jessica to abandon her fantasies for the day.

Using the rim of the trampoline like a monkey bar, Sarah did a perfect handstand, twisted her body and came down feet first onto the tramp.

Show off, Jessica thought.

Sarah was a natural athlete who excelled at every sport she picked up. Tennis, gymnastics, cheerleading, soccer. It exhausted Jess. She and Sarah cheered during seventh and eighth grade and Jessica was actually good at it. Good enough to make captain that second year. But it was Sarah who was the team's star tumbler. Jess grew sick of the coach praising how great Sarah's tucks were when Jess, with her long, gangly legs struggled to get a basic back handspring. Rather than compete with her twin—and lose—Jess quit.

Well that and Mari-Beth's "so over" cheerleading hints.

Sarah slid next to Jess on the rim.

"Mommy's looking for you. She wanted to know if you guys were going to sleep in the basement tonight?"

"Gross. There are spiders in the basement," Jessica said with an exaggerated eye roll.

"Daddy sprayed last night. It's probably fine."

"Fine for you and your friends, maybe." Jess pouted.

"Wow. So Mina's moved up to friend status?"

"Please! What I meant was, I don't want to sleep in the basement. Not even with the rejects from the soc project," Jess explained. Her shoulders caved. "You know, I hate it here. I wish daddy's band would get a record deal and blow up. Then we could move."

Sarah sat thoughtfully, neither acknowledging nor ignoring her sister's comment. Jess had been wishing to be somebody else since they were old enough to talk.

Jess wished their dad wasn't "just" a music teacher/aspiring musician. She wished their mom had gone on to become a great artist instead of deciding to be a stay-at-home wife and mother. She wished she were light like Sarah. She wished they would win the lottery and strike it rich.

She wished. She wished. She wished.

"Well, just remember to take me with you when you find that castle with your *real* parents," Sarah said.

It was their inside joke. Because of Jess's constant million-dollar dreams and tastes, Sarah teased that they were probably a product of infant switching like *The Parent Trap*. Somewhere out there was a twin who liked cold pizza and didn't mind sitting in the smoky basement while their dad's band jammed.

There had to be. How else to explain why Jess's tastes had never fit in with the rest of the Johnson clan.

Sarah leaned and gave her twin a quick hug, ignoring that Jessica tensed under the affectionate gesture.

"Hey, isn't that Mina?" she asked.

Jessica followed Sarah's gaze until she spotted the silver BMW 7 Series doing the stop and stutter crawl of someone trying to find the right address.

"That car is so hot," she said, desire in her eyes. "Mrs. Mooney is always so stylish. Too bad Mina's such a wannabe."

Sarah tipped precariously as she walked to the opposite end of the trampoline before balancing herself on the edge.

"How come you don't like her?"

Jessica made pitiful eyes at her sister. It pained her to explain the obvious. "I don't need a reason not to like her. You're too friendly with everybody."

Sarah stood up and bounced on the tramp, doing a perfect toe touch, body upright, feet snapping up to her hands while her toes remained pointed. She did consecutive toe touches fluidly like most people did jumping jacks.

"Ready to come down?" Sarah asked, not even winded.

"No. Just . . . can you send her up here?" Jessica said.

"You're one of a kind, Sis," Sarah said, another inside joke, before jumping down.

Jess played along. "And don't you forget it."

She watched the Mooneys' BMW pull in front of her house. The freshly detailed car looked completely out of place in their crumbling, driveway junked wit half a dozen of her father's unfinished projects. A partially painted door for the basement, sawed off pieces of molding for the dining room, hammers, nails, and paint brushes littered the drive, forcing Mina's mother to pull up only the nose of the big Beemer.

Mina, Jacinta, and Kelly filed out of the car, blabbing.

Mina's voice carried across the yard, "I'm not saying LL Cool J doesn't have a bangin' body, but I can't be scheming on the same dude as my mother."

Mina's mom stepped out of the car, midchatter. "You girls wish there was a rapper, today who had the full package like Uncle L, body, lyrics, acting resume."

"Ice Cube," Kelly said.

"She said nice body, Kelly," Mina said.

"Princess, I'm kind of with your moms on this one," Jacinta said.

"Kelly?" Mina gave her an I-know-you're-with-me look.

"I already answered wrong. So I'm out of this." Kelly laughed. "Shoot, I'm still in mourning over B2K."

She and Mina bowed their heads momentarily before breaking into hysterical laughter.

A chill broke Jessica's arms out in gooseflesh. She shook involuntarily and rubbed her arms. Seeing the girls arrive together stabbed at her. It wasn't being left out of their girls' club chatter, but having to be around it all night. The soc project was old. Worse since this was their third weekend together, back-to-back. Thank God Mina's— the last—was already scheduled for next weekend.

Get this over with! Jessica thought.

Jess had fallen into a social black hole thanks to the project. She couldn't wait to shake off the weekends with her classmates, ridding herself of every memory, like a dog drying off after a bath.

Jessica winced when her mom, a petite blonde, emerged from the house wiped her hands dotted with paint on her paint-stained T-shirt then extended it to Mrs. Mooney. To her credit, Mina's mom didn't draw back even though she was pristine in a mint-green pantsuit.

"How are you, Mariah? I haven't seen you since the girls cheered together."

Jessica watched Jacinta's face go into overdrive, her thick eyebrows scowled in confusion as she stared openly at Jessica's mother. You could practically hear her brain tick as she tried to connect something from the white face with Jessica's dark one.

"Jessica!" her mom called out. Spotting her on the tramp, she scolded, "Come on, your company's here. Girls go on and put your bags in the house."

Jessica reluctantly lowered herself from the trampoline and made her way to the driveway.

"You remember, Mrs. Mooney, Mina's mom, right?"

"Hi," Jessica said.

"Hi," Mina's mom said. "I don't know about you, Jessica. But if there's one class Mina better pass it's this one. She can get an A in sleepovers with her eyes closed. Oops, no pun intended."

Mina and Jessica's mothers shared a good laugh. Jessica obliged with a polite teeter.

"So Mina's cheering for JV this year?" Jessica's mom asked.

"Yes. She considered going out for an all-star cheer squad this year. But I'm telling you, the costs for the travel and gym fees . . ." Mina's mom shook her head. "And she wanted to do all-star in *addition* to JV. That girl will pick my pockets dry if I let her."

Jessica unconsciously looked toward the BMW. Their pockets weren't that dry, she thought.

"You don't have to tell me," Jessica's mom said. She swatted Jessica on the butt. "I have that times two. Now Ms. Jess here has decided she has modeling aspirations. It never ends, does it?"

"No. It doesn't." There was a comfortable pause, filled only by the girls coming back out of the house, with Sarah along. "Well, you girls have fun or . . . I don't know what I'm supposed to say when the sleepover is homework," Mina's mom said. "You girls get some work done. How about that?"

Mina pecked her mom on the cheek. "See you."

"Jacinta, your aunt is doing pick-up, right?" Mina's mom asked.

"Yes," Jacinta said.

"Well, it was good to see you again, Jennifer," Mina's mom said. Her keys jangled in rhythm with her heels as she made her way across the crowded driveway back to her car.

Looking every bit the stylish mother of Jessica's dream, wide stunner shades and camera-ready smile, Mariah waved one last time. The BMW ran silently, easing out of the driveway as if it floated on air.

Jessica's mom waved as the car backed away. She tweaked Jessica's shoulder. "Okay, girls. I was right in the middle of painting. So, I'll get out of your way."

"Mom, can I go over to Sherri's?" Sarah asked.

"Honey, wait until Dad gets home. I'm right in the middle of this."

"Sarah, hang with us," Mina said.

"God, Mina!" Jessica frowned. "You act like this is your house. You can't just invite Sarah without asking if it's okay with me."

Mina side-glanced Jacinta then Kelly, letting a silent "whatever" pass between them.

"Sorry. I didn't think it was a big deal since she's your sister," Mina said.

Sarah tried to joke away the awkwardness. "I don't want to mess up the soc flow."

Jessica cut her eyes at the girls. "Believe me, there's no flow to mess up."

Mina made prayer hands at Sarah and pleaded with her eyes for Sarah to stay. Mina and Sarah had always gotten along. Having easy-going Sarah around, even for a little while, might make the long evening ahead less of a chore.

"I don't know why you'd voluntarily hang out with them," Jessica said. "But hey, whatev."

Mina wrapped her arm around Sarah's, tugging. "Just hang out until your dad gets home."

Jessica was already heading back to the trampoline. She wasn't ready for the girls to breech her house, one of her last havens away from them.

Jacinta's eyes roamed the expansive stretch of the trampoline.

"Okay, ya'll . . . I have a thing about trampolines. I broke my arm once on one."

"We'll boost you," Kelly said.

Jacinta stopped a few inches away.

"It's not that. I'm just not comfortable on 'em."

Everyone stopped and stared in her direction. Jessica pulled herself onto the tramp and looked down on the girls.

"You live in a bad neighborhood and that's fine, but you're afraid of a bouncy mat?"

"Man, shut up," Jacinta said.

Mina pulled herself onto the trampoline. She laid on her stomach and leaned over. "Come on."

"Come on what?" Jacinta frowned.

"I'll pull if Kelly and Sarah push."

"Why can't we just go in the house?" Jacinta said.

Jessica sat with her arms crossed, making no moves to give Jacinta a hand.

"Nobody questioned you when you had us parading through your nabe last Friday," Jessica said.

"It's not that bad," Sarah said to Jacinta. "Grab onto the edge."

Jacinta did, throwing darts with her eyes at Jessica the whole time. She pushed on the edge of the trampoline, while Mina pulled on her wrists and Sarah and Kelly gave her butt a shove. She fell onto the tramp's matting with an ungraceful whoomp.

Not trusting her legs to stand, Jacinta crawled toward the center, bouncing as Kelly and Sarah stepped onto the trampoline with a double thud.

"Aren't there supposed to be some kind of nets, fence, or something around this whole thing?" Jacinta asked.

Jessica and Sarah shared a look and laughed.

"Well there *should* be," Sarah said.

"Our father is the Anti–Mr. Fix-It," Jessica said.

"He starts things," Sarah said.

"But never finishes them," the twins chorused.

Suddenly, Jessica was glad Sarah was there.

"We've had this thing for three years and that's how long he's been putting up the net guards," Sarah said. "We jump near the middle. But our mom has a heart attack anytime I do any tumbling on it."

"Once Sarah did a back flip and sprained her butt from landing on the frame." Jessica said.

Sarah rubbed her lower back. "We should never speak of that out of respect for my buns."

Mina scooted over to look down at the ground five feet below. "I'd be too afraid to tumble this high without nets."

Jessica's bored tone returned.

"Sarah's a daredevil. She doesn't care."

Kelly stared back and forth between the sisters. "It's so weird that you guys are twins."

Sarah smashed her face against Jessica's. "Nah. Look closer. It's like staring in a mirror."

Jessica pushed Sarah away, playfully. "Not really."

"You can see the resemblance," Mina said, meaning it. Sarah and Jessica had the same oval-shaped eyes. What made it drastically different were that Jess's were hazel.

"If you took those contacts out, it would be a little more obvious," Jacinta said, snatching the words from Mina's mind.

"Who said I cared if we looked alike?" Jessica said, her face icy.

"So, does her majesty treat you like she treats everybody else?" Jacinta asked.

Sarah wisely kept quiet. It was answer enough for the girls.

"After next weekend, promise me you'll act like we never met," Jessica said, clasping her hands together in a plea.

Jacinta pushed herself toward the center, keeping her distance from the edges. "Trust, that's a promise I can take to my grave."

"So, are you guys making any progress?" Sarah asked.

Again there was silence. Kelly decided to be the politically correct one. "I think so. I mean, Cinny and Jessica haven't ripped each other's eyes out." With a smile hidden in her eyes she looked at her project mates. "I'd say that's progress, right guys?"

"Definite, progress," Mina said, not joking. She wasn't expecting much for the day. Jessica had made it clear she wasn't into sharing.

"I'm just not interested in being friends with any of you," Jessica said with a shrug.

"And none of us are shedding any tears because of that," Jacinta shot back. It's not like . . ."

Mina touched Jacinta's leg, gently pressing her to quiet down. Jacinta took the hint.

"In class you guys all sit together and Mina and Kelly eat lunch together. That's fine for you all, but I don't care," Jessica said. "I wouldn't be caught dead talking to any of you if it weren't for this class."

"Your honesty is like, woah," Kelly said.

"I still don't get why you think you're the shit." Jacinta shook her head. "I don't mean no harm, but you not exactly high rolling." She swiveled around and scoped out the houses on Jessica's street. "Just going by how you and your little friend, Mari, dogging out everybody who not on your 'list,' I'm still trying to figure out how you got on the list anyway."

Sarah picked at her sneakers. She wanted to excuse herself. Jess was more than able to defend herself. But Sarah's twin vibe was tingling. She wouldn't leave Jess to brave it alone.

Three curious faces loomed in front of Jessica.

"Mari and I have been friends since sixth grade. There's no mystery behind it," Jessica said. But the nervous shift in her eyes toward Sarah said otherwise.

"I can vouch for that," Sarah said. "Ever since that first day of school in sixth grade they've been close."

Jessica's heart ached. She loved her twin more than anything at that moment for not revealing how she really felt about Jess's best friend. It was no secret from Jessica that Sarah disliked Mari-Beth with a passion.

Jess had lost count of the number of arguments they'd had about "the blond-haired, blue-eyed socialite in training," as Sarah called Mari. Their last argument had been over the summer and had all started over hair.

Jessica was going to Bermuda with the Lintons and needed her hair extensions done. Her parents made it clear they were no longer up for including the costly expense in their summer budget. Their household's income shrank once school was out. They couldn't foot the bill for the extensions and give her spending money to summer on a tropical island. After throwing a major tantrum, Jessica fled the kitchen, feeling sick to her stomach.

Sarah followed her sister to her room, always there to commiserate with her twin. She listened as Jess went on about how she couldn't spend several weeks swimming with her own short, hard-to-manage hair. How, within days, she'd look like a chicken who'd lost a fight. It was too embarrassing. She'd rather stay home than face the Lintons with a nappy-head.

Sarah offered solutions: find some stylish hats and call it her summer trend, get a good perm before she left and wear her short hair slicked back, get African twists. Finally, Jessica revealed the truth. She'd already hinted to Mari-Beth, days before, that her parents might squash the extensions and Mari-Beth had said Jess would be uninvited if she didn't have the wavy locks.

Not that she'd said it exactly like that. But Jess knew what it meant when she said, "God, I've never seen your real hair. Isn't it like really short and kind of frizzy?"

Jess never had the chance to answer because Mari dropped the boom shot. "You know, we're going to spend a lot of time hanging out on the catamaran and swimming. It's not like we'll have a lot of time for you to blow dry and curl and all that. Maybe I should just bring Katie."

Jessica immediately regretted sharing the exchange with Sarah. Because Sarah had gotten all wound up and started in about how insensitive Mari-Beth was and how she didn't understand how Jess could stay friends with somebody so shallow.

"As usual she's just using you, Jess," Sarah said. "Don't do it Mari's way and you're yesterday's news."

"Using me for what?" Jessica spat. "We live in a tiny three-room shack on our father's fat teacher's salary." Her eyes rolled in mock exaggeration. "Oooohh what on earth could Mari want from me?" She tapped one finger on her lip, pretending to think. "Oh, I know, maybe she wants Dad's old raggedy pickup. Or Mom's hip, trendy minivan. Or, oh, I know, she wants to renovate our house and make it her guest house. I mean everybody wants to vacation in Woodberry Ridge!"

"Jess, you're playing dumb on purpose. You know exactly what I mean," Sarah said. "You're like her shadow, doing exactly what she does. And everything is great as long as you keep being the shadow and not a real person. But the first time you decide you don't want to go along she's on to the next friend."

"Don't you and your friends do things for each other?"

"Yeah, but I don't change how I look for them," Sarah said. Her voice had grown louder and more agitated. "And it never gets me in trouble. And I don't constantly try to get out of doing stuff with you and Mom and Dad because of them. Or quit a sport because they think it's not cool."

"But you also don't get to lunch at the Folgers club on Saturdays or play tennis there or swim there with your friends," Jessica said, lowering her voice. She didn't want their mom to come refereeing. "You never get invited to travel on vacations with your friends. I mean real places like Bermuda. I do."

Sarah looked as if she'd been slapped. But she hadn't argued back. She didn't hang around with people like Mari-Beth, a pampered princess whose parents didn't mind footing the bill for Jess to tag along if that's what "Mare" wanted. The only family vacation the Johnsons took were a few days in Ocean City, the beach resort, two hours away. And those weren't guaranteed.

Jess felt bad when Sarah stood abruptly and headed to her room. She hadn't meant to throw it in Sarah's face. She was just upset about missing out on the trip over something as small as how her hair was done. She followed behind her sister.

"Look, I'm sorry that I like spending so much time with Mari. But I do," Jessica said, in a warm tone heard by few outside of her home. "And even if she is using me, it's not like I'm not getting something out of it, too."

"Forever is a long time to be a shadow," Sarah said.

Jessica gave her twin's shoulder a squeeze, the closest she ever came to hugging. They weren't identical, dress-alike, Bobbsey twins, and they didn't agree on much. But they were still sisters.

"It's not all bad. It's not like she asked me to kill somebody," Jessica said, meaning it as a joke.

"I hope she never does," Sarah said, her voice heavy. She went to her room across the hall. Before shutting the door, she said, "I still have the money Gramps sent us for our birthday. If you want it for your hair you can have it."

They hadn't argued about Mari-Beth since. Unless you counted Sarah making jokes here and there about having the bail money ready in case Jess needed to steal some extensions from the Beauty Emporium to get her hair done for school.

With only a twinge of guilt, Jessica had taken Sarah up on the offer. Now she felt she owed Sarah again, for not putting her and Mari's friendship on the chopping block of scrutiny in front of her classmates.

Jessica sent a silent thank-you with her eyes across the tramp to Sarah.

Sarah pretended not to see the look. There was so much she wanted to say about Jess's friendship with Mari-Beth and none of it was good.

Jess was the more outspoken and independent twin. She was the one who put her foot down when they were four, refusing to dress in the same clothes as Sarah anymore. Yet, Sarah could list a dozen times she'd watch Jessica do something stupid in the name of pleasing Mari-Beth. And those were just the things she knew about. Watching how Mari-Beth worked, Sarah knew there had to be plenty more.

Jessica gave into anything Mari asked, no matter the consequence. And Mari was so slick about it. She never came right out and demanded. To get her way, Mari-Beth played the sympathy card, turning her tears off and on when she needed. Or, she'd make a subtle threat, like saying she'd take someone else on vacation instead of Jess. Mari-Beth had a wicked streak a mile long when things didn't go her way.

Sarah had plenty of reasons to dislike Mari-Beth and the feeling was mutual. Mari-Beth saw Sarah, or anything that wasn't about Jess being at her beck and call, as competition that gobbled up Jess's time.

Sarah was lucky if she was in the top ten of things taking up Jess's attention. The most time they spent together was dinner, back and forth to school on the bus and the one weekend a month their parents called Johnsons Only, their mom's idea when the twins turned twelve and their weekends began to drown in sports and sleepovers. If it wasn't for JO weekends, Sarah and Jessica might never bond.

But Sarah sensed the tension, tight as a violin string, between Jessica and her project mates. Plus, she was an invited guest in the circle today. She wouldn't add any fuel to whatever fire was burning among the girls.

Kelly watched the silent exchange between the twins. She didn't buy that Mari-Beth was the world's best friend and she told them so.

"That's weird. I knew Mari-Beth in elementary school. She's always been into excluding people. If she didn't like yellow and you were wearing that color that was enough for her to not speak to you that day." Kelly rocked, trying to steady herself on the tramp's mat. She frowned. "Have you guys always lived here?" She was apologetic. "I don't mean to sound cold, but Mari-Beth has taunted people for way less."

"I know that's right," Mina murmured. She promised herself she wasn't going to go the extra mile to get to know Jess. Two cheer seasons from hell were all she needed to know. Kelly and Jacinta were on their own with today's research.

"The first day of sixth grade our teacher made us all say our names and one thing about ourselves. Mari's one thing was she had transferred from McStew. I introduced myself to her after class. We lived happily ever after," Jessica said.

"Oh, so you were jocking her?" Jacinta said.

"I introduced myself. There was no 'jocking,'" Jessica said, making air quotes. She rolled her eyes in exasperation.

"What does your dad do?" Kelly asked.

"Why?" Jessica wrapped and unwrapped a piece of hair around her finger. She looked to Sarah.

"He's a music teacher in PG County," Sarah said, proud. "He's the sax player with The A-Town Express. It's his jazz band. They play small clubs and stuff all around the region."

"Oh that's ya'll father? I've seen him play," Jacinta said, remembering the band from her cousin's wedding last year. The guy playing the sax had been about six-foot-five and thin with mahogany skin. Jessica obviously took after him in build and complexion.

"I asked because . . ." Kelly considered holding back then blurted. "Mari-Beth has got to be getting something out of you guys' friendship. Unless she's changed a whooolllllle lot. And anyone who tells some- one they're odd but then invites them to hang out the next day . . . hasn't changed."

Jacinta burst out laughing at the memory of Kelly's sleepover and Mari-Beth's "invitation."

"Well, she is the bossiest person ever. That's my problem with her," Sarah said. She sent Jess an apology with her eyes and promised herself she'd say no more.

"That's your *only* problem with her?" Jacinta quipped.

Mina hugged her knees to her chest to hide her smile. Cool air wisped up her pants leg. She braved a comment, fidgeting to ward off the chills. "Bossy, I can take. Mari is a good candidate for burning at the stake. She's a straight up witch. "

Jacinta laughed heartily and Kelly chuckled. Sarah didn't respond.

"That's my best friend you guys are ragging on," Jessica said. "And if it's open season, then I'll start with Mina and her wannabe friend who's all up in Lila's butt."

"Don't go there, Jess. Lizzie's never done anything to you," Mina said. "But Mari-Beth has a list of enemies as long as this street." She stretched her arms out for emphasis. "You don't make enemies by being an innocent bystander."

"And you don't become an Upper by wishing," Jessica shot back.

Mina contemplated for a second. If she had any ground to lose when it came to getting into the café, it was probably lost the day Jessica was placed in her group. "If I'm making any of this up, you can call me mud over the PA system Monday morning . . ."

"Is that a promise?" Jessica mewed.

"Didn't you, Mari, Katie, Belinda, and Jenny start the slam book with all these racist jokes in it? And someone had wrote that LaMont Dozier was a jiggaboo?" Mina said.

Jessica's eyes fluttered quickly then blinked hard one time, registering blank as she stammered. "That happened a million years ago."

"Yeah. But did ya'll start it?"

"Yeah. So," Jessica said. "We were like twelve. Just being stupid."

"Well how come only you got in trouble for it?" Mina said.

The neighborhood's chatter grew in the absence of any answer from Jessica. The soft idling of a car as it whispered by made the silence on the tramp louder.

"And ya'll were girls, real close. The glam pack," Mina said.

"Squad," Jessica said in irritation.

"I remember how tight you guys were. Always dressing alike and walking down the halls side-by-side so no one could walk beside or near you."

"Yeah. You were wishing you could be down even then, huh?" Jessica said.

"Oh most definitely." Mina laughed at the memory. "For a minute, it was like all I thought about. But when you got in trouble for the slam book, I knew what was up."

Jessica tried to put the coolness back in her voice, but it came off shaky. "You don't know anything."

"That's why I'm asking you. I know what I heard back then," Mina said, warming up as the sun suddenly blazed bright through some clouds above the trampoline. She unzipped her jacket. "That your clique put you out there and you got suspended because of it."

"Umph, that's messed up," Jacinta said.

Kelly's eyes were wide and curious. "How come no one else got in trouble?"

"Basically, what I heard was that a teacher found Katie writing in the book," Mina said. Her hands danced as she recounted the story. "He took it from her and asked Katie to rat out who else was responsible. But Katie wouldn't. Then the principal told her that school policy considered slam books with racial slurs a hate crime." She stretched her legs out, making the tramp bounce slightly, and stared at Jessica. "So Katie blamed Jessica. I mean I guess she did. Jess was the only one who got in trouble."

"So what, Mina? What's your point?" Jessica snapped.

"I just think the understanding you and Mari have is that you'll do whatever she says," Mina said. "All Katie got was a one-day suspension. You got a week. No one else even got in trouble."

"It wasn't a big deal. When Mr. Josephs started talking hate crime, Mari thought I'd get in less trouble since I was black. How can it be a hate crime if a black person wrote it? Simple," Jessica said. "It's not like this big conspiracy or anything."

"So your girl let you get suspended for a week," Jacinta sneered. "So that's on your record but not hers. You stupid."

Jessica's face crumbled into an angry scowl. Having Jacinta call her stupid was the insult of the worst kind. She fought back. "How are *you* calling *me* stupid?" Jessica's voice rose with indignation. "We'll see who's the stupid one when you're in jail serving time for having your friend, Angel's, back."

"Man, please." Jacinta refused to waste anger on Jessica. "I don't sell drugs. Don't use them. Don't place myself where Angel does his dirt. So yeah, you're the stupid one." She turned on the voice she used to mock their suburban lilt. "When Kel Bell, Katie-Did, and Mari-Mare are all off at Yale and Harvard and stuff, you'll be at the junior college still trying to erase the black mark on your record."

Jacinta laughed suddenly. "And you are black, you know? All the weave and fake eyes in the world won't change that." She pretended to think, then said, "Oh, but you know that already. That's what your friends used to get themselves *out* of trouble."

Jessica sat ramrod straight and shook her finger in Jacinta's general direction as she lashed out. "What do you know, Project Queen?" She turned her anger back on to Mina. "And for all you think you know, Mina, the only person who actually gets it is Kelly. Like she said at her house that night, it's not easy being popular. If you don't have the stomach for it you'll never know what real popularity is like. So *you* won't ever know. You don't have what it takes to roll with the Uppers."

"My clique would never ask me to get suspended for them," Mina said. "I'm not that pressed to get suspended for anybody, for that matter."

"Look, you guys . . ." Sarah said, alarmed at the nasty turn in conversation.

"Kelly, I think it's crazy that you'd rather hang around with a middle grounder like Mina," Jessica said. "But, I'll respect that you've decided the pop game isn't for you." She turned her nose up at Jacinta. "But I'm not going to be judged by someone like you. Do us all a favor and go back to Sam-Well next year, with the other hood rats." Not finished, Jessica looked Mina in the eye. As usual, she felt a certain special disgust for Mina. "You're in the middle of the pack. You'll always be in the middle of the pack. Stay out of my way unless you want to see how it feels at the bottom."

She stared at Mina one second longer to bring her point home, then hugged her knees to her chest and watched the kids across the street play an energetic game of kickball.

Mina slipped her hands under her legs to hide the trembling. She tried to take comfort in having Jacinta and Kelly on either side of her. But their closeness couldn't keep her stomach from diving. The steely taste of bile rose in her throat.

Jessica's mom peered from the front door. "Girls? Is anyone hungry or thirsty?"

"I think you guys could use a break," Sarah said, in a low voice. She peeked her head up. "We're coming in for a drink, Mom!"

The girls filed off the trampoline. Jessica sauntered into the house, while the other girls helped Jacinta work her way down.

"Sarah, I'm sorry," Mina said, her eyes dewy with unshed tears. She didn't want to cry, but at this point it was cry, or throw up.

"Why?" Sarah asked.

SO NOT THE DRAMA **3 1 5**

"I hate your sister," Mina said. A tear slipped from her eye and she quickly dried it with her shirt sleeve.

"I knew you guys didn't get along. But I didn't know it was this bad," Sarah said, eyeing the house to check on Jessica's whereabouts. The girls huddled around her, no one anxious to go inside.

"Ya'll two couldn't be more different. Your sister is off the hook," Jacinta said.

"Jess is just really . . . serious about her status in school," Sarah said, voice low. "For whatever reason, Mina, it's like she sees you as a threat."

Mina nodded, unable to talk without the dam breaking on her tears. She was grateful when Kelly rubbed her arm with a warm smile.

"Isn't it weird how people find each other?" Kelly said. "Mari probably saw that Jessica would do anything to be friends. They're a good match. Scary. But good."

Mina managed a tiny laugh.

"They're like Frankenfriends. A friendship built in somebody's evil lab," Jacinta said.

"Stop, ya'll. She's still Sarah's sister," Mina said. She didn't want to disrespect Sarah. And for once it wasn't about climbing the popularity ladder. She felt bad for Sarah, having to live with Jess's poison 24/7.

Sarah's smile was grateful. "I'm used to people not liking Jess. And you know she doesn't care who doesn't like her."

"We know," the girls said, muffling their chorus with a round of "shh" and giggles.

"Come on," Sarah said. She led the girls into the house.

Hours later, Jessica was sorry to hear the light twitter of their father's horn signaling Sarah to hurry up. He was dropping her off to

Sherri's on his way to pick up another band member for their late-night gig.

The soc sleepover, so far, had been bearable because of Sarah. The last few hours had passed with them talking in the pit, the Johnsons' damp, dark, and clammy finished basement. Well, Mina and Jacinta talking to Sarah and Jessica adding a comment here and there, usually because of something Kelly asked her.

Mina and Jacinta hadn't uttered a word to Jessica since coming into the house. Jessica hadn't cared while Sarah was there.

"See you guys," Sarah said. With a wave, she disappeared up the stairs.

The thought of sitting in the pit with the girls, by herself, made Jessica scramble behind her.

"Why don't you just hang out with us the rest of the night," Jessica said, hoping she didn't sound like she was begging, though she was sure she did.

"She's already waiting on me. We're going to the movies," Sarah said. Thrusting her arms into a jacket, she slowed when she saw that Jessica was upset. She lowered her voice. "Jess, it'll be okay."

"This stupid project is taking forever to end," Jessica said, sniffing back tears.

"Turn on a movie. Then you guys don't have to talk," Sarah suggested. She wanted to recommend that Jess try being nice. But after seeing how she talked to Mina, Sarah knew they were past that option.

Jessica blinked back the tears. She straightened up and flipped her hair off her shoulders. "I'll be fine. It's just when you were here I didn't have to make conversation. Have fun," she said, then marched off into the kitchen.

Keeping herself hidden, she watched from the bay window as Sarah hopped into the truck and gave their father a kiss on the cheek. The truck pulled off and was gone in seconds.

Kelly's soft voice came from behind, startling her. "We were just talking and . . . maybe it's not such a good idea if we spend the entire night."

"Are you like the spokesperson or something?" Jessica said.

"I think I'm the only one who hasn't gotten into some kind of fight with you," Kelly said, honestly.

"I don't care if you guys want to leave. Just don't turn around and tell Mrs. Simms that I didn't do my part," Jessica said. She rose to her full height warding off defeat. She'd spent an entire night in the hood and yet they couldn't stand to be in her house for twenty-four hours. It ranked right up there with being called stupid by Jacinta as the most insulting thing ever.

"I think we should stay. But, you know, only if it's going to be productive," Kelly said.

It didn't escape Jessica's attention that even though Kelly had turned down the offer to hang out with Mari-Beth and her, after the first sleepover, Kelly was now the closest thing Jessica had to someone she could relate to. The script was flipped and it was *Outer Limits* meets *Roswell* strange.

Kelly's invitation to "Come on back downstairs," was the only white flag Jessica needed.

She strode by Kelly and descended back into the basement, her confidence in place.

Jacinta and Mina, their heads together on the sofa, the room's lone piece of furniture, stopped talking the second Jessica's foot hit the bottom landing of the stairs.

"I think we should stay the whole night. Jess is up for it," Kelly announced, relishing her role as mediator.

"Too late. I already called my aunt," Jacinta said. She tucked her leg underneath her as she slipped her cell phone into her pocket. "She's on her way."

Kelly's face cracked. "But I thought we said . . ."

"What? Am I supposed to apologize or something to get you guys to stay?" Jessica said, speaking only to Kelly. She folded her arms.

Kelly looked from Mina, who was unusually quiet, back to Jacinta. She spoke with her eyes, frustrated that they changed their minds while she was upstairs smoothing things over.

Jessica leaned against the clammy, moist wall. She wiped her hands in disgust and remained standing in the middle of the doorway. Her eyes drooped with boredom masking the raging embarrassment swelling in her chest. *They* were walking out on *her*, a twist of epic proportions.

"I'm not going to beg you guys to stay," Jessica said.

"We don't want you to," Jacinta said. She looked at Mina, waiting on her to finish the sentence.

Mina cleared her throat. Her eyes flitted nervously between Kelly, Jessica, and the walls dotted with portraits of Jessica, and Sarah posed and at play as she mumbled, "It's not like we're going to get anything done."

"Come on, don't do this," Kelly said.

"You can stay, Kelly," Jacinta said.

"It's a group project!" Kelly exploded. "What good is it if half the group isn't here?"

"We're just not spending the night. We've been here all day, Kell," Mina said.

"But spending the day wasn't what we agreed on," Kelly said. "It's not right, you guys."

"I tell you what," Jacinta said. She addressed Jessica this time. "Just ask us to stay and we'll stay."

Kelly nodded, eager to save the project from imploding. "That's fair."

"How is that fair?" Jessica said, eyebrows scrunched.

"If you ask us to stay, chances are you won't treat us like we're something stuck on the bottom of your shoes," Jacinta said.

"And if I don't?" Jessica said. She thought the whole challenge was ridiculous.

"Then it means we'll probably spend the rest of the night not saying or doing anything since we're so beneath you," Jacinta mocked.

"But we'll finish out the project like we agreed we'd do it," Kelly said.

"Kelly, if me and Cinny are in one corner and you and her are in another, that's not what we planned either," Mina said.

"I'm not taking sides with anyone," Kelly said, quickly.

Jessica caught the panic in Kelly's voice and felt betrayed. She shifted a step away from her.

"I mean . . . it's not going to be like that," Kelly said.

"It won't if she asks us to stay. But Kelly, things won't change just 'cause you want us to stay." Jacinta pointed at Jessica. "It's *her* sleep-over."

"Jessica, just ask us to stay," Mina said. She made herself look into Jessica's hurt and angry eyes. A part of her felt bad but she shushed that part, refusing to hear it.

"Why? So you can go back and tell everyone at school I begged you to sleep over at my house?" A strangled chuckle escaped her throat. "No thanks."

"This isn't about school," Mina said.

"Um, class project, Mina. Yeah, it is," Jessica said, her sarcasm growing as her anger took hold. "Remember, me not being caught dead with you guys outside of Del Rio High, ever, otherwise."

Mina shook her head and looked at Kelly, hoping she got the message. But Kelly stood her ground. "Just stay. It's like almost eight o'clock. We can . . . go to bed early," she said.

"Alright. Last chance, Jess-eh-ca," Jacinta said. "Are you gonna ask us to stay or what?"

Jessica's eyebrow was so high it nearly hit her forehead. She pursed her lips and her arms tightened against her body. "Or what."

She ascended the stairs, slow and deliberately, leaving them sitting there.

"You guys, I think this is wrong," Kelly whispered, angry.

"And when did you become such a big fan of hers?" Jacinta said.

"It's not about that."

"Kell, we have more than enough info to write our observations," Mina said. She didn't want Kelly to be angry. But she was ready to go.

"Mina, come on. You've known Jessica longer than us. You know she's just being . . . herself," Kelly said. "Why are you acting like you can't stand it any longer, now?"

"That's just it. I do know her," Mina said. "If some brand-new side of her had come out today, I could see your point. But it didn't. I'm not going to spend the rest of the night waiting on her to crap on me some more."

Jessica's voice floated down to them. "Jacinta, your aunt is here."

"Come on we gone," Jacinta said. "Let's go get our bags."

She and Mina got up and walked up the stairs. Mina stopped midway up the stairs and peered down into the basement. "Kelly, are you coming?"

Kelly came to the bottom of the stairwell. She looked up at Mina, her face tight. It was her only answer before walking away and disappearing back into the basement.

Soc
9-23-05
Observations by Jessica Johnson

I don't know what I hate more, these stupid sleepovers, Jacinta, or Mina. I can't believe they bailed. CAN'T BELIEVE! I tried being honest. That's why I told them if it weren't for this project we'd never socialize outside of school. I wasn't trying to be mean. I really don't care about becoming friends with them. So what do I get for trying to go with the flow of the project and letting them know how I really feel? A revenge of the losers' mutiny.

If this gets out, every pop wannabe will think they can take on the glams. But I think Mina has enough sense to keep it quiet. She only went along because of Jacinta anyway. Like I said, she's weak. And Jacinta isn't friends with anyone that matters. This better be between the four of us. I don't want to have to explain to Mari how I lost control and had two nobodies walk out on me.

Can't believe Kelly stayed. She might reach that potential after all. She never said a word about them walking out, even when my mom asked where the girls were. I made up some story about Mina having cramps and wanting to go home. I don't think she bought it. But she didn't ask anymore either.

I'm majorly impressed that Kelly ended up being the one with the most guts. I'll take a million nights with her over one with the other two any day. Thank God I won't have to. Last sleepover is next weekend. FINALLY.

Sociology
September 23, 2005
Jacinta Phillips
What did I say from the start? That I thought Jessica was phony. I was expecting her crib to be laid out and huge. I can't figure out how she lives in this little boxy house with all the rooms on one floor except for

the basement and still acts like she was born into royalty. I bet her girl, Mari-Beth, never spends the night there. I just kept staring at her house wondering where the rest of it was. And I'm not busting on her house. It just doesn't match her royal highness's constant 'tude.

It's not like she comes from mad poverty or anything. She has a nice house with two parents. Shoot, her mother seems like she'd bake you cookies. I gotta say, it was crazy strange to hear her call this white woman Mom. Still, her pops obviously stay on his grind teaching and playing music enough to keep them all laced with nice things. Jessica's hair weave alone gotta cost them a couple bones every few months. She already have a lot more than some!

I know us walking out on her had to be a first. Kelly could have come if she wanted. Hey, want to play peacemaker, get left behind.

I loved the look on Jessica's face when we said we were leaving. For once she tripped right off her pedestal. Her eyes bugged for a few seconds, even though she tried to play it off. For all the mouth Jessica have, she just a pretender. A real bad chick would have never got herself suspended just 'cause some snotty rich girl told her to. I'd still be snatching those girls bald to this day. Jessica, your bad girl card been REVOKED.

Sociology
September 23, 2005
Observations by Kelly Lopez

I can't believe Mina and Cinny left like that. Right now, Jessica is sitting across from me scribbling her notes. The pen can barely keep up with how fast she's writing. She's hurt and angry and I don't blame her. We said we'd spend the night over at each person's house. I didn't want to stay there, either, especially by myself. But I wasn't going back on my word. I would have never gone upstairs and gotten Jessica if I had known Mina and Cinny were planning to leave all along. That's what made me so mad. They turned on me. If Mina and Cinny are mad at me after this, so be it. I'm not going to start going along with people, again, just to make friends.

I know that Jessica has issues. But no more than anybody else. I mean come on. I have issues with my mom and making friends. Jacinta has a mother who's addicted to drugs and a friend who sells drugs—it's like the world's worst conflict. But they can't spend another few hours, half of them sleeping, over at Jessica's to hear her admit that she's a snob and isn't particularly concerned if we care or not. I know she hurt Mina's feelings, but according to Mina it wasn't the first time.

I'm glad I stayed. It's not like Jessica and I ended up having a tear-jerker confessional or anything. But her mom hung out for awhile and showed me some old photos. I saw lots of pictures of the twins. Sarah was a little light-skinned baby in her dad's dark arms and

Jessica was a dark-skinned baby in her mom's white arms. And for me, it didn't seem so crazy anymore that Jessica is cruel to people and quick to pick and choose who gets to hang out with her clique. I think she acts that way just because she can. The way we treat people is the only thing any person has any real power over.

Soc

9/23/05

Observations by Amina Mooney

This is crazy. I feel like I'm hiding out, even though Cinny's aunt only lives a few streets away from my house. Her Aunt Jacqi almost took me home and I screamed NO so loud she almost ran off the road. But if I called myself walking up in the house at 8:30 at night when I was supposed to be somewhere (for homework) my mother would have driven my butt right back over to Jessica's. But my head hurts and I wish I could go home.

That nervous stomach I used to get around Jessica had gotten better. Now it's back. Only tonight, it's not just because Jess seems to save up her thickest nastiest attitude, so she can hurl it at me. It's also because I don't want to become her! The way she said she'd make sure I suffered at the bottom if I got in her way was on the psycho tip. It's not like she's hanging on to friends who have her back. I'd rather be the school's loneliest geek than kick it with someone like Mari.

After the slam book thing, the whole school joked on Jessica, calling her (behind her back, of course) the racist black girl. I felt sorry for her. When it happened, I always said JZ, Michael, and Lizzie would fess up and take the hit with me. Even suspension! I'd like to think they would anyway. I still feel a little sorry for Jessica because she definitely has some of the most sometimey, uncaring friends ever. Okay, I'm done. I said I felt A LITTLE, sorry for her.

Mostly, what I feel is relief. This project is almost over. And if I didn't learn anything from tonight, I figured out that my friends are the shiggity. I miss kicking it with them. Right now I'd much rather be at Lizzie's than here. No offense, Cinny. But I need a serious dose of life before the soc project.

I Got My Own Beef to Squash

"I got the rock in my hands
There ain't no tellin' what I'm gonna do wit it."
—Bow Wow, "Basketball"

Saturday afternoon, Michael snatched a hat from a shelf full of them, smashed it on top of his head, changed his mind, and flung it back. He glared at the hats as if his indecision was their fault.

Mina knew she was the reason he was angry. She'd burst into his room, speech prepared for why he and JZ had to make up, right now—a rambling speech full of admissions of her guilty conscience for being the cause of the disagreement. The only time he looked away from the hats was when she said, "I know I let this whole soc project get out of hand."

"Ya think?" Michael sneered.

She felt silly when he finally got a word in edgewise to let her know he was on his way to JZ's. It was then she noticed how tense he was, concentration etched on his face as if what he chose to wear would make a difference. After four of the strangest days in the clique's friendship, no e-mails, no phone calls, and no lunch together, Michael was ready to make the first move and squash the beef she started and here she was preaching to the choir. Obviously, she had blown his calm with all of her blathering.

Now she sat silently, holding herself back from stirring up his anger even more.

He stared at the shelf full of baseball caps, fedoras, knit caps, and hats, his chest heaving. Without turning around he said, his voice straining to be patient, "Look, me and JZ don't roll like I do with you. We not gon' have no girl chat session and work out our differences over some deep conversation."

"I just wanted you to know I'll help if you want," she said.

"No. You gotta let us do this our way. Alright?"

Mina nodded. "Can I come?" she whispered.

His shoulders heaved and fell hard, his patience with her at an end.

Mina wished she could take the question back. Making up would be private for them. She had no right to intrude. But it was out there now. She waited for him to deny her, so she could stand up and exit gracefully.

He surprised her, pulling himself back from saying what he really wanted to say with a shake of his head. He turned to her. "Would it matter if I said no?"

She wiggled her eyebrows and shook her head.

"That's what I thought."

He laced up his kicks, threw a lid on his head, and held his hand out to her, helping her off the bed. He grabbed his basketball out of the corner as they headed up the stairs and out into a day that begged for being outdoors. With the warm autumn sun at their back, they took their time on the stroll.

"I've gotta make up with Lizzie," Mina confessed.

Michael snorted softly, answering with the same smart, "Ya think?"

"You think she'll forgive me?" Mina fretted.

He bounced the basketball as he walked, letting the steely ping serve as his conversation.

Mina talked over his silence. "I still can't believe you two didn't come to the Ria on Thursday. I mean we deserved it I guess, but . . ." She quieted for a second. The memory of Lizzie and Michael standing up her and JZ made her throat ache. She struggled to swallow, needing to purge herself of the anxiety. "It's like we don't know how to talk to each other anymore."

"Ya'll don't know how to or just you?" Michael said, never missing a bounce with the ball.

"I . . . well, we," Mina said. She was willing to own up to her part, but it took two people to beef. "What? Are you saying it's all me?"

He shrugged. Mina tried to keep her voice nonchalant but it squeaked as she said, "Be honest, Mike. If you saying this is all totally me, just say so. I mean . . . I'm trying to figure out how to make it right."

"I'm not saying anything, Mi. I got my own beef to squash, remember?" He flung the ball down, pushing it off his fingertips with force, slamming it back to the ground each time it bounced back up to his hand.

Mina left him to his thoughts. She hadn't meant to make this about her. She was grateful Michael let her come along. If it went wrong between him and JZ, she'd do what she could to set things right.

There was no sign of life in JZ's cul-de-sac. The ping of Michael's bouncing ball competed with chirping birds and rustling leaves, but no human sounds.

Mina ventured down the long drive toward the front of JZ's house but stopped short when she realized Michael was heading to the backyard. She scurried behind him, rounding the corner on to JZ's backyard.

JZ stood on the basketball court shooting three-pointers, sweat raining down his face.

He squinted up at the net, wiped his face then took a shot, landing it easily.

"Hey, Jay," Mina called out, before taking a seat on the sideline bleacher, a party of one. She melted into the background, doing her best not to intrude more on the boys' reconciliation. At least she hoped it ended in them making up. Her stomach rumbled in anticipation of the first words.

"What's up, girl?" JZ said. He kept taking shots, while Michael took his time, lingering on the edge of the court, bouncing his own ball.

He threw a quick head nod when JZ finally turned his way.

JZ threw his own nod then sank another three-pointer.

Michael sauntered to center court, his back to JZ as he faced the opposite net.

"Wassup, kid?"

"It's all you, playuh," JZ said. He dribbled, prepping for his next shot.

Mina exhaled in relief, under her breath. So far so good.

Michael took a few shots at his basket. Each time he hit the backboard dead center, sinking the ball. He rebounded for himself, working up his own sweat, took a few more jumpers, than laid the ball up into the net. When he returned to the three-point line, JZ was there, hands out waiting for the ball. Michael flung it to him, then crouched low set to play defense.

Mina sat riveted, as they played one-on-one, showing no mercy to one another as they fought to make baskets.

JZ dribbled, faked to the left then drove to the basket from the right with Michael on his back. Michael reached in, stole the ball, and laid the ball in for a smooth two points.

On his turn, JZ immediately shot from three-point land, his body a pretty arc as the ball left his palm. A money shot. Mina smiled. Basketball season would be better than football.

On his turn, Michael dribbled slowly, thoughtfully as if he had all the time in the world. He eyed JZ, in the defensive position, pretended to drive to the basket then took the jumper from the three.

It missed. Mina frowned, torn, unsure who or even what she was rooting for. She held her breath with each fling of the ball as if its final destination would determine whether the boys actually made up.

JZ chased down the rebound, returned to the three-point line, and immediately drove to the basket. He knocked Michael over as he laid the ball into the net.

Mina cringed as Michael fell back hard on his butt, legs splayed. Her heart leapt happily when JZ extended his palm, helped Michael up, and passed him the ball.

They played, their soft grunts and the ball's hollow bounce the only communication between them.

Mina was spellbound. She silently cheered each time either of them made a basket and slammed her eyes shut, wincing, when they didn't.

After nearly an hour the game's silence was broken.

"You thirsty?" JZ asked.

Out of breath from the intense one-on-one, Michael nodded.

They headed to a full-size outdoor cooler and were swallowed, for a second, by billowing puffs of cold steam.

JZ held up a Gatorade and nodded across the court to Mina. She shook her head. He held up a bottled water and she nodded.

He walked over and parked next to her on the bleacher, handing her the chilled bottle.

"Thanks, Jay," she whispered, feeling out of place now that the game was over.

Michael joined JZ and Mina on the bleachers, wincing as the icy liquid froze his insides. He downed half the bottle before speaking. "Good game, kid."

He extended his fist.

JZ chugged his drink, offing it in one long swallow then gave Michael a pound. He returned to the cooler to get another drink. When he sat back down and spoke, his voice was raspy from their workout. "Your skills gold, son. The coaches don't know what they missing."

Michael shook his head. "You know me. I love balling, but it ain't nothing but a hobby for me."

"Rather rip your skills on the stage, huh?"

"Yeah. I gotta do me, nahmean?" Michael said.

JZ nodded. "Do your thing, playuh."

"You know I will," Michael said. "You know how I do."

JZ knocked knees with Mina. "We cool?"

Mina had goose bumps. She wanted to jump into his arms for a long hug, but knew JZ would think she was crazy. Instead she settled for the wink he gave her, assuring her he already knew the answer to his question.

Making up Is Hard to Do

Mina stared at the screen.

This had to work.

Mina had recruited her parents to help her. They sat in the front seat of her father's Navigator, the truck parked just down the street from Lizzie's house. They quietly waited for Mina's word that step one, reaching Lizzie, was complete.

Mina looked down at her father's OGO, a wireless e-mail pager, and watched as her buddy list announced Michael, then Jacinta, and her cousin, Keisha, were online. Luckily her Away message was on. She didn't want to be distracted chatting with everyone else. She was incognito, watching as her friends appeared and disappeared online.

For a second she could actually hear her heart's whump-whump-whump-whump it was so silent in the truck. Staring intently at the screen she grew frustrated as everybody except Lizzie logged on and off.

A flurry of nerves tickled her belly when Lizzie's name finally glowed bright. She took several deep breaths to get her nerve up and closed her eyes.

If her plan didn't work, she'd go old school and apologize to Lizzie at school tomorrow. But it had been three weeks since their first argument and she'd lost count how many they'd had since. Stepping to Lizzie with an "I'm sorry" felt weak. She needed to do it right.

She drew confidence from the guys' happy ending the day before and ignored that Lizzie hadn't IM'ed her. Unless Lizzie had trashed Mina from her buddy list, she could see that Mina was now online. If Mina needed any confirmation that things were bad, Lizzie not pinging her was it.

Mina sucked in a mouthful of air, exhaled noisily and let her fingers go. No surprise, she would have to do the ice breaking. She quickly changed her IM status to Available before dashing off a message.

BubbliMi: Hey. What's up?

She waited.
And waited.
Her words stared back at her like an echo. It felt just like yelling "hello" into a huge, empty black space and getting nothing back but your own voice. She forced her fingers to move again, refusing to give up.

BubbliMi: Look, I know ur pissed. But I need 2 talk 2 u

She stared at the screen, waiting. Her feet dug into the carpet as her knee tapped away, the anxiety spreading from one limb to another. When Lizzie's response appeared, Mina nearly stopped breathing.

Liz-e-O: What do you want, Mina?

She read the message three times. No mistaking the tone. It was glacial. But a snitty answer was better than none.

Time to play the game.

BubbliMi: Things have been pretty bad b/w us the last 3 weeks. Thought we might talk.

Liz-e-O: U had ur chance 2 talk and made it clear how u felt. Not sure what else there is 2 say!

BubbliMi: we both played a part in the madness but there's a better way than having a shouting match at lunch or online.

Liz-e-O: Omigod r u seriously trying to say I should be to blame for all this?!

BubbliMi: :::sighing::::: Can we talk? Offline? Face-2-Face? Jus us!

She knew Lizzie wouldn't just say yes or no that fast. She was on the other end feeling Mina out, wondering what she was up to. Just like Mina would have done her if the roles were reversed.

It took Lizzie exactly three minutes and twenty seconds to reply.

Liz-e-O: Ok when? Where?

BubbliMi: Right now.

Liz-e-O: What?

BubbliMi: Can u come open the door. I'm sitting down the street from ur house w/my parents.

Liz-e-O: Serious?

BubbliMi: Ask ur 'rents. They're in on it too.

Liz-e-O: How r u IM'in me?

BubbliMi: My dad's OGO. See u in 60 sec.

As Mina's fingers tapped, her father looked back at her.

"Is it a go?"

"Yes. We can pull up to her house now," Mina said.

She was still nervous but the worst was over. Lizzie was willing to talk. Good thing since Mina had gotten her parents and Lizzie's involved in the big "makeup" scenario.

After leaving Michael and JZ yesterday, she went home and talked things over with her mother. She knew she was going to make up, but she didn't know how and she didn't know how to handle it if Lizzie said thanks but no thanks.

Her mom broke it down for her, like Mina knew she would. It occurred to Mina that she could have asked her mom this after the mall incident. But then that would have been too much like doing right, as her mother always said.

"Okay, I need to ask you something," Mina said to her mom as they sat watching TV.

"I kind of figured you might," her mom said.

"Why?"

"Because you're sitting with me tonight instead of bugging me about going out or having Lizzie over."

Mina nodded. "Yeah, well, you know we've been off and on. But that's the thing. What if I want to bring other people into the clique and Lizzie isn't cool with it? Does it mean we're growing apart?"

The thought terrified her.

"I won't tell you how to handle it. And I can't answer if you're growing apart." Her mom shrugged. "Maybe you are. But, if you can't figure out a way to bring Lizzie into your new circle, it's you who's not being true."

"But I don't want to spend half the time me and Lizzie are out making sure she's okay and not feeling left out," Mina said. "When it was the guys, she and I at least had a girls against guys thing. But now with Jacinta and Kelly, I keep thinking Lizzie will feel like I'm saying she's not enough friend for me or like I need a black best girlfriend."

Mina's mother laughed. "Sweetie, you're trying to prevent something from happening without even knowing if Lizzie cares. Look how long you guys have been friends and she's hung in there being the only white girl."

Mina couldn't argue.

"This is as simple as asking Lizzie how she feels," her mom said.

Mina rolled her eyes.

"What?" her mom asked.

"I hate when JZ's right. He said the same thing at the Ria, Thursday," Mina said. *"Well will you and Daddy help me?"*

"Of course," her mom said.

And they hatched a plan that Mina came to think of as the Lizzie Ambush. Since Lizzie's parents knew they were coming, she was the only one in the dark. There was no Plan B if she refused to see Mina, unless you could count their mothers forcing Lizzie and Mina to meet and make up as a plan. Mina was sure it could come to that if they didn't quit bickering.

But it hadn't come to that.

As the Mooneys' Navigator pulled up to the O'Reillys' house, Mina shook off the last of her jitters.

"Thanks, Mom and Dad," she said, grateful for the backup.

"Is it too late to trade her in for a son?" her father asked, the chuckle in his voice overwhelming the gruffness. "Girls are way too much work."

Mina's mom laughed. "Yeah, Jack, it's too late . . . she's almost paid for anyway."

Mina tuned them out. She couldn't joke right now.

When the truck stopped, she stepped out. Lizzie stood on the porch step, confusion still clouding her face. She peered at the Mooneys' truck as if it were a mirage.

Mina's parents hugged Lizzie as they made their way into the house.

Mina walked up and sat on the front step, waving in response to Lizzie's parents' hollered "hello."

"Did my parents know you guys were coming?" Lizzie said.

Mina nodded.

"Something else I was left out of huh?" Lizzie said. "What did you want to talk about? I'm pretty tired of fighting."

Mina blurted, "Liz, I'm sorry! The way I've been acting is messed

up. And calling you prejudiced was just out of line! I jumped to con-
clusions." She stood, pacing the small stoop. "I took some of the stuff
I learned in soc too far." She paused, half-expecting Lizzie to laugh
at the gross understatement. "If you want to bounce on our friendship, I'd totally understand. Since, basically, that's what I did to you.
But if you're into second chances, I'd really like one."

She stopped long enough to look Lizzie in the face and smiled at
the shock on it.

"Wasn't expecting this, huh?" she grinned.

Speechless, Lizzie could only shake her head.

"I mean it, though," Mina said. "I kind of went off the deep end
with my new 'insight into human behavior,' as Mrs. Simms would
call it."

Lizzie laughed. "Yeah, you did. But if you're ready to forget it
then so am I."

Mina bear-hugged her.

Lizzie nodded through the smothering embrace, caught off guard
by emotions she'd been trying to bury. Since their disagreement,
everything felt like a dream. Things had been up and down so long
Lizzie wasn't sure which part felt more like a dream—the fight or
Mina standing there apologizing. Mina hugged tighter, crushing
Lizzie's doubts away. When Mina finally let go, Liz spoke softly. "I've
really missed hanging out and cracking up in class."

"Me, too." Mina put her pinky out. "Girls fo' li-yife?"

"Girls for life," Lizzie replied, linking her pinky with Mina's then
shaking once. Her smile faded. "And look, about the Raheem
thing—"

Mina put up her hand. "No, let's squash it."

But Lizzie kept going. "I shouldn't have said those things. There
was a part of me jealous that you and Jacinta were suddenly so close,
after just one sleepover. Then when you stuck up for Raheem, it just
. . . it seemed like you were being blind on purpose, not caring what
I thought anymore . . ."

"The next time I'll talk it out with you instead of jumping the gun like that," Mina said.

"If the all-mighty soc class taught you anything, there won't be a next time," Lizzie said, only half-joking.

Mina took the shot in stride. She deserved it for taking everything too seriously.

Lizzie surprised her by taking some of the blame. "And I'll admit how I really feel instead of trying to make you think you're imagining things."

"If we're being honest . . . I need to ask you something," Mina said. She sat. Lizzie joined her.

"Okay, what?" Lizzie said.

"Is it weird for you being the only white person that hangs with me, Michael, and JZ?"

Lizzie hunched her shoulders. She was quiet for a long time before answering.

"No. Well, it hasn't been for a really long time. I mean when I first moved to The Woods and the guys would tease me calling me Vanilla Chip . . ."

Mina giggled. "Sorry. Yeah, they were wrong."

Lizzie laughed. "Totally. But we were nine. Now hanging with them is just . . . normal." Lizzie frowned. "Why? Is it weird for you guys?"

"No. No, that's not why I asked," Mina said, quickly explaining. "I tripped a little with the soc project. But Jacinta and Kelly are actually cool. I want us all to be friends. But if it's gonna be weird for you . . . I won't."

Mina stared, hoping to read something in Lizzie's eyes, which were crinkled in thought.

Lizzie frowned and twirled a strand of hair around her finger. Spend time with the girls Mina had gotten to know well enough to consider friends, girls who filled Mina's last three Saturdays, maybe even sided with Mina if they knew she and Mina were on the outs.

Jealousy cramped her brain. She didn't want to become a fifth wheel with her own best friend. It scared her. She was already odd-man out. She didn't know anything about any of the soc girls.

"Look, if it's too weird it's not a big deal," Mina said.

"You wouldn't ask me if it weren't a big deal," Lizzie said. She made a face. "We're not turning into the glams are we?"

Mina threw her head back, laughing. "Trust, no worries there. As a matter-of-fact, I think I may be over my whole Upper crush any-way."

Lizzie's eyes bucked.

Mina shrugged. "Okay, not totally. But, you try spending a month with Jessica Johnson. Life on our side of the pop crowd isn't that bad."

"I feel so out of the loop," Lizzie confessed. "You guys have been hanging out on weekends and . . . I guess they know as much about you as I do."

Mina stretched her eyebrows. "Come on now. We girls. No one knows more about me than you." Mina put her arm around Lizzie. "If having them hang out with us is weird, you get the ultimate best friend veto."

"Promise?" Lizzie said.

"Best friend rule number four," Mina said.

Lizzie squinted. Mina and her crazy rules. Lizzie had no room in her brain for them, school, and lines. Then the rule popped into her head like a light.

Mina saw the recognition and they chorused, "Best friends never lie."

"If you veto, I'll respect that," Mina said. "But something tells me, you'll like 'em too."

They hooked arms and headed into the house.

No One at Del Rio High Goes It Alone

"I cannot take it anymore. I'm so glad I'll never fit in."
—Pink, "Stupid Girls"

Mina pushed back furniture and made space in her family room. She was excited to be hosting the final sleepover. Happy that the exhaustive project would officially be over, and over in less than a week. It had been the longest month of her life.

No regrets, she thought, sweeping over the room with an eagle eye.

Her semester had been turned upside down out the gate. She'd nearly lost her best friend. Caused a rift, if only temporary, between Michael and JZ. And a picture window still sat between her and the café. But she had no regrets.

High-pierced laughter and banter floated from the family room as Jacinta, Kelly, and Jessica invaded the Mooney residence.

"Mina, the girls are here," her mom called.

Mina bounced upstairs. She doled out hugs to Kelly and Jacinta and managed a polite, "Hey, Jess."

"Uh-oh, she must want something," Jacinta said.

Mina smacked at her. "Paranoid much?"

"Okay, Mina, Dad and I will be back in a few hours," Mina's mom said. She winked at the girls. "Have fun . . . I mean, get some work done."

Mina blew her a kiss. The girls sang good-bye.

Mina led the way to the family room. "I told Michael we might come down to his house later."

"Michael?" Jessica frowned. "The guy with the bald head you're always with?"

Mina nodded.

"Look, can, for one night, you guys not force me to hang out with your friends?"

"Fine, Jessica," Mina said. She flopped on a chaise lounger. "I think we're all happy this is the last one."

"Not me," Kelly said, sitting at the foot of the chaise. "Except for some parts, I've enjoyed it."

Jacinta pulled up an ottoman to the chaise. "Enjoyed it is pushing it for me. But it wasn't as bad as I thought it would be."

"What about you, Jessica?" Kelly said.

Jessica sat in a leather rocker, across the room from the girls, and crossed her long legs.

She inventoried the spacious room, big oak bar on one wall, 36" flat screen on another, pictures of Mina plastered everywhere like a shrine. It was simple and plush at the same time. I'd even settle for a house like this, Jessica thought.

The Cove sleepover was bad, because she feared for her life. But she'd been dreading being in Mina's territory. Seeing the comforts of her home made Jessica want to race down the street screaming. Life wasn't just unfair, it sucked.

She realized all of the girls were staring at her.

"What?" Jessica frowned.

"Did you enjoy any of the project?" Kelly said.

"No."

The room was mute except for the television, playing low in the background.

"Alrighty, then," Mina said. "My mom left us some chili upstairs if anyone is hungry."

"I'm not hungry yet," Jacinta said. She clicked the TV onto

MTVJams and turned up the volume. "I'm trying to catch that new Chris Brown. The one with Lil' Wayne in it."

"Yeah, that's hot," Mina said.

"He's going to be in town for the Jingle Jam, around Christmas," Kelly said.

Jacinta and Mina looked at each other. Kelly caught the exchange and laughed.

"Don't even ask," she said.

Mina wrapped her arms around Kelly's neck. "Kell, that's my future husband, for real. If you get us tickets we won't ask again."

"Yeah, right," Kelly said.

"Hmmph, see Mina's not so innocent," Jessica said.

Mina frowned. "What are you talking about?"

"At least I'm up front about things."

"What do you mean?" Kelly said.

"Kelly why do you think Mina and Jacinta want to be friends with you? For the same reason anyone else would, the hookup to celebs." Jessica snorted. "Just because she does it all sweet doesn't change that she's asking you for something."

"It's not like that," Mina said to Kelly. "Kelly brought it up, Jess. It's not like I went asking her."

"But you still asked." Jessica fixed her hazel eyes on Kelly. "You still need to find a clique. Would you rather be around girls who pretend they're your friends and then turn around and leave you hanging, like they did at my sleepover? Or"—Jessica ignored Mina's shocked indignation—"hang with the glams? Obviously, we'll expect you to bring what you can to the table like everyone else. But at least you know that up front."

"We didn't leave Kelly hanging last weekend, we left you hanging," Jacinta said.

"I didn't care that you guys left," Jessica said with a haughty head swish. "Kelly was the one who thought she was talking on your behalf and then you dogged her by calling your aunt behind her back."

Kelly's head swung back and forth between the dueling girls. Memories of Maisy ditching Mari-Beth for her in the fifth grade flooded her mind. At the time, Kelly was so glad to have a friend she never thought about how Mari-Beth felt. But being between the two of them was bad. She wasn't about to relive that.

"We only called Cinny's aunt because we were sick of you," Mina spat. "I wanted Kelly to come with us. But I couldn't make her."

"Kelly did what she felt she had to," Jacinta said. "And if she doesn't want to hook us up with tickets we not gon' ice her. She's cool with me."

"Oh you not gon' ice her?" Jessica mocked. She rolled her eyes. "Your father wasted his time sending you here. The hood's already in too deep."

"Cinny don't!" Mina yelled as Jacinta raised up from the ottoman.

"I'm not scared of you." Jessica stood up, ready for the altercation. "If you hit me I'll sue your ass."

Kelly froze, watching, as Mina ran across the room behind Jacinta.

"I told you don't say shit about my family out your mouth," Jacinta said, reaching to slap Jessica.

"And I told you I'm not scared of you." Jessica's head ducked away from the oncoming hand.

Mina grabbed Jacinta's arm midswing, catching an elbow in her mouth.

"Ow! Ahhh, my mouth," she cried, dropping Jacinta's arm.

Jacinta whirled around. "Mina, I'm sorry."

"Your bullying doesn't scare me, Jacinta!" Jessica raged.

"Man, shut up," Jacinta said. She walked Mina over to the chaise. "Let me see."

Mina took her hand down from her mouth, sure blood would fly. But her hands were dry.

She held her head up to Jacinta.

"I'm sorry. Your lip swelling but I didn't bust it," Jacinta said. "Can I get some ice out of your refrigerator?"

Mina nodded.

"What the hell is wrong with you guys?" Kelly whispered. She stared at them, eyes blazing. "What is wrong with you?!"

Jessica fluffed her hair then plopped back into the rocker.

Jacinta ran to get the ice.

"How can three intelligent people be so . . ." Kelly's mouth worked but no words came out. "Have any of you guys paid attention in class? I don't care if none of us becomes friends. But how can you still hate each other so much after all we've been through and learned from Mrs. Simms?"

Jacinta came back down the stairs with the ice in a paper towel. She walked over, handed it to Mina and sat on the chaise, head down from Kelly's reprimand.

Kelly's eyes were moist. "This is stupid. The class was wasted on us if this is how we're ending our month together." She wiped angrily at a tear slipping down her cheek. "I guess you guys want me to feel . . . honored or something that you're fighting over me. But I don't. It makes me sick. I don't want to be friends with any of you if I'm just the last pick in the Del Rio High draft."

Mina reached out for Kelly's shoulder but Kelly moved away. "You don't pick friends, you make them." She looked at Mina. "I thought at least you knew that."

Mina's swollen lips made her words jumble. "Kell, I'm sorry. I wasn't trying to treat you like a prize in a race. I don't care about the tickets."

"This isn't about the stupid tickets," Kelly said. "I thought we were becoming friends. But if we're only friends because it means Jessica loses 'the pick,' I don't want to hang out with you." Kelly swiveled and raised an eyebrow. "You either, Jess. I'm not picking sides. And I'm not picking a clique."

"You'll regret that," Jessica said matter-of-factly.

"Well it won't be the first time I'll be by myself," Kelly said. "It's great that you're honest about my place if I hung with you and Mari-Beth. But that only makes it easy for me to say no thanks."

Jessica shrugged. "Fine, Kelly. But no one at Del Rio High goes it solo. Pick a clique or not, you'll be labeled anyway."

"I don't care," Kelly said. She sat on the ottoman and faced Jacinta and Mina. "I guess I was wrong that we were becoming real friends."

Mina shook her head. "No. Don't let Jess . . ."

"It's not about what Jess said. It's how you guys are acting," Kelly said.

"Kelly, believe what you want. I already told you, you're cool with me," Jacinta said.

"I don't get it. How can I be the only one changed by this project?" Kelly said.

"You're not. I've definitely learned a lot about myself," Mina nodded.

"Me too," Jacinta said.

"Then how can you three still be no nicer to each other than you were on the first day?" Kelly said.

"Everybody isn't meant to be friends," Jessica said. "What's wrong with that?"

"I was willing to dump my prejudices about you, Jessica," Mina said. "All you did was confirm what I already thought."

"Oh and what was that, Mina?" Jessica rolled her eyes.

"That you're nasty and bitter and happy being nasty and bitter."

"Well, should Mrs. Simms give you an A for that insight?" Jessica said.

"You've never even tried to be nice to me this whole time," Mina said. Her voice shook with anger. "No matter how much I stay out of your way, you find a reason to be nasty to me."

"Maybe because you're always right on the back of my heel, trying to get where I am," Jessica snapped.

Mina pulled the ice away from her mouth. She ran her tongue

across her lip, wincing at the fatness. "If that ever was true, it's not anymore." She wiped at her mouth. "And if you only hated me because you thought I was following behind you, you can sink your fangs into the next 'wannabe.' Whether I'm at the middle of the pack or the bottom of the pile at least I have real friends."

Jessica clapped. "Oh yay. And they lived happily ever after."

Mina shook her head. She looked at Kelly. "See what I mean?"

"Jessica, can we at least not be enemies?" Kelly said.

Jessica shrugged.

"Ain't it too late for all that?" Jacinta frowned.

"I don't know what the other groups went through. But I don't want to get in front of the class with it obvious that we didn't get it," Kelly said. "I know you guys don't either."

"You're right," Mina said.

Jessica picked at her fingernail. A nod was her only agreement.

"Cinny?" Kelly said.

Jacinta folded her arms. "I don't like her."

"As if I said I liked you." Jessica scowled.

"Stop it!" Kelly said. "I don't care who likes who. I said, for the sake of our project grade, we need to figure out how we're going to prove we're eliminating our biases. And if we're not, there should be a good reason. It has nothing to do with liking each other."

"If Jessica goes along, you can," Mina said to Jacinta.

"There we go again letting her decide how we doing stuff," Jacinta said.

"No. We're all agreeing, that's it. Majority rules." Kelly raised an eyebrow. "All!"

"Fine," Jacinta said.

"Jessica, there's gotta be something you feel differently about since we started," Kelly said, looking over her shoulder at Jessica.

Jessica sat silent, her face blank.

Kelly turned back to Mina. "Mina?"

"Well . . ." Mina didn't want to cause more drama. She treaded carefully. "First, Kelly, I thought you were going to be like a pretty-girl snob." She added quickly. "But that was literally before you ever said anything. I thought Jacinta was going to keep acting hard . . ." Mina looked at Jacinta. "I was surprised you actually hung out with us that first Thursday at the Ria. It definitely helped to squash my first impressions. And I was cool with Kelly really fast since we ate lunch together all the time."

Mina stopped and cracked her knuckles, hoping someone else would jump in so she could skip over Jessica. But Kelly pressed. "I know you and Jessica have never been friends but . . ."

"All right . . . well, I used to think the glams were cool, in middle school," Mina said. She stared across the room at Jessica. "Now, I think . . . well, I feel bad that your friends don't have your back. Because everybody should be able to count on their clique and I don't think you can."

Jessica rolled her eyes. "I don't need your sympathy."

Mina continued. "Even though this has nothing to do with friendship . . ." She shrugged. "I'm saying, I feel like I know you a little better . . . enough to eliminate my prejudices against you." She sat back on the chaise lounge, glad to be done. "Cinny's turn."

Jacinta nudged Mina in the side before scooting to the edge of the chaise. "I thought you were all about yourself. But, you've stepped in every time to stop me from fighting . . . and only a friend would bother to keep somebody out of trouble." Jacinta looked over at Kelly. "Even though you quiet, I respect that you stand up for yourself. So, no doubt, my prejudices against ya'll are gone." She folded her arms, inhaled then finished in one big exhale. "Jessica, I can't see us ever getting along."

"Big surprise," Jessica said, her eyes dull with boredom.

"Even if I could get over the way you treat people like dirt, we don't have anything in common," Jacinta said, shrugging.

"Agreed," Jessica said. She raised her eyebrow. "My turn?"

Kelly nodded.

Jessica leaned up in the rocker and sat near the edge of the seat.

"If eliminating prejudice means would I ever be friends or friendly to you guys, then, nope, I haven't done that for Mina or Jacinta," Jessica said, unapologetically.

Kelly's back was turned to Mina and Jacinta, giving Jessica her full attention.

"At least tell us why," she said.

"Mina annoys me." Jessica frowned. "And do I really need to explain why I still think Jacinta is a project queen? How many times did she jump in my face ready to fight?"

"'Cause you never know when to shut up," Jacinta shot back.

Kelly turned and frowned at Jacinta. "Okay, okay. I didn't mean to start a new argument."

"Look, Kelly," Jessica said, ignoring Jacinta's remark. "If you care at all about your status at DRB High, I can get you the hookup with the glams."

For the first time since she'd started playing the mediator, Kelly was silent. She pushed herself to the middle of the ottoman and looked from Mina and Jacinta on the lounge to Jessica in the rocker.

Jessica sat back in the rocker and crossed her legs. The buzz of the television settled back over the quiet room.

"Feel better, Kelly?" Jacinta asked.

"Better? I don't know," Kelly said. "But, at least we have something to go on for our report. Are we going to put together our final presentation tonight?"

"Please, no," Mina groaned. "Can't we just meet up one more time. If I have to think about school one more Saturday, the entire day, my head is gonna explode."

"Can't we just get this over with?" Jessica said.

"Maybe Mina's right," Kelly said. "Let's meet . . . on Tuesday and finish everything."

"We can even do it here, after my cheer practice," Mina volunteered. She gave Jessica a halfhearted smile. "Unless you want to do it at your house."

Jessica shook her head. "Nope. Here is fine. One last time, right?"

Mina, Kelly, and Jacinta nodded.

The sound of the new Chris Brown came from the television.

"Oooh there it is!" Jacinta yelped. "Okay, no more homework. At least while Chris is on." She turned up the volume.

Jacinta and Mina danced and sang at the top of their lungs. They pulled Kelly up from the chaise, holding her arms forcing her to move along with them.

As the girls twisted her body this way and that, Kelly looked over at Jessica, sitting back in the rocker, distant, and felt bad for her. She also felt bad for herself. Since Jessica made it clear that she felt the same since day one, it would probably be a long night of Kelly playing referee.

Soc
September 30, 2005
Observations by Amina Mooney
Here's what I learned about ME:

❀ I tend to go a tiny bit over the top about things (just a bit). When I love something, I love it to death and when I don't love something ... well it can get ugly! Not saying that's a bad thing but, I have to keep that in check and be just a little more middle of the road now and then.

Here's what I learned about other people:

❀ Having even one thing in common with someone goes a looonnnngggg way. Say for example ... hmmm ... shar-

ing a class together (Cin, Kell, heyyy) or liking the
same kind of cereal (shout out to my girl Liz and Cap'n
Crunch).

⚜ Some people get too comfortable being with people who
think exactly like themselves so they cut off anyone
else (ahem, Jessica).

It's not that I'm happy Jessica still hates me. I hate
being hated. But I don't care as much. I don't need a
house to fall on me. I can see she just won't ever like
me. Everybody won't always like me (shudder). I could
use some serious Dr. Phil, Oprah, or Tyra Banks psychology for that realization. On the other hand (bright-
siding it for myself) the people showing me love show it
to me whether I make them mad or get on their nerves
or what. Didn't think I needed a soc class to show me
that . . . but, sort of did. I love my peeps, they wish me
well everybody else can go to . . . ha-ha!

Soc
9-30-05
Jessica Johnson

I did it! I survived!

I walked through the hell of wannabes and it only
left a light stench of loserdom on me. I can easily shed
the stink with a weekend at the Club with Mari. I
can't wait to get back to my life! Thank God the rest
of the night was spent with MTV as background. If I
never see another video it would be too soon. But
videos saved me from having to talk anymore—
obviously Kelly's goal. They screeched the rest of the

night until Mina's parents got home and shut the "party" down.

Kelly keeps surprising me. I can't keep inviting her to the glams. She'll think we're desperate or something. But I know she'd come in handy. Who knows, maybe she'll see for herself how stupid it is to swim the waters alone. The glams will take her in . . . after making her suffer for not making the choice sooner, of course.

All I can say for this "project" is it's over. If there is a God in Pop Heaven he will see to it that I won't have to say a word to these girls (minus Kelly on occasion) the rest of this semester, in class or out. At least I can say I'm earning my stripes the hard way for my LL course.

Eliminating prejudice? Let me put it this way. I can be in the same room as Mina without retching. How's that?

Sociology
September 30, 2005
Jacinta Phillips

Mina, you're mad cool with me. This is the second time you stopped me from tearing into Jessica. Only a friend would bother to stop you from doing something you'd regret later. But man, that's one regret I wouldn't mind taking. Oops but sorry about the lip! You still got a little bobble head 'burb girl thing going on. But I think your heart in the right place.

Speaking of heart . . . Kelly. I'm gonna admit this in writing only once—but I've never been more wrong about a person. This chick is standing up to snotty ego-power tripping chicks and even to me (and my stuff wasn't an act, Jessica). Tonight she took on all of us at once. This is the same girl that tucked her hair behind her ear anytime you looked her way and asked her to say a peep a month ago. She called us out though. And she was right.

The project and the things Mrs. Simms talks about has changed how I look at things and at people. I'm not going all bobble head saying that everybody will be holding hands, singing Kirk Franklin gospel jams (Silver and Gold . . . Silver and Gold . . . I'd rather have Jesus than . . .) just kidding. Seriously, I might stop to think before I crack on somebody. BUT . . . it also proved to me that some people are gonna think what they want, even if the facts say how you think is wrong. Score one for the soc class. It's not a slam-dunk . . . but it's a three-pointer.

Sociology
September 30, 2005
Observations by Kelly Lopez

I think I'm all sleepovered out. New friends or not, staying home with Grand next weekend sounds pretty good to me.

I kind of lost it, tonight. I was so sick of hearing them argue and fight. There's no way the other groups in the class went through this kind of struggle just to conclude that it's okay if you play soccer and I like Chess, we can still be friends. Just no way. I couldn't take it anymore. Not Jessica's sarcasm or Jacinta's humor. I feel like we failed this assignment. And this IS NOT about us becoming friends. We spent a month of weekends together and still Jessica only sees what we represent (Jacinta = projects, Mina = clique climber, and me = connections). I believe Mina and Jacinta have seen beyond those things in each other and in me. But the way they let Jessica get to them, just my opinion, says they're letting how she sees them bother them. Why? Jacinta is a great big sis to her brothers and sister, Mina will be a friend to just about anybody and me . . . well, I'm more than connections. Heck, I don't have any—my parents do. So I don't get mad when Jessica goes on about my connections. I know I'm more than that. And I can ignore the people who don't see me for me.

I'm glad I made some friends. And I definitely feel like Mina and Cinny are my friends. I just know if all three of us tried harder we could have gotten Jessica to see things our way, too.

Hail, Hail, the clique's All Here

"Who you wit'? Throw up your set."
—Juelz Santana, "Dipset"

The moment Jessica's mother's minivan pulled into the Mooneys' driveway Saturday morning, Mina felt ten pounds lighter. She managed a polite, straightfaced, "See you, Jessica," without any fist-pumping or happy-dancing. The second Jessica was gone, Mina made Kelly call her grandmother and Jacinta her Aunt Jacqi to beg for a very late evening pickup or, in Jacinta's case, permission to stay out most of the day before walking home.

The whole plan almost backfired because Kelly's grandmother was already on her way out of the door when the phone rang. It took Mina's mom to get on the phone and assure Mrs. Lopez that yes, it was okay and the girls hadn't coerced Mariah into letting them stay.

Once the permissions were out of the way, Mina called Lizzie, asked her to join her for pizza at Rio's Ria around one o'clock, and then walked with Kelly and Jacinta first to Michael's, then JZ's. After hanging at JZ's for a few hours, the five of them walked to Rio's Ria.

The entire clique, except Lizzie, sat at a big table at the Ria. Mina was nervous. She had brought them together as a clique, for the first time, for a reason, and she needed to hurry. Lizzie would be here in twenty minutes. If they didn't get down to business, things might get all crazy again with Lizzie wondering why everyone else was there before her.

"Okay, listen, I need a favor," Mina said. "A big one."

"No tickets," Kelly giggled.

"No for real," Mina said. She rushed through her planned speech. "There's one person missing from the table and that's Lizzie. She's on her way. But first I wanted to know if you guys would help me plan a party for her for getting the lead in *The Wiz*."

"Hmmm . . . my first gray party," Jacinta said.

"We could have it at my house if you want," JZ said.

"Thanks, Jay. But we'll do it at my house," Mina said.

"Let me handle decorations," Michael said.

"Wait." Mina looked at Kelly and Jacinta. "Are ya'll okay with helping? You haven't hung out with Lizzie yet. I'm hoping she'll get to know you like I did . . ." Mina smiled. "And still like you anyway."

"That's wrong," Jacinta said.

Mina laughed. "But ya'll are cool planning with me?"

"I'm in," Kelly said.

"Well, do you think Lizzie be cool around Raheem? 'Cause I'd invite him," Jacinta said.

"Yeah, it'll be fine. Lizzie's cool," Mina said. "It wasn't Raheem that she was tripping over. It was just some stuff she and I had to work out and we did."

"Can Angel come?" Jacinta said.

Mina winced. "What if Angel . . . you know brings trouble?"

"He wouldn't do that," Jacinta said.

"Who's Angel?" Michael said.

"Raheem's friend," Mina said. "Look. Okay we'll talk guest list later. Here's the thing. Homecoming is in two weeks. I want to have the party next week. So we gotta get the word out fast."

"I think I can get a DJ," Kelly said.

"Hold up," JZ said. "I need to weigh in on this. Ya'll might pick some dude only playing that Top 40 mess."

"Why don't we send out invitations online," Michael said. "You know word will spread quick if we just drop dime with the right people."

Ideas circulated around the table as excitement mushroomed. Bickering over music, guest list, and décor broke down any shyness anyone might have felt from being thrown into the motley crew of planners.

The noise of friendly arguing was music to Mina's ears. She had brought old and new together without her world imploding. Well, she still needed Lizzie for a true temperature check. But so far so good.

"Mina, tell him that's corny," Jacinta demanded.

Michael fixed Jacinta with a hard look. "I know she didn't just call my stuff corny!"

Mina shook her head. "See, I knew ya'll would fit right in." She looked at the clock. "I'll be back. I want to catch Lizzie before she walks in."

She left them to yammer about the details.

The O'Reillys' Toyota Camry pulled up to the curb as she walked out of the Ria. Mina waved to Miss Marybeth.

"Your mom is bringing her home, right?" Lizzie's mom said.

"Yes. See you, later," Mina said.

Lizzie hopped out of the car. "Where are the guys?"

"Already inside." Mina wrung her hands, a sheepish grin on her face. "Confession."

Lizzie's eyes rolled. "This isn't another ambush is it?"

"Sort of," Mina winced. "But a good kind."

Lizzie craned trying to see inside the Ria. It wasn't too crowded. But it was still early. The Ria would have its usual Saturday traffic jam of bodies by three o'clock.

"Who's in there?"

"I'm having a party for you," Mina said.

Lizzie frowned. "Now?"

"No. I mean, I'm planning a party for you. A little welcome the new Drama Diva type thing," Mina said.

Lizzie groaned. "Lila will love that."

"This is my way of saying sorry *I* was a diva and congratulations," Mina said.

"What's the catch?" Lizzie said, still peering into the restaurant.

"Jacinta and Kelly are helping to plan it." Mina stood still, waiting for the reaction. She stared Lizzie in the eye waiting for a flinch, wince, or squint to give away anything.

"And they're okay with it?" Lizzie said.

"Yes," Mina gushed. "We've already started planning. I wanted you in on it too so you wouldn't start getting all suspicious and crazy."

"Umm . . . yeah, that's more like you than me." Lizzie arched her brows. "Remember your surprise thirteenth party and how you drove me crazy trying to figure out what was going on?"

Mina's shoulders shook as she laughed. She'd been a nutcase. Her mother vowed to either (1) never throw her another surprise party or (2) do so without telling Lizzie so Mina would have no one to pester. Lizzie nearly lost her mind trying to keep Mina in the dark.

"Okay, yeah that's totally me. But are you okay with it? This is a good chance to see if you need to use that veto or not," Mina said.

Lizzie had her fears about the friendship. But Mina was trying awfully hard to make it work. The least she could do was try. It could be worse. Mina was never short on plans. This was the least painful yet.

What Does It Matter What We Thought Then?

"I gotta shake it off. Gotta make that move."
—Mariah Carey, "Shake It Off"

Tuesday evening Mina, Kelly, Jacinta, and Jessica sat in Mina's sunroom planning for their final presentation. The room was quiet. No one seemed to know how to start.

Mina gazed outside at the trees. The leaves, starting to turn a rich gold and red, shone through the dark evening. She daydreamed about the party. It was only two days away. With Lizzie at her side, yesterday, she'd invited Craig and he said yes. It was all she could think about.

Kelly broke the silence. "So, how should we start?"

Mina pulled herself back to the present. "Let's just exchange first impressions, read them, react, then get our points together for the report."

They took out their impressions and swapped. The room grew silent once more, as they read over the notes that revealed what they had thought of one another the moment they met.

Mina finished first. Her face was tight with anger. Jacinta's mouth was pooched out in an expression they had all come to know as her poor attempt at pretending she wasn't mad about something. Kelly put her paper down and kept her eyes down. Only Jessica finished and looked around the table, expressionless.

Kelly moved them along once more. "Maybe we should . . ."

Mina cut her off, her voice tinged with hurt. "I don't get it. Why does the fact that I'm talkative and friendly offend you guys?" She wasn't quite sure why that bothered her. The clique called her Mouthy Mi all the time. But the impressions made it seem like she went on endlessly just to hear herself speak. And she couldn't help the jealousy she felt from Jessica writing she could probably "deal" with Kelly. That was more then Jessica had ever done for Mina.

It was like she hadn't made any impression outside of being a popularity-seeking chatterbox. Was she really that shallow?

No, wait, she didn't need the answer to that—the comments said it all.

Jacinta sniffed, her offense clear. "I figured ya'll all thought I was ghetto. But that doesn't make me stupid." She glared at Jessica.

Jessica met Jacinta's eyes but said nothing.

"What's with this, 'Hello, contractions are our friend.' Why do you care how I speak?" Jacinta asked.

Jessica's tone was clipped. "We were supposed to be honest. I was. Your whole ghetto I don't need to prove anything to anyone 'tude, was my first impression . . . and you're still like that. So my impression isn't that wrong."

"I don't have to prove anything to anybody. But it doesn't make me stupid because I talk a certain way," Jacinta said.

"Then why not try to make a better impression?" Jessica said. "I don't see why you guys are mad. I'm not getting all upset over Mina calling me evil or Jacinta making fun of me because I'm mixed."

"I said using your *powers* for evil. I didn't say you were," Mina said with an eye roll.

Silent bitterness festered until Kelly's quiet voice dented the tension. "I could be upset that you guys felt I didn't make much of an impression other than I had on a pair of cute pants, looked scared, and lived in a nice neighborhood." She looked at each person as she regurgitated their comment about her. "But I'm not. The question is, are we still only those things to each other?"

Mina's eyes darted around the table. She chuckled. "She's right. It doesn't matter what we thought then. We girls now, right?" She looked at Jessica and hitched her shoulders. "I mean, most of us."

"I'm totally not offended to be left out of that clique," Jessica said.

"We know," Mina and Jacinta sang. They snickered.

Jacinta shrugged it off. "On the real, none of these observations surprise me."

"Me either, really," Jessica admitted.

"So, we're all stereotypes, huh?" Mina asked.

"Looks like it," Kelly said. She playfully offered each girl her hand, "Hi, I'm the Boogee Latina Princess."

"Hi, I'm the Ghetto Chick," Jacinta said.

Mina squawked in a high-pitched voice, "Hi, I'm the Bubbly Chatterbox."

They waited for Jessica to flip a smart remark. But she played along.

"Hi, I'm The Ice Queen," Jessica said.

Mina laughed. "Okay, I need a digital recorder. Can't believe you called yourself that."

A smile tugged at Jessica's mouth. "I mean ice as in I don't care what you guys think."

"Hey, whatever. Nobody saying you're wrong," Jacinta laughed.

Jessica's eyes popped. "Oh my God. Did you just use a contraction?"

Jacinta arched an eyebrow. "Umph, watch it, you're damn near close to acting friendly."

"Well, it'll be one of the last times," Jessica said without venom.

Kelly enjoyed the momentary lightness before bringing them back to their goal. "Okay, well, let's get this report together."

They took advantage of the truce to write and plot their presentation.

P*A*R*T*Y

"Go Shorty, it's yo' birthday!"
—50 Cent, "In Da' Club"

The room pulsed with a dull sheen from hundreds of large metallic silver stars hanging from the ceiling. The words "Ease on down the road," "Slide some oil to me," and "The Wiz" were graffitied all over the walls in funky glow-in-the-dark gel ink. The blackness of the dark room hid the fact that the words were written on black witches' caps. Other props from the school's production littered the room, a fake street light with half-torn flyers on it, a bashed-up trash can, and a wall-sized poster of a condemned building. It looked like someone had taken an inner-city street and dumped it in the middle of Mina's family room.

The eerie glow from the ink made the ninety some odd people packed into the room look like beings from outer space and the spacious party area their mothership. Bass boomed, vibrating framed photos to shake off the wallflowers.

Mina raised her arms, moving closer to Craig as they shook in time to the bass line. He pulled her into him, smiling down at her as their bodies bumped in sync. Every few minutes someone would pass and say hello or comment on the party being hot or blazing, making Mina's grin wide.

Popularity points dinged in her head like coins falling from a slot machine as she counted the number of Uppers in the room, including the one she was getting her grind on with. So she still cared a little bit about rising within DRH's cliqueosphere.

Café here I come, she thought.

She had planned this perfectly. The fact that she might kill two birds with one stone—celebrating Lizzie's lead in *The Wiz* and kicking up her café campaign—put pep in her step and she swayed against Craig, delirious with pleasure.

The turnout was phenomenal. The theater set was there, including Lila and her flunkies, the jocks, even the glams stopped in, refusing to be left out.

Whatever else was behind the turnout, Mina knew two things were to thank: (1) DJ Beatz and (2) Homecoming.

Beatz' jams were always hotter than a tea kettle. And if some people were there just to say they had gone to a Beatz party that was good enough for Mina. Because Beatz party was her party and she wouldn't let a soul forget it.

With Homecoming next weekend, people didn't mind setting off the Blue Devil spirit a week early and the clique's party was the perfect vehicle.

She rolled her shoulders to the music and put the few tense weeks of planning out of her head. Craig's voice tickled her ear. "Ay, JZ trying to get your attention."

Mina glanced down at her watch. It was nearly eight. It wasn't a surprise, but she wanted Lizzie to make an entrance. So Mina nagged her into showing up fashionably late.

She headed upstairs, where her parents manned the refreshments and directed new guests down to the family room.

"Do you want me and Daddy to come down there and show ya'll how to groove?" her mom teased.

Mina groaned. "No. Not if it's anything like your vouging." She laughed. "Thanks for letting me have the party."

"So where is this Craig I keep hearing about?"

"Mom, I can't do a formal intro. He'll think I'm going all girl-friend on him," Mina said.

Her dad frowned. "Okay, what does that mean?"

"I'll find a way to casually introduce you when he's with a bunch of people. Nothing one-on-one . . . yet," Mina said, pecking her dad's cheek. "Oooh Lizzie's here."

The O'Reillys came in.

"See how cute you look!" Mina squealed. She made Lizzie turn around so she could see her in the gauchos and high boots she and Michael begged her to wear. "Hi, Mr. and Mrs. O'Reilly," she said before dragging Lizzie off.

"Oh my God. It sounds like a lot of people are here," Lizzie whispered, pulling back.

"What is this, stage fright?" Mina giggled. "This is your big debut. Lila needs to know you're gunning for her spot."

"Please don't say that around her," Lizzie said.

"I won't have to. After tonight you'll be on shine. Then when you rip it at the production, she'll know," Mina said, grinning.

She shuttled Lizzie to the top step entrance to the family room. Mina waved her hand, got DJ Beatz attention and the music went down to a thumping whisper. Beatz's deep voice boomed over the speakers, "The Drama Princess is here! Introducing Lizzie-O, the new Dorothy of Detroit!"

Clapping broke out. A sea of well-wishers surrounded them, wishing Lizzie good luck with the play.

Lizzie gaped, looking from the crowd to Mina. Her face reddened from a mix of excitement and embarrassment. "I can't believe how many people you got to come."

Mina winked. "Didn't I say I'd get us in before the semester ended? But this is about you tonight. With Michael's help it was no problem getting the theater clique here. And of course, JZ made sure all the jocks showed up."

Lizzie's eyes swam over the partygoers, the decorations. Was that Lila in the crowd? She laughed out loud. So Mina's persistence (pushiness) worked on just about anybody.

JZ broke through the ring of bodies. He pulled Lizzie into the thick crowd and signaled for Beatz to pump it up. The dance floor flooded again and the party jumpstarted itself.

Jacinta wished Lizzie congratulations as she passed them. She stood by Mina and frantically fanned herself. "Girl, this party is blazing! Beatz is off the hook tonight."

"I know. Kelly really came through on the hookup!" Mina shouted, pointing at Kelly dancing with Angel. She gave her a thumbs-up and laughed at Kelly's shy smile.

"So much for him being her phone boyfriend." Jacinta nudged Mina.

"I guess," Mina said. She stared at Angel, wondering if anything about him could give him away to her parents. After a quick introduction to her mom and dad, Mina ushered Raheem and Angel downstairs, hoping their crazy parent radar didn't pick up anything odd. But minus his Incredible Hulks, Angel fit into the crowd, thankfully, like all the other guys.

JZ's voice rose over the thumping music. Mina saw his body bouncing. His mouth was moving, but she couldn't understand over the music. She walked deeper into the family room, leaned in toward the crowd, listened again to catch on.

As she walked to the center of the room, Mina tugged Jacinta's sleeve, then grabbed Kelly along the way closer to JZ and Lizzie. Michael came up, dancing behind her. They bounced along, joining JZ's call:

"Who you wit'?"

"Rolling with that clique!" they responded before all six yelled, "The Del Rio Bay Clique, 'cause you know we roll thick."

Can We Get Extra Credit for the Friend Part?

"I'm sky high. Sky, sky high."
—Kanye West, "Touch the Sky"

Monday morning, Mina was still riding high from the party. But she put the fresh memories of spending nearly the entire party dancing with Craig aside as she waited for Mrs. Simms to get class started. A month of work was about to come to a head and Mina was excited to put an official end to the soc project. Had anyone accomplished the lofty goal of eradicating prejudice from their lives?

The students' voices rose and fell in eager waves. The air was thick with expectation.

Mrs. Simms let them chatter. The excitement coursing through her classroom was exactly what teaching was about for her. Before the noise reached a level that would disturb the other classrooms, she stepped in. "Well, I'm sure you've all found out that this project was neither as easy nor as hard as you expected."

A murmur of agreement went through the room. It brought a pleased smile to the Guru's face. She looked around the room expectantly. "Well, any volunteers to go first?"

Jacinta and Mina both shot up their hands, snickering at their anxiety.

"Okay, great. Jacinta, Mina, Jessica, and Kelly will go first."

The girls walked to the front of the room. A silent signal passed between them and they all struck a pose. Kelly kept her head down.

Her thick auburn hair waterfalled, covering most of her face. Jacinta mocked chewing gum, smacking loud and hard. Mina twirled her hair around her finger and danced from foot-to-foot in an anxious fidget. Jessica's face was stony.

Soft murmuring went through their classmates. Who knew the report required a skit? Some threw anxious looks to their group mates, questioning the sufficiency of their presentation.

"Hi, I'm the Boogee Princess," Kelly said in a soft, breathy voice, eyes downcast.

Giggles and whispers ran through the class.

"Hi, I'm The Ghetto Chick!" Jacinta asserted, sullenly, her hands on her jutting hip.

More whispers filtered through the room.

"Hi, I'm the Bubbly Big Mouth!" Mina said in a high, pitchy voice. She flipped her hair and cocked her head.

"Hi, I'm The Ice Queen," Jessica swished her hair and folded her arms.

Some laughter and lots of confused stares and whispers rippled through the room.

Jessica stepped ahead of her group mates. She spoke crisp and clear, like the narrator of a documentary. "These are the first characteristics we saw in each other when we met. Our first impressions were based only on seeing one another and talking in class for about thirty minutes."

Mina stepped up. "But, over the course of the semester we got to know one another by spending the night at each other's houses. In one way, our first impressions were right. Kelly's family is wealthy. Jacinta's family does live in low-income housing. Jessica can be very stand-offish. And I am very talkative and curious."

Jacinta joined in. "By spending one night in each other's environments, we quickly learned that, no matter how much money somebody has, or whether they are black, white, Asian, or whatever, we're all working toward the same things. We want friends who see past the outside and say, 'Hey, you cool with me.'"

In a strong voice, Kelly summed it up. "It may sound cliché, but what we found was that we're not all that different. Most of our differences were outside of our control. We couldn't control who our parents were or what they do for a living, which meant we couldn't control where we lived or how we were brought up."

Mina added, "So, we've decided to eliminate prejudice and respect our differences. But we found out it takes more than respecting differences for everyone to get along."

"We're not going to hold our differences against each other," Jessica said. "But it didn't translate into a unanimous decision to like one another."

Mina piped in, brightly. "But *some* of us have decided to become friends." She frowned and looked at Mrs. Simms. "Can we get extra credit for the friend part?"

Mrs. Simms roared with laughter.

Mina smiled and grabbed Jacinta's hand. They all clasped together and took a theatrical stage bow. Mina, Kelly, and Jacinta burst into a fit of nervous laughter. Jessica started back to her seat.

Mrs. Simms beamed and enthusiastically applauded the girls.

Mina, Kelly, and Jacinta gave one another dap and headed for their seats.

"Who you wit'?" Mina whispered.

Kelly and Jacinta chanted back, "Rolling with that clique, the Del Rio Bay Clique. 'Cause you know we roll thick."

Sociology
October 10, 2005
Jacinta Phillips: Last Impressions
   This group of girls is unbelievable! But what's more unbelievable is that they're my girls. I never saw it

coming, it just happened. In a way, I know I'll always be the project chick to them because I see things a certain way—in a way they could never see it, based on where I'm from. I'll always be able to add a new twist. Still it feels good to have a group of friends that at least tries to understand you. Could I ask for anything more?

Sociology
October 10, 2005
Observations by Kelly Lopez: Last Impressions

The poor little rich girl with no friends is dead! At least it feels that way.

I'm not the same girl that started this class, keeping to myself, afraid to speak my mind.

I have a whole gang of good friends and it's new. It's scary. But it's real!

I finally found the right friends, people who won't give me the cold shoulder just because I won't do everything they ask.

Soc
10-10-05
Jessica Johnson: Last Impressions

I didn't come into this project looking for friends or even approval. I still think that people will judge you within seconds and a lot of times nothing you do or say will change that first impression.

Mina still annoys me. Jacinta is still someone I wouldn't

even take a second look if we passed one another in the hallway. And Kelly is still someone who has potential if she were around the right people.

Right now, it's all about survival. Mina swims around in a school of fresh fish to get through. But I'm the shark they're watching out for.

Soc

10/10/2005

Observations by Amina Mooney: Last Impressions

My mother told me that your friends are a reflection of who you are. That you should never take making a new friend lightly because if that person was trouble, you would be too or at least people would see you that way.

When I look at myself through my friends, I like what I see: someone who is able to look at a situation and turn it over and over again until all of the possibilities are explored. There aren't just two sides to every story, for me there are six: JZ, Lizzie, Michael, Cinny, Kelly, and ME.

SO NOT THE DRAMA

A Del Rio Bay Novel

PAULA CHASE

ABOUT THIS GUIDE

The following questions are intended to
enhance your group's reading of
SO NOT THE DRAMA
by Paula Chase

DISCUSSION QUESTIONS

1. The issue of popularity is a large part of DRAMA. The book begins with Mina narrating and saying: "Popularity is a drug. You get a taste of it and suddenly the looks you get from people, the way you get treated, the things you get away with . . . you need it. You honest to God, need it." Is popularity addicting? If so, how far are you willing to go to be popular and remain popular?

2. Is popularity important to you? If yes, why? If no, why?

3. Of the five girls in the book, Mina, Lizzie, Cinny, Kelly, and Jessica, who are you the most like? Who are you most different from?

4. Several times throughout the book Mina hints to other people about being dramatic (Michael, Lizzie) but it isn't until the end that she realizes that sometimes she's the cause of drama and she reacts very passionately to those around her. Who is the Drama Queen/King in your circle of friends? What do they do to earn that label? Is being passionate such a bad thing? Why or why not?

5. The clique escapes from their everyday worries at Cimarra Beach and Rio's Ria, where few adults tread. Are there places like that in your community? What are they? If not, describe your "dream" teen hangout. Is there a way you can help your community create a place where teens can hang out safely?

6. The girls decide to use sleepovers as a way to move the soc project along. If you were in their group would you like doing sleepovers with people who weren't already your friends? What other activities could groups use to complete an assignment?

7. The soc class kept the students on their toes, forcing them to react and analyze their reactions. Would you like to be in a class like that? Make up an assignment that you think would fit well into Mrs. Simm's soc class.

8. Thinking about where you live—are there communities like The Woods, Folger's Way, The Melting Pot and Pirates Cove there? Which Del Rio Bay nabe is your neighborhood most like?

9. Jessica ends the soc project feeling the exact same way about Mina and Jacinta as she did going into the project. Why do you think Jessica didn't change? Do you know someone like Jessica? Would you ever attempt to befriend someone like that?

10. At the end, when Mina says, "There aren't just two sides to every story, for me there are six: JZ, Lizzie, Michael, Cinny, Kelly and ME," she's talking about how she is reflected in her friends. How many sides do you have to your story? What do you think the people you hang around with say about you?

Enhance your book club:

1. *So Not the Drama* is set in a very teen-friendly world (most of the hangout spots are within walking distance and the clique hangs out a lot without supervision). When discussing the novel, tie it into a teen-friendly activity. Discuss the book for half the session and then go out for pizza or to the mall, or to have the book club discussion at a local park or beach.

2. Contact the author, and arrange for a virtual visit (via chat session or teleconference) to talk about the book with your club. Visit *www.paulachasehyman.com*

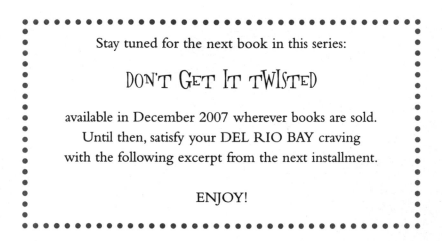

Stay tuned for the next book in this series:

DON'T GET IT TWISTED

available in December 2007 wherever books are sold.
Until then, satisfy your DEL RIO BAY craving
with the following excerpt from the next installment.

ENJOY!

The Frenzy

R U down?

Mina Mooney stood over her desk, staring at the three words on her monitor. Her stomach rumbled. From hunger or anxiety, Mina wasn't sure.

Two seconds ago, it was definitely hunger.

Sick of leftover turkey, mashed potatoes and all the other food they'd eaten on Thanksgiving and all of yesterday, she'd been ravenous at the thought of sinking her teeth into something that wasn't stuffed or covered in gravy. When her mom burst into the room, plopped down on the bed, rousing Mina from a sound sleep with a tickle to the neck and a proposal that they cook a very un-Thanksgiving family breakfast, Mina eagerly shook off the early—if you could call ten thirty a.m. early—morning haze fogging her head.

That was five minutes ago. Now . . .

She wanted to be sure that she understood Craig Simpson's words correctly. He *was* asking her out. Wasn't he?

Mina swiveled the chair with her knee half-sitting, half-standing stance. She scrolled the screen and read the short exchange, again.

Bluedevils33: Ay what up?
BubbliMi: Nuthin' ready to go eat.
Bluedevils33: O. U know 'bout the Frenzy?

Mina knew. It was all JZ had talked about for the last two weeks since football season ended. It was the big bash Coach Banner held for the varsity football team at his McMansion in Folger's Way, Del Rio Bay's ritziest neighborhood, to celebrate the end of the season.

BubbliMi: yeah. heard they had strippers last year.
Bluedevils33: LOL. whatever. people b x-ageratin! It's not that bad.
BubbliMi: I figured . . . but u never know! Y'all ballers can get out of control—ha ha.
Bluedevils33: tru dat. But naw it ain't nothin' like that.
BubbliMi: I'll have 2 take ur word 4 it.
Bluedevils33: No u can see 4 urself. u want go w/me to the party?

And that's when Mina had shut down, unable to move, type, blink or breathe. It was while she was trying to come back to her senses when the last message came in.

Bluedevils33: R U down?

Mina stared at the screen, letting the words sink in. She wanted to type "seriously?" but figured that sounded stupid.

She rested a knee in the chair, a big grin on her face. Craig was finally asking her out. Exactly four weeks ago they had spent the night bumping, grinding and getting their dance on at a party Mina had for her best friend, Lizzie. Since then she and Craig talked more at school than they had before and IM'ed when they were online at the same time, but nothing drastic had changed between them.

NOW, he was asking her out. And not just any date—not the movies or grabbing a slice at Rio's Ria, the hot hangout spot in Del Rio Bay—Craig was asking her to go with him to the annual Blue

Devil's Football Frenzy. She ignored the images the word "frenzy" brought to mind and instead tried to picture the forty-member football team playing rowdy rounds of Spades, Madden football or Checkers.

Yeah, right.

JZ had already given her and the clique an earful about the Frenzy. Board games and PlayStation were never mentioned.

JZ and a few other select junior varsity football players, those who were definitely making varsity next year, were invited to the Frenzy. JZ was the main reason the JV football team had gone on to win the county championship. The invite to the Frenzy was a not so subtle acknowledgment that next year's tryouts were only a formality. JZ's future place on the varsity food chain was set.

The only reason JZ wasn't on varsity football this season, as a freshman, was because of his father. He wanted sports second on JZ's priority list. But JZ was a die-hard athlete—football in the fall, basketball in the winter and track in the spring to stay in shape. He trained like a pro, running several miles a day and lifting weights several times a week. Even if sports were second on JZ's schedule, because Mr. Zimms said so, football and basketball were first in his every thought.

And being on the JV team had actually brightened JZ's star, not dulled it. The minute he stepped on the field in September, it was obvious to the coaches he was varsity material. They'd been drooling over the thought of having him move up ever since.

Now the varsity basketball coaches were going to get the chance the football team hadn't had, because when football season ended, JZ's dad relented and agreed to let him try out for varsity. JZ made the team easily. The only "catch," was if JZ's grades suffered even a little, his father was going hardcore and making JZ cut out the sports until next season. So all JZ talked about lately was basketball and the Frenzy.

According to JZ, the Frenzy was wild. Coach Banner basically let his "boys" have the run of the house for the night, no chaperons. JZ also mentioned nude foolishness in the hot tub and drinking, *Real World* high school edition.

Other than pointing out to JZ that she thought the details of the party were probably rumors or exaggerated, Mina hadn't given the Frenzy much thought. Until now. Now she had an invitation from a varsity football hottie.

Was she down?

Mina wanted to type YES in all caps just so Craig would know how down she was.

She couldn't believe that only three letters stood between her and her first date with the guy she'd crushed on for months. Her first date, period.

It wasn't even eleven a.m. and this day was quickly moving toward best-day-ever status.

And to think, in her haste to throw down on some pancakes and bacon, she'd almost walked right by her computer without as much as a glance.

Thank goodness she'd logged in to see if Kelly had sent a message confirming whether or not she'd come over later and hang at JZ's with the rest of the clique. Mina was anxious for the six of them to get together. They'd only squeezed in a few IM's and phone calls over the week-long break. Mina didn't mind family time, but five straight days of it was enough. She was ready to kick it with her friends, especially now that she had something more interesting to share than an account of her family's insanely competitive game of Trivial Pursuit on Thanksgiving night.

Mina's head turned toward the loud clanging of pots and pans coming from downstairs, her attention slipping just for a second from the three words on the screen. She tipped over to her bedroom door, leaned her head out of the room and waited on her mother's call asking for (requiring) help cooking breakfast. When it didn't come, Mina scurried back over to the desk and sat down, her heart pounding and her hunger completely forgotten.

The loud tinkle of another IM from Craig rang out.

Bluedevils33: Yo, Mina u there?
BubbliMi: Sorry! Listening out 4 my mom . . . I'm supposed to be downstairs cooking.
Bluedevils33: Word. I let u go if u answer me. U down w/the Frenzy?

This time Mina didn't think. She typed, quickly.

BubbliMi: Mos' def!!
Bluedevils33: Cool. U be @ the Ria tonite?
BubbliMi: Trying to be. Not sure tho'.
Bluedevils33: I can give u a ride if u want.

The thought of being in the car with Craig made Mina's heart race. Everything was moving so fast.

BubbliMi: Naw I'm cool. If I go it'll be w/my girls. I see u there if we go.
Bluedevils33: Aight. Later.
BubbliMi: C U

Mina stared at the conversation on the screen, reading over it quickly again and again. It felt like a dream. If her heart wasn't practically beating out of her chest, she would swear she was still sleeping.

"Mi-naaa!" her mother called from downstairs. "What's taking you so long?"

"Coming, Ma!"

Smiling like an idiot, Mina closed out the IM box and signed off.

She stood up and jogged down the hall to the bathroom. If Craig could see her now, bed head and stank morning breath, he'd run screaming in the other direction. She laughed out loud at her fuzzy-headed image in the bathroom mirror.

Stank breath and all, she had a date!

She had a DATE . . . and only one problem—her parents didn't allow her to date, yet.

Thoughts of her parents' dating rules wouldn't dampen Mina's excitement. And her parents had plenty of rules.

Mariah and Jackson Mooney's Guide to Dating included the following little lovelies:

→ First and foremost, no solo dating until age fifteen. (*That was going to be a tough one to battle*).

→ For group dates there must be at least six other people going. As far as Mina was concerned, going to the movies with six or eight other people wasn't a date but a field trip.

→ Mariah and Jack must KNOW the parents of each person on the date.

→ This was Mina's *favorite:* absolutely no car dating until age fifteen, i.e. parental drop-offs only. It was why Mina had quickly turned down Craig's offer for a ride to Rio's Ria.

→ If the "date" takes place at a party, the 'rents must first speak to someone who is chaperoning the party before giving approval.

Mina bounced happily down the stairs, the rules swirling in her head. As she walked into the kitchen Mina convinced herself she had a solid argument against each one:

First, this wasn't a solo date because JZ would be there (even if the last thing on his mind, that night, would be keeping up with Mina).

It was a group date, sort of. Couldn't she count the forty other people and their dates (if they brought any) as a group? She was sure to know a few other girls there.

Okay, so she couldn't do squat about her parents knowing everyone else's parents. That rule was just ridiculous. Not that she was going to tell them that, but . . .

As far as car dating, at this point if her parents let her go she didn't care if they dropped her off. Maybe she could get them to drop her off down the street from the house or over at Kelly's and she'd walk to Coach Banner's house. Mina didn't know how far Kelly lived from the coach but they lived in the same neighborhood.

Talking to the chaperons . . . well, if it came to it, she'd have her parents talk to Coach Banner. Not sure how. It wasn't like she had his number or anything. But where there's a will there's a way and all that jazz.

Mina's resolve wilted a little. Maybe the arguments against the rules weren't so solid . . . but they were all she had.

"Morning, Mom," Mina chirped. She stood by her mom's side at the stove. A mix of hickory and seasoned salt floated toward her nose, making her stomach growl. "Still need help?"

Mariah Mooney looked up from flipping a pancake. She put her hand on her hip. "I thought we were fixing this breakfast *together*?"

Mina giggled. "Sorry. I was checking to see if Kelly was coming over today. I'll help."

She put her hand out and her mom quickly relinquished her pancake flipping duties then moved on to the grill where bacon popped quietly.

"Where's Daddy?" Mina scooped a pancake, peeking at its underside to test its brownness. The pancake needed a few more seconds.

Mina's mom paced between the bacon and a pan of fried potatoes. She shook her head. "Still in bed." She grabbed another spatula from a nearby drawer and stirred the potatoes around. "If I had known a Mooney un-Thanksgiving breakfast meant me cooking by my lonesome, I would never have suggested it."

Mina leaned over and kissed her mom's cheek. "Forgive me?"

Mariah smiled. "No. But thanks for gracing me with your presence, Miss Social Butterfly. So can Kelly join you guys today?"

Mina frowned. In all the excitement of Craig IM'ing her, as far as she'd gotten was opening the inbox. She never actually looked at the new messages.

"Probably," Mina said, rushing on and ignoring her mom's perplexed expression. "Hey, Ma, remember Craig Simpson?"

Mariah chuckled. "Oh, you mean the boy you refused to introduce to me and Daddy at your party?"

A slice of regret cut through Mina. Now she wished she had been more assertive about introducing Craig to her parents. They were sticklers for "knowing" her friends. Even though her mom had heard Craig's name mentioned a few times since the school year started, when he showed up at the party for Lizzie, Mina didn't want Craig to think she was singling him out for a grand introduction. It felt too formal. Instead, she'd flipped the whole "group" concept on her parents and waited until Craig and a few other guys from the football team were upstairs getting a drink before introducing all of them to her parents. It seemed like a good idea at the time.

"I didn't refuse," Mina reminded her mom. She flipped two pancakes and took a step back from the stove so she could face her mom. "I just didn't want Craig thinking that I was going all girlfriend on him. I did finally introduce y'all."

"Uh-huh. To him and about four other guys." Mariah shrugged. "For the few minutes I talked to him he seemed like a nice guy."

"I couldn't risk Daddy asking him a million questions. It would have been too embarrassing," Mina said. Her face grew hot just thinking about it.

"Oh, Lord, Mina." Mariah rolled her eyes. "God forbid your dad asks the guy's last name, where he lives, who his parents are . . ."

"Exactly!" Mina shook her head. "We were dancing together not running off to Vegas."

Mina's mother laughed hard. "Girl, where do you get all that drama from?" She smiled and tried to sound serious. "Alright. Well what about him?" She moved the pan of potatoes off the burner and covered them before moving back to the bacon.

"Well . . ." Mina stepped back over to the pan of pancakes, slipping them out of the pan and onto a plate.

"Hold on, sweetie," her mom said. She peeked around the corner of the kitchen and called out, "Jack! Breakfast is almost ready!" She popped back around and faced Mina. "Sorry. Now what about Craig?"

Mina's words rushed out in a stream. "Heaskedmeout."

Mina watched her mom's eyes crinkle the way they did when she was happy. Maybe she had a chance.

"Really?" Mariah smiled.

"Yes," Mina gushed. "Ma, Craig is like . . . do you know how many girls would love to go out with him?! And he asked me. I mean, I was hoping he would. I thought he would after the party. But he didn't. He . . ."

"Slow down, baby girl." Mariah chuckled. She slid the bacon on to a plate, tore a paper towel off a roll and dabbed at the grease on each slice. "Okay, I get it. You really like this guy even though you didn't want to introduce him. Guess you're ashamed of the parental units."

Mina rolled her eyes. "Ma, parental units? Okay, please come back to the new millennium."

Mariah carried a bottle of syrup and tub of butter over to the table. "Sorr-eee." She leaned against the counter, arms folded, smile still tugging at her mouth. "Just teasing. I'm glad he asked you out. It's exciting huh?"

Mina's head nodded in an excited bobble.

"First dates are exciting. And he's nice looking from what I remember," her mom said.

"Understatement of the year," Mina said. She turned the stove off and dropped the pan into the sink, which had water waiting. The pan sizzled as she exclaimed, "Mom, he's FINE!"

Mariah's voice turned serious and professional. "Uh-huh. Well, where is this date? And when would it be?"

Mina knew that voice. It meant the preliminary nice-nice chit chat was out of the way and the rules were coming. Scared her mother would see the worry on her face, Mina focused on the dish water as she washed out the pan.

"It's a um . . . a party," she said. "The varsity football team's annual end-of-the-season party. It's in three weeks."

"Well, you know how Daddy and I feel about . . ."

"It wouldn't just be me and Craig, Ma. JZ will be there," Mina sputtered. She rinsed the pan, dropped it on the rack to dry and wiped her hands on a towel.

"Okay. Anyone else we know? And how were you planning to get there?" Her mother's questions poured nonstop. "Who throws this party? It's a team party, which means lots of people you don't know. Who else besides Craig and JZ do you know? I mean really know?"

"Coach Banner has the party for the team," Mina mumbled. She fiddled with the towel, for once wishing she had another dish to wash to keep herself from looking at her mom. "You and Daddy could drop me off or I could ride with JZ. And I'm sure I'll know other girls there."

"Do parents chaperone?"

"I'm not sure. I mean Craig didn't go into all that," Mina said.

"I have to be honest, Mina." Mina's mother walked over and stood behind her at the sink. "A team party? I'm not comfortable with that as a first date. How can you and Craig enjoy a date around a bunch of guys blowing off steam from the football season? How is that giving you both a chance to get to know each other?"

"It's just dancing and stuff," Mina said, her heart galloping. "And we already know each other. I see him everyday in school."

She could feel any chance of approval slipping away fast. Her stomach fell as her mother went from gathering information on the party to explaining why it wasn't going to happen.

"You know Daddy and I both agreed you wouldn't officially date until next year." Mina's mom put her hand up to stop Mina from interrupting. "Now, there's some wiggle room in there for going out. We don't expect you to stay in your room every weekend," Mariah said. She went to a cabinet and took out plates. "But we don't know Craig well enough. And even if we did, a team party isn't an ideal first date."

Mina pleaded. "But you've met him. You said he's a nice guy——"

Her mom interrupted, "I said he, *seems* like a nice guy. I don't know him."

"Well, what am I supposed to do to help you know him better?" Mina asked anxiously, thinking she found a loophole in the denial.

Her mom chuckled as she walked over to the table. "We'll get to know him over time, Mina." She glanced over at her daughter's exaggerated pout. "I think you knew what the answer would be when you asked. Hanging out in a big group is fine and totally acceptable . . .

"We *will* be in a group," Mina said.

"A group of football players, not a group of your friends," her mom said, sternly. "Being around your other girlfriends would at least help take some of the pressure off the date. You're moving too fast. Especially with someone who . . ."

"You don't know," Mina mocked, making a face.

Mariah's gaze was stony. "Don't be smart," she warned. "You're not going out on a date with this boy. At least not to this party."

A tear fell down Mina's face. She swiped at it angrily. She fully expected her parents to at least consider letting her go out with Craig. Even as her mother attempted to make sense of the decision, Mina couldn't see any good reason for her to squash the date.

She sulked. "So, now I'll look like a total baby when I call to tell him I can't go."

"I'm sure he'll understand," her mom said absently, checking to make sure all of the stove burners were off.

Mina began to rant. "Yeah, right. Hundreds of girls in school would kill to date Craig and he asks me out. Me! Now he'll probably regret going after the . . . the girl with the curfew and the parents with all the rules!"

Mina's mom rolled her eyes and spoke in a tone that made it clear she was nearing the end of her patience. "Cut the drama, Amina! If he liked you before, he'll like you now . . . rules and all. All we're saying is take it slowly. Hang out with Craig with your friends and learn to be comfortable with one another that way. What's the rush on the solo date?"

"It's not a rush. But he asked me out, and now I'll look like a little girl saying I can't go because my mommy won't let me."

"Well, then that's what you'll look like, honey. The answer is no," her mom replied matter-of-factly then added gently, "At least it's no for this party, anyway."

Mina stomped off, her mother's warning at her back. "Uh-uh, no you're not stomping off, Ms. Thing!"

Mina eased her steps, but nearly collided with her father at the top of the stairway.

"Morning, baby," Jackson Mooney said. He stood in the middle of the landing, preventing Mina from getting past.

"Morning," Mina mumbled, her head down. The hot steamy tears came faster as her father played referee.

"Uh-oh. What did I sleep through?" he asked, raising his voice so his wife could hear the question as well.

"Your daughter's just being a Drama Queen," Mariah answered, not unkindly. "What else is new?"

Jackson put his arm around Mina and she buried her face into his stomach.

"What's the matter?" her dad asked.

"Mom said . . . I can't . . ." Mina's voice, thick from crying, hitched as she talked through the tears. "Craig asked me out . . . and Mom said I can't go . . . because you two don't . . . know him."

Jackson looked over Mina's head at Mariah who stood at the foot of the stairs, shaking her head. Her jaw was firm but her eyes were soft. He got the message—*don't take sides, not right now.*

"Well, come back down and we'll talk about it. Let me hear the whole story," Jackson said.

Mina's head shook no furiously.

"Breakfast is ready," her mom said.

I'M NOT HUNGRY! Mina shouted to herself. But she kept her voice quietly in check as she responded. "I don't feel like eating."

Mariah threw her hands up in frustration and walked back to the kitchen muttering, "So much for a big family breakfast."

Jackson whispered down to Mina. "We'll talk about it later. Okay?"

"I know the answer will still be no," Mina said, wiping at the tears. She poured on a little extra poutiness. "Mommy seemed like she was speaking for both of you."

Mina looked up at her dad, hope in her glossy eyes. *Please say she wasn't,* they pleaded.

But Jackson knew better than to disagree with his wife until he knew all of the facts. He changed course. "Well, you know our rules. But I can't weigh in on it without knowing the whole story." He tugged Mina down a step. "Come on and eat."

Mina's body went rigid. She refused to move. "I'm seriously not hungry, Daddy."

"Okay. Well we'll talk later, then," her dad said.

Mina nodded as she left her father standing on the stairway. She walked up the stairs and down the hall to her room. She shut her bedroom door quietly then threw herself violently onto her bed, letting the tears stream down her face. As much as she wanted to go out with Craig, not being able to go wasn't the truly bad part. The embarrassment of telling him she couldn't go was the worst!

Her head pounded from the good, hard cry, but Mina ignored the throbbing. *Fine, I'll just stay here in this room until I'm old enough to date him,* she thought, fully prepared to remain in her tantrum.

Mina threw a pillow over her head and listened to the pulse in her temples beat. The house telephone bleated beside her, vibrating against her pulsing head.

"Mina, telephone," her mom called. "It's Michael."

Mina reached her hand up to her night stand and grabbed the phone, taking it under the pillow with her. She snapped at her mom through the phone, "I got it!"